*A young wo...*
*A hus...*
*Stirring...*

# THE

## Scandals

**VOLUME SIX**

When the debauched Marquis of Sywell won Steepwood
Abbey years ago at cards, it led to the death of the Earl
of Yardley. Now he's caused scandal again by marrying
a girl out of his class – and young enough to be his
granddaughter! After being married only a short time,
the Marchioness has disappeared, leaving no trace of her
whereabouts. There is every expectation that yet more
scandals will emerge, though no one yet knows just
how shocking they will be.

The four villages surrounding the Steepwood Abbey
estate are in turmoil, not only with the dire goings-on at
the Abbey, but also with their own affairs. Each of the
eight volumes in THE STEEPWOOD SCANDALS
contains two full novels that follow the mystery behind
the disappearance of the young woman, and the
individual romances of lovers connected in some way
with the intrigue.

# THE STEEPWOOD

# *Scandals*

### *Regency drama, intrigue, mischief...*
### *and marriage*

# THE STEEPWOOD
# *Scandals*

## Volume 6

*Gail Whitiker & Anne Ashley*

*M&B™ and M&B™ with the Rose Device
are trademarks of the publisher.*

*Harlequin Mills & Boon Limited, Eton House,
18-24 Paradise Road, Richmond, Surrey TW9 1SR*

*First published in Great Britain in 2002*

THE STEEPWOOD SCANDALS © Harlequin Books S.A. 2007

The Guardian's Dilemma © Harlequin Books S.A. 2002
Lord Exmouth's Intentions © Harlequin Books S.A. 2002

*Special thanks and acknowledgement are given to
Gail Whitiker and Anne Ashley for their contribution to
The Steepwood Scandals series.*

*ISBN: 978 0 263 85500 5*

052-0407

*Printed and bound in Spain
by Litografia Rosés S.A., Barcelona*

# The Guardian's Dilemma
*by*
*Gail Whitiker*

Originally hailing from Pembrokeshire, **Gail Whitiker** now lives on beautiful Vancouver Island on the west coast of Canada. When she isn't indulging her love of writing, you'll find her enjoying brisk walks along the Island's many fine beaches, or trying to catch up on her second love – reading. She wrote her first novel when she was in her teens, and still blesses her English teacher for not telling her how bad it really was.

# Chapter One

*August 1812*

'*Elope!*' The shocked exclamation burst from Oliver Brandon's lips as he turned to stare at the young woman standing by the window. 'What in the world are you talking about, Sophie? Gillian would never do such a thing.'

'Wouldn't she?' Mrs Sophie Llewellyn glanced at her brother with an expression of amused indulgence. 'You know what a headstrong young girl our stepsister is. She has the determination of three and she has shown in the past that if she is pushed too hard, she will rebel. Do you not remember that little incident several years ago?'

Oliver snorted. 'Gillian was ten years old when she set off for Dover on her pony. At seventeen, I expect her to have more sense.'

'And at seventeen she should have, dearest, but that is not to say that she has. For all her protestations to the contrary, Gillian is very young. She has been pampered and cosseted most of her life and has not half the maturity you or I had at that age.'

Oliver's dark brows arched upwards in surprise. 'Are you saying I've spoiled her?'

'No, but she has certainly been indulged. And not only by you, so you needn't look at me like that.' Sophie's mouth twitched. 'I too am guilty of having given in to her whims. But Gillian has such a sweet, amiable nature that one cannot help oneself. However, you cannot deny that she likes to have her own way, Oliver, and when she doesn't get it, she can become...'

'Troublesome?'

'I prefer to use the word challenging.' Sophie smiled as if hoping to soften the criticism. 'Troublesome has such a disagreeable connotation to it, don't you think?'

'Hmm.' Oliver clasped his hands behind his back and joined his sister at the window. It was easy to discern the resemblance between the two. They both had the same dark, wavy hair and finely sculpted features of the Brandon side of the family, and the same height and physical stature of their late mother's Howden connections. But that was where the similarities ended. In matters of personality and temperament, they were as different as night and day. Oliver might be only four years older than his sister, but his brooding countenance and serious nature often made him appear considerably more.

At thirty-five, he was as fit as a man ten years his junior, but unlike such greenheads, there was nothing of the dandy about him. He did not wear his hair in a Brutus crop or pad his calves to show a shapelier leg. He had no need to, given his propensity for strenuous exercise, both in the boxing ring and with the foil. But he was not so easily moved to laughter as was his sister, nor so trusting of the outside world.

In contrast to both of them was their seventeen-year-old stepsister, Gillian Gresham; a blonde, blue-eyed child who no more resembled either of them than did a rose a cornstalk. She had the round face and bubbly personality of her late mother, and standing at just over five feet tall, she barely reached Oliver's shoulder. She was a happy, good-natured child, inclined, as Sophie had said, to cajole people into giving her what she wanted, but in such a way that no one could truly resent her for it. And she was forever falling in and out of love. Oliver had had more than his share of emotional battles with her over the past two years.

Gillian had come to live at Shefferton Hall when her mother, Catherine, had married Oliver's father just over nine years ago. She had become his legal ward when Catherine had succumbed to pneumonia two years later. Surprisingly, Oliver had grieved deeply over his stepmother's death. More so, perhaps, than he had over his own mother's. The bond between them had been surprisingly strong, and Oliver knew that Catherine had come to feel the same respect and admiration for him as he had for her. It was the reason she had left Gillian in his care, and that she had died at peace, secure in the knowledge that her only daughter would be well taken care of.

The guardianship hadn't been bad to begin with, Oliver admitted. Gillian had been an amusing little minx and, for the first few years, had behaved in a manner suitable to her age and in way that gave him little cause for concern. But over the last four years she had developed into a very determined young woman indeed. So much so that when she thought she was right, there was little hope of convincing her otherwise. At times, even his mild-mannered sister had been tempted to throw up her hands in despair.

At the moment, however, Gillian was happily engaged in the garden below, gathering a colourful selection of roses and placing them in a large straw basket. The fact that the basket was being held by a handsome officer who seemed only too happy to perform such a menial task accounted for a large part of *her* happiness, Oliver reflected moodily, and for considerably less of his.

'Challenging may be the more agreeable word, Sophie, but I think troublesome is the more appropriate one,' he muttered. 'At least when she was ten I had no need to worry about *who* she might be running off to Dover with.' Oliver's brow furrowed as he studied the disturbing scene below. 'I do not like Sidney Charles Wymington. I have no doubt he has a flattering tongue and that his looks are as elegant as anyone might wish, but his glib manner disturbs me very much. He is forever offering opinions on matters that do not concern him, and he is seldom caught without an answer. And I, for one, do not trust a man who is never at a loss for words.'

A twinkle appeared in the depths of Sophie's bright green eyes. 'You are seldom at a loss for words yourself, Oliver, and I have never held that against you.'

'Thank you, my dear, but I do not use my eloquence to curry favour as does Mr Wymington.' Oliver's mouth curved in a rueful smile. 'Nor, I think, do I do it half as well. He seems to live very comfortably for a half-pay officer, don't you think?'

Sophie lifted her elegantly clad shoulders in a shrug. 'I have heard that he does, though I have never stopped to consider the reasons why. However, if it makes you feel any better, Gillian has informed me that he is hopeful of a posting in the near future.'

'Really.' Oliver's dark eyes narrowed as he turned to look out the window again. 'If that is the case, it cannot come soon enough.'

It was not the first time Oliver had expressed negativity towards one of Gillian's suitors, nor the first time he had scoffed at her claims of the gentleman's being the most romantic in all England. Because Oliver himself was not a romantic. He and Sophie had been raised in a home where love and affection had had no place. His parents had tolerated one another, but there had been little more to their marriage than that. Perhaps that was why his father had not grieved overly much when his first wife had died only four years after Sophie had been born.

His father's second marriage, to Catherine Gresham, had started out better than his first, but it had not ended well. Catherine had died most unexpectedly of complications arising from an illness, and after that, Oliver's father had withdrawn even further into himself. So much so, that when he lost his life in a boating accident, many people wondered whether or not it had been a deliberate act of suicide.

Thank goodness his sister's marriage had turned out as well as it had, Oliver reflected now. Rhys Llewellyn had fallen in love with Sophie the first time he'd met her, and hadn't been in the least intimidated by her unusual height. Indeed, he had professed himself delighted to meet a lady who could look at him without risk of serious injury to her neck. More importantly, he had called her beautiful at a time when Sophie had been least willing to believe it, and in the end, his repeated assurances had won her heart and her hand.

Oliver had never experienced that kind of gentle, all-encompassing love. Nor had he known the kind of soul-searing passion that could turn one's heart and one's life inside out. He knew what it was to experience physical desire, but he had sated those urges with Nicolette, a pretty little ballet dancer who'd become his mistress the year he turned four-and-twenty. He still frequented her bed whenever he felt the need to lose himself in the softness of a woman's arms, but other than that, there had been precious little female intrusion into his life. Which was probably why his view of marriage as a whole was somewhat tainted.

Oliver harboured no delusions that people wed solely for love. He knew that women looked to marriage for social advancement and security, while men—especially those in restricted financial circumstances—hoped to avail themselves of money and a convenient lifestyle.

Sidney Charles Wymington was just such a man. Oliver was sure of it. Which explained why he had been less than pleased when Gillian had started coming to him with praises spilling from her lips about the man. Why should he celebrate the fact that his ward was keeping company with a fellow who had little to recommend him other than his handsome face and his practised charm?

After all, Gillian was an heiress. Her mother had left her an inheritance of some twenty-five thousand pounds, with the instructions that the money be re-

leased to her on the occasion of her twenty-first birthday *or* upon the day she married; the latter proviso
having been made in order to prevent Oliver from
having to use his own funds to provide the necessary
dowry. Catherine had been convinced of Oliver's suitability as a guardian for Gillian, and equally confident
that he would *never* allow her to enter into an unac-
ceptable alliance. As a result, she had put no further
restrictions on the inheritance than that.

Therein lay the problem. Oliver had no idea
whether Gillian had told Mr Wymington about the
conditions of her inheritance, but he *did* know she
hadn't troubled herself to conceal the depth of her
feelings for him. And if it came right down to it,
Oliver knew that Wymington wouldn't hesitate to use
those feelings to his own advantage.

'Then what would you suggest I do, Sophie?'
Oliver said at length, a note of frustration creeping
into his voice. 'Gillian is headstrong, as you say, but
I cannot believe she would knowingly disgrace herself—or us—by doing something imprudent.'

'You are her legal guardian, Oliver. You could forbid her to see him.'

'What, and run the risk of alienating her even further?' Oliver shook his head. 'I would far rather cast
Mr Wymington in the role of the villain than myself.
Unfortunately, I have checked into his military rec-
ords and found nothing to condemn him, other than
a slight propensity towards gambling.'

'Unless it is a propensity which causes him to lose
vast sums of money in a single night, I doubt it will
be enough to sway Gillian's opinion of him.
Especially if she believes herself in love with him—'

'In love!'

'Well, you cannot ignore the possibility, my dear.' Sophie's expression softened. 'You see how she behaves with him. Most young ladies would have the good sense to conceal their affections, but Gillian seems to want *everyone* to know how she feels about the man. Which is why I think it would be a good idea if you were to separate them for a while.'

'And how do you suggest I do that? Even if I were to tell Wymington to keep away from Gillian, I do not trust him to listen to me.'

Sophie sighed her agreement. 'I doubt he would. If Mr Wymington knows that Gillian is an heiress and his intentions are what you say, he will be more than willing to bide his time. He will have to if you do not intend to give your approval to the match.'

'Unless he decides to elope with her, as you suggested earlier. Which given the terms of Catherine's will *any* man might be tempted to do. '

Sophie had the grace to look embarrassed. 'Well, perhaps I was being a touch melodramatic in saying that she would elope. For all Gillie's headstrong ways, I do not believe she would knowingly disgrace us. But I still think it would be wise to send her away for a while. With any luck, her absence will force Mr Wymington to look elsewhere for a wealthy bride, and give Gillian time to come to her senses.'

'That's all very well, my dear, but where do you suggest I send her? She has no family who would welcome her. At least, none whom I would trust not to try to take advantage of her fortune themselves.'

'You could send her away to school,' Sophie said slowly. 'Do you remember me telling you about the Guarding Academy for Girls?'

Oliver began to pace. 'No. Should I?'

'I suppose not. A friend of mine, Lady Brookwell, mentioned it to me in passing a few weeks back. She said that her eldest daughter, Elizabeth, was there and that she was very pleased with her progress. The headmistress is a woman by the name of Eleanor Guarding and from what Lady Brookwell tells me, she is quite a unique person. Not at all the sort one usually finds running schools of this nature.'

Oliver stopped pacing. 'And where is this Guarding's Academy for Girls?'

'In Northamptonshire. I believe Steep Abbot is the name of the village.'

'Steep Abbot?' He frowned. 'Why would that name be familiar to me?'

'Possibly because it is where the Marquis of Sywell was murdered three months ago.'

'Good God! And you would have me send Gillian there?'

Sophie chuckled as she let the curtain fall back across the window. 'I hardly think Gillie is in danger of suffering a similar fate, my dear. From all I've heard, Sywell was not undeserving of his reward. But the reason I mention it is because the teachers at the Academy are purported to be more liberal-minded than most. They strive to impress upon their girls the importance of thinking for themselves.'

Oliver sent her a sharp glance. 'Gillian does quite enough thinking for herself as it is, Sophie. That is one of the problems I am trying to overcome.'

'You miss my point, dearest.' Sophie walked back towards the green velvet settee and sat down. 'The staff at Guarding's attempt to expand the intellectual minds of their pupils by providing tutelage in subjects not normally offered to young ladies. How many schools do you know of, for example, where girls are given extensive instruction in advanced mathematics and archaeology, as well as in Latin, Greek and philosophy? And from what I understand, Mrs Guarding is herself something of an emancipationist and historian.'

'A female emancipationist?' Oliver frowned. 'The last thing I need is someone else filling Gillian's head with nonsense. I suspect Mr Wymington does quite enough of that as it is.'

'All right. Then what would you say if I told you that the teachers at the Guarding Academy would be far more likely to impress upon Gillian the importance of knowing what she stands to gain *and* to lose in a marriage to a man who is not her social or financial equal, than would a teacher in a fancy London seminary?'

Oliver thought about that for a moment. Sophie was an intelligent woman and he respected her opinion, but sending Gillian away to a girls' school was not going to be easy. He knew that in his ward's mind she had long ago finished with that kind of schooling. 'What could I say that would persuade her to go?'

'That, I'm afraid, is something you are going to have to work out for yourself, Oliver. I merely put forward the suggestion as a solution to the problem of how to separate Gillian from Mr Wymington for a while.' Sophie smiled as she rose to kiss her brother affectionately on the cheek. 'After all, a year spent at a boarding school might be time enough for her to see the gentleman in a different light. And if Mr Wymington is the adventurer you think, it may be all the time we need.'

\* \* \*

Oliver gave his sister's words considerable thought over the next few days, and the more he thought about it, the more he came to see that the plan had merit. Gillian had always resented the fact that young ladies were not offered the same quality of education as young gentlemen, and by the sound of things, spending the better part of a year at Mrs Guarding's Academy would give her precisely that opportunity.

In the end, however, it did not come down to a matter of choice as to whether or not he sent her away to school, but rather, how quickly could he get her there. Gillian's conversations were becoming far too full of Mr Wymington for Oliver's liking. It seemed that every utterance was prefaced by 'Mr Wymington said this,' or 'Mr Wymington thinks that,' until by the end of the week Oliver was sick to death of hearing about Mr Wymington. But even in his frustration, he saw the way Gillian's face closed down whenever he expressed negativity towards the man, and knew that he was fighting a losing battle.

It was that stubbornness which convinced him that Sophie was right. Gillian *was* impulsive, and she was used to getting her own way. She was also at the age where, like most young women, her thoughts were turning more frequently towards marriage. Oliver could not be sure that if he pushed her too hard, she wouldn't do precisely what Sophie had suggested and elope.

For that reason, little more than a week after his conversation with her, he contacted the headmistress at the Guarding Academy for Girls in Steep Abbot, and then, a few days later, told Gillian of his plans.

Needless to say, she was not pleased.

'You intend to send me *where*?' she echoed in disbelief.

'It is called Mrs Guarding's Academy for Girls,' Oliver informed her calmly. 'I thought that since you did not have occasion to finish your lessons with Monsieur Deauvall and Miss Berkmore, you might welcome the opportunity to do so now.'

'But I have no wish to go to school!' Gillian cried petulantly. 'I am nearly eighteen years of age, Oliver! I have far more important things on my mind than silly lessons. Mr Wymington says—'

'I don't give a…that is to say,' Oliver said, catching himself just in time, 'I don't think anything Mr Wymington has to say on the matter is relevant, Gillian. I am your legal guardian and I will be the one to decide how and where you complete your education. And after due consideration, I have determined that the Guarding Academy is the place for you to do that.'

Gillian stamped her dainty little foot and set her blonde curls dancing. 'But I don't want to go to any stuffy girls' school!'

'From all I've heard, the school is anything but stuffy. The headmistress is a female emancipationist and the teachers are all somewhat radical in their thinking. A young lady with your intelligence and personality should get on very well there.'

'But I do not wish—'

'Gillian, the discussion is at an end. We leave for Steep Abbot in a week's time. I have already sent a letter to Mrs Guarding advising her of your enrolment, and have received a letter back confirming your place. I would advise you to make whatever arrangements you feel are necessary and then tell me when you are ready to depart.'

Gillian's face darkened. 'What about Mr Wymington?'

'What about him?'

'Oh, how can you be so heartless, Oliver! You must know that I care for him. And it cannot have escaped your notice that he holds me in considerable esteem.'

'It hasn't escaped my notice at all, but neither has the fact that you are only seventeen.'

'I shall be eighteen in January, but what has that to do with it? Jane Twickingham was betrothed to Lord Hough when she was only sixteen, and you have told me yourself she was a silly little chit. What has my age to do with Mr Wymington's courting me?'

Oliver's eyes turned the colour of stone. 'Since when did Mr Wymington's visits take on the aspect of a courtship? He has not sought my permission to address you.'

As if realising she had said more than she should, Gillian's pretty cheeks flushed. 'Well, no, of course not, because we are only acquaintances. But that is not to say that I...that is, that he—'

'Gillian, what do you really know of Mr Wymington?' Oliver asked, deciding to try a different approach. 'That he is charming, I have no doubt. That he knows how to turn a young girl's head, I have seen with my own eyes. But what do you *know* of the man's character or background? Has he spoken to you of his family? Do you know where he comes from or who his people are?'

'Of course I do.' Gillian lifted her chin in defiance. 'We have spoken of all those things. Mr Wymington has nothing to hide from me.'

'Then what has he told you of himself?'

'That his parents are dead, and that he has a sister living in Cornwall to whom he is not close. He also told me he has hopes of achieving a higher rank in the militia.'

'I see. And what is he now—a lieutenant?'

'Yes.'

'Has he the funds to purchase his next commission?'

'I do not believe he has,' Gillian admitted reluctantly, 'but he did tell me he was like to come into a considerable amount of money.'

Oliver was immediately on his guard. 'Did he say how?'

'Well, no, not precisely.'

'Did he say *when* he might expect this good fortune?'

Gillian coloured. 'No, nor did I ask. Why should I when one day I shall have money enough for us both?'

*That* was precisely what Oliver had been afraid of hearing. 'And I suppose you told him that?'

'Yes.' Gillian's golden brows drew together in a frown. 'Why would I not?'

Oliver suppressed a sigh. There was no point in answering the question. His naïve young ward might not realise how tempting was the carrot she dangled in front of Mr Wymington's nose, but he certainly did. 'I'm sorry, Gillian, my mind is made up. We leave for Steep Abbot in a week's time. Say goodbye to whichever friends you wish to and then begin your preparations to leave.'

'But—'

'And you are not to see Mr Wymington again.'

'But that is not fair, Oliver! Why can I not say goodbye to him? He is a friend, and you told me I may say goodbye to whomever I wished.'

'You know very well I was not referring to gentlemen when I said that. You may write Mr Wymington a farewell note, but that is all. And I wish to read it before you send it away.'

Oliver could see that Gillian was angry. There was a defiant sparkle in her bright blue eyes and her chin was thrust out in the gesture he had come to know so well.

'I think you are being beastly about this, Oliver,' she flung at him. 'You are sending me away to some dreadful school because you do not like Mr Wymington and because you do not wish me to see him.'

'I am sending you to Steep Abbot so that you may complete your education,' Oliver replied with equanimity. 'I do not share in the opinion that all a young lady need know how to do is arrange flowers and engage in polite conversation. You are far too bright for that, as you yourself have told me on more than one occasion.'

'I do not have to listen to you!'

'Ah, but you do. At least until the occasion of your twenty-first birthday. I promised your mother that I would look after you until that time, and I intend to keep my word. Now, I would ask you to respect my wishes and abide by my instructions. We leave in six days.'

'Six!' Gillian's eyes widened in dismay. 'You said we were leaving in seven!'

'I was, but your decision to argue has persuaded me to move it up a day.'

'But you cannot—'

'And for every objection you make, we shall leave one day sooner. The choice is yours, Gillian.'

With that Oliver turned and walked towards the door. He could feel his ward's eyes boring into his back, but he did not give way. He had learned that the only way to deal with Gillian was to be firm, regardless of what Sophie or anyone else thought. He was doing what was best for the girl and with any luck, she would eventually come to realise that.

In the interim, it did not lessen his awareness that had looks been sufficient to kill, he would have been lying on the floor suffering his final moments even now!

# Chapter Two

*September 1812*

Helen de Coverdale sat in the small, walled garden behind the main body of the school building and breathed a sigh of pure pleasure.

What a glorious morning it had turned out to be! With the sun so warm and the air so mild, it was hard to believe that the first of September had already come and gone. In fact, if she closed her eyes and tried very hard, she could almost convince herself that it was the fragrance of spring flowers perfuming the air rather than the dusky scent of autumn signalling the end of yet another summer.

How quickly time passed, Helen thought wistfully as she gazed out towards the gardens. Indeed, with the arrival of each new year, the days seemed to tumble over one another with ever-increasing speed. When she was a child, the summers had stretched on endlessly. She remembered long, golden afternoons spent in the Italian countryside, when there had been nothing more pressing to do than paint pictures of olive groves and fields of brightly coloured flowers. She remembered sitting with her grandmother in the little stone house, listening to her tell the same wonderful stories she had told Helen's own mother when she had been a child growing up there. How blissful those days seemed now, and how very long ago. Before the long years of war had begun to change everything.

Thank goodness her memories of the past hadn't changed, Helen reflected silently. They would always be there for her, reminding her of a time when her future had loomed bright and hopeful. Before the heartbreak of love and the harsh realities of life had intruded to shatter her expectations and chase away her dreams.

Helen picked up the letter she had placed on the seat beside her and smiled as she read it over one more time. It was from her dear friend Desirée Nash. Desirée lived in London now, but before that she too had been a teacher at the Guarding Academy. She had taught Latin, Greek and philosophy for over six years, until a most unfortunate incident had forced her to leave.

Helen's smile faded as she thought back to that dreadful time. In the spring of last year, Desirée had been caught in a compromising position with the father of one of the students. The fact that she had been completely innocent of any wrongdoing meant nothing. The episode had been witnessed by Mrs Guarding and two of the girls, and it had effectively put an end to Desirée's future at the school. It had also been a particularly difficult time for Helen. She and Desirée had become close in the brief time they'd known each other, and Helen had shed many a tear as a result of her friend being so cruelly sent away. But she knew there was nothing she could have done. There was nothing anyone could have done. It was simply the way young single women were misused by society.

But now, Desirée was having the last laugh on them all. She had gone up to London and become the companion of an aristocratic lady, and had then fallen in love with the lady's dashing young nephew. Now, she was betrothed to marry him. Her letter was to inform Helen of the date of the wedding, and to say how very much she hoped her dear friend would be able to come up to London for it.

Helen sighed as she carefully refolded the letter. How wonderful it would be to go to London and see Desirée married. How satisfying to see her take her place in society as Lady Buckworth. Indeed, after everything she had endured, it seemed only right and fitting that she should. Unfortunately, as much as Helen would have loved to go, she knew it was impossible. The school was operating short of the full complement of teachers as it was, and there were new girls arriving all the time. Mrs Guarding had informed them that three new girls would be coming in at the end of this week alone.

Which simply meant there was no way Helen could take the time necessary to attend Desirée's wedding. She could not afford to risk losing her position here. While she knew that being a teacher was not a profession many people would envy, it was all she had, and in her own way she was happy with it. She valued the company and friendship of the other women who worked here; women who, like herself, had been forced to make their own way in the world. And it was certainly a vast improvement from the positions she had held in the past. Better to be a schoolmistress in a country school than a governess in a fine house where one lived in constant fear of being caught alone by the master.

'Helen, Helen, come quickly. Mrs Guarding is looking for you!'

Helen looked up to see Jane Emerson hurrying across the grass towards her. Jane was a pretty little thing with big brown eyes and dark hair. She taught dance and deportment at Mrs Guarding's and was well liked by both the staff and the girls. But her appearance in the garden now with the news that Mrs Guarding wanted to see her came as something of a surprise.

'But why would she wish to see me?' Helen asked, hastily slipping the letter into her pocket. 'I have no classes until this afternoon.'

'Yes, but Miss Gresham and her father are here.'

Helen blinked. 'Miss Gresham?'

'One of the new girls.' Jane stopped for a moment to catch her breath. 'Mrs Guarding is gathering…everyone in the hall to meet them.'

'But I thought none of the new girls were due to arrive until the end of the week?'

'That was what Mrs Guarding told us, but Miss Gresham is here now and we must all take our places. Come, Helen, we had best make haste,' Jane urged. 'You know how Mrs Guarding hates to be kept waiting!'

'I apologise for our early arrival, Mrs Guarding,' Oliver told the headmistress in the privacy of her sitting-room, 'but I thought it best that Gillian begin her studies here as soon as possible.'

Mrs Guarding inclined her head. 'No apology is necessary, Mr Brandon. I have asked my staff to assemble downstairs and it will be only a few moments before they are there. But in the interim, is there anything you would like to tell me about your ward?'

Oliver glanced at the older woman in surprise. 'Why would you ask?'

'Because given Gillian's age, I thought there might have been another reason for your haste in bringing her here.'

'I'm not sure I take your meaning.'

The headmistress looked at him in the same manner she might have regarded a tardy pupil. 'Mr Brandon, I am very proud of the reputation I have built here at Guarding's, but I am well aware that education is not the only reason parents send their daughters away. Especially to a school like this.'

'Like this?'

'Yes. One where the main focus is *not* to prepare young women for marriage.'

As a man accustomed to plain speaking, Oliver appreciated the headmistress's forthright style. He was also glad he had left Gillian in the corridor beyond. 'You are quite right, Mrs Guarding. I did have another reason for bringing my stepsister here, and under the circumstances, I see no reason why you should not be made aware of it.' He paused, took a deep breath, and then laced his hands together behind his back. 'Gillian has developed an unfortunate *tendre* for a gentleman of whom I do not approve. I had hoped that by separating them for a while, she might eventually find her affections cooling, and that the gentleman might find another target for his.'

A gleam of understanding appeared in the headmistress's eyes. 'Am I to assume that your ward's inheritance has something to do with the gentleman's interest?'

'I believe it has. Because of her wealth, Gillian will be pursued by a great many gentlemen. Some will love her for who she is while others will court her for what she has. I am hoping that when the time comes for her to make a choice, she will have the maturity and good sense to recognise the difference. At the moment, she hasn't,' Oliver said flatly. 'She has been swept away by the romantic ramblings of a handsome officer and believes herself in love with him. That is why I have brought her here.'

'I see.'

'It is also why I would like to make a request of you.'

'And that is?'

'The gentleman's name is Sidney Charles Wymington. He's a dashing fellow to be sure, but I want it made clear that Gillian is to have absolutely nothing to do with him.'

Mrs Guarding's eyebrows rose in inquiry. 'Have you reason to believe he would attempt to contact her here?'

'Regrettably, I have no reason not to believe it,' Oliver replied without hesitation. 'Mr Wymington has become rather persistent of late in his attentions. That is why Gillian is not to be allowed contact with any gentlemen who might call for her. She is also not to receive correspondence from anyone other than family members and female friends.'

Mrs Guarding nodded. 'I will ensure that my staff are made aware of your wishes, Mr Brandon.'

Oliver hesitated, not sure whether he detected a note of censure in the woman's voice, and even less sure why he should be disturbed by it. 'It is not my intention to sound like an overbearing parent, Mrs Guarding. Gillian is an amiable child but at times she can be…impulsive.' He gave the headmistress a rueful smile. 'She has done an excellent job of winding her tutors and her family around her little finger, and I regret to say she has become accustomed to getting her own way. I simply wish to prevent her from making a terrible mistake.'

The reluctant explanation brought a smile to Mrs Guarding's face. 'I understand your dilemma, Mr Brandon. It is an unfortunate truth that all too often young women are guided by their feelings rather than by their good sense, and I would not wish to see your ward come to grief. However, having said that, I must remind you that Miss Gresham is not a prisoner here. I cannot restrict all of her activities nor force her to remain on school property. If she is not to leave the grounds or to venture into the village unescorted, you must be the one to tell her that. I shall then endeavour to enforce your instructions as best I can.'

'That is only fair,' Oliver conceded. 'Gillian is well aware of my feelings regarding Mr Wymington, but as I've said, she's a strong-willed girl used to getting her own way. I am hoping that you and your staff will be able to strengthen and refine certain aspects of her character. I have been assured that moral development and intellectual growth are encouraged here.' Oliver took a deep breath. 'I wish her to understand that a young lady in possession of a considerable fortune cannot always be ruled by her heart, since the gentlemen who are courting her seldom are.'

Helen accompanied Jane to the dining-hall and smiled at the other teachers who were gathered there. They were a quiet group of women, made that way by their upbringing as much as by their choice of livelihood. They had all been forced to seek employment as a result of neither having had the good fortune to secure a husband, nor being in the enviable position of not needing one.

Helen had come to the Guarding Academy with a slight advantage over the others in that she had once been a pupil here. But she had never had cause to regret her decision. Even now, as she approached the beginning of her third year, she still enjoyed the opportunity of working with the young women in her care. That was not to say that all the young ladies *liked* being shown the best way to apply watercolours to a page, or how to conjugate Italian verbs. Indeed, with travel on the Continent so restricted, many of them felt there was little need for any language other than French in their daily lives, and some even balked at the learning of that.

For all of the attendant aggravations, however, Helen was not unhappy. There was a sense of belonging here; a feeling that they were all part of a small community, and that was important to Helen. She had spent too many lonely years forced to live without it.

The sound of approaching footsteps caused the low murmur of voices to cease, and in silent expectation the ladies turned towards the door where three people had just entered. Mrs Guarding led the way, followed by a very pretty young woman of about sixteen, and behind her, a gentleman who looked to be somewhere in his late thirties.

The young lady was dressed in the first style of fashion, from the brim of her attractive straw bonnet to the tips of her dark brown kid boots. She wore a short pelisse of deep lilac trimmed with white, and her light blonde hair was attractively arranged in loose curls around her face. She had high, round cheeks, a pert little nose, and a soft, rosebud mouth. But Helen could tell from the petulant expression on that mouth that the young lady was anything but pleased at the prospect of becoming a pupil at Mrs Guarding's Academy.

The gentleman behind her was equally well dressed. He was garbed in a dark blue jacket over fawn-coloured breeches, and was wearing a pair of highly polished Hessians. The perfectly tailored garments accentuated the width of his shoulders and the musculature of his legs, but there was nothing foppish about him. The fabric of his single-breasted waistcoat was tastefully subdued, while his snowy white cravat was well but not fussily tied.

Unfortunately, it was not the manner of his dress that gave Helen cause for alarm. As she slowly raised her eyes to his face, icy fingers tightened around her heart, and for a moment, she could scarcely breathe.

*No! It could not be! Not now, after all this time, surely it was not him…*

'Ladies, thank you for gathering so promptly,' Mrs Guarding began in her usual brisk manner. 'I am very pleased to introduce our newest student, Miss Gillian Gresham. Miss Gresham comes to us from Hertfordshire and will remain with us until the spring.

I know you will all make her feel welcome at the Guarding Academy.'

The young lady introduced as Miss Gresham glanced briefly at the cluster of women in the room, but she did not smile, nor did she respond to a whispered comment made by the gentleman beside her. She kept her eyes on the floor, refusing to look up or even to acknowledge him.

Helen bit her lip. She wished with all her heart that she *could* smile, but her face was frozen from top to bottom. *Dear heavens, was the gentleman truly the young woman's father? She would not have thought him old enough…*

'I would also like to introduce Mr Oliver Brandon, Miss Gresham's guardian,' Mrs Guarding went on to say. 'Mr Brandon has been good enough to donate an excellent selection of books from his own library for our use, and we are exceedingly grateful to him for his kindness. And now, Miss Gresham, Mr Brandon, if you would be so good as to follow me, I shall introduce you to the members of my staff.'

Helen nervously clasped her hands in front of her as the three began their perambulation. She kept her eyes down, wishing with all her heart that she could turn and run from the room, but she knew she dare not. Mrs Guarding would never forgive such a breach of etiquette from a member of her staff. Worse, it would only serve to draw attention to herself, and that was the last thing Helen wished to do. Which meant that she would just have to stay and see it through.

Perhaps he would not recognise her, she thought with sudden hope. After all, it had been nearly twelve years since he had last seen her and her appearance had certainly changed from the time she was a young

woman of nineteen. There was also the possibility
that he might not remember her, given that the room
in which he'd found her had been very dark. And
considering the awkwardness of the situation, he
could have had only the briefest glimpse of her before—

'And this is Miss Helen de Coverdale,' she heard
Mrs Guarding say. 'Miss de Coverdale has been with
us for two years and instructs the girls in the areas of
watercolours and Italian.'

Helen was aware of Miss Gresham and her guardian stopping in front of her and knew there was nothing she could do but acknowledge the introduction.
She slowly raised her head and smiled tentatively at
the young woman. 'Good morning, Miss Gresham.'

'Good morning,' came the lack-lustre reply.

Finally, with a reluctance borne of fear, Helen
turned her head and looked at Oliver Brandon, trying
all the while to ignore the butterflies swirling madly
inside her stomach.

He, too, had changed over the past twelve years.
His face, a striking mixture of lines and angles, was
no longer that of a youth but of a man; one who had
experienced life, both the good and the bad of it. He
had a slender nose poised above a firm chin, a beautifully sculpted mouth and eyes that glowed a rich
shade of brown. His hair was so dark as to appear
almost black, as were his brows and lashes.

And he was tall. Helen had to tilt her head back to
look into his face. Unfortunately, as she did, she saw
the change in his expression, and felt her breath catch
painfully in her throat. She recognised a brief flicker
of surprise, followed by confusion, and then disbelief

as forgotten memories stirred to life like the cold ashes of a long dead fire.

Helen's heart plummeted. It seemed that her hopes of escaping recognition were to be dashed. The man knew exactly who she was. And it was clear from the look on his face that time notwithstanding, he thought no better of her now than he had all those years ago.

Oliver stared at the young woman standing before him and felt as though he'd gone tumbling backwards in time.

*Good God, was it really her? After all these years, could it possibly be the same woman?*

He blinked hard, wondering if it was just his memory playing tricks on him. It had, after all, been years since he'd last seen her, and what he had seen of her at the time hadn't been all that much. But if it wasn't the same woman, it could surely have been her twin. The resemblance was uncanny. She had the same dark, lustrous hair and the same exotic beauty of the woman he had encountered so briefly all those years ago. But if it was the same woman, what the hell was she doing here?

*How had a nobleman's whore become a teacher at a private girls' school?*

'Mrs Guarding, might I have a word with you in your study?' Oliver said finally.

The headmistress glanced briefly at Miss de Coverdale, and then nodded. 'By all means, Mr Brandon. Miss Emerson, would you be so kind as to show Miss Gresham to her room?'

'Yes, Mrs Guarding.'

'Thank you, ladies. You may all return to your classes.'

As silent as little grey mice, the teachers filed out. Oliver saw a few cast surreptitious glances his way, but he noticed that none of them met his eye. And Helen de Coverdale did not look at him at all. She turned and walked away, not scurrying as the others had, but seeming to float across the floor, her movements slow and graceful, indicative of a poise and refinement he would not have expected in one of her class. At the door, she hesitated.

Oliver held his breath. Would she turn and look at him? If she did, it would be tantamount to an admission of familiarity. He waited as the seconds seemed to drag into hours.

In the end, she did not turn. Helen de Coverdale left the room and quietly closed the door behind her. She did not look back at him once.

Oliver slowly let go the breath he'd been holding. *It had to be her.* He'd seen the tell-tale flash of recognition in her eyes. She'd known who he was as surely as he'd known who *she* was. Which meant that his suspicions had to be right.

Helen de Coverdale *was* the young woman he'd stumbled upon in a darkened library, clutched in the passionate embrace of the married lord who had employed her.

Helen sat on the stone bench in the rose garden and thought back to the one and only time she had seen Oliver Brandon. It seemed a lifetime ago now, and in many ways, it was. She had been employed as a governess to Lord and Lady Talbot at the time. A dreadful position, and one which, had she had a choice, she would have turned and run away from as far and as fast as her legs would have carried her. Unfortunately,

she hadn't had a choice. She had taken the job because she'd needed money to live on after her father
had died. But she had seen the look in Lord Talbot's
eyes the first time he had spoken to her, and had
known what it would portend. Men had been looking
at her like that since she was a child of thirteen, their
hungry eyes lingering on her face and on her already
ripening body.

Helen hadn't always had to worry about her appearance, of course. Before her father had died, her
life had been very different. Robert de Coverdale had
been a barrister, and as his only daughter, Helen had
been a most eligible young lady. Indeed, her father
had held out great hopes of her achieving a respectable marriage, perhaps even to a titled gentleman of
some fortune.

What he had *not* expected was to see his only
daughter fall in love with an impoverished clergyman
who had come to the village during the summer of
her seventeenth year.

Helen shuddered as she cast her mind back to her
youth. Her father had refused to countenance an alliance between his daughter and Thomas Grant, the
young vicar who'd claimed to love her. He'd said it
was so far beneath her as to be laughable, and he had
forbidden Helen to see him. And dutiful daughter that
she was, Helen had obeyed. But it had taken years to
recover from the heartache of losing Thomas. He had
been her first true love, and the loss of that love had
nearly destroyed her.

Over the next two years, more unhappiness had
plagued Helen's life. Her mother had died in a freak
riding accident, and her father, devastated by the loss
of the woman he had loved more than life itself, had

fallen into a series of personal and financial disasters. Unable to cope with a life in ruin, he had eventually taken his own life, and suddenly, Helen had discovered what it was to be dependent upon others. She'd had no relations in England. Her mother's family was still in Italy, and her father's only brother had been killed in the Americas. She'd had no one to turn to and no reputable avenues left open to her. It was then she started trying to disguise her natural beauty. She'd had no wish to appear attractive to the men who passed her in the street, or desirable to the husbands of other women.

Unfortunately, not even the wearing of plain clothes or the scraping back of her hair into a matronly style had been enough to disguise the true loveliness of her features. Helen had not been able to make her heavily lashed eyes appear any the less noticeable, or her full-lipped mouth any the less appealing. She hadn't been able to hide the fact that she wasn't as slim and dainty as were so many of the English ladies she met. She had inherited her mother's lush, exotic beauty, and it was that lushness which men found so attractive, Lord Talbot included. He had been hosting a shooting party at his country estate in Somerset that fateful weekend. The huge house had been filled with guests, many of whom had come all the way from Scotland to partake of the sport and to enjoy the lavish entertainments Lady Talbot had planned for the evenings.

Helen had not been invited to enjoy any of the amusements, of course. She had been included in the outing to Grovesend Hall simply to look after the children, but as a lowly governess she was not expected to participate in any of the festivities. So after tucking her two little girls into bed, she had gone down to the kitchen for a glass of warm milk and had then headed for the library. Lady Talbot had told Helen she could avail herself of his lordship's libraries. She had discovered Helen's passion for reading, and had assured her that as long as the master was not about, she was welcome to browse through his extensive selection of books.

Helen often wondered if Lady Talbot had known of her husband's philandering ways and had simply turned a blind eye to it. Whatever the case, Helen had made a terrible mistake that night. Believing that Lord Talbot would be busy entertaining his guests, she had made her way to the library—which was located well away from the source of the revelry—and had begun to look for something to read.

That was where Lord Talbot had found her.

Helen shivered as she went over it again in her mind. She remembered turning around at the sound of the door opening and seeing the look on his face; a look that had caused her to immediately forget all about books. Like most of the gentlemen, Lord Talbot had been drinking since noon and was well on his way to being in his cups. Knowing that, she had pulled her shawl more closely around her, had quickly retrieved her candle and her drink, and had gone to move past him.

For a drunkard, Lord Talbot had moved with terrifying speed. The milk and the candle had gone flying as Talbot pulled her roughly into his arms and started kissing her.

Repulsed, Helen had struggled against him, fighting to avoid the wet, slobbering kisses he had pressed upon her neck and mouth. She'd sensed that her struggles were only adding to his excitement, however, and given that he had the advantage of both size and weight, Helen had been left in no doubt as to the outcome. He pushed her back towards the settee, his mouth smothering the scream that left her throat as his other hand closed painfully over her breast.

At that precise moment, the door to the library had opened and Oliver Brandon had walked in.

Helen hadn't known who he was at the time. He had simply been a guest in her employer's home. But during the long, agonising moments in which he'd stood frozen in the doorway, Helen had seen the look of shock on his face. And she had watched it change to one of disgust as he'd placed his own interpretation upon the scene before him. He'd muttered an apology and abruptly withdrawn, not even guessing at the true nature of the horror taking place.

Helen closed her eyes as the humiliating memories came flooding back. The only good thing about it was that Mr Brandon's appearance—however brief—had given her the chance she'd needed to escape. Distracted by the sound of the intrusion, Lord Talbot had momentarily looked up, and in doing so, had loosened his grip. In that blessed moment, Helen had broken free and bolted for the door. She had raced towards the stairs as tears of anger and humiliation had streamed down her face and had run all the way to her room. Once inside, she'd turned the key in the lock, wedged a small writing-table against the door and pushed the bed against that. She hadn't slept a wink all night.

The next morning, she'd left Grovesend Hall for ever. She had returned to London, where she had lived off her wits until she had been able to secure another position in the south of England. She had never seen Lord or Lady Talbot again. She hadn't seen Oliver Brandon either. Until this morning, when he had brought his sixteen-year-old ward to be a student at Mrs Guarding's Academy.

But it had been clear from the look on his face that he had not forgotten who *she* was. And he would surely be wondering how and why a woman of such loose morals had ended up becoming a teacher in a private girls' school. Especially one where he was intending to leave his own stepsister as a pupil.

# Chapter Three

Oliver was silent as he accompanied the headmistress back to her study. His mind was spinning, turning over in ever-increasing detail the memories of that fateful night so very long ago.

He had never forgotten what he had seen in the library at Grovesend Hall. He remembered with distaste the sight of Lord Talbot's hand clutching the young woman's breast, and the lustful expression on his face when he'd turned around and seen Oliver standing there. Even now, the memory of it repulsed him.

The problem was, Oliver hadn't known William Talbot well at the time. Yes, they had frequented the same clubs, and they'd often run into one another at social occasions, but the difference in their ages had prevented them from forming any kind of a close friendship. But for whatever reason, Talbot had taken a liking to him and Oliver had been young enough to be flattered by his regard. So when the wealthy peer had invited him to come to his country house for a weekend shooting party, Oliver had accepted with alacrity.

He shook his head now, as he so often did when he thought back to the naïveté of his youth. He hadn't known that Talbot was such a reprobate. But even if he had, Oliver would never have expected the man to flaunt his mistress in front of his guests during a crowded soirée. What would his wife have said if *she'd* been the one to discover them in the library?

Fortunately, or unfortunately, it hadn't been Lord Talbot's wife who had stumbled upon that sorry sight, but Oliver himself. He had opened the door to the library, wanting only to escape from the noise and revelry going on in the other rooms, and had come face to face with his host and a young woman locked in a passionate embrace. Obviously, the sound of his arrival had immediately served to catch the young woman's attention, if not Talbot's, and she had glanced up and stared at him across the darkened room.

For the space of moments, Oliver had been treated to the sight of one of the loveliest faces he had ever seen. A cascade of thick, black hair fell nearly to her waist, framing a face of such arresting beauty that he felt as though he was staring into the face of an angel. Her dark eyes had reached into his soul, tugging at the very core of who he was.

The memory of those eyes had stayed with him for years.

Then, belatedly aware that he had stumbled upon a lover's tryst, Oliver had withdrawn. He'd closed the door and gone back to the ballroom, trying to lose himself in the crowd of revellers and merrymakers. But for some reason, the memory of what he'd seen had stayed with him, disturbing him to such a degree that even he himself hadn't been able to explain it.

The next morning, he'd left Grovesend Hall and headed back to London. He hadn't said a word to anyone about what he'd seen. Not even to Lord Talbot who, obviously too drunk to remember, had been surprised and disappointed by his young guest's hasty departure. Nor had he seen the raven-haired beauty again.

Until this morning when he had arrived at Mrs Guarding's Academy for Girls. Her name was Helen de Coverdale. And unless he did something about it, she was about to become one of the women who would have a direct influence on his impressionable young ward.

'You wished to speak with me, Mr Brandon?'

'Hmm?' Oliver glanced across at the headmistress, and realised she had been waiting for him to begin. 'Oh. Yes. I wanted to ask you about…one of your teachers.'

'Miss de Coverdale.'

It wasn't a question and Oliver frowned. 'How did you know?'

'Because she was the only one who elicited any kind of response from you. Forgive me for speaking plainly, Mr Brandon, but are you acquainted with Miss de Coverdale?'

'No. At least, not formally,' Oliver amended quickly. 'I was not aware of her name until today. But I remember seeing her…many years ago under considerably different circumstances. I was wondering how she came to be in your employ.'

Mrs Guarding walked towards a fine black lacquer desk and sat down behind it. 'Would it surprise you to learn that Miss de Coverdale was once a pupil here?'

'Yes.' Oliver picked up a particularly fine cloisonné vase from the table and turned it over in his hands. 'Am I to assume she comes from a privileged background?'

'Not privileged, but certainly genteel. Her father was a barrister. Her mother, I believe, was of foreign birth. Helen was with us for a few years and showed great promise with her drawing. And of course, she spoke Italian beautifully. After she left, I heard nothing more about her. Until three years ago when to my great surprise, I received a letter from her, asking if I would consider giving her employment as a teacher.'

'Which you agreed to do.'

'Most happily. I was delighted to have a teacher with her skills.'

Oliver nodded, pausing for a moment to deliberate upon how best to phrase his next question. 'Does she have any…gentlemen friends?'

'If she has, I am not aware of it. Miss de Coverdale seldom leaves the building.'

'Not even to visit family?'

'She has no family in England. Her parents are both dead and I have never heard her refer to anyone else in conversation.'

'I see.' Oliver crossed his arms over his chest. 'Mrs Guarding, did Miss de Coverdale provide you with suitable references when she came to you?'

He saw a brief flash of annoyance darken the headmistress's eyes. 'Of course. Have you any reason to believe she would not?'

His shrug was purposely evasive. 'I am merely curious as to the nature of Miss de Coverdale's past employment.'

Mrs Guarding abruptly rose and crossed to the bell pull. 'Miss de Coverdale's work as governess to the children of Lord and Lady Peregrine was spoken of in glowing terms. The letter was written by Lady Peregrine herself, if that is of any consequence.'

Oliver smiled faintly. He had put the headmistress on the defensive, and her message to him was quite clear. She did not care to entertain intrusive questions about her staff, nor did she feel compelled to answer them. 'I shall take up no more of your time, madam. I ask only that you provide me with periodic reports as to Gillian's progress. I have reason to believe she will experience some difficulties in settling in, but I am sure everything will be fine once she comes to know the other girls.'

'I am confident she will fit in very well, Mr Brandon. But I shall keep you apprised of her progress.' The door opened and a black-garbed maid entered. 'Molly will show you out.'

Oliver bowed. 'Thank you.'

As Oliver followed the maid down the hall, he admitted to feeling a certain degree of frustration. He was no further ahead *after* his conversation with Mrs Guarding than he had been before it. It was clear the headmistress thought well of Miss de Coverdale, and it was equally clear there was nothing in her past that would have precluded her from being taken on as a teacher here.

But how could a woman who had been employed in a household where she might well have been the lord's mistress, receive a glowing report from the lord's wife? Had she been that good at concealing the nature of her relationships? Oliver wondered. Or had she simply been fortunate enough to end up in a

household where the wife knew of her husband's behaviour, and had been equally willing to turn a blind
eye to it?

Helen set her easel close to the base of the linden
tree and checked to make sure that the footing was
secure. 'Now, girls,' she said, turning to smile at the
eight young women who were gathered around her,
'I thought today we might begin work on a new landscape. Miss Tillendon, did you not express the opinion that it would be challenging to paint the varying
shades of blue in the sky?'

'Yes, Miss de Coverdale.'

'Then I think that is what we shall undertake. Now,
to begin with, we should spend a little time studying
the sky. We should look up and see how the colours
in it change. Notice the way the blue is lighter there,
and how the clouds come across it and make it appear—'

'Miss de Coverdale, who is that gentleman?'
Rebecca Walters enquired suddenly.

Helen abruptly turned away from her study of the
sky to glance in the direction Rebecca was pointing.
To her astonishment, she saw Oliver Brandon striding
down the path towards them, his face set in grim
lines. He covered the distance between the school and
the pasture in short measure, but then, as if uncertain
of his welcome, stopped at the edge of the field and
leaned against the fence.

Helen felt a quick surge of colour to her cheeks.
What was Oliver Brandon doing out here? Surely he
wasn't expecting to have a conversation with her right
in the middle of her lesson? But why else would he

have come? He would hardly be interested in watching a group of young girls learn how to paint.

'The gentleman's name is Mr Brandon,' Helen said, seeing no reason not to tell them. 'He is the guardian of one of our new students, Miss Gresham.'

'But why is he watching you?' Lydia McPherson piped up.

'He isn't watching me, Miss McPherson. He is watching all of us attempt to paint the sky.'

'I think he is looking at you, Miss,' little Eliza Howard said shyly. 'He is too old to care about the rest of us, or about our paintings.'

The girls started to giggle and Helen felt the blush in her cheeks spread to the rest of her face. '*If* he is looking at me, it is only because he wishes to see how I conduct my classes. His ward is to be a pupil here. No doubt he wishes to see what kind of teacher I am.'

'I shouldn't mind his watching *me*,' Rebecca Walters said on a sigh. 'He's ever so handsome.'

Elizabeth Brookwell gave a disparaging snort. 'You think all gentlemen are handsome.'

'I do not!'

'Yes you do!'

'Ladies, please!' Helen interrupted firmly. 'It is not for us to wonder why Mr Brandon has chosen to stand by the fence and watch us. He is perfectly within his rights to do so, and I am sure it is nothing more than curiosity. Now, kindly return your attention to the sky. If you will recall, I was remarking on the number of shades of blue to be seen. Who can tell me how many different shades there are?'

The question served to focus the attention of most of the girls back on their work, and gave Helen a legitimate reason to ignore Oliver Brandon. But she could not so easily dismiss the awareness of his presence standing some thirty feet away. It was all very well to say he was only there to observe the activities of girls at their lessons. It was another thing entirely to believe it.

Oliver stood by the gate and watched Helen de Coverdale conduct an art class for the small cluster of girls gathered around her. They had each brought easels, paints and papers with them, and from what he could see, they were all diligently trying to replicate the ever-changing shades of blue in the afternoon sky. Even from this distance, however, it was obvious that most of them would never be called upon to make a living from their art. But what about the woman standing in the middle of the circle? What had happened to bring about such a change in her life?

There was no question in Oliver's mind that Helen de Coverdale was wasting her time here. With those full pouting lips and that blatantly sensual figure, she could have been one of the most sought after courtesans in London. Wealthy, aristocratic gentlemen would have vied with one another to offer her their protection, while handsome young bucks would have been lined up outside her door.

And who could blame them? Oliver had never seen such a combination of innocence and sensuality in a woman before. Her skin was itself a palette upon which an artist might sketch. But unlike canvas, it invited touch. Even from this distance, he had an overwhelming urge to run his fingers over her face and see if it felt as warm and as soft as it looked. And her movements fascinated him. Helen de

Coverdale walked amongst the girls with the same languid grace she had demonstrated in the dining-hall; her hips following her legs in a movement that was decidedly provocative, yet totally instinctual. Her attire, a simple, round gown of unadorned muslin, was not designed to flatter her figure, yet the voluptuous curves of her hips and the fullness of her breasts caused it to appear enticing in spite of it being so plain. Furthermore, in direct contrast to what was expected of a woman in her position, she did not hide her hair under a cap or restrain it in a matronly style. The glorious tresses rippled freely down her back, falling almost to her waist in a dark, shimmering stream.

Yes, she was certainly a woman to be desired, Oliver acknowledged. And given what he had seen of her conduct in the library at Grovesend Hall, she was not inexperienced in the arts of love. But if that was the case, what was she doing here? Sophie had assured him that the teachers at the Guarding Academy were all of the highest moral character. Yet what he had witnessed of Helen de Coverdale's conduct in the past had been impropriety, plain and simple. How could a woman like that be hired to teach moral rectitude to the young women in her care?

Suddenly, Oliver straightened. The lady in question had broken away from her girls and was walking towards him.

Without thinking, he pushed himself away from the gate and removed his beaver. She might be a lightskirt, but she was a woman, and his manners were too deeply ingrained to allow him to treat her any differently. Besides, to demonstrate such shocking lack of manners in front of a group of young girls who were even now casting secretive glances in their direction would have been the height of rudeness.

Nevertheless, Oliver kept his voice polite but cool as he sketched her a brief bow. 'Good afternoon, Miss de Coverdale. I hope my study has not disturbed you.'

'It has not disturbed *me*, Mr Brandon, but I fear you are affecting the concentration of some of my girls,' Helen said quietly. 'They are easily distracted by the presence of strangers, especially those about whom they are curious.'

Oliver had expected her voice to be as seductive as everything else about her, but he was surprised to discover that her eyes were not brown as he had first thought, but a most unusual shade of dark green flecked with bits of amber and gold. 'I apologise for any disruption I might be causing, Miss de Coverdale. I was simply curious to see if you were as good an artist as Mrs Guarding led me to believe.'

The beautiful eyes grew wary. 'You discussed me with Mrs Guarding?'

'Of course. As I discussed all of the teachers I met this morning. I thought it only wise since my ward is to be a pupil here.'

Oliver knew he didn't owe her an explanation, but neither did he wish to make her feel as though he had singled her out. *Why* he should be concerned with her feelings, he had no idea. After all, it was not *his* conduct that had engendered his current opinion of her.

'Does your ward like to paint?' Helen surprised him by asking.

'Paint? Yes, I suppose she does. Gillian is skilled in a number of areas, including those of a more creative nature.'

'Good. Then I look forward to the opportunity of working with her.'

'That is what I would like to speak to you about, Miss de Coverdale,' Oliver said stiffly. 'I think there are things which need to be clarified—'

Suddenly, a clattering behind them, followed by smothered gasps and then a burst of feminine giggles, brought an abrupt end to their conversation.

'Miss de Coverdale, come quickly!' one of the girls cried. 'Rebecca's easel has fallen over and she is all spattered with yellow and blue paint.'

Helen's eyes widened as she turned to survey the spectacle. 'Dear me! Miss Walters, did I not tell you to make sure your easel was securely placed?' She turned back around and Oliver was surprised to see not anger, but laughter bubbling in the depths of her beautiful eyes. 'Forgive me, Mr Brandon, I fear I must return to my class.'

'But it is important that we speak—'

'I am sure whatever you need say to me can wait, sir.'

With that, she turned and hurried back towards her class. The girls were all clustered around the unfortunate Rebecca, ineffectually dabbing their small white handkerchiefs at the spots of yellow and blue paint on her smock. Oliver listened as Helen put one of the older girls in charge, and then watched her escort the stricken Rebecca back to the school. Once again, she did not spare him a second glance.

Oliver bit back a sigh of vexation. He was not used to being summarily dismissed, and certainly not by a woman like Helen de Coverdale. But she had made her position clear. Obviously if he wished to have any kind of private conversation with her, it was either going to have to be before her classes, or after them.

Helen was somewhat surprised that she did not see Oliver Brandon again that day, but she was not in the least surprised to receive a summons to the headmistress's sitting-room later that afternoon.

'I hope you do not mind my asking you here, Helen,' Mrs Guarding began, 'but I think you know the reason why.'

Helen sighed. She had long since come to realise that Eleanor Guarding was not only an intelligent woman but an intuitive one. She had obviously seen the look on Oliver Brandon's face this morning—as well as on her own—and the interview now was about achieving an understanding of what those looks had been about. For the good of the school, of course.

'Not at all,' Helen said, taking the indicated seat in front of the headmistress's desk. 'I am sure you noticed my reaction to Mr Brandon.'

The headmistress smiled. 'I am used to young women blushing in the presence of a handsome gentleman, but I thought your response indicated something more than just a touch of simple embarrassment.'

Helen was dismayed to feel fresh colour rise to her cheeks. 'It isn't what you think.'

'Oh? What is it you perceive I think it might be?'

'I am not *acquainted* with Mr Brandon,' Helen said carefully. 'I merely saw him at the home of one of my employers, many years ago.'

'Really. And yet it struck me there was some discomfort on your part. Why would that be, if you had done nothing more than see him?'

'Because I saw him while I was being…' Helen broke off, finding it difficult even now to say the words. 'While I was being most…rudely treated by the man whose daughters I had been engaged to look after.'

'I see.' There was a moment's silence during which all that could be heard was the ticking of the mantel clock. Then Mrs Guarding nodded. 'It would be foolish of me to pretend an ignorance of what goes on in the world, Helen. You would not be the first woman to be unjustly put upon, and I sympathise with you for what you had to endure. I take it Mr Brandon did not realise what was happening at the time?'

'No. I am quite sure he believed he was witnessing a mutually agreeable embrace. He said nothing, but he left the room very quickly.'

'And you have not seen him since?'

'No. I left Lord Talbot's employ the very next day.'

Mrs Guarding laced her fingers together on the desk in front of her. 'Well, I think we need say no more about it. I apologise if my question seemed intrusive, but for the good of the school, I had to ask.'

'I understand.'

'My other reason for inviting you here was to inform you of Mr Brandon's concerns with regard to his ward.'

Helen frowned. 'Concerns?'

'Yes. It seems Miss Gresham has been keeping company with a gentleman by the name of Sidney Wymington. Mr Brandon is not happy with her choice of companion and has sent her here to place her beyond Mr Wymington's reach.'

Helen glanced at the headmistress in confusion.

'But if he has sent her here for that reason, why is he still concerned?'

'Because he is of the opinion that Mr Wymington may try to get in touch with Miss Gresham here. As such, he has asked me to advise my staff that she is not to receive letters from the gentleman, nor to entertain him here. She is also not to leave the school grounds unescorted.'

At the headmistress's words, Helen felt a mixture of anger and resentment kindle in her breast. Why did men always feel they had the right to meddle in other people's lives? Especially those of their wives or daughters? Oliver Brandon was interfering in his ward's life in exactly the same way her own father had meddled in hers; an interference which had cost Helen the love of the man she had dearly hoped to marry. Why was everyone so willing to accept such high-handed treatment?

'Do you agree with what he is asking you to do?' she asked stiffly.

Mrs Guarding picked up her teacup and raised it to her lips. 'It is not for me to agree or disagree, Helen. Mr Brandon's ward is my pupil; therefore, I have no choice but to act in accordance with his instructions. He has made me aware of certain facts and I must now do whatever I can to ensure that Miss Gresham and Mr Wymington do not meet.'

'But what if he is wrong about the gentleman?' Helen felt compelled to ask. 'What if Mr Wymington is a perfectly amiable man who loves Miss Gresham and who has the best of intentions at heart?'

'That possibility certainly exists, but it is not up to you or me to make it known to Mr Brandon. He has paid his ward's tuition in full and has also made a most generous donation of books. I am in no position to challenge him about what he does and does not feel is right for his ward.'

'But he is interfering in a young girl's life!'

'A young girl who is legally in his care,' the headmistress reminded her. 'As such, one who must be expected to abide by his decisions. I do hope I have your co-operation in this, Helen. I cannot have individual members of my staff acting of their own volition in matters such as these.'

Helen bit back the words she longed to speak and vented her frustration in a sigh. She knew there was only one answer she could give. Whatever her own feelings in the matter, they could have no place here. For the good of the school, she had to comply with Mrs Guarding's wishes. But not for the first time in her life, the rules by which she was forced to live sat ill upon her conscience. 'Yes, of course you have my co-operation.'

Mrs Guarding looked considerably relieved. 'Thank you. I know you have strong feelings in the matter, my dear, but we really have no choice. If we do not do as Mr Brandon asks, he will simply remove his ward and demand a refund of the tuition he has already paid. And then we shall be in forfeit of both his good opinion and his funding.'

'Yes, I know,' Helen murmured reluctantly. 'But it does not make me any the happier for knowing.'

'We must do the best we can.' Mrs Guarding smiled. 'Thank you too for telling me the truth about the manner of your first introduction to Mr Brandon.'

'Why would I not?'

'Because it is not always easy to tell people about things we are ashamed of, especially if they happened in our distant past. And it takes even more courage to admit them to me.'

Somewhat reluctantly, Helen began to smile. 'I had no idea what Mr Brandon might have told you. In the event he told you what *he* remembered seeing all those years ago, I thought it would be in both of our interests to tell you what *really* happened.'

'And that is why we need say no more about it.' Mrs Guarding raised the teacup to her lips again. 'As far as I am concerned, the matter is closed.'

# Chapter Four

Perhaps because of what Mrs Guarding told her about Gillian Gresham, Helen found herself taking a keener interest in the girl than usual.

That she was resentful at having been forced to come to Guarding's was obvious. The girl attended classes but remained stubbornly uncommunicative throughout. Even when she was compelled to answer a question, she did so grudgingly and more often than not, with the very minimum of conversation required. Most of the teachers soon began to express frustration at dealing with the child, and as the end of Gillian's first week approached, Helen was more inclined to believe that Oliver Brandon had done his half sister a disservice by forcing her to come to Guarding's, rather than a good turn.

Of course, Helen knew better than most what it was like to have other people make decisions for one, especially in matters of the heart. She knew the hurt that resulted from being told that the man you loved was totally unsuitable—whether he was, in fact, or not—and she knew that because of the resentment Gillian was feeling towards Oliver, everyone else would be made to suffer too. For that reason alone, Helen knew she had to try to get closer to her. It wasn't Gillian's fault she was here. Like most women, she had very little say about what she could and could not do with her life.

'Miss Gresham, you have a very nice grasp of colour and balance in your paintings,' Helen complimented her one afternoon. 'Your use of different shadings in the greenery of the new and old leaves is very good.'

Gillian shrugged. 'I like to paint. And I paint what I see.'

'So do all the other young ladies, but they do not have as good an eye as you when it comes to colour.'

Gillian looked up at her, and for a moment her face brightened in a smile. It was a fleeting gesture, there and then gone, but it was enough to make Helen marvel at the change it wrought in the girl's appearance. Goodness, it was like the sun coming out after a summer storm. It also made her more determined than ever to break through the barrier of silence and to find out what was really going on in Gillian's mind.

Happily, the opportunity arose a few days later. Helen had taken a book out to a secluded area of the garden to read. It was one of her favourite places and she often retired there to sit and write letters, or to indulge her love of reading. It was there Gillian came upon her. 'Good afternoon, Miss de Coverdale,' she said politely.

'Good afternoon, Miss Gresham.'

'I hope I am not disturbing you, but Mrs Guarding told me I should come outside and take some fresh air.' Gillian flounced down on the seat next to her. 'She said I was looking peaky. Do you think I am?

Helen pretended to do a study of the girl's face. 'I think perhaps you are a trifle pale, but I would not say peaky.'

'That was what I thought too. I do not think anyone has ever called me peaked before.' Gillian sighed again, and then glanced at the book Helen was reading. 'Are you sure I am not disturbing you?'

'Not at all. I was just about to stop for a while anyway.' Helen closed the book and set it aside. '*Othello* is a diverting tale, but I confess I do not like it as well as some of Mr Shakespeare's other works.'

Gillian's eyes opened wide. 'Oh, but how can you not! It is so very romantic. Indeed, Mr Wymington quotes to me from it frequently.'

The mention of the notorious Mr Wymington's name did not escape Helen's notice, but she decided to ignore it for the moment. Better not to express too much curiosity this early in the game. 'Well, you have been here over a week now, Miss Gresham. What do you think of Guarding's?'

Gillian shrugged and some of the gaiety left her eyes. 'It is not as dreadful as I thought it would be. The teachers are all very nice, and so are the girls, but some of them are frightfully intelligent. Annabelle James is brilliant at maths, and Mary Putford knows how to speak French, Italian *and* Greek fluently.'

Helen arched one dark brow in surprise. 'Miss Putford is fluent in Greek? Dear me, perhaps I should ask her if she would be willing to take classes once a week.'

Gillian shrugged again. 'I expect she would. She confided to me that she would very much like to be a teacher one day.'

Helen glanced at the girl in surprise. Mary Putford

was a pleasant girl and one generally acknowledged
by all as being exceedingly bright, but to the best of
Helen's knowledge she seldom mixed with the other
girls. How interesting to discover that in the short
time Gillian had been here, she had somehow managed to get close enough to Mary to know that she
both spoke Greek *and* that she was interested in
teaching it.

Clearly there was more to Gillian Gresham than
met the eye.

'So, does that mean you are not entirely sorry to
be here with us rather than back home in
Hertfordshire?' Helen enquired with a smile.

'Not entirely, though I would never tell Oliver
that.' Gillian watched a small green caterpillar inch
its way through the grass at her feet. 'I want him to
suffer terrible feelings of guilt for having left me here.
I intend to make sure he knows that if I waste away
to nothing, it will all have been his fault.'

Helen was careful not to smile, though she was
very much tempted to. 'I hardly think he will believe
that, Miss Gresham.'

'Nor do I, but it pleases me to think he might. I
would certainly not tell him that I do not miss stuffy
old Shefferton Hall at all.' Gillian sighed. 'The only
problem is that I *do* miss my dear Mr Wymington.'

Thinking it might sound strange if she did not enquire about a gentleman who had now been mentioned twice in conversation, Helen said, 'And who
is Mr Wymington?'

Once again, the change in Gillian's appearance was
remarkable. She clasped her hands together in front
of her and her smile grew positively radiant. 'He is
the most kind and considerate gentleman I have ever

known. He is a lieutenant in the militia, and surely the most handsome man in the entire regiment!'

'Is he indeed? And is there an arrangement between the two of you?'

The girl's animation vanished like a candle being extinguished. 'I only wish there were. Oliver does not care for Mr Wymington. That is why he sent me here. He does not wish me to see him ever again.'

Helen had to exercise a certain amount of care as regards what she said next. She knew it would be wrong to encourage Gillian to go against the wishes of her guardian, but she did want to hear Gillian's side of the story. After all, it was entirely possible that Oliver Brandon's reasons for wishing to separate the two were entirely groundless. 'Why doesn't your guardian like Mr Wymington?'

'Because he thinks he is only after my money. I'm an heiress, you see, Miss de Coverdale. When I turn one-and-twenty, I shall inherit a great deal of money.'

'And is Mr Wymington in possession of a good income himself?'

'No. At least, none that he has ever mentioned to me.'

Which probably meant he wasn't, Helen reflected silently. Lower-ranking officers did not earn a great deal of money, and half-pay officers even less. 'Then it is entirely possible your guardian is right,' Helen replied, willing for the moment to give Mr Brandon the benefit of the doubt. 'It is not unheard of for young gentlemen who are in, shall we say…restricted financial circumstances to be attracted to wealthy young women,' she pointed out. 'Especially when they are as pretty as you.'

The young woman's face brightened again. 'Do you really think I am pretty?'

'Of course, but I am sure Mr Wymington has told you that.'

The blush in the girl's cheeks deepened. 'Miss de Coverdale, may I ask you a question?'

'You may.'

'It is rather personal.'

'I shan't answer it if it is too personal.'

'Well, it is just that…why would someone as beautiful as *you* not be married?'

Helen blinked her surprise. 'Good Lord. Whatever made you ask such a thing?'

'Because you are not like the other teachers here. Oh, they are all very pleasant, to be sure, but none of them are anywhere near as lovely as you. And I know that gentlemen are attracted to pretty ladies. So I simply wondered why you were not married.'

'Perhaps no one has ever asked me,' Helen said in as light-hearted a tone as she could manage.

'But you have been in love, haven't you?'

*Oh yes, I have been in love*, Helen thought wistfully. *But like your guardian, my father did not approve of the gentleman I loved either, and he had him sent away too.*

'I think it would be best if we were to talk about your hopes for the future, Miss Gresham, rather than sit here and discuss something which is of no importance to either of us.'

'But love *is* important,' Gillian said desperately. 'Surely it is the most important thing in the world!'

'It is important, to be sure,' Helen agreed, 'but there are many things which take precedence over it.

Like the value of a good education, for example,
which is why you are here.'

Gillian snorted. 'I am here because Oliver does not
wish me to see Mr Wymington and because there was
nowhere else he could send me.'

There was an unknowingly wistful note to the girl's
voice and it tugged at Helen's heart. 'I am sure your
guardian only has your interests at heart, Miss
Gresham. He is older than you, and he knows what
is best.'

'But how can he know what is best when he has
never been in love?' Gillian cried in frustration. 'How
can he know…how sweet it is to be close to someone
you love when he has never experienced those feelings himself?'

Helen blinked in surprise. A gentleman as handsome as Oliver Brandon had never fallen victim to
love? How very strange. 'Are you sure he has never
felt that way?'

'Oh yes. I have spent most of my life in Oliver's
house, and I know him better than anyone. Except
perhaps his sister, but even Sophie knows what it's
like to be in love.'

'Is she a married lady?'

'Yes, and a most happy one. I like her very much.
We have the most interesting talks, even though she
is very sensible.'

Helen hid her smile, amused by the notion that in
Gillian's mind, being sensible *and* being interesting
were not necessarily synonymous. 'What does she say
about your association with Mr Wymington?'

'She doesn't say very much at all,' Gillian admitted. 'But then she hardly would, being Oliver's sister.
She would never express an opinion contrary to his.'

'Has she met Mr Wymington?' Helen enquired.

'Once. I introduced them at a musicale.'

'And did she appear to like him?'

Gillian frowned. 'I do not know. I cannot recall her saying very much about him at the time.'

'But she did spend enough time in his company to form an opinion of him?'

'Oh yes. Sophie is very good at forming opinions of other people. And she is seldom wrong.'

'Then, if she is good at judging other people's characters, and she is seldom wrong, why would she not tell Mr Brandon he had made an error in judgement with regard to Mr Wymington if she truly believed he had?'

It was a neatly worded exercise that forced Gillian to acknowledge the fact that a woman she considered eminently sensible had made her own decision regarding Mr Wymington and that it might be less than favourable. Unfortunately, Helen could also tell from the look on Gillian's face that she was not about to concede the point so easily.

'Sophie is very capable of forming her own opinions, but she is not always given to sharing them. But I do not believe she would tell me she liked Mr Wymington if she knew her brother would object.'

This time, Helen decided to let it go. She had a sneaking suspicion that Oliver's sister did *not* approve of Mr Wymington and that Gillian was perfectly well aware of it. But her reluctance to admit it naturally begged the question why?

What was there about the dashing young gentleman that both Oliver *and* his happily married sister could object to?

* * *

Oliver read the letter from Gillian, the third he'd received since he'd left her at Guarding's, and frowned in consternation.

Miss de Coverdale has such a refreshing out-look on everything, Oliver. Indeed, I almost feel as though I am talking to someone my own age, rather than someone closer to yours...

Oliver sighed. Obviously she thought him quite de-crepit.

Miss de Coverdale...Helen as I like to think of her...has also told me about the scandalous events which have taken place in Steep Abbot. It seems the old Marquis was murdered right here in the Abbey and that everyone has a dif-ferent opinion as to who did it.

Many believe it was his wife, while others say it was his faithful servant. Really, Oliver, it is quite fascinating. The girls talk about it inces-santly...

Oliver threw down the letter and began to pace. Wonderful. Not only was his ward forming a close friendship with a woman of questionable morals, but she was gossiping with her about the scandalous go-ings-on in the village where she lived. Where was the high moral fibre Sophie had spoken of in reference to the teachers at Mrs Guarding's excellent academy?

Still, he supposed gossiping about a society murder should be the least of his concerns. Far more troubling was the fact that Gillian and Miss de Coverdale were

spending so much time together, and that *Helen* had
such a *refreshing* outlook on everything. What was
he to make of that? Was the woman encouraging
Gillian in her foolish notions? Was she suggesting
that his silly young ward follow her heart and act in
a manner Miss de Coverdale might herself have
thought appropriate at that age?

It was enough to set Oliver ringing for his valet.
He did not like what he was hearing at all. He had
not sent Gillian to the Guarding Academy to be corrupted by a woman like Helen de Coverdale. He *knew*
he should have said something to the headmistress
that first day. He should have voiced his concerns
about Miss de Coverdale's past and taken pains to
ensure that Gillian was not exposed to her influence.
In fact, he should have stayed and *spoken* to the
young woman himself instead of allowing his conscience to be assuaged by Mrs Guarding as regards
the lady's character.

And that's what he was going to do now. The only
way he could find out what was going on in Steep
Abbot was to return there and see with his own eyes
precisely what effect Helen de Coverdale was having
on his ward—before any more damage was done!


Helen didn't know whether to be flattered or flum-
moxed by the letter she had just received. It was from
Oliver Brandon, and it requested the pleasure of her
company on a drive with him that very afternoon, if
she could spare him the time.

Helen thoughtfully tapped the parchment against
her bottom lip. As it happened, she did have some
free time, given that it was her weekly half-day, but
she had not thought to spend it with Mr Brandon. She

had expected him to ask for a meeting to discuss the incident that had happened in her past well before now. Gillian had been at Guarding's nearly two and a half weeks. Why was he bothering to spend time with her at this late date?

Helen frowned as she put the letter on her desk. Was it possible the visit had something to do with Gillian herself? Was he concerned, perhaps, as to how well she was settling in, or as to how competent she was in her studies? Helen knew that Gillian wrote frequently to her guardian. Was it possible she had expressed unhappiness or dissatisfaction with the school, and that he was coming to see to the matter himself?

As quickly as the thought came, Helen dismissed it. No. If Mr Brandon was curious to know how his ward was progressing, he would have written to Mrs Guarding directly. The headmistress was kept fully apprised of the progress of each girl, just in case such an enquiry might arise.

Then what else could it be? Had Gillian taken a personal dislike to her and written to Mr Brandon about that? Helen didn't think so. In fact, she was rather pleased with the friendship that had sprung up between them, and she was sure it had contributed to Gillian's adapting more easily to her new environment. Even the other teachers were commenting about her sudden willingness to participate in class, and about how quick Gillian was to help the younger girls with their problems.

So if it wasn't an interrogation about her past, and it wasn't in response to a complaint from Gillian, what could Mr Brandon possibly be coming to see her about?

At precisely twenty-seven minutes past three, Helen closed the door to her room and walked briskly toward the stairs. The soles of her worn leather boots made a soft clicking sound against the wooden floor, but she barely heard it over the thudding of her heart. She had tried to tell herself she had nothing to worry about, but after much deliberation, she had concluded that the reason Mr Brandon wanted to see her today was to talk to her about her past. It was the only logical explanation.

But in recognising that, Helen also recognised that Oliver Brandon was *entitled* to know what had happened. And she felt sure that once she told him the truth—embarrassing as that might be—everything would be fine. After all, Oliver Brandon was a gentleman. As a gentleman he would understand.

He was already waiting in the hall by the time Helen descended. He looked extremely dashing this afternoon, wearing a multi-layered greatcoat over a dark jacket and light-coloured breeches. He seemed to her even larger than usual, and with his hair somewhat dishevelled by the wind, there was a roguishness about him that Helen found distinctly attractive.

She made a show of attending to her gloves, not wanting him to see how affected she really was. 'Good afternoon, Mr Brandon. I hope I have not kept you waiting.'

Oliver turned at the sound of her voice and sketched her a perfunctory bow. 'On the contrary, Miss de Coverdale, you are exceedingly punctual.'

The formal tone gave Helen a moment's pause, but she told herself to ignore it. It was only natural that his speech would be short. No doubt his impressions of her prevented him from being anything but distant.

In the courtyard, a stylish curricle drawn by two perfectly matched blacks awaited their arrival.

'Oh, what a splendid pair,' Helen commented with approval. 'Do they go as sweetly as they look?'

'They do indeed. Are you at skilled at tooling the ribbons, Miss de Coverdale?'

'I used to be,' Helen admitted as he settled her into the passenger seat, 'but a great deal of time has passed since then, and I should not like to comment upon my abilities now.'

'It is not something one forgets,' Mr Brandon observed, climbing up beside her.

'No, but neither is it a skill which improves with lack of practice. However, on such a lovely day as this, I am quite content to sit back and enjoy someone else's skill.'

And truly, it was a perfect mid-September day. The slight briskness in the air encouraged the wearing of gloves and a light coat, but it was not so cold as to be uncomfortable. Helen wished she might have had a prettier gown to wear, but such things were not available to a young woman in her position. The dark green spencer over the plain cambric gown did very well, as did her poke-bonnet tied with a matching ribbon. The newest thing she owned was a pair of buttery-soft kid gloves, a much-cherished Christmas present from her friend Desirée.

Mr Brandon gathered up the reins and set the pair to a brisk trot. His hands were firm but never harsh on the reins, and Helen enjoyed watching him employ his skills at keeping the pair to a steady trot. She also liked the fact that he seldom used the whip. She had seen far too many young men try to demonstrate their skill with the tool, only to have the horses suffer for their inadequacy. But when Mr Brandon employed the whip, it was with such a light hand that Helen knew it was the sound of the snap more than the touch that set the horses to responding. Besides, with a pair of high-steppers like these, it would hardly be necessary.

They drove for a few miles in silence, enjoying the loveliness of the autumn day. Helen wished she could have said she was enjoying Oliver's company as much, but with every minute that passed, her feelings of apprehension grew. The knowledge that she was going to have to talk about an incident which had caused her so much pain and embarrassment was not conducive to serenity.

Finally, when she could bear the silence no longer, she turned to him with the question on her lips. To her surprise, she was forestalled by one of his.

'Where did you learn to speak Italian, Miss de Coverdale?'

Helen blinked. 'I…beg your pardon?'

'Italian.' Oliver favoured her with a piercing gaze. 'It is an unusual language for an Englishwoman to be teaching, is it not?'

'Well, no, not…really,' Helen stammered. 'My mother was Italian.'

'But not your father.'

'No. He was English. My mother met him while she was visiting friends in Canterbury. They married soon after.'

'Did they return to Italy?'

Helen shook her head. 'My father was already established in England so there was no question of their living abroad.'

'And was your mother happy to leave Italy?'

Helen's eyes softened. 'I don't think she was ever truly happy in England. She hated the dampness of the weather and the persistently grey skies. And I know she missed her family very much. She was one of eight children.'

'Good God, eight?'

Helen smiled. 'Italians are known for having large families. Unfortunately, my father had no desire even to visit Italy, so in the end, my mother decided to spend her summers there. And she took me with her.'

'Your father didn't mind?'

Helen shrugged. 'Theirs was an unusual marriage. My father was passionately in love with my mother, and there was nothing he could deny her. So the separations were allowed as long as they did not extend beyond a month.'

'And did *you* like Italy, Miss de Coverdale?'

'I loved it,' Helen said, with, for the first time in his company, a complete lack of reserve. 'The bright, sunny days were such a welcome change from the dreary English winters, and I found the people very open and spontaneous.'

'And that was where you learned to speak the language,' he said, making it a statement of fact rather than a question.

'Yes. My entire family conversed in Italian, so it was only natural that I would pick it up. But even when we were back in England, my mother continued to speak to me in the language. Never when my father was around, of course, but he was away so much of the time, it wasn't a problem.'

'Your father objected to you and your mother speaking in her native tongue?'

'My father thought it was rude to speak in a language that only two of the three people in the room could understand,' Helen told him. 'However, my mother was of the opinion that one must use a language to stay conversant in it.'

'Just as one must practise driving to keep one's skills up,' Oliver said distantly.

Helen flashed him an amused glance. 'Just so.'

They drove on again in silence. A few other carriages passed them, but for the most part, they had the road to themselves. Helen didn't even trouble to hide her pleasure at being driven out on such a beautiful day. She even endeavoured to make light conversation about some of the places they passed, but as her attempts were often met with silence she soon gave up.

Finally, when the silence again became uncomfortable, she took a long, deep breath and turned to face him. 'Mr Brandon, I must confess to a certain…surprise at having received your letter. It is most unusual for a schoolmistress to spend time alone with the parent of one of her girls.'

'I seldom trouble myself with what is or is not usual, Miss de Coverdale,' Oliver replied blandly. 'I wished to speak to you alone and perceived this to be the best way of doing that.'

'But…what did you wish to speak to me about?'

Oliver sent her a mocking glance. 'Do you really need ask, given the nature of our first acquaintance?'

Helen quickly averted her eyes. So, it was as she had expected. 'I see. You wish to ask me about… what you saw in the library that night.'

'Yes, but only as it affects your relationship with my ward.'

'I beg your pardon?'

'I will be honest, Miss de Coverdale. I might not have found this interview necessary had Gillian's letters to me not been filled with such glowing praise about *you*.'

Helen's eyes opened wide. 'She wrote to you about me?'

'Frequently. And in the most flattering of terms.' When she made no answer, Oliver's lips curved in a sardonic smile. 'You seem surprised, Miss de Coverdale. Did you not expect Gillian to speak well of you?'

'I had no idea how she would speak of me. I thought we had established a friendship, but I...'

'Yes?'

Biting her lip, Helen looked away. 'If your ward thinks well of me and has written to tell you as much, why did you feel it necessary to speak to me about...something of which she has no knowledge?'

'Because it is not Gillian's ignorance of the event which concerns me,' Oliver informed her. 'She told me you had a *refreshing* outlook toward certain subjects. I am simply curious to know which subjects those might be.'

Frowning, Helen shook her head. 'I cannot honestly say, sir. We talk of so many things it is difficult to remember the nature of every conversation.'

'Then let me see if I can narrow the field somewhat. Did Mrs Guarding apprise you of a situation with regard to a Mr Sidney Wymington?'

Helen grew wary. 'Yes.'

'And has my ward also made mention of that gentleman?'

Knowing there was no point in denying it, Helen inclined her head. 'Yes, she has.'

'Then I'm sure you can understand why I might wish to speak with you in private regarding the matter.'

Helen's brow furrowed. 'In truth, sir, I cannot. Unless you have some reason to believe I would not adhere to your wishes.'

'Miss de Coverdale, let us not mince words. I saw you in the library with Lord Talbot. I know you were not there to discuss the merits of literature and given that knowledge, I think you can understand why I was so surprised at finding you here, acting out the part of schoolmistress.'

An angry flush suffused Helen's face. 'I do not *act* the part, sir. I *am* a teacher and I take great pride in what I do. Have you reason to doubt my abilities?'

'Not at all. Mrs Guarding spoke most highly of your skills.'

'Then I do not understand—'

'The issue I wished to address, Miss de Coverdale, is one of morality, not proficiency.'

'Morality!'

'Yes. Since you are aware of my feelings with regard to Mr Wymington, I am sure you can understand why I would be concerned about any…influence you might have on Gillian in regard to that situation.'

'I do not understand your concerns at all,' Helen replied, her voice curt. 'If you do not wish your ward to have anything to do with the man, what makes you think I would?'

'Because given your behaviour in the past, I am not sure you have as high a moral character as I would like.'

His words struck her like a slap across the face and Helen swallowed hard, fighting to keep her composure. 'Mr Brandon, I understand how you might have been tempted to form certain…opinions of me based upon what you saw. But to still hold me in such contempt for a perceived indiscretion twelve years later demonstrates to my way of thinking a shocking narrowness of mind.'

'Narrowness of mind!'

'Indeed, sir. You formed an impression of my character based upon what you thought you saw—'

'Based upon what I *did* see.'

'No, sir. Based upon what you *thought* you saw, and have held it to this day, without even giving me a chance to explain.'

'Then explain yourself now,' Oliver snapped. 'You have not once tried to deny that you *were* the woman I saw in Lord Talbot's arms that night.'

'No, because it would be foolish of me to try,' Helen flung at him. 'We both know it was me, but what you do not understand is that I was not there of my own accord.'

'Were you a servant in his house?'

'I was the governess.'

'And had Lord Talbot *asked* you to come to the library?'

'Of course not, but—'

'Then why, as a servant in the house, were you in the master's library with your hair unbound at that time of night, when you had no reason or permission to be there?'

Helen's cheeks burned. 'I had gone to procure a book. And I frequently wear my hair unbound.'

The expression on Oliver's face was not encouraging. 'Miss de Coverdale, I can find nothing in what you have just told me to justify your conduct or to make me change my opinion of you. If you felt no compunction about behaving in such a fashion, how do I know you would not counsel an impressionable young woman to do the same? Or in this case, to take up with a man I have refused to let her see!'

Oliver had not raised his voice, but the condescension in his words cut Helen to the bone. Not only was he accusing her of having behaved in a wanton and disgraceful manner, he was saying she was quite capable of persuading Gillian to do the same. He was insinuating that her character had not improved at all in the past twelve years, and that he was perfectly within his rights to believe that his assessment of her was still correct today.

And Helen resented that. She resented the implication that she was not worthy to keep company with his ward. She resented his belief that what he had witnessed twelve years ago had been the truth, even when she had tried to tell him it was not. And most deeply of all, she resented *him* for having brought it all back; for making her relive the feelings of shame and degradation she had felt on that dreadful night. Feelings she had fought so long and so hard to overcome.

'Mr Brandon, I do not think there is anything else which needs to be said between us,' Helen said, finally turning to look at him. 'Obviously the testimonials of people who know me far better than you, and who are willing to vouch for my respectability, mean nothing, so I would ask you to be so good as to take me back to Guarding's.'

Oliver reined the team in, but he did not turn the carriage around. 'I do not understand why you evidence such surprise at my comment, Miss de

Coverdale. I was a witness to what took place in the library at Grovesend Hall, not the cause of it.'

'Nor was I, Mr Brandon, but since you obviously aren't willing to believe that, I do not see that we have anything further to discuss.'

'Miss de Coverdale—'

'For the last time, sir, would you please take me home,' Helen said stiffly. 'I have done nothing to deserve such treatment from you, and unless you have an apology to offer, there is nothing more I wish to hear.'

Oliver had no intention of offering an apology, and as if finally realising that Helen had indeed, no intention of speaking another word to him, he cursed softly and turned the team around. He flicked the reins and set them to a brisk trot.

Not another word was spoken the entire way home.

# Chapter Five

Helen decided not to tell Gillian she had driven out with her guardian. After all, what would be the point? Nothing would be gained by such an admission. Gillian would want to know the details of what they had talked about, and Helen had no intention of telling her. Yes, there was a chance Gillian might find out about the meeting and then accuse Helen of holding something back, but it was a slim chance at best. Gillian certainly wouldn't hear the truth from her stepbrother. Why would he bring up a subject that would expose him to a barrage of questions he would be no more anxious to answer than Helen?

Thankfully, the subject did not arise, and when Helen heard from Gillian that Oliver had been called away to London on business, she could not find it in her heart to be sorry. The man had insulted her in every possible way. He had all but called her a trollop, and then accused her of corrupting the innocents in her care.

Was it any wonder his company was something Helen was all too happy to avoid?

\* \* \*

Sunday mornings were typically reserved for service in Abbot Quincey, and at nine o'clock Helen and Gillian set off for church. They were accompanied by three of the other teachers, Jane Emerson, Ghislaine de Champlain and Henriette Mason, as well as by a few of the girls. Mr and Mrs Guarding always took the youngest ones in their carriage, but the older pupils and the teachers were quite happy to walk. It afforded them an opportunity to enjoy the beauty of the countryside, and to escape, if only for a few hours, the somewhat confining atmosphere of the school.

Abbot Quincey was the largest of the four Abbey villages. It boasted a fine old church, the living of which was held by the Reverend William Perceval, a kindly man with a wife and four daughters, and a younger brother to Lord Perceval. Helen had always enjoyed the Reverend Perceval's sermons. In the quiet of the village church, and in the companionship of her friends, she experienced a sense of peace and contentment as the gentle words of forgiveness flowed all around her. Unfortunately, on this particular morning, Helen found little to take comfort in. The memory of Oliver Brandon's visit and the disturbing things he had said to her stayed with her the entire time, intruding painfully into the serenity of her thoughts.

Fortunately, not everyone was as disconsolate as she. Jane Emerson sat quietly beside her on one side of the wooden pew and Gillian sat on the other, the girl's gloved hands folded primly in her lap as she listened to the words of the sermon. It was a particularly moving lesson on the value of patience and the importance of forgiveness in everyday life.

Helen was quite sure Oliver Brandon had never heard that particular sermon before.

As Gillian continued to sit quietly through the service, Helen found herself envying the girl's placid air of repose. How lucky she was to be seventeen and still so innocent to the ways of the world. There were no ghosts lurking in her past. No disturbing memories ready to haunt her at the slightest provocation. There was nothing anyone could say that would humiliate Gillian the way Oliver Brandon had humiliated her.

Helen sighed as she ran her gloved finger along the spine of her prayer book. Of course, she supposed he wasn't entirely to blame for what had happened between them. She should have told him *exactly* what had happened in the library with Lord Talbot. She should have *forced* him to listen and to make him understand that she had *not* been there of her own volition. But the truth was, she had been so shocked by his heartless accusation that she had been left completely at a loss for words. Indeed, she had been nearly speechless with anger.

How dare he infer that she was corrupt and immoral! He, who knew nothing of her character or her circumstances. Surely his own narrow-mindedness was every bit as grievous a flaw. After all, *she* was the one who had been willing to be conciliatory. She had even been willing to risk a scold for having been foolish enough to put herself in such an ignominious position to begin with. But she was *not* willing to be labelled a scarlet woman. If that was the make-up of the man, she was better off having nothing more to do with him. Gillian too, was better off away from such bigotry.

At length the service came to an end and people began to get up and move about. Helen rose along with the others and filed out of the church, blinking a little as she stepped into the bright sunshine. There were no formal classes at Guarding's on Sunday afternoons, but the girls were expected to return there for the midday meal. After that, they could go to their rooms, or to the common area where they might apply themselves to their embroidery or their scriptures. Sunday evenings were generally reserved for the reading of psalms by Mrs Guarding, and if she was so inclined, a discussion of the sermon given by Reverend Perceval that morning.

Helen stopped briefly to have a word with the vicar and his wife, while Gillian struck up a conversation with a young woman from the village. Indeed, so animated was their discussion that, when it finally came time to leave, Helen had to call Gillian away. It was only on their way back to Steep Abbot that she discovered the reason for the girl's excitement.

'Miss de Coverdale, who do you think murdered the old Marquis of Sywell?'

Helen caught her breath in dismay. 'Good heavens, Miss Gresham, I have no idea. Nor do I think it a suitable topic for us to be discussing after church on a Sunday morning.'

'But everyone else is talking about it!' Gillian cried. 'Imagine being murdered in your own bedroom. Apparently the murder weapon was his own razor and there was heaps of blood everywhere! That would be quite a shock to whoever found him, don't you think?'

'I think it would be very shocking indeed,' Helen allowed, knowing that the thought had crossed her own mind several times.

'Frances Templeton thinks one of the girls who worked as an upstairs maid murdered him,' Gillian said. 'She said Sywell was wretched to her, as he was to all of the servants. Personally, I am more inclined to believe it was his wife. After all, she would have inherited everything upon his death, wouldn't she? Or so she would have thought.' Gillian didn't even bother waiting for a reply. 'Louise wouldn't have known when she murdered her husband that the Abbey wasn't really his. But given her *belief* that it was, and that she would inherit, I think that would have been reason enough for her to do it, don't you?'

'I am really not acquainted with the details of the story, Miss Gresham,' Helen said, hoping the Lord would forgive her for the lie. Everyone knew it was all but impossible to live this close to the Abbey and *not* be aware of all the rumours and speculation going on about its former occupant. But that was still no reason to encourage an impressionable young woman like Gillian to gossip about it.

'Oh, bother,' Gillian said, clearly disappointed. 'I find the whole subject fascinating. I mean, when you think about it, there are an endless number of people who could have murdered him, and for any number of reasons!'

'Which is why it would be foolish of us to attempt a discussion of the subject,' Helen said in a firm voice. 'Certainly we cannot do so with any degree of intelligence. Not that murder has anything to do with intelligence, but I think that on such a beautiful day as this, we should be able to find something more pleasant to talk about.'

'Oh, very well.' Gillian was silent for a moment. 'What do you think of my guardian?'

Helen all but stumbled. 'I *beg* your pardon?'

'I asked you what you thought of Oliver.'

'I know *what* you asked, Miss Gresham. I am simply wondering *why* you asked it.'

'Well, he is very handsome, don't you think?'

The abrupt switch to a topic Helen found even more disturbing than the murder at Steepwood Abbey left her feeling somewhat shaken. 'I have not given it any consideration at all. After all, the only time I've spent with Mr Brandon was on the morning you arrived,' she said, sending up another prayer for forgiveness.

'And when he came to take you driving.'

Helen came to an abrupt halt. 'How did you know about that?'

'Elizabeth Brookwell saw the two of you drive off together. Oh you needn't worry, I am not going to give you a scold,' Gillian assured her. 'I admit, I was a little put out that you didn't tell me, but then I realised you were probably just waiting for the right time to bring it up. Otherwise, I would be just as like to believe you were trying to hide something.'

Botheration, Helen thought. She should have realised that *someone* would have seen them drive off. 'I can assure you I have nothing to hide. The outing was not motivated by any feelings of personal affection on your stepbrother's part.'

'Then why did he take you driving?'

Helen started walking again. 'He wished to speak to me about something.'

'About me?'

'Partly.'

'And what else?'

'About matters which do not concern you.'

'Were they matters which concerned you?'

'Gillian, it is impolite to ask so many questions.'

'I know, but you won't give me answers otherwise. Oliver really is very nice, you know,' Gillian said, her enthusiasm not in the least dampened by the rebuke. 'Oh, I know he comes across as being terribly serious, but he isn't that way all the time. I've heard him laugh with Sophie quite often—'

'I am not interested in who Mr Brandon laughs with—'

'He drives very well too, do you not think? I don't know any other gentleman who handles a pair as well as Oliver. And he is a superb hunter.'

'Miss Gresham, why are you telling me all this?'

'Because I think the two of you would make a splendid match.'

*That* all but caused Helen's knees to buckle. *Herself and Oliver Brandon?* It did not even bear thinking about. 'I would thank you not to make such ridiculous suggestions, Miss Gresham. I am not looking for a husband—'

'But if you were—'

'If I were, I would still not consider Mr Brandon. We have absolutely nothing in common.'

'He thinks you're beautiful.'

Helen opened her mouth to answer, and then abruptly closed it again. No. She was not about to attempt a response to a comment like that. Apart from the fact that she was not at all sure Gillian hadn't made it up, it could have absolutely no bearing on the situation. Oliver Brandon had already told her what he thought of her. And given her knowledge of what he'd said, the fact that he thought her beautiful—if indeed he did—made for a very shallow compliment indeed.

Unfortunately, Gillian's questions and revelations

about her guardian were not the only shocks Helen was to receive that afternoon. Just before they reached the school gates, they heard the sound of a carriage coming up behind them. Perpetually curious, Gillian turned around to look, but Helen, assuming it was the Guardings returning home, merely moved to the side of the road.

She couldn't have been more wrong. As the equipage drew to a halt beside them, Gillian's startled exclamation caused Helen to stop and whirl around.

'Oh, my dear Miss de Coverdale,' Gillian whispered in tones of barely concealed delight. 'I vow the angels have heard my prayers! Only look! Here is none other than my dear Mr Wymington come to pay me a visit!'

# *Chapter Six*

Helen could only stare in horror at the gentleman pulling the carriage to a halt beside them. *Mr Wymington?* Dear Lord, what was she to do? The one man she had been warned to keep Gillian away from was the very one who had found them! What would Mr Brandon say if he were to learn of this?

'Miss Gresham, we must continue towards the school!' Helen whispered urgently. 'You know this meeting cannot take place!'

Unfortunately, Gillian was lost to everyone but her beloved Mr Wymington. She stared at him like one in a dream, her lips parted, her eyes glowing with happiness as he jumped down from the seat and began to walk towards them. And as much as Helen might like to deny it, she could not find it in her heart to blame Gillian. The young man walking towards them was truly the embodiment of the romantic hero. Standing tall and dashing in his regimentals, with a shock of golden blond hair and eyes that were as blue as the summer's sky, he was easily one of the most handsome men Helen had ever seen.

'Mr Wymington!' Gillian cried, pouring her heart into the expression of his name.

The gentleman looked similarly elated at finding the object of his affection so close at hand and quickened his pace, causing a swath of wavy, blond hair to fall across his forehead. His smile, which had been somewhat tentative at first, widened to an expression of such heart-shattering beauty that Helen knew there was absolutely nothing she could do to prevent the meeting from taking place. However, knowing she must do whatever she could to make it as brief and as harmless as possible, she stepped in front of Gillian, placed the girl securely behind her, and addressed the man in a clear and no nonsense voice.

'Good afternoon, Mr Wymington. My name is Helen de Coverdale. I am a teacher at the Guarding Academy for Girls.'

Mr Wymington looked at Helen and offered her the same dazzling smile he had just given Gillian. 'Miss de Coverdale, I am genuinely delighted to make your acquaintance. And I feel compelled to say this is truly the most incredible of coincidences. I knew Miss Gresham was attending school near Steep Abbot, but it never crossed my mind that I would be fortunate enough to see her here.'

'But is it not wonderful that you have!' Gillian cried breathlessly.

Helen saw nothing wonderful in it at all. 'It is coincidental indeed, but what has brought you all the way from Hertfordshire on a Sunday, sir?'

'Do not fear, my reasons are entirely justified. I have come to visit my sick uncle.'

'Your uncle?' Gillian's delicate eyebrows shot upwards in surprise. 'You did not tell me you had an uncle residing in the area.'

'Indeed, I think I may have neglected to mention it,' Mr Wymington said somewhat sheepishly. 'But I do in fact have one. He lives just outside Abbot Quincey.'

'But we were just *in* Abbot Quincey,' Gillian said, her face alight with joy. 'Is that not the most amazing coincidence, Miss de Coverdale?'

'Amazing indeed,' Helen muttered, feeling it was all far *too* coincidental for her liking. 'But I'm afraid we cannot linger, Mr Wymington. We are expected back at school. If you will excuse us—'

'Oh, but why must we leave so soon?' Gillian turned to her in dismay. 'Mr Wymington has come all this way to see me—'

'To see his uncle,' Helen reminded her.

'Oh. Well, whatever the reason, he is here now. Even better, he has had a chance to meet you.'

The gentleman bowed graciously. 'I consider myself most fortunate to have had the pleasure of meeting *two* such beautiful ladies.' He glanced at Helen with unfeigned interest. 'What subjects do you teach, Miss de Coverdale?'

'Italian and watercolours,' Gillian offered impulsively. 'And she is very good at both.'

A swift rush of colour stained Helen's cheeks. 'Miss Gresham is prone to exaggeration, sir.'

'In some areas, perhaps, but not in this I shouldn't think. Otherwise you would not be employed at such a reputable establishment.'

Helen glanced at him in surprise. 'You are familiar with Mrs Guarding's Academy, Mr Wymington?'

If Helen had thought to catch him out, his answers

were to come as a disappointment. The man was no fool. He proceeded to tell her when the school had been established and who the headmistress was, then further surprised her by expressing familiarity with some of the papers Mrs Guarding had published, as well as a knowledge of her beliefs and of the precepts upon which the school had been founded.

For a moment, Helen could understand Gillian's attraction to him. But she could not shake the feeling that the meeting had been far from coincidental. 'How long do you intend to stay in Abbot Quincey, Mr Wymington?' she enquired.

'That depends entirely upon my uncle. He is not in the best of health, which is why I have come to see him. But I cannot say how long he will wish me to stay.' Mr Wymington's expression turned endearingly humble. 'He is a very independent gentleman and I shouldn't wonder that he'll try to send me back to London just as soon as he can, with the assurance that he is quite capable of looking after himself.'

'If I were ill, I know I should very much like to have you taking care of me,' Gillian said impulsively.

Helen only just managed not to gasp. 'I'm sorry, Mr Wymington, but we really must be on our way.'

'Of course. It was most inconsiderate of me to detain you. But I cannot deny that I have enjoyed meeting the two of you.' He smiled at them and bowed. 'Your servant, Miss de Coverdale. Miss Gresham. I hope I shall have the honour of seeing you both again in the near future.'

Gillian nodded fervently. 'Oh yes, we must arrange—'

'Good afternoon, Mr Wymington,' Helen said, before Gillian had time to commit any further indiscretions.

Tipping his hat, Mr Wymington returned to his carriage and headed back in the direction from whence he had come. Gillian watched the carriage until it rounded a corner and disappeared from sight. Only then did she let out a long, ecstatic sigh. 'Oh, is he not the most handsome of gentlemen, Miss de Coverdale? Indeed, he appears even more handsome to me than he did when last I saw him. Do you think it is possible for someone to grow even more handsome in the space of three weeks?'

'I very much doubt it,' Helen muttered, far less pleased with the outcome of the day than Gillian was.

'But you cannot disagree that he is handsome. Or that he is charming! Did you not think so?'

'His manners were all that were pleasing, yes.'

'Then why were you so abrupt with him?'

Helen turned and starting walking briskly in the direction of the school. 'I was not abrupt.'

'Yes, you were. I know you, Miss de Coverdale, and I know when you are being abrupt.'

'If I was short with Mr Wymington, it was only because I was not pleased at finding him here. Nor will your guardian be when he finds out.'

Gillian's face went white. 'Oh, but he mustn't find out! You mustn't tell him! If Oliver were to learn that Mr Wymington was here, there is no telling what he might do.'

'I cannot keep secrets from your guardian, Miss Gresham. Especially about this.'

'But you heard what Mr Wymington said. He came to visit his sick uncle.' Gillian scurried to keep up with her. 'Surely you cannot hold such noble motives against him.'

'I do not hold them against him. I am merely suspicious of his timing. Do you not find it disturbing that Mr Wymington suddenly decided to visit a sick uncle who just happens to live in Abbot Quincey, when he never even mentioned the *existence* of the man to you before?'

'What I find disturbing is that you are starting to sound like Oliver. Why is everyone so suspicious of Mr Wymington? Why can't anyone believe that the man is attracted to me and not to my money?'

*Oh, Gillian, there is so much you need to learn*, Helen thought sadly. *And we are only trying to prevent you from learning it the hard way.*

'Miss Gresham, whatever your own feelings with regard to Mr Wymington, you cannot ignore the fact that your guardian wishes you to have nothing to do with him.'

'But he has no right—'

'He has every right. Mr Brandon has let it be known that you are not to see Mr Wymington, or to correspond with him.'

'But that is not fair! Mr Wymington has done nothing wrong. Oliver doesn't like him because he reads Shakespeare to me and tells me I am pretty. What is wrong with that? Is that not the way two people who care about each other express their thoughts and feelings?'

Helen abruptly came to a halt. 'Miss Gresham—'

'Oh, do call me Gillian. At least when we are alone.'

'Very well, Gillian. You have to understand that Mr Brandon—'

'Oliver.'

'That Mr Brandon is concerned with your welfare. Many young women are taken in by a gentleman's blandishments and marry against their parents' wishes, only to come to regret it later.'

'But why is Oliver so convinced that Mr Wymington is bad?' Gillian's face mirrored her confusion. 'There is absolutely nothing evil about him. Surely you just saw that for yourself. What is there not to like about Mr Wymington?'

*What was there not to like indeed?* Helen thought in the privacy of her room later that evening. She had found Mr Wymington to be all that Gillian claimed him to be; a well-spoken and charming gentleman whose appearance and manners were only to be admired. She did not know him well, of course, but on first meeting, there was nothing to which she could take a dislike.

Unfortunately, Oliver Brandon had made his wishes clear. There was to be absolutely no association between Gillian and Mr Wymington. He had told Mrs Guarding to advise her staff of that fact, so Helen could hardly claim ignorance of his wishes. But what if Oliver's dislike of Mr Wymington had nothing to do with the man personally? What if his feelings of animosity arose from something else altogether? After all, it was not unheard of for fathers or brothers to suffer feelings of jealousy the first time their daughters' or sisters' attentions moved in another direction. Was it possible Oliver was reluctant to lose his stepsister's affections? Because if he was, he could be doing Gillian a tremendous injustice.

*Just as your father did you.*

Helen closed her eyes and willed the painful thoughts away. No, this was not the time to dwell on that. Their two situations were not the same at all. *Her* father had not wished her to marry beneath her, whereas Mr Brandon did not wish Gillian to marry a fortune-hunter. The reasons for their objections were entirely different.

Unfortunately, when it came right down to it, Helen knew that the end result would be the same. Gillian would not be allowed to follow her heart and marry the man she loved any more than Helen had. The only difference was that Helen was quite sure Gillian would not accept her fate so meekly. Nor that Oliver would escape so lightly!

Oliver tossed back the last of his cognac and stared glumly at his surroundings. He shouldn't have come here tonight. The club was painfully devoid of company. He could usually count on at least one or two of his friends being present but tonight it seemed they had all found better things to do. And he was not in a mood to be alone.

He frowned as he poured himself another drink and crossed one booted ankle over the other. Fact was, he'd been blue-devilled ever since his return from Northamptonshire, and it was all as a result of his encounter with Miss Helen de Coverdale. What was he to make of this young woman who had turned up so unexpectedly in his life again? She was a beauty to be sure. Even now, the memory of her face lingered in his mind like a sweetly haunting melody. But why was he suffering feelings of guilt over what he had said to her? He had only spoken the truth; they'd both known that. And he had only brought the subject up because of Gillian's welfare. So why had Helen glared at him as though *she* had been the injured party?

'Brandon. Good God, man, where the hell've you been?' came an affected drawl behind him. 'Thought perhaps you'd headed for the Americas.'

The husky voice—familiar despite the length of time since he'd heard it—caused Oliver's lip to curl in distaste. He raised his glass in an attempt to disguise his annoyance. 'As you see, I have not.' He glanced up as the man staggered towards the vacant chair across from him. 'Looking a bit foxed this evening, Lord Talbot.'

'Humph, no reason why I shouldn't be.' The heavy man grunted as he sat down. 'Just lost a packet to Clapham! Bloody fool swore he didn't know one card from the other.'

The remark served to restore a little of Oliver's flagging spirits. 'I'm surprised he took you in. Everyone knows Clapham's a master when it comes to cards.'

'Yes, well, I'll be damned if he gulls me like that again. Told him he'd best stay out of my sight.' Talbot raised his hand to summon a waiter. 'So, what brings you to London? Business or pleasure?'

Oliver rested his glass on his knee, but his eyes were sharp on the peer's face. 'A little bit of both.'

'Huh! More pleasure, I'll wager.' Talbot's smile suddenly turned sly. 'Did you know Carter tried to lure your little Nicolette away?'

'Really?' Oliver shrugged, careful not to let his displeasure show. He wasn't concerned that he might lose Nicolette, since it had been some time since he had wished to spend a night in her bed. But he was disappointed that a man who had once called himself a friend had tried to go behind his back in such a way. 'No, I hadn't heard.'

'Didn't think you had. Not that it mattered, because she would't have him.' Talbot reached for the glass the waiter had just brought and downed the contents in one gulp. 'Told him to take himself off. You must keep her well satisfied to make her turn down a nabob like that.'

'We have an understanding,' was all Oliver said.

'Then you're a lucky man. Most wenches would switch beds for nothing more than the promise of a pretty bauble or two.'

'Is that your experience of women?' Oliver enquired mildly.

'For the most part. But there's always more to be had, so I don't trouble myself about it.'

'No, I'm sure you don't.' Oliver steepled his fingers in front of his face. 'Speaking of being lucky, I seem to remember one mistress you must have been sorry to lose.'

Talbot glanced at him in surprise. 'One of mine, you say?'

'Yes. Do you remember the night I caught you and a young lady in the library at Grovesend Hall?'

The peer's expression was blank. 'Grovesend?'

'Yes. Nearly twelve years ago.'

'Good God, man, I barely remember what I was doing twelve *hours* ago, let alone twelve years.'

Oliver smiled faintly. 'I think you would remember this particular night. I walked into the library and found you in an embrace with a young woman by the name of Helen de Coverdale.'

'Helen de…what?'

'Coverdale. I believe she was your governess at the time.'

'A governess.' Talbot's eyes clouded. 'We went through an endless succession of governesses. Why would you expect me to remember one in particular?'

'Because this young lady was exceptional,' Oliver said quietly. 'She had long, black hair, and was, as I recall, exceedingly lovely.'

'Really?' Talbot was silent for a moment. 'Long black hair, you say?'

'Yes.'

'And pretty?'

Oliver filled his glass again. 'Exceptionally.'

It was evident from the look on Talbot's face that his recollection of the past was faulty. So much so, that Oliver began to wonder if he would remember it at all. But then, very slowly, Talbot began to smile. 'Wait a moment. Yes, now that I think about it, I do remember a governess like that. Couldn't tell you what her name was but I remember the long black hair. Fell almost to her waist. And she had the most seductive eyes I'd ever seen.' The peer's smile broadened, but in a way that sent chills down Oliver's spine. 'Yes, damn it, she was beautiful, but she wasn't my mistress.'

Oliver's hand froze halfway to his lips. 'She wasn't?'

'Cold little bitch,' Talbot spat out. 'Wouldn't have anything to do with me. I'd been trying to bed her from the day she walked into the house, but she wouldn't have any part of it. Told me to…well, never mind what she told me to do.'

A flurry of emotions tumbled through Oliver's

mind. 'But you were with her that night. When I walked into the room, you were holding her—'

'Of course I was holding her,' Talbot snapped. 'And I would have done a damn sight more if you hadn't walked in when you had.'

'Then...she wasn't your mistress?'

Talbot shook his head. 'Never so much as kissed her. She left the next morning. Never saw her again. But by God, if ever I did, I wouldn't mind picking up where I left off.' He rose unsteadily from the chair. 'She had the most beautiful... *Ouch!* Damn and blast the bloody table!' he shouted, kicking the offending object aside. He rubbed his hand over the sore spot on his thigh and then limped away, seemingly unaware he'd been halfway through a sentence.

Oliver was more relieved than he cared to admit. What an idiot he'd been. No wonder Miss de Coverdale had been so angry with him. She hadn't been lying to him at all. Obviously, Talbot had come upon her in the library and thought to take advantage of the situation. And Helen, being so much smaller, wouldn't have had a hope of defending herself.

All the way home Oliver thought about the things he'd said to her—and wished he could take every one of them back. Well, there was one thing he knew for a certainty. The moment he concluded his business here, he was going back to Steep Abbot. The sooner he straightened out this mess with Helen, the better.

The only question was, would she be willing to listen to anything he had to say?

In a quiet section of deserted hallway, Helen glanced from the letter in her hands, to Gillian's radiant face, and then back to the letter again. She did not even attempt to hide her feelings of alarm. 'How did Mr Wymington get this to you?'

Gillian was beaming. 'Does it matter?'

'Yes, Gillian, it does. If you are using one of the other girls to pass these notes along, it must stop immediately.'

'But there is nothing in the letter to which anyone could object.' Gillian's happiness shone through her eyes. 'Mr Wymington has simply written to tell me that his uncle's health is improving and that he will soon be returning to Hertfordshire.'

'And that he wishes to see you before he goes.'

'Well, yes, but I am sure it is only because he would like to say goodbye.'

Helen folded up the letter and handed it back to her. 'You must know that I cannot go along with this.'

Gillian's face fell. 'But why not? What does it matter to you if I see him?'

'It matters nothing to me, but it matters a great deal to Mrs Guarding. *And* to the future of this school. What do you think Mr Brandon would say if he were to learn that you had both been seeing *and* receiving correspondence from Mr Wymington, and that I had been privy to it?'

Gillian had the grace to look contrite. 'I imagine he would be a little annoyed, but—'

'He would be *exceedingly* annoyed. So much so that in his anger he might do something to jeopardise the continued operation of this school.'

'Oliver wouldn't do that!'

'Are you so sure?'

For once, Gillian didn't have a ready answer. She merely crossed her arms and walked up and down the length of the room, the jerkiness of her steps evidence of her agitation. 'Then you will not let me see Mr Wymington?'

'I think it best for everyone that you do not.'

Gillian turned and walked the length of the room again. Suddenly, she came to an abrupt halt. 'Wait! I have just had the most marvellous idea. What if I were to meet Mr Wymington—and you were to come with me?'

*'Me!'* Helen gasped.

'Yes. That way you could be sure that nothing untoward was taking place. After all, Mr Wymington could hardly say anything that Oliver would object to if you were standing right there. And since he has suggested that we meet at his uncle's cottage, there will be the presence of another chaperone as well!'

'It is not a question of chaperonage—'

'Oh, please, Miss de Coverdale. I know you think this is wrong, but I do like him so very much. In fact...I love Mr Wymington,' Gillian said, a note of desperation creeping into her voice. 'And I am quite sure he loves me.'

'Has he ever told you that?'

'Not in so many words, but I can tell from the way he behaves when we are together. Oh, please, can you not allow us just this one chance to be together?' Gillian pleaded. 'It would mean so very much to me. And you needn't worry about Mrs Guarding finding out. Since Mr Wymington has said that his uncle's cottage is in the countryside outside Abbot Quincey, there is very little likelihood of anyone seeing us. And I truly have no wish to jeopardise that lady's reputation or the future of the school.'

'I understand that, Gillian, but it is not that simple...'

'If you let me see him just this once, I promise I shan't contact him again,' Gillian implored. 'I shall do as Oliver wishes and apply myself to my studies. I shall be as good as anyone could wish me to be. But please, Miss de Coverdale, please say that you will let me see him. Oliver would not allow me to say goodbye to him before we left Hertfordshire, and I should so very much like to do that now, in person. Is that so terribly wrong?'

Helen breathed out a long, heavy sigh. What a muddle this was turning into. Nothing good could come of allowing a meeting to take place between Gillian and Mr Wymington, she felt sure of it. If Mr Brandon found out, he would be furious. He would certainly take Mrs Guarding to task for her negligence, and then ensure that Helen was made to suffer the consequences. She had to be mad for even *contemplating* such foolishness.

The problem was, though it defied all logic, Helen knew that in some deeply buried part of her heart, she *wanted* Gillian to see her young man one more time. She knew what it was like to be separated from the one you loved. She had not been allowed to see Thomas once her father had learned of her feelings for him, and it had nearly broken her heart. More than that, she remembered how she had felt towards her father after that painful episode. She had come close to hating him for what he had done to her. Did she really wish to be the cause of Gillian resenting Oliver in such a fashion?

Helen took another long, deep breath, and then sent a prayer heavenward that she was not about to do something she would regret for the rest of her life.

'Very well, Gillian. I shall accompany you on a

visit to see Mr Wymington. But I shall remain in the room the entire time, whether his uncle is there or not, and I shall allow the visit to take place *only* on the condition that you do not attempt to see or to correspond with him again. Do I have your agreement?'

'Oh yes, Miss de Coverdale, yes! And thank you so very much! I knew you would understand!'

Helen wasn't sure she understood at all. But there was one other motivating factor she hadn't told Gillian about. One she scarcely liked admitting even to herself.

Retribution. She wanted to strike back at Oliver Brandon for what he had said to her. She wanted to hurt him as much as he had hurt her, and the only way she could do that was through Gillian.

Helen knew it was a dreadful way to feel, and not in the least charitable, but given Oliver's wretchedly unfair opinion of her, she could not help herself. He had not asked her for an explanation as to what had happened with Lord Talbot. He had simply assumed the worst, believing her to be a willing participant in the seduction.

And that was what had angered her the most. It was not the first time Helen had been judged because of her appearance, but that did not mean people had a *right* to believe her prone to certain types of behaviour simply as a result of it. She had never encouraged uninvited attention. Indeed, she went out of her way to avoid it. Unfortunately, some gentlemen seemed to believe that being a governess meant she was ripe for a tumble.

But that was simply not the case. Not even after her father's death, when things had been at their worst, had Helen had any desire to become a man's mistress. She knew it would have afforded her a far more enviable lifestyle than the one she had, but her sense of honour and self-worth were far more important to her than pretty clothes or sparkling baubles.

Yes, she would allow Gillian one last opportunity to see her young man. The child deserved that much. And if Mr Wymington turned out to be the honourable gentleman he seemed, she might even quietly encourage Gillian to keep her hopes up with regards to an eventual match. She would not purposely try to undermine Oliver's authority, but she would remind Gillian that in the fullness of time, she would be in a position to make up her own mind.

Yes, Helen decided with growing certainty. That much she would be willing to do—*if* Mr Wymington turned out to be the kind of man Gillian truly believed he was.

# *Chapter Seven*

Helen did not inform Mrs Guarding of the planned
visit to Abbot Quincey for two reasons. The first was
because she had no desire to lie to that good lady.
The second was because she could not bring herself
to feel that what she was doing was entirely wrong.
Gillian was not a foolish girl. She was merely a young
woman blinded by her feelings. But Helen was not.
If it turned out that Mr Wymington was *not* the
charming gentleman he pretended to be and that he
was only after Gillian's money, Helen felt sure she
would be able to see it.

But to do that, she had to spend time in his company. She had to see how he behaved with Gillian.
And if she were able to discover any kind of flaws in
his personality, she would be in a better position to
warn Gillian about them. Surely that was worth any
risks that might be involved?

The visit began well enough. Mr Wymington
greeted them at the door of the small, well-tended
cottage, and then endeavoured to put them at ease by
playing the part of the genial host. Gillian, as a result
of having been cautioned by Helen beforehand, was

somewhat more restrained than usual. She returned his greeting with the proper decorum, and smiled at him in a manner that even a dowager duchess would have approved of.

Helen's only concern was that there was no sign whatsoever of Mr Wymington's uncle.

'Alas, he suffered a bit of a relapse this very afternoon,' Mr Wymington informed them as he led the way into the tiny sitting-room. 'It forced him to retire in something of a foul mood to his bed. He did, however, ask me to pass along his most sincere regrets that he would not be able to make your acquaintance this evening.'

Gillian's disappointment was evident. 'Oh dear. I was so looking forward to meeting him.'

'As he was you, my dear Miss Gresham, but I told him his health must come first. And I live in hope that there will be other opportunities for the two of you to meet.'

'Perhaps you should have Dr Pettifer in to see him,' Helen suggested, anxious to keep the conversation from becoming too personal. 'A relapse can be very serious in a man your uncle's age.'

'I suggested that to him myself, Miss de Coverdale, but he told me that if the good Lord intended to call him home, there was nothing any mortal man could do to stop it.'

'But surely we could pay him a very brief visit?' Gillian persisted. 'Do you not think the sight of two happy, smiling faces would make him feel better?'

Mr Wymington laughed. 'I am sure it would do wonders for his spirits, but I doubt it would do much for his heart. The sight of two such lovely faces standing by his bed might be more than it could stand. I know it would put a serious strain on mine.'

Gillian dimpled prettily, obviously finding the remark very much to her liking. Helen did not. She did not like to believe that Mr Wymington was lying, but for some reason she was hard pressed to think otherwise. As much as she wanted to believe that the cottage belonged to his uncle, and that the poor old gentleman *was* asleep in another room, she was finding it difficult to do so. She couldn't help wondering if this wasn't all a ruse of some kind; a fabrication intended to make them believe that it *was* his uncle's cottage and that Mr Wymington truly had a valid reason for being in the area.

She also wondered if Mr Wymington was really as pleased to see her as he pretended to be.

In the end, however, Helen was forced to admit that it was likely only scepticism on her part. Mr Wymington behaved like a perfect gentleman the entire time. He entertained them with humorous tales of his adventures in the militia, and served them tea and biscuits, apologising all the while for the basic fare and saying that, as a poor bachelor, he was woefully inexperienced at such feminine arts as entertaining.

Gillian, of course, saw nothing of his faults. She saw only a handsome gentleman who smiled at her with uncommon warmth, and whose gaze softened every time she looked at him. She hung on his every word and laughed at even the most inconsequential of his remarks, evidencing no awareness that once again she was baldly exposing her feelings to him.

Perhaps that was why, as the visit progressed, that Helen was better able to understand Oliver Brandon's concerns about his ward's behaviour. There was no question of Gillian's being infatuated with Mr Wymington. It was clear that she could—and would—see absolutely nothing bad about him. And that was a most precarious position for a young lady of fortune to be in.

'Well, I think it is time we were on our way, Mr Wymington,' Helen said abruptly. She placed her cup and saucer on the small table and stood up. 'Thank you so much for your hospitality.'

'Yes, it was very good of you to have us,' Gillian agreed. She also rose, but far more reluctantly than Helen. 'What a shame the time has gone by so quickly.'

'It is a shame indeed, Miss Gresham.' Mr Wymington's voice was warm, his eyes gently caressing as he looked at her. 'But hopefully the months until you are home again will pass swiftly.'

'They cannot pass swiftly enough for me,' Gillian cried, forgetting for a moment the warning Helen had given her.

'Come along, Miss Gresham,' Helen said briskly. 'We must not overstay our welcome.'

'Ah, but you could never outstay your welcome, Miss de Coverdale,' Mr Wymington said gallantly. 'I trust you will remember that my door is always open to you as well as to Miss Gresham.'

The look that accompanied his words was almost as warm as the one he had given Gillian, and for some reason, that troubled Helen. She knew there was nothing in his words to which she could take exception, and yet, once again, she did.

'Thank you, Mr Wymington. But now we really must be leaving.'

With that, Helen turned to lead the way out of the

cottage. All of a sudden, she was in a desperate hurry to get back to Guarding's.

She shouldn't have come here today. She knew that now. She had made a mistake in allowing Gillian to see this man. Unfortunately, only time would tell how big a mistake it really was, and what would come of it.

After a somewhat prolonged goodbye at the gate, Gillian finally allowed Mr Wymington to hand her up into the carriage. Helen observed the way he held on to her hand, frowning as she saw the manner in which he gently pressed her fingers, and bit her lip when she heard Gillian assure him in the most fervent of tones that she would be counting the days until she was back in Hertfordshire once more.

At last, Mr Wymington turned to smile at her. 'I am so pleased you came along, Miss de Coverdale. And it was very kind of you to arrange this meeting. I am well aware of Mr Brandon's feelings regarding the association between Miss Gresham and myself.'

'It will be the only time, Mr Wymington,' Helen told him quietly. 'Mr Brandon has made his wishes clear with regard to the situation, and while I admit I had my reasons for allowing Miss Gresham to see you today, it will not happen again. I trust you will not endeavour to contact her in the future.'

Mr Wymington inclined his head fractionally. 'Perhaps I can communicate with you directly, Miss de Coverdale. That way you can convey my sentiments to Miss Gresham without anyone being aware of it. For surely *you* are free to receive correspondence from gentlemen?'

Helen glanced at him sharply. 'I am free to receive whatever correspondence I wish, Mr Wymington, but you should know that I am as bound by Mr Brandon's wishes as Miss Gresham is. And I will not violate his trust.'

'Ah, but that is just the thing, Miss de Coverdale,' Mr Wymington said, his voice a silken whisper. 'By bringing Miss Gresham here this afternoon, that is exactly what you have done.'

'Miss de Coverdale, Mr Wymington, what are the two of you whispering about?' Gillian called from the carriage.

Helen sent the girl a worried smile. She was not at all pleased with the way the conversation was going, but she could hardly stand here and continue it now with Gillian only a few feet away and listening to every word they said.

'Mr Wymington, I *beg* you not to pursue this,' Helen said in a low, urgent voice. 'It can have no future. Mr Brandon has made his feelings very clear with regard to you and your relationship with Miss Gresham.'

It seemed to Helen that just for a moment a look of cunning appeared in the man's brilliant blue eyes, replacing the expression of amusement that had been there only moments before. 'I sincerely regret that you have chosen to side with Mr Brandon in this matter, Miss de Coverdale,' he said softly. 'I thought perhaps that by bringing Gillian here this afternoon, you were evidencing sympathy towards our plight. But I see now that such is not the case. However, I am not one to be so easily cast aside.' He reached for her hand and raised it to his lips. 'Perhaps we can arrange to meet, just you and I, to discuss the matter further. Perhaps I can convince you that I am not so shabby a fellow as Mr Brandon would have you believe.'

Then, as he pressed his lips to her hand, he raised his eyes to hers—and Helen felt her insides go cold.

He was looking at her in exactly the same way so many other men had, so many times before.

'Miss de Coverdale, are you coming?' Gillian cried imperiously.

Helen only just managed to conceal her shudder as she withdrew her hand. 'I doubt there will be any need for us to meet again, Mr Wymington. Good day to you, sir.' Then, pausing as she hurried towards the carriage, added, 'I do hope your uncle makes a speedy recovery.'

If Helen had expected him to give himself away, she was again to be disappointed.

'I shall indeed extend the wishes of two such lovely ladies to him,' Mr Wymington said with aplomb. 'Thank you, Miss de Coverdale. *Arrivederci ad un altro giorno.*'

Helen's foot faltered on the step. The expression, spoken in near-perfect Italian, was not one to signify a farewell. It simply meant goodbye—until another day.

Gillian waited all of twenty seconds before commencing the inquisition.

'There, *now* what do you think of my dear Mr Wymington?' she demanded, clearly very pleased with herself and with the visit. 'Is he not a perfect gentleman? Is he not as wonderful as I have been telling you?'

'He is a handsome gentleman with very nice manners,' Helen forced herself to say, 'but beyond that, I do not believe I am in a position to offer any kind of

informed opinion about him. I still know very little
of his character.'

'But how can you say that? Did you not hear him
evidence concern towards his uncle? Did you not find
his stories amusing, and his speech and company all
that could be admired?'

Helen turned away to hide her sigh. It was painful
having to listen to Gillian go on about the man. The
excitement and hopefulness in her voice was evidence
of her infatuation, and it was obvious that she wanted
Helen to share that enthusiasm.

Helen could understand that. Had she been
Gillian's age, and at her stage in life, she would probably have felt the same way. But she wasn't Gillian's
age and she certainly wasn't in her situation. At one-
and-thirty, Helen had far more experience of life than
Gillian ever would. She knew what motivated men
like Sidney Wymington, and she was deeply troubled
by their meeting this afternoon. Certain aspects of his
character worried her, as did the manner in which
they had parted. If what Helen was beginning to suspect was true, Gillian was destined to fall very hard
when she learned the truth about him.

But even more frightening than that, was whether
or not she would learn the truth before it was too late!

Helen was tidying her room after the last class of
the day when she heard the sound of a knock on the
door. She turned around—and drew a startled breath.
'Mr Brandon!'

'Good afternoon, Miss de Coverdale. I hope I
haven't come at a bad time?' he said hesitantly.

Helen glanced at him in surprise. His voice lacked
the hard edge it had held before, and there was some-

thing almost apologetic in his tone. Nevertheless, she kept her voice cool as she leaned against the edge of her desk, suddenly finding herself in need of its support. 'A bad time for what?'

'To speak with you?'

'I thought we had said all that needed to be said.'

Oliver took two steps into the room. 'On the contrary, there is a great deal more I would say to you. If you will give me the chance.'

Helen's first impulse was to say no. After all, what more could he possibly wish to say? What other insults had he to fling at her? Then, she glanced into his eyes and saw something that gave her pause. 'What is this about, Mr Brandon?'

'Something which is very important to both of us. But especially to you.'

*Something important to her?* Helen sighed. 'Very well. I have a few minutes before tea. What have you to say to me that is so terribly important?'

'I wonder…' Oliver glanced around the room. 'Is there somewhere we might go that would be more conducive to conversation?'

For the first time, Helen allowed herself a smile. 'I have always found my classroom to be most conducive to conversation, Mr Brandon. It is one of the functions it serves.'

To her surprise, Oliver smiled too. 'Yes, I am sure it is. But I think it is still quite pleasant outside. Perhaps you would care to join me for a stroll about the gardens?'

Deciding that a breath of fresh air might not be such a bad idea, Helen picked up her shawl and draped it over her shoulders. She led the way to the backstairs and then out into the late afternoon sunshine. Soon, they were walking together down the length of the gravelled drive. The large trees provided cover from both the road and the school and would, with any luck, prevent her from being treated to a barrage of questions in class tomorrow morning about the gentleman she had been seen strolling with this afternoon.

'Very well, Mr Brandon, we are outside in surroundings which are hopefully more conducive to adult conversation,' Helen said, trying to keep the sarcasm from her voice. 'What is it you wish to say to me?'

'To tell you the truth, Miss de Coverdale, I hardly know where to begin,' Oliver admitted slowly. 'I fear the errors I have made are grievous indeed. But I suppose I should commence by extending my most humble apologies for the mistake I made so many years ago, and for the tremendous embarrassment I have caused you as a result.'

It was not at all what Helen had been expecting to hear. An apology? From Oliver Brandon?

Too shocked to do more than stare at him, Helen waited for him to continue.

'By chance I met someone in London a few nights ago,' Oliver continued. 'Someone with whom we are both acquainted, but whom neither of us has seen in a very long time.'

The remark brought a frown to Helen's face. 'I cannot imagine who you are talking about, sir. There are few people I know in London any more.'

'Nevertheless, this is someone with whom you are acquainted. And not happily, I regret to say.' When Helen continued to look blank, Oliver said softly, 'Lord Talbot.'

The name caused Helen to stumble awkwardly. *Lord Talbot!*

Immediately, Oliver reached for her, the warmth of his hand closing firmly around her arm. 'Are you all right?'

'Yes, I'm...fine. That was clumsy of me. I wasn't watching where I was going.' Helen pretended to concentrate on the ground ahead of her, but all she could see was Lord Talbot's face. It loomed like a dark spectre in her mind, bringing back all of the unpleasant memories of the past. She was also aware of Oliver's hand still resting on her arm, and of the comforting warmth it offered. 'Please...go on.'

'I chanced to encounter Talbot at my club.' Oliver withdrew his hand as they walked on. 'And as is so often the case, he had been drinking. Apparently, he had just lost a large sum of money to a man most gamblers know to avoid.'

'Mr Brandon, I have no wish to hear about Lord Talbot's losses or about his drunkenness,' Helen interrupted. 'In fact, I have no wish to hear *anything* about him.'

'Not even a confession he made to me whilst in his cups?'

'No, because I cannot imagine what kind of confession he might make to you that would be of any interest to me.'

'What about one which pertained to that infamous night in the library?'

Helen stared at him in surprise. Then, warily, she nodded. 'Go on.'

'Lord Talbot admitted to me that he had forced himself upon you that night,' Oliver said. 'He told me it had been his intention to seduce you from the mo-

ment you first walked into his house. He also told me
that you refused to have anything to do with him.'

Helen listened to his words, too surprised by what
he was saying to offer any kind of comment. She
knew she should have been delighted at hearing
Oliver Brandon—the only other person who had been
a witness to her humiliation—say that she was not to
blame for what had happened. She should have been
happy and relieved that after all this time, she had
finally been vindicated.

And yet, she wasn't ecstatic or happy or even particularly relieved. It was almost as though he was
talking about someone else. Someone she didn't know
any more. All she felt was a strange kind of numbness
around her heart. Because when it came right down
to it, what had she really gained from Lord Talbot's
admission?

Yes, Oliver Brandon now knew that she hadn't
been to blame for any part of the seduction he'd witnessed that night. But that did not change the fact that
he'd had to hear it from Lord Talbot himself before
he'd given it any credence. He hadn't rushed to ask
*her* about the truth of the matter. In fact when she
had tried to tell him, he had put his own interpreta-
tions on it and, once again, made her feel culpable.

Furthermore, Helen knew that the *only* reason the
peer had made *any* admission of guilt was because
he'd been in his cups. Had he been sober, he would
never have embarrassed himself by admitting that a
lowly governess had spurned his advances.

'Thank you for telling me, Mr Brandon. It is…
good to know that your fears have finally been laid
to rest.' Helen managed a fleeting smile. 'Hopefully,
you will no longer worry about the time Gillian

and I spend together, or about any topics we might choose to discuss. And now, I think I should return to the school.'

'But...is that all you have to say to me?' Oliver reached for her arm and turned her around to face him. 'After the shoddy way I treated you, have you no words of reprisal? No harsh expressions of condemnation? I thought you would have been pleased with the news.'

Helen sighed. 'I see nothing to be pleased at in being told something I already knew, sir. It was you who jumped to the conclusion that I was in the library with Lord Talbot of my own choice. You put your own interpretation on what you saw there and you weren't inclined to believe me when I tried to tell you differently, so I fail to understand why I should feel happy now that you have finally learned the truth from someone else.'

Oliver appeared taken aback by her response. 'I simply thought you might have enjoyed being given the opportunity of telling me I was wrong.'

Helen tried to rally a smile, but this time, even that simple gesture eluded her. 'It really doesn't matter what you think any more. I have tried to put the past behind me and move on with my life. Your coming here and reminding me of what happened twelve years ago forced me to take an unpleasant step backwards, but that is all. I was foolish to let your bad opinion weigh upon my mind, and I would be even more foolish to allow myself comfort now that you have changed it. A great man once said that truth is always the strongest argument. I have always believed that to be the case. Sometimes, it is just a matter of waiting for others to recognise it. And now, I would bid you a good afternoon, Mr Brandon. And... goodbye.'

# Chapter Eight

Helen was quite sure that her conversation with Oliver would be the last one she would ever have with him. He had offered his explanation and his apology, and as far as she was concerned, the matter was closed. She saw no reason for their paths to cross again, except, perhaps, as it concerned Gillian. To her surprise, however, Oliver seemed reluctant to let it go. It was almost as though he felt obliged to make up for the error in judgement he had made all those years ago, and for the embarrassment he had caused her as a result. So when Gillian told her that he was planning an outing to Castle Ashby, and that she was to be included, Helen had naturally felt compelled to object.

'But there is no reason for Mr Brandon to include me on such an outing. Our acquaintance is not of the kind that would warrant my being invited to participate in a family excursion of this kind.'

'But did you not say you would enjoy visiting the castle if you ever had an opportunity to do so?' Gillian retorted.

'Of course, but that does not mean I thought to do

so with you and Mr Brandon.' Helen's brow furrowed as she walked around the empty classroom collecting slates. 'I hope *you* did not suggest to your guardian that I come along.'

'Well, I suppose I *might* have mentioned your passion for the Italian Renaissance once or twice,' the girl admitted. 'And I understand that Castle Ashby has a particularly fine collection of paintings from the period, as well as some splendid tapestries.'

'Be that as it may, it was still no reason to ask Mr Brandon to include me in your visit. If he has arranged an outing, it is because he wishes to spend time with *you*.'

'But he told me I might bring along whomever I wished. And when I thought about everything Castle Ashby had to offer from an educational point of view, I immediately thought of you.'

Helen pressed her lips together. She was beginning to understand why Mr Brandon felt it necessary to warn people about his ward. Gillian was very good at getting her own way, but in such a manner that one seldom felt as though one was being manipulated. Such was the case here, in that an innocent family outing had suddenly become an opportunity for an *educational* experience.

'Oh, do say you will come with us, Miss de Coverdale,' Gillian urged as the silence dragged on. 'It would make the outing far more enjoyable for me. And I am sure Oliver would be grateful for your company.'

'Grateful?'

'Yes. He often complains that my constant chattering about inconsequential matters bores him excessively.'

Helen found the notion of Mr Brandon's being grateful for having her along for *any* reason hard to accept. Why would he, when she was little more than a stranger to him?

'Besides, if it makes you feel any better, I have also asked Elizabeth Brookwell to join us,' Gillian said. 'Her mother is a good friend of Sophie's, so he can have no concerns about the connection.'

'Yes, but will he not mind the intrusion of yet another person? I cannot help but feel that his desire to spend time with you has suddenly blossomed into a full-blown party.'

'Oliver won't mind.' Gillian gave her a confident smile. 'He can be very accommodating when he wishes to be.'

'I am surprised to hear you in such charity with him,' Helen remarked. 'I thought you were still angry at him for sending you here.'

'Oh, I always *get* angry with Oliver, but I seldom stay angry with him. I am not *happy* with him for taking me away from Mr Wymington, of course, but I did promise I would not mention that subject again, so I shall not. But I can assure you that Oliver will be pleased to hear I have invited you and Elizabeth along. Besides, four is a much nicer number than three for an outing, don't you think?'

Helen made no reply, for in truth, she could not think of one. She wasn't even sure that anything she might say *would* make a difference. Gillian's mind was made up and she was beginning to learn that once it was, there was very little chance of it being changed.

But what about Oliver Brandon? How would he feel about having her come along when only a few days ago she had told him, in no uncertain terms, exactly what she thought of him and of his apology!

On the appointed day, Oliver arrived at the Guarding Academy at promptly half-past twelve. And, as Gillian had predicted, he did not seem in the least concerned at the prospect of escorting three ladies to Castle Ashby, rather than one. In fact, he seemed decidedly pleased at the unexpected mix of company awaiting him. He settled the two giggling girls in the carriage first, and then turned to offer his hand to Helen.

'I am delighted you agreed to join us, Miss de Coverdale. Gillian told me she had invited you but I was not sure you would come.'

A blush danced across Helen's cheeks. 'Your ward can be very persuasive when she wishes to be, Mr Brandon. She all but told me that because the visit was to be of an educational nature it would be remiss of me, as her teacher, not to come along. Unfortunately, she also appealed to my love of art and that made it very difficult for me to refuse.'

Oliver's eyes crinkled with amusement. 'Then I am grateful for Gillian's *persuasiveness*, as you have so nicely phrased it. There have been times in the past when I have been tempted to call it otherwise, but since it has convinced you to make up one of our party, I shall not condemn her for it. And now, let us be off. A most pleasurable day awaits.'

Castle Ashby was a sprawling Elizabethan house set in the countryside six miles east of Northampton. It had been built in the early sixteen hundreds and contained a wealth of paintings from the Italian

Renaissance period, along with fine examples of the
seventeenth-century Dutch school. Oliver had already
determined that the Marquis and Marchioness of
Northampton were not at home, and so had applied
to the housekeeper to show them around.

The girls exclaimed at length over the elegant fur-
nishings and priceless hangings inside many of the
rooms, and while they were initially awed by the
stateliness and grandeur of the house, they both
agreed they would be most happy to be mistress of
such a fine establishment. Helen would have preferred
them to stay close, but they were more inclined to
walk ahead, talking in excited whispers, and leaving
her frequently in the company of Mr Brandon alone.

Helen was very conscious of his eyes on her as
they stopped in the dining-room to admire the beautiful dishes and exquisite appointments. She felt very
plain indeed against the opulence all around her, and
suddenly wished she'd had something more fashionable to wear than the plain muslin dress under a man-
tle of twilled sarcenet. But she knew it would have
been foolish to spend her hard-earned wages on such
unnecessary extravagances. A stylish pelisse like the
one Gillian was wearing, or even the shorter one
Elizabeth sported, would have cost far more than her
meagre income allowed.

Fortunately, Mr Brandon did not seem displeased
with her appearance. In fact, Helen was quite sure she
saw a flicker of admiration in his eyes, and she took
comfort in the knowledge that she was not an embarrassment to him. *Why* she should worry about what
Oliver Brandon thought of her, she would not even
allow herself to consider.

'Have you visited Castle Ashby before, Miss de

Coverdale?' Oliver enquired as they slowly walked the length of the picture gallery.

Helen shook her head. 'I have not had the pleasure, sir. I've often thought it would be a splendid house to see, but there is seldom a carriage available to bring us this distance, and I would not undertake a journey like this on my own.'

'Then I hope you see all you wish to today so that you can remember it long after you have returned to Guarding's.'

Helen risked a quick glance at him as he stopped to admire a particularly fine painting of the current Marquis's father. She wished she could bring herself to feel more at ease in his company, but something about him made her feel gauche and tongue-tied. Which was silly, given that he had done nothing but try to make her feel at ease ever since they had left the school.

'It was very good of you to allow me to come today, Mr Brandon,' Helen said, feeling it was the least she could do. 'I cannot help but feel that I have intruded on a family outing.'

'On the contrary, you have spared me the tedium of having to listen to the unending chatter of two excitable young girls.' A wry but indulgent glint appeared in Oliver's eyes. 'You offer far more interesting and intelligent comments about the paintings and their artists than I would have heard otherwise, Miss de Coverdale, and I confess myself impressed by the depth of your knowledge.'

His candid answer brought a smile to Helen's lips. 'I would be a poor teacher indeed if I did not know more about my subject than my pupils. But I own, it is a pleasure to talk to someone who is truly *interested* in the subject, rather than to a group of girls who learn it because they know they must.'

'I can understand your feeling that way. When I was at school, there were many subjects I learned because I had to rather than because I wished to. I suppose it is the nature of education.' Oliver hesitated, and then gruffly cleared his throat. 'I am also pleased you agreed to come today, because I was not sure you would *wish* to be in my company again, given the nature of our last conversation.'

Helen purposely fixed her gaze on the painting in front of her. So he too had suffered doubts as a result of that meeting. She was glad, and even a little relieved. Mayhaps Oliver Brandon was not as narrow-minded as she had come to believe.

'I do not recall there being anything in our speech to make you feel that way,' she replied. 'A misunderstanding was laid to rest and the air cleared between us, but that is all, I think. We did not part in anger.'

'No, but I know I offended you, and I regret that very much,' Oliver said quietly. 'You were right to express your disappointment in my behaviour, for I can assure you I felt it most keenly myself.'

Helen raised her eyes to his and was momentarily shaken by the expression she saw within them. 'I...thank you for telling me, sir, but as I said before, what happened in the past is over and done with. Perhaps it would be best for both of us if that is where we left it.'

His gaze travelled over her face, touching briefly on her mouth, and then searching her eyes. 'You are a most admirable woman, Miss de Coverdale. I was wrong to think otherwise.'

Having no answer to give him, Helen merely inclined her head, and the two walked on in silence.

'Gillian seems to be settling well into her new environment,' Oliver commented when they had walked on some way.

Relieved that the conversation had taken a more neutral turn, Helen smiled. 'Yes, I believe her initial feelings of resistance have been overcome. The staff are all delighted with her progress and she is very popular with the girls, especially the younger ones.'

'I am glad to hear it.' Oliver clasped his hands behind his back and moved towards the next painting. 'In truth, I did not know if sending her to Mrs Guarding's Academy was the right thing to do. My sister, Sophie, suggested it. She spoke very highly of the school's reputation and of Mrs Guarding herself and it was she who convinced me of the wisdom of sending Gillian there.'

'To finish her education?' Helen couldn't resist asking.

Oliver slanted her a rueful glance. 'That, and to distance her from Mr Wymington.'

Helen bit her lip and looked away. Her feelings of guilt at having broken the rules and allowed a meeting to take place between Gillian and Mr Wymington were growing by the day, but she was still not convinced that Oliver Brandon's reasons for wishing to keep the two apart were entirely justified.

'Gillian seems to think you are being unfair in not allowing her to see Mr Wymington,' Helen said, deciding this might be a good time to find out. 'Is he really so unsuitable?'

'If you were to meet him you would not think so.' Oliver bent forward to study the detail on the painting in front of him. 'From outward appearances, he is all that is charming.'

'Then why do you object to him?'

'Because I do not trust him. I do not believe for a moment that his intentions towards my ward are honourable.'

'You do not believe that he is in love with her?'

Oliver turned towards her and his burning eyes held her still. 'I believe it is her fortune to which he is most keenly attracted, Miss de Coverdale. I think he merely gives the impression of caring for Gillian in order to disguise his true intent.'

'That is a strong accusation to make without proof.'

Oliver shrugged. 'Perhaps, but how would you suggest I go about obtaining such proof? If I were to ask him the nature of his feelings, he would hardly be so foolish as to tell me something I did not wish to hear.'

'Do you not think you would be able to tell the difference between feigned affections and those which are genuine? Surely if Mr Wymington was only pretending to love Gillian, something in his voice or his manners would give him away.'

Oliver sighed. 'Even if that were the case, what good would it do me? Gillian is the one who must be convinced of his unsuitability, not I.'

'Mr Brandon, have you given any consideration to the possibility that what you are looking for simply isn't there?'

'I beg your pardon?'

Helen knew she was delving into matters that were, by all rights, none of her business, but given what was at stake, she felt she had the right to ask. She'd already begun to suspect that Oliver was correct about Mr Wymington's character, but she needed to know if his reservations stemmed from feelings of genuine mistrust, or from something more personal.

'Perhaps you can find nothing to object to in Mr Wymington's manner because there is nothing to object to.'

Oliver studied her in enigmatic silence for a moment. Then he said, 'Women put much stock in intuition, do they not, Miss de Coverdale?'

'Yes, I suppose we do.'

'Well, it may surprise you to hear it, but so do I. Mr Wymington has done absolutely nothing for which I can fault him,' he told her candidly. 'There are no marks against his service record, nor any man willing to speak out against him. And yet, something here,' Oliver pointed to the area just below his heart, 'tells me he is not to be trusted. I believe the words he speaks are not the sentiments of his heart, and I am afraid that if I allow Gillian to marry him, I would be making a most grievous mistake.' Oliver's mouth curved in a sad, almost wistful smile. 'Ours is not a perfect world, Miss de Coverdale. I doubt either of us is so foolish as to believe that the majority of marriages are made for love. And yet, in Gillian's case, I find myself hoping that the man who marries her will do so *because* he loves her, rather than because he has any less noble reasons at heart.'

A smile tugged reluctantly at Helen's mouth. 'Your confession is safe with me, Mr Brandon, but I do hope you are not wrong about Mr Wymington. Sometimes the biggest mistakes are made by those who have the best intentions of others at heart.'

His gaze held hers momentarily. 'You sound like you speak from experience. Might I hazard a guess that something similar has happened in your life?'

'Oliver?' Gillian suddenly called from the bottom of the stairs, 'when are you and Miss de Coverdale coming down? Elizabeth and I are anxious to see the gardens.'

'We are coming now,' Oliver replied calmly. 'Go ahead and we shall meet you there.'

'Very well. But do not be long! There is so much to see, we would not wish to leave you behind.'

Helen carefully bit back a smile. At times it was hard to tell who had brought whom on the excursion today. In truth, however, she was not ungrateful for Gillian's interruption. Oliver's question had caught her off guard and she hadn't known what to say. She could no more imagine telling him about her own unhappy love affair than she could believe he would be interested in hearing about it. And yet, just for a moment, something in his eyes had reached out to her; almost making her want to talk about some of the secrets she had locked away so deeply in her heart.

They made their way back outside, and once there, Helen stopped to admire the beautiful countryside in front of her. 'How lovely it all is,' she whispered. 'I do not think I could ever grow tired of looking at such beauty.'

'The view is very fine to be sure,' Oliver agreed, 'though I feel I am the more fortunate one. From where I stand I have the benefit of two very different but equally lovely views.'

Helen was not of an age to pretend an ignorance of what he was saying, yet the softness of his voice and the genuine warmth with which he offered his compliment caused her to blush like a schoolgirl. 'You are too kind, Mr Brandon.'

'Kindness has very little to do with it, Miss de Coverdale. ' He indicated a bench where they might sit down. 'You are a remarkably beautiful woman, and I am sure I am not the first to tell you that. But come, enough of flattery. You said that something similar had happened in your life. Would you not be willing to tell me about it?'

Once again, Oliver's seemingly genuine desire to learn about her past put Helen in a definite quandary. What possible good could come of revealing intimate details of her life to him? There was certainly no romantic interest between them. It was not as though he needed to know things about her that might help determine her suitability to becoming his wife. So what interest could he possibly have in hearing about what had happened in her past?

Helen mulled that over for a while. As she did, however, she began to wonder whether divulging something about her own past might not help Gillian now. Perhaps by disclosing details of her own thwarted love, she might be better able to make him understand what she was trying to say. Was that not worth the embarrassment such a disclosure would bring about?

'It seems a long time ago now,' Helen began reluctantly. 'And indeed, it is in the measure of years. But I still remember how…difficult it was at the time.' She took a deep breath and then raised her eyes to his. 'When I was little more than Gillian's age, my father prevented me from…marrying the man I loved.'

Oliver's gaze remained steady on her face, but his eyes were suddenly filled with questions. 'I assume he had a good reason for doing so?'

'He believed he did. My father informed me that…the gentleman was beneath me in every way, and that I was foolish to have allowed my feelings to become engaged. He told me that as his daughter, I could do better than to marry a poor clergyman.'

'I see.' Oliver eyes were dark, the expression in them unreadable. 'And were you truly in love with your poor clergyman, Miss de Coverdale?'

There was no mockery in his voice, not even a hint of reprisal. Only a gentle note of concern that told her he was not unsympathetic to her plight. Nevertheless, Helen turned away, strangely uncomfortable at talking to Oliver about her involvement with another man. 'Yes, I loved him,' she admitted. 'Thomas was extremely dedicated to his calling, and to the people in his care. He had great hopes for the parish and for the work he wanted to do there.' Her smile grew unknowingly wistful. 'I believe his passion for his work and for other people was part of what I loved about him.'

'And do you love him still?'

Helen raised startled eyes to his. 'It was a very long time ago.'

'Perhaps, but I have heard that first loves are often the hardest to forget.'

*He had heard.* So Gillian was right. Oliver Brandon hadn't been in love, for if he had, he would surely have remembered the pains and the pleasures of his very first *affaire de coeur.*

'I suppose they are, but time changes many things.' Suddenly restless, Helen got to her feet. 'In the years that followed, my life went through many changes, none of which were particularly pleasant. My mother died, and after her death my father just seemed to give up. He lost all interest in life. He stopped going to work, and eventually began to drink. I suppose he did so to forget the pain, but it made life very difficult for those close to him. He died less than a year later. By that time, we had amassed such a staggering debt that it became necessary to sell the house just to cover the tradesmen's bills and the cost of the servants' wages.'

'Is that when you were forced to seek employment?'

Helen nodded, but did not look at him. 'I had no choice. I had no relatives in England with whom I could stay, and I had lost touch with my mother's family in Italy, so there was nothing I could do but look for a paying position.'

'What about your clergyman? What did he do when he learned of your troubles?'

Helen fixed her gaze on a distant field. 'He never did. Thomas married within six months of our parting. He moved to Derbyshire soon after and was given the living of a fine church there.'

'That must have come as a great disappointment to you.'

'Young men in the church are often ambitious, Mr Brandon. Thomas knew the Dean wished him to take a wife, and since it was not going to be me, he chose…someone else.'

'Pity he did not wait a little longer,' Oliver commented wryly. 'Had he done so, he would have been able to have both the woman he loved *and* the life he'd chosen for himself.'

Helen said nothing. There didn't seem to be any point in admitting that she had often wondered about the same thing herself. 'Sometimes it is best that we not know what is around the next corner. If we did, we might be tempted to spend our entire lives waiting for tomorrow to arrive.'

Oliver studied her face, and then reached out to gently brush his fingers against her cheek. 'Sometimes tomorrow is worth waiting for, Miss de Coverdale. We just have to be wise enough to realise it at the time.'

The touch of his hand and the softness in his voice were nearly Helen's undoing. She could not risk exposing any more of her vulnerabilities to him. It was too easy to get lost in the tenderness of his gaze. Too easy to read meanings into words that weren't there.

'Oliver, Miss de Coverdale, come quickly!' Gillian cried from further down the garden. 'We have found the most delightful gazebo hidden in the trees. Oh, do come and look!'

The intrusion of the high-pitched voice into her conversation with Oliver came as a relief to Helen. It shattered the mood of intimacy that had begun to form between them, and brought her abruptly back to earth. 'I think we had best rejoin the girls, Mr Brandon. No doubt they will be wondering at our constantly lagging behind.'

'I shouldn't worry about it,' Oliver said, nevertheless getting to his feet. 'They will put it down to our age, as young people are inclined to do.'

Helen smiled and would have walked on had she not felt the gentle pressure of his hand on her arm. 'Thank you for telling me about your young man, Miss de Coverdale. I know it was not an easy admission. But given the situation between Gillian and Mr Wymington, I can understand why you felt I needed to know.'

Helen looked down at his hand, aware of the warmth emanating from it, and gave him a regretful smile. 'It was not only because of Gillian's feelings for Mr Wymington I told you this, Mr Brandon, but because of her feelings for *you*.'

'I'm not sure I understand.'

Helen took a deep breath. 'After my father forbade me to see Thomas, my feelings towards him began to change. I could not understand why he would not allow me to see the man I loved, nor condone a relationship neither my mother nor I saw anything wrong with. But my father would not change his mind, and I resented him for that. Nor did I ever fully forgive him.'

'Is that what you see happening between Gillian and myself?'

'I cannot speak for your ward, sir, but the situations are not so very different. Gillian doesn't understand why you do not wish her to see Mr Wymington, any more than I understood why my father refused to allow me to see Thomas. But I fear that if you forbid the association outright, there is a good chance she will come to feel the same kind of resentment towards you that I felt towards my father. And I would truly hate to see that happen. I know how much Gillian loves and respects you, but sometimes, in the foolishness of youth and the idealistic fantasies of love, young women lose sight of that.'

Oliver was silent for a few minutes. Then, he nodded. 'Your compassion does you credit, Miss de Coverdale, as does your loyalty to my ward. But I'm afraid it is a risk I shall have to take. Gillian might only be a stepsister to me, but I love her as dearly as I do my own sister, and because of her impulsive nature, I worry about her twice as much. I would not wish to see her marry ill and find out too late that she has been deceived. I would never forgive myself if that happened. For as you've said yourself, a mistake once made, no matter how innocently, stays with us for a very long time. Isn't that right, my dear Miss de Coverdale?'

# Chapter Nine

Helen thought about what Oliver had said for a long time after she returned to the school: '...*a mistake once made, no matter how innocently, stays with us for a very long time...*'

Had he been referring to the mistake he'd made with her twelve years ago? Helen thought it likely, given the note of regret she had heard in his voice. She also remembered what he'd said about Mr Wymington, and the more she thought about it, the more she realised that he was right. Mr Wymington was not as harmless as he seemed; a conclusion confirmed a few days later when a small parcel arrived from the gentleman. The package was addressed to Helen but inside was a sealed enclosure for Gillian.

The remarks Mr Wymington made in his note to Helen were both pleasant and innocuous, expressing again his delight at having met her and at having seen them both in Abbot Quincey. But they were also followed by a request that she forward the enclosed letter to Miss Gresham at her earliest convenience.

Helen did not pass the note along, of course, nor had she any intention of doing so. But when a second letter arrived a few days later, accompanied by a note which suggested in more forceful terms that she forward the letter, Helen knew she had to do something. It seemed she had not mistaken the look in Mr Wymington's eyes. He was just as determined as Gillian when it came to getting what he wanted—and what he wanted was Gillian.

Helen thought back to some of the remarks he had made just before she and Gillian had taken their leave of him, and in particular, to the remark he had made about Helen having compromised herself by allowing Gillian and Mr Wymington to meet. Had he intended the remark as a threat? Helen hadn't thought much about it at the time, but now she realised it was a very good possibility. Was it also his plan to tell Oliver what she had done if she did not allow him to see Gillian or to allow her to receive correspondence from him?

Helen couldn't be sure, but she knew it was imperative that she find out. She had inadvertently put herself in an exceedingly awkward position and the only way she could see her way clear to getting out of it was by being truthful to all. There would be time enough to worry about the consequences later.

So saying, she sat down at her desk and wrote another letter to Mr Wymington, asking him to do her the favour of meeting with her. She told him they had a most urgent matter to discuss, and suggested they meet in Abbot Giles, the village the farthest removed from the school. She then addressed the letter to his uncle's cottage in Abbot Quincey and gave it to one of the kitchen lads to post.

Not that it would matter if anyone did see her, Helen reflected as she threw her shawl about her

shoulders and went out for a walk. No one apart from
Gillian and herself knew what Mr Wymington looked
like, so if anyone did see them together, she could
simply say she had run into an old friend. But she
knew she couldn't afford to wait any longer. She had
to speak to Mr Wymington and find out exactly what
his intentions towards Gillian were. Because the
sooner she did, the sooner she could tell Oliver
Brandon that he was wrong—or right—in his assumptions about the man.

Not surprisingly, at the thought of Oliver Brandon,
Helen experienced again the strange fluttery sensation
in the pit of her stomach. She was astonished at how
much her feelings towards him had changed. She was
no longer angry or even resentful about what he *believed* had taken place with Lord Talbot. Indeed, she
had been touched by Oliver's apology and by his concern that she understand the reasons behind it. More
than that, during their outing to Castle Ashby, she had
been given a glimpse into another side of the man.
She had experienced first-hand his concern for his
ward, and she had listened to him express his own
doubts as to the wisdom of what he was doing for her
now.

On a more personal note, Helen had found herself
opening up to him and telling him personal things
about her own life and even about her feelings for
Thomas. And he had been a marvellous listener. At
no time had she felt that she was boring him, or that
he was listening to her out of a sense of obligation.
His interest in her past had been genuine, as had the
look of concern in his eyes when she had revealed
her feelings of resentment towards her father.

Yes, something had definitely happened between

them at Castle Ashby. Unfortunately, Helen suspected it wasn't anything good. At least, not for her. She had begun to care about a man who had never known what it was like to be in love. She had given her heart to someone who would not only not want it, but who would likely have no idea what to do with it once he discovered it was in his possession.

Oliver spent the days following his outing to Castle Ashby in something of a brown study. Because it wasn't the castle or his ward that lingered on his mind, but Helen de Coverdale. Certainly, he couldn't deny that his opinion of her had changed over the last few weeks. Whereas for the past eleven years he had believed her to be a beautiful, sensual woman willing to use her appearance and her feminine wiles to make her way in the world, he now realised how wrong he had been. Helen had been nothing more than a victim of circumstances; a woman trapped by her own beauty in a situation totally beyond her control. What he had seen of her that night in the library had not been a tempting seductress trying to coax money or jewels from her lover, but an innocent young woman fighting for her virtue.

Why the hell hadn't he seen it at the time? Oliver demanded of himself. Had he been so blind to the truth that he hadn't been able to see the look of un-bridled lust on Talbot's face and the unmistakable look of fear on hers? Because it was all he *could* see now that he thought back to that night. Unfortunately, it had taken an admission from Lord Talbot himself to force Oliver to look back and see beyond his own ignorance.

It was a wonder Helen was even speaking to him!

Still, perhaps it was a good thing it had taken such a jolt to make him see the truth, Oliver reflected. Because her graciousness in accepting his apology was just another indication of the kind of woman she really was. He saw the patience she exhibited towards her pupils, and the gentleness with which she talked to the little girls. And he had seen more than once her willingness to laugh. Would he ever forget the look in Helen's eyes when she had turned to find one of her girls spattered in paint? There had certainly been no anger in her expression. Indeed, she had been forced to bite her lip to keep from laughing. She was a warm and caring woman who gave more to others than she asked for herself. And in doing so, she commanded affection from her girls, respect from her peers, and the unwavering loyalty of the woman who employed her.

As to hearing that Helen had been in love with another man, Oliver hadn't wanted to admit, even to himself, his feelings upon learning that. Certainly there was no reason for him to have had *any* kind of feelings in the matter. Nor had he the heart to tell her that had he been in her father's place, he would probably have done the same thing. He knew better than most the social implications of such a marriage. But when Helen's life had been turned upside down by her father's death, and she had been forced to make her own way in the world, she had done so with courage and dignity. Not, as he'd first believed, through the use of artifice and temptation.

Yes, there was much to admire in Helen de Coverdale, Oliver acknowledged, and he cursed himself for the ridiculous concerns he'd entertained. Imagine believing that she would be a bad influence on his ward. In point of fact, Gillian would do well to study the example set by such a woman. And that was something else Oliver was pleased about. Gillian was in a much better frame of mind than she had been when he'd left her at the school a few weeks ago. She seemed to have made a place for herself there, and he was delighted with her association with Elizabeth Brookwell, whom he knew to be a nicely mannered young lady from a good family.

More than that, however, Oliver was relieved that Gillian had not made a single mention of Mr Wymington. She had not acted the part of a lovelorn waif nor professed herself wretched with despair. Instead, she had laughed and acted like a young woman who hadn't a care in the world.

Yes, Sophie had been right in her suggestion that he send Gillian to Steep Abbot. Oliver had no doubt that by the time she returned to Hertfordshire at the end of the year she would be over her infatuation with Mr Wymington and eager to travel to London for the Season. Hopefully, she would meet a man more suitable to her station and they would marry and settle down, leaving Oliver free to get on with his own life.

And then suddenly, it hit him. What did he *want* to do with the rest of his life? What was he to do once Gillian married and moved away? How would he keep himself occupied in the empty halls of Shefferton Hall?

And why did an image of Helen de Coverdale keep popping up in his mind?

Abbot Giles lay due west of the Guarding Academy. It was a small village, boasting a church and a vicarage, and it could be reached by walking through the grounds of the Abbey, a building that until a few months ago had been the home of the contemptible Marquis of Sywell.

Helen sighed as she thought about the story of the bizarre murder, and about Gillian's unending fascination with it. She had refused to gossip with her about it, not because she was lacking information on the subject, but because there was simply too much information to be had. And after the shocking revelations of the past weekend—revelations which had been passed on to her by Jane Emerson, who had in turn heard them from Aggie Binns, the washerwoman in Steep Ride—it seemed there was even more grist for the rumour mill.

In discussion with the investigators, it appeared that the Earl of Yardley had finally disclosed the nature of his business with the Marquis of Sywell on the night he had visited him. It seemed that the Earl had gone to the Abbey to speak to Sywell about his purchasing the Abbey, and apparently, they had agreed—reluctantly on the Earl's part—on a price of two hundred thousand pounds!

Helen had gasped at the staggering sum, as had most of the villagers. To think that the Earl would be willing to pay such an amount of money for something he already owned! But even more astonishing was the Earl's willingness to pay that same amount of money to Sywell's widow. After all, she had had nothing to do with the Marquis's behaviour, the Earl had stated, or with Sywell's reprehensible conduct in acquiring the Abbey in the first place. Why should she not benefit from that which would rightfully have been hers?

That news, of course, had unleashed a flurry of

speculation in the villages. Why was the Earl willing to pay so much money for the Abbey? Was it just a ruse on his part to draw Sywell's widow out of hiding? Many believed it was. Because there were many who believed, like Gillian, that Louise had committed the murder and that she was now in hiding for her life.

Still others believed that the Earl had simply set forward a most generous offer and that Louise would be a foolish young woman indeed not to accept it. And if she were truly innocent of the crime, why would she hesitate to come forward and accept it?

Helen shook her head in confusion, wondering what to make of it all. Certainly, it had become the most widely talked about scandal in years. The girls at Mrs Guarding's Academy were constantly being reprimanded for whispering about it. But even Helen could not deny that it made for diverting conversation. Indeed, she might have tossed it around in her own mind a good deal longer, had she not looked up to see Mr Wymington standing across the road from her. At the sight of the dashing man who had the power to affect both Gillian's future and her own, Helen immediately forgot all about the Marquis and his unfortunate demise. Instead, she took a deep breath, squared her shoulders, and walked forward as calmly as she could to greet him.

'Mr Wymington, thank you for agreeing to see me.'

'I would have been foolish indeed not to meet so beautiful a lady.' Mr Wymington offered her a sweeping bow. 'I take it by Miss Gresham's absence that she is not aware you are seeing me today?'

'No. I thought it best I say what I had to in private.'

'Of course.' He nodded towards the carriage behind

him. 'Would you like to take a drive while we talk or would you prefer to walk?'

Helen glanced at the carriage and shook her head. She was not sure she was comfortable with the idea of being alone in a closed carriage with him. 'Thank you, but it is a lovely day and I think we would do just as well to walk.'

'As you wish, Miss de Coverdale.'

'By the by, how is your uncle?' Helen enquired as she fell into step beside him. 'I do hope he is feeling better.'

'He is much recovered, thank you. But he continues to regret the fact that he was deprived of the pleasure of meeting you and Miss Gresham the other evening.'

A tiny smile pulled at the corner of Helen's mouth. 'I am relieved to hear he is on the mend.'

'Decent of you to say so since you are not even sure he exists. Oh, come, Miss de Coverdale, you must not take offence,' Mr Wymington said when he saw her look of surprise. 'I was aware from the moment of my telling you he was ill that you did not believe he was there. Like Mr Brandon, you are suspicious of my motives with regard to Miss Gresham.'

'You are a man for speaking plainly, Mr Wymington.'

'I am when I feel myself to be with like-minded people.'

'Like-minded?' Helen frowned. 'Why would you consider us to be so?'

'Because you and I were not born as fortunate as some, Miss de Coverdale. We must struggle to make our living, rather than be handed it on a silver platter. You have chosen to seek your rewards by being a schoolmistress, and I through…other means.'

A flutter of anxiety rippled up Helen's spine. 'What other means do you refer to, sir?'

'My dear Miss de Coverdale, I cannot believe you are as naïve as all that. You know full well there are many other avenues for those like us to earn our keep, rather than by hard work alone.'

'Perhaps you should explain yourself, Mr Wymington. I understand that you are at present a half-pay officer in the militia. Are you not content with your station in life?'

'Good God, why should I be?' He laughed harshly. 'The life of an officer is hardly one to be envied. My expenses are always higher than my earnings and I am ill content for them to remain so. I do not apologise for being desirous of a better life.'

'If it is advancement and glory you crave, why not seek a higher commission?'

'Because I haven't the blunt to buy one,' Mr Wymington admitted, his boyish smile evidence of his lack of concern. 'But if I were to marry a wealthy young woman, that would bring about an end to all of my problems, wouldn't it?'

'And I suppose Miss Gresham is the young woman you had in mind?'

'What do you think?'

'I begin to think you are no better than Mr Brandon suspected.'

For a disreputable man, Wymington possessed the smile of an angel. 'No better perhaps, but no worse. I am very fond of Gillian. She is lovely enough to amuse me and has money enough to afford us both a very comfortable life. More importantly, she loves me enough to do whatever I ask.'

'Does that include going against the wishes of her guardian?'

'If necessary. A woman will always choose the man she loves over the parent who raised her. That is the way of the world.'

'You sound very sure of yourself, Mr Wymington,' Helen said coldly. 'Which is surprising, given the circumstances. You must know that I will not allow you to use Gillian in such a manner.'

'And what would you do, fair Helen? Tell her that you have met with me in private and discovered that I really am the scurrilous cad her guardian believes me to be?'

'My name is Miss de Coverdale,' Helen reminded him, 'and why would I not?'

'Because she would not believe you. Oh, I have no doubt she respects you well enough, but she would not take your word over mine. Nor, I think, would she be pleased to hear of our little rendezvous today. I know Mr Brandon would not.'

Helen wasn't in the least surprised by the remark. 'Are you threatening to tell him?'

'If I had to. I am no one's fool, Helen. A man must use whatever means are at his disposal to secure his ends and to ensure his future. It would not be my wish to inform Mr Brandon or Miss Gresham that we had met in secret, but I would do so if I felt it necessary to protect my interests.'

'And what if I told you I intend to tell Mr Brandon about the visit myself?'

'You may tell him whatever you wish. But I suggest you bear in mind the fact that he will not be as angry about our visit today as he will be about the fact that you arranged a secret meeting between Gillian and myself at a deserted cottage.'

It was an undeniable truth, and in light of it Helen fell silent. It seemed her doubts about Sidney Wymington were well founded indeed. He was not above using blackmail to achieve his ends, and if it came right down to it, Helen had no doubt he would twist the truth in any way necessary to make her part in this affair appear as black as his own. The only difference was, he could sway Gillian to his side. She could not. As Wymington had said, Gillian might like and respect her, but if it came to choosing sides, she was far more likely to go with him than with anyone else. Worse still, if Wymington were so inclined, it was very possible he could turn Gillian against all of them.

'Miss Gresham does not turn one-and-twenty for nearly four years,' Helen said quietly. 'In the absence of Mr Brandon's approval to marry, do you really think she will wait for you?'

'She will wait as long as I wish her to,' came Wymington's cocksure reply. 'Once she is back in Hertfordshire, it will be easy enough for me to see her. While she is here, I have only to keep assuring her of my unwavering devotion, which is easy enough to do by sending her the right kind of messages.'

Helen's feelings of concern veered sharply to anger. 'You are not to communicate with her!'

'And how do you intend to stop me, Helen? It is a simple enough matter to get letters to her. You may not be willing to forward my notes, but there are plenty of young ladies at the Academy who are.'

Helen came to an abrupt stop in the middle of the road. She realised now that she had been foolish to think she could persuade this man to give up his quest. Because in doing so, she had jeopardised not only Gillian's future, but her own.

'I think we have said all that needs to be said, Mr Wymington.' Helen's voice was flat, but her eyes flashed with anger and resentment. 'You may threaten me if you wish, but it will do you no good. I *shall* tell Mr Brandon of your conduct. I shall write to him this very day and tell him you are every bit as conniving as he suspected, and that he was right to try to keep you apart. I shall also tell Gillian what kind of man you are, and do everything in my power to change that innocent young girl's opinion of you.'

Mr Wymington breathed a sigh of resignation. 'You may do whatever you wish, my dear Helen. And you are, of course, entitled to your opinions. But in the end, we shall see who comes out ahead. You were wrong to threaten me, my dear. Because I am in a much better position to win than you. A few words in Gillian's ear will rob you of her affection, and a carefully worded note to Mrs Guarding, of your employment. Not that you need have any worry about finding other kinds of work.' Wymington stepped in close and grasped her chin in his hands, tipping it back and forcing her to meet his eyes. 'You are an exceptionally lovely woman. I doubt you would have difficulty in finding a man to take you in. I would set you up as my own mistress, but I doubt you would pleasure me in bed given the way you feel about me now.'

'Hateful man!' Helen jerked her head away. 'How dare you speak to me in such an insolent manner!'

'I am only speaking the truth, my dear. You may enjoy teaching your little girls how to speak the language of love, but we both know that isn't where your true talents lie. You have beauty enough to dazzle any man, and you would be foolish not to make the most of it before it is too late.'

'I will hear no more of this, sir!'

Wymington pretended to be hurt. 'I do wish you would call me Sidney. We are going to be seeing a good deal of each other over the next little while.'

'I will *not* see you again,' Helen said, fighting against the feelings of dread that were even now twisting her stomach into knots. 'Whatever the outcome of this meeting, I shall see to it that you are not allowed to continue in your plan. I will not allow you to ruin that young woman's life.'

Wymington chuckled, but the sound was sly and, at the same time, disturbingly sensual. 'Ruination is not always as bad as it is made out to be, Helen. Gillian may be young, but she longs for adventure and romance, and I can give that to her. Come now; be honest with me. Have you not longed for such adventure in your life? Would you have turned down an opportunity like this, had you found yourself in a similar position at her age?'

His words tore at Helen's heart, and for a moment, she could not speak the words she had to say. She *had* been in a position like this once; hopelessly in love with a man she could not have, and desperate to be with him. So desperate, that when Thomas had suggested they run away together, Helen hadn't even stopped to consider the consequences. She had agreed to an elopement, knowing they would be married as soon as they crossed the Scottish border.

Of course, the elopement had never taken place. Somehow, her father had learned of their plans and had immediately put a stop to them. He'd threatened to go to the Dean with news of Thomas's disgraceful behaviour, and he would have, but for Helen's fevered intervention on his behalf. She had promised her father that if he would let Thomas remain in the church, she would never see him again. And that was exactly what had happened.

But in the months that had followed, Helen had learned just how hard was the task she had set for herself. To live in the same village as the man she loved and to know she could say nothing to him beyond good morning or good afternoon had been torture of the most excruciating kind. But she had not faltered. She had stood by her promise and done everything her father had asked of her. But she could not deny that she *had* been willing to give up everything to be with Thomas.

Was that not exactly what Wymington was talking about now?

Helen took a long, deep breath and then stepped away from him. 'I have nothing more to say to you, Mr Wymington. Other than to advise you that you have made an enemy today.'

'I am sorry to hear that, Helen, but I shall not endeavour to change your mind. I shall only say goodbye until we meet again. And we will meet again.' Mr Wymington bowed, but when he straightened, Helen saw there was nothing of respect in his eyes. 'You can be quite sure of that.'

# Chapter Ten

There was only one thought in Helen's mind as she hurried back towards the school. She had to talk to Gillian. She had to convince her that Mr Wymington was a liar and a cheat, and that for her own good, she must never see him again. But how was she to do that? How could she even *begin* such a conversation?

*The only way you can begin it*, Helen told herself. *By telling Gillian the truth about everything that's happened—including the meeting you had with him today.*

Helen tugged thoughtfully at her bottom lip as she passed through the shadow of Steepwood Abbey. Yes, she would certainly have to reveal what Mr Wymington had said to her, but the question was, would Gillian believe her? She already suspected Helen of siding with Oliver in the matter. Indeed, ever since their visit to Castle Ashby, Gillian had taken to remarking how attentive Oliver had been to her, and how much he seemed to have enjoyed her company.

Naturally, Helen had been quick to deny it. She

has assured Gillian that Mr Brandon had merely been playing the part of an attentive host, and when reminded of the amount of time they had spent alone together, had replied that neither she nor Mr Brandon had wished to intrude on the good time the two girls seemed to be having.

Gillian hadn't believed a word of it, of course. And judging by the complacent smile she'd given Helen, the girl had formed her own impressions as to what was going on between her guardian and her teacher. In which case, Helen knew there was very little chance of Gillian believing her in this.

It did not make for an enviable situation, and when Helen got up the next morning she was no closer to knowing how to resolve matters than she had been when she'd gone to bed. She continued to think about it throughout the day, but had still not reached a decision when they set off for church on Sunday morning. Unfortunately, matters quickly went downhill and in a manner Helen couldn't even have begun to anticipate.

It all started when Oliver showed up unexpectedly after the service and invited Gillian and Helen to join him for a drive.

'Oh, Oliver, how splendid of you to suggest it,' Gillian exclaimed. 'I should love to go for a drive, and I'm sure Miss de Coverdale would too.' She slid a knowing glance towards her teacher. 'After all, the two of you got along so well at Castle Ashby.'

Helen felt her face go three shades of red. 'Thank you, Miss Gresham, but I do not think my joining you today would be appropriate.'

'Of course it would,' Gillian said, refusing to be denied. 'It will be far more pleasant than returning to school. Will you treat us to some refreshments as well, Oliver?'

'I think that could be arranged.'

'In that case, I shall certainly not join you,' Helen said quickly.

'Do you not eat, Miss de Coverdale?' Oliver enquired, a twinkle forming in his eyes.

'I do, sir, but not at someone else's expense.'

'Excuse me, Miss de Coverdale?'

Helen turned as Sally Jenkins came running up to her. 'Yes, Miss Jenkins, what is it?'

'Pardon the interruption, miss, but I was told to give you this.'

Helen glanced down at the small package Sally was holding out to her and frowned. 'What is it?'

'I don't know, miss. The gentleman said I was to give it to you as soon as you came out of church.'

'What gentleman?'

'Mr Wymington, miss.'

Helen heard Gillian's sharp gasp of dismay beside her, but it was Oliver's reaction she feared the most. She glanced up at him to see his smile disappear and an expression of disbelief settle upon his features. 'Wymington is *here*?'

'I d-don't know. Miss Jenkins, did the gentleman *say* his name was...Mr Wymington?'

'Yes, Miss. He made me repeat it twice so I wouldn't forget.'

'But...where did you see him?'

'Over by the commons. He told me I was to give this to you because you had left it in his carriage.'

'In his *carriage*?' Gillian's expression reflected her feelings of shock and dismay. 'But...when were you in Mr Wymington's carriage?'

'I wasn't.' Helen's heart raced as she stared at the package in her hand. 'I have no idea what this is all about.'

'But you have *seen* Mr Wymington?'

That question came from Oliver and there was no mistaking the tone of voice. Helen looked up, and shivered at the iciness of his gaze. 'Mr Brandon, I think it would be best if we discussed this in private—'

'I asked you a question, Miss de Coverdale. Have you seen Mr Wymington in or around Steep Abbot?'

Helen sighed, painfully aware there was nothing she could do but tell him the truth. 'Yes. I arranged to meet with him on…Friday afternoon in Abbot Giles.'

'You *arranged* to meet him?' Gillian echoed in disbelief. 'But I don't understand. Why would you wish to do such a thing?'

'Perhaps before you answer that, you should open the box and see what Mr Wymington has returned to you,' Oliver said in a cold, disapproving voice.

Helen risked a quick look at Gillian, saw the doubt and bewilderment in her eyes, and then glanced down at the package. She folded back the paper with fingers that were visibly trembling, and to her astonishment, found herself staring at one of her new kid gloves.

'That is your glove, Miss de Coverdale,' Gillian exclaimed. 'I have seen you wear it on several occasions.'

Helen stared at it in bafflement. It certainly *looked* like her glove, but how could Mr Wymington possibly have gained possession of it? She hadn't left it in the cottage the afternoon she and Gillian had gone to see him, nor had she taken it off when she had met him in Abbot Giles.

'It is one very much like it, I admit, but I...cannot be sure it is the same.'

Oliver picked up the glove and examined it. 'Where did you get these gloves, Miss de Coverdale?'

'A very good friend sent them to me.'

'From London?'

'Yes.'

Oliver nodded. 'I know the shop where they are made. The workmanship is quite distinctive and they do not come cheap. Gloves like these would not be common property around here. I can only assume it would have to be yours.'

'But there is no way Mr Wymington could have come into possession of it.'

'Why not? Were you wearing them when you met him in Abbot Giles?'

'Yes, but I did not take them off. And it is impossible for me to have left it in Mr Wymington's carriage, because I have never *been* in his carriage.'

'Why then would he say you had?' Gillian demanded.

Searching her mind for a plausible explanation, Helen could only shake her head in dismay. Something warned her that Wymington had planned this. He'd wanted her to be humiliated in front of Gillian. He had wanted to discredit her, and to make her look deceitful, and he had more than succeeded.

'Go back to school with Miss Brookwell and wait for me there, Gillian,' Oliver said abruptly.

'But Oliver—'

'Do as I say, child. I wish to speak to Miss de Coverdale alone.'

Looking very unhappy and more than a little confused, Gillian turned and slowly walked away. She glanced back over her shoulder a few times, her face a study in dejection as she looked from one to the other of them.

Oliver waited until she was well beyond their hearing before he turned to Helen and said, 'Now, Miss de Coverdale, would you care to explain what this is all about?'

Awkwardly, Helen cleared her throat. 'Truly, sir, I have no idea—'

'Pray do not take me for a fool, Miss de Coverdale.' Oliver's expression darkened ominously. 'Whether or not this *is* your glove is hardly the issue here. What is, is that you have been in contact with Sidney Wymington, and that you have chosen not to tell me about it.'

'But I have a good explanation—'

'If there is an explanation, I doubt it will be good,' Oliver snapped. 'Since you said you had *arranged* to meet Wymington, I can only assume you knew what he looked like. Does that mean you had occasion to see him prior to your Friday afternoon meeting in Abbot Giles?'

Reluctantly, Helen nodded. 'Yes, but—'

'And was Gillian with you?'

At that, Helen stopped. She didn't dare tell him that she had taken Gillian to see Mr Wymington in Abbot Quincey. Not without explaining why. But surely she could reveal the details of their chance encounter on the road. Surely he would not hold her culpable for that. 'Yes she was. Mr Wymington happened to come upon us as we were walking home from church.'

Sparks danced in Oliver's eyes. 'Did you not think that a little strange given that Mr Wymington resides in Hertfordshire?'

Helen's temper began to flare. 'Of course I did.'

'Yet on the strength of that meeting, you arranged to meet him again in Abbot Giles?'

'Well, no, not precisely.'

'Not precisely?'

Helen closed her eyes. It seemed that with every word, she was digging herself deeper into a hole. 'I arranged to see him again…after I had met with him at his uncle's cottage in Abbot Quincey.'

For a moment, there was complete silence. Then, like a volcano, Oliver's anger began to erupt. 'You met with him in the privacy of a family member's home?'

'Mr Brandon, I can assure you—'

'I want no assurances, Miss de Coverdale, other than to be told that Gillian did *not* accompany you on that visit.'

'I fear I really must be allowed to speak—'

'Damn and blast it, woman, answer my question! Did Gillian go with you when you went to see Wymington?'

Helen cringed at the anger in his voice. 'Yes, but if you would just let me explain—'

'No! I will hear no more! I let it be known in no uncertain terms, that Gillian was not to be allowed *any* contact with Mr Wymington, and yet today I learn that not only have you been in contact with him, but that you have exposed Gillian to him as well. Well that is not satisfactory, Miss de Coverdale. By God, it is not!'

A very short time later, Oliver jerked the horses to a halt in front of Mrs Guarding's Academy. 'Has Mrs Guarding returned from church?' he demanded of the young lad who came running to hold the horses.

'Aye, sir. A few minutes ago.'

'Good.' He tossed the reins to the boy, ordered him to hold them until he returned, and then, taking the stone steps two at a time, flung open the front door and climbed the stairs to the headmistress's sitting-room. He barely waited for an answer to his knock before he opened the door and walked in.

'Mrs Guarding, I have come to express my extreme dissatisfaction with you and a member of your staff.'

The smile of welcome that had been forming on the headmistress's face died within seconds of his greeting. 'Mr Brandon, whatever has happened?'

'Only that which I tried to prevent by warning you well in advance of its likelihood.'

'Would you care to sit down?'

'I am far too agitated to sit, madam.' Oliver began to pace the length of the room. 'I have just learned that my ward has been in contact with Sidney Wymington, and that Miss de Coverdale had a hand in the meeting taking place.'

'Miss de Coverdale?' The headmistress's disbelief was plain. 'I am sure there must be some mistake. I cannot believe Helen would do such a thing.'

'I regret to inform you that she has. I have just learned of the entire sorry affair. I thought to take

Gillian and Miss de Coverdale for a drive, but whilst talking to them, a package was delivered to Miss de Coverdale by one of the students. It seems she left one of her gloves in Mr Wymington's carriage.'

Mrs Guarding gasped softly, and then leaned against the corner of her desk. 'Are you sure it was her glove?'

'I don't give a damn if it was.' Oliver's voice was cold and deliberate. 'The fact is, she has seen the man on three different occasions, the most recent of which was a meeting that she arranged herself in a nearby village. But far more distressing to me is the fact that she has allowed Gillian to be in contact with him as well.'

By now, Mrs Guarding's face had gone ashen. 'Mr Brandon, I really have no idea what to say.'

'There is nothing to say, madam,' Oliver interrupted harshly. 'I put my trust in you to keep Gillian safe from that man, only to discover that my faith has been sorely misplaced. Especially in regard to Miss de Coverdale. I begin to wonder if everything she's told me has been a Banbury tale.'

'Mr Brandon, I can understand your being angry. And while I have no idea what has transpired here, I do intend to find out. But you have no reason to doubt that anything else Miss de Coverdale has told you is anything but the truth.'

'Good God, madam, do you really expect me to believe that?' Oliver's laugh exploded as a harsh burst of sound. 'The woman went behind my back and did *exactly* what I asked her not to. She knew how I felt about Mr Wymington, yet she wilfully allowed this abominable meeting to take place. Well,

that is not acceptable. I demand you take measures
to remedy the situation at once.'

Mrs Guarding nodded, but her eyes were deeply
troubled. 'Yes, of course. I shall speak to her at immediately upon her return.'

'I expect you to do more than speak to her, Mrs
Guarding. I want Miss de Coverdale dismissed. If
she is not, I shall ensure that no young lady of quality ever sets foot in this establishment again.
Furthermore, I intend to remove Gillian before the
end of the month and take her back to Hertfordshire,
where with any luck, I shall find a suitable young
man willing to marry her.' Oliver turned on his heel
and headed for the door. 'Business matters compel
me to leave first thing in the morning, but I shall
stay at the Angel for the night. You may let me know
of your decision there.'

Helen did not see Oliver again that afternoon. She
knew he had spoken to Mrs Guarding, and she assumed he would talk to Gillian, but beyond that she
had no idea of what he was planning to do. She sat
on the edge of the bed in her tiny room and picked
up the letter that had been waiting for her upon her
return from church. With a heavy heart, she read the
damning words again.

Dear Helen
I trust Miss Gresham and Mr Brandon were
suitably impressed by the gallant return of your
misplaced glove. A simple gesture, I thought,
but highly effective. You are no match for me,
my dear. You would do well to remember that.
SCW

This, then, was what Mr Wymington had referred to when he'd said he would do whatever was necessary to achieve his goal. The entire performance had been planned with a view to discrediting her in front of Gillian. Obviously, he had convinced one of the girls—with heaven knew *what* kind of trickery— to remove the glove from her room and to bring it to him. Certainly, he had timed the delivery of it well. He knew that she and Gillian would be together after church and by making sure that the glove was delivered to her in such a way, it would have been obvious to Gillian that they had met. The fact that Oliver had been there to witness her disgrace had been an unexpected bonus.

Helen tried to ignore the tearing pain in her chest as she thought about Oliver and the way he had reacted. Would she ever forget the way he had looked at her when she had mentioned Mr Wymington's name? Would she ever be able to banish the memory of the disappointment and anger that had appeared in his eyes during the conversation that had followed?

She feared not. She hadn't realised until that moment just how much his good opinion had meant to her. She had been so pleased when they had been able to resolve their differences from the past. And she had enjoyed, more than she cared to admit, the time she had spent with him at Castle Ashby.

But all of that was gone now. She had done something she'd known all along to be wrong, and had lost not only his respect but her own credibility. Even now, he would be questioning the validity of everything she had told him. He might even begin to believe she *had* invited Lord Talbot's advances, regardless of what the drunken peer had admitted to. And what about Mrs Guarding? What would she do if the headmistress turned her away?

Helen's face crumpled. After all, she had blatantly disregarded the rules. She had ignored her instructions and had taken matters into her own hands. What choice would the headmistress have but to turn her away?

When a tentative knock came at the door, Helen froze. 'Yes?'

'Miss de Coverdale?'

Helen gasped, and quickly opened the door. 'Gillian, what are you doing here?'

'I had to see you.' The girl walked in and collapsed on the bed. 'Oliver is furious.'

'Yes, I'd expected as much. Did he scold you very badly?'

Gillian's bottom lip trembled. 'He didn't say much to me at all. I don't think he could find the words. But I am terribly afraid he is going to take me away.'

There was such a plaintive quality to the girl's voice that it nearly broke Helen's heart. 'Oh, Gillian, I am so sorry.'

'Why did you have to tell him I had been in contact with Mr Wymington? He would never have found out if you hadn't.'

'I could not lie to him, Gillian. It was bad enough we did something without his knowledge. To compound that by lying would have made it even worse. Besides, he already knew I had seen Mr Wymington myself.'

'But *why* did you arrange to see Mr Wymington in Abbot Giles?'

Helen had been expecting the question, but somehow, it didn't make the answering of it any easier. 'Because I was…troubled by something he'd said to me when we were leaving his uncle's cottage.'

'Why? What did he say?'

Helen wished there was some way she could soften the blow Gillian was about to receive, but she knew in her heart there was not. 'Gillian, Mr Wymington hasn't been completely honest with you about his feelings.'

Gillian went very still. 'What do you mean?'

'I mean that your guardian has been right all along. Mr Wymington admitted to me that…the reason he is courting you is because he is interested in securing a wealthy bride.'

*'No!'*

'I wish I could say it wasn't so—'

'No, it isn't true!' Gillian sprang to her feet, her blue eyes blazing with anger. 'You are only saying that to make me *think* he doesn't love me. But he *does* love me! He told me so himself!'

'Mr Wymington would tell you whatever he thought he had to to make you believe him, Gillian, don't you see that?' Helen took the girl by the shoulders and gave her a gentle shake. 'He's not a wealthy man, but he knows that by marrying you he will become one.'

'But the money is mine!'

'Yes, but when a woman marries, everything she owns becomes the property of her husband. You would have absolutely no say in how your money was spent, or on what.'

Suddenly, Gillian jerked free of Helen's hands. 'You like him, don't you!'

Helen blanched. *'What?'*

'You like Mr Wymington,' she repeated. 'That's why you went to see him, isn't it?'

Helen flinched at the accusation in Gillian's voice. 'Of course it isn't. What nonsense!'

But Gillian only shook her head and began to back towards the door. 'No, it isn't nonsense. He told me you would say terrible things like this. He told me you would...try to make me think badly of him, because you were jealous and wanted him for yourself. But I didn't believe it.' Gillian looked at her with a haunted expression. 'I didn't *want* to believe it.'

'Gillian, what do you mean he *told* you that's what I would say? Have you been in contact with him?'

'That's none of your concern,' Gillian cried.

'Yes, Gillian, it is. Have you had a letter from him?'

'All right, yes, I have!' Her tone was defiant. 'And I want the others he sent to you for me. You had no right to keep them! They were mine!'

Stunned, Helen rocked back on her heels. Dear God, how could everything have gone so terribly, terribly wrong? 'Gillian, listen to me. Mr Wymington had no business sending you letters. He was wrong to try to contact you, and he was certainly wrong to try to do it through me. Mr Brandon expressly forbade any correspondence between the two of you.'

'I do not think that is the case at all,' Gillian said, her voice ringing with condemnation. 'You like Mr Wymington and you didn't like the idea of his sending letters to me.'

'That is utterly ridiculous!'

'No, it isn't. Mr Wymington is a wonderful man! Any woman would be proud to have him by her side.

And you're just an old spinster who can't find a gentleman of her own,' Gillian flung at her. 'That's why you tried to take mine.'

Helen gasped at the cruelty of the indictment. 'I would never do such a thing!'

'Yes, you would. Well, I hope Mrs Guarding does dismiss you!' Gillian said as she threw open the door. 'I hope she sends you away as soon as possible. Because I never ever want to see you again!'

# Chapter Eleven

Mrs Guarding sent for her thirty minutes later.

Helen went to the headmistress's office with a heavy heart. Her world was falling apart and there was absolutely nothing she could do to stop it. First Oliver had turned against her, then Gillian, and now, she was to be taken to task by Mrs Guarding. Would this wretched day never end?

'So you were, in fact, a willing accomplice to the meeting between Gillian and Mr Wymington,' Mrs Guarding said at the end of Helen's recounting of the events.

'Only in that I allowed it to take place.' Helen breathed a heavy sigh. 'I had to know if Mr Wymington was truly as reprehensible as Mr Brandon believed him to be. I thought that by going and listening to his conversation with Miss Gresham, I might be able to discover something about him which would confirm Mr Brandon's suspicions.'

'Which you did.'

'Yes.'

'And that is why you arranged to meet with him again in Abbot Giles,' Mrs Guarding said slowly.

'I know you think I was inclined to disbelieve Mr Brandon because of my past, Mrs Guarding, but I had to find out the truth. I thought that if I could go to Gillian with proof of Mr Wymington's duplicity, she would be able to see that her guardian was right.'

'And yet, in spite of what you were able to learn about Mr Wymington, Gillian is enamoured of him still.'

Helen's head fell forward in despair. 'Yes.'

Mrs Guarding got up and slowly began to walk around the room. 'You say that Gillian and Mr Wymington have been exchanging letters.'

'I can only assume that some of the girls have been helping the messages go back and forth. Mr Wymington was not above using trinkets or sweets to encourage them, and indeed, the girls would have no reason to believe they were doing anything wrong. It was only the staff that were told there was to be no communication allowed. No doubt the girls thought it all very romantic. A kind of Romeo and Juliet relationship, as it were.'

'Hmm, and look where love got *them*,' Mrs Guarding muttered. 'Well, we are in a fine mess, my dear. Mr Brandon has threatened the future of the school if I do not dismiss you, yet your reasons for doing what you did—if not the manner in which you did them—are only to be commended. Especially in light of Mr Wymington's true nature. Unfortunately, I am once again caught in the middle of the problem, forced to choose between what I feel to be right and what is best for the school.'

Helen closed her eyes. 'I am so very sorry, Mrs Guarding. I had no idea it would come to this.

Certainly, it was never my wish to cause you so much aggravation.'

'I know, my dear, but unfortunately, being sorry doesn't make the problem go away.' Mrs Guarding sighed again. 'Go back to your room, Helen. I shall take the evening to think the matter over and advise you and Mr Brandon of my decision in the morning.'

'Has Mr Brandon returned to Hertfordshire?'

'No. He has taken a room at the Angel, but he has asked for my decision before he leaves in the morning. Did I mention that he has also advised me of his intention to remove Gillian from the school?'

Helen gasped. 'No!'

'I believe he intends to settle her in marriage as soon as possible.'

With every word, Helen's spirits plummeted even further. 'She will hate that above all. I wonder she did not mention it to me.'

'I am not sure she knows. Mr Brandon possibly would not wish to upset her to the point where she might do something foolish before he can get her home.'

That made sense, Helen reflected sadly. Oliver didn't trust Gillian at the best of times. In the state she was in now, there was no telling *what* she might do.

'By the way, it would probably be best if you did not see Gillian until I've made my decision,' Mrs Guarding advised. 'No doubt she will be feeling extremely troubled by all that has happened.'

Helen remembered the acrimonious tone of the girl's voice; the stinging words of condemnation she had thrown at her, and regretfully nodded her head.

'Yes, I have no doubt that she is, at the moment, a very troubled young lady indeed.'

Helen went back to her room and thought long and hard about the situation she found herself in. And the more she thought about it, the more she realised it was not only her future that was at stake here, but Gillian's. The child had to be kept safe from the likes of Sidney Wymington, but how? Wymington certainly couldn't be trusted to keep *his* distance. Events of the past few weeks were evidence of that. And knowing the man as well as she did, Helen was convinced he would do everything in his power to continue his clandestine courtship.

But was Oliver's intention of taking her back to Hertfordshire and settling her in a marriage of convenience the right answer? He would no doubt choose someone respectable. An older man, perhaps; someone who was steady and reliable, and who would have a settling effect on Gillian. But Gillian was in a highly emotional state right now. How would she react to Oliver choosing a husband for her and *forcing* her into marriage? '...How can he know what is best for me when he has never been in love himself?' Gillian had complained. 'How can he know how sweet it is to be close to someone you love when he has never experienced the feeling himself?'

There was no need for Helen to try to answer the question. Oliver's intervention in such a way would surely bring about the end of his relationship with his ward. If Gillian could not choose the man she would spend the rest of her life with, she might very well choose never to see Oliver again!

\* \* \*

Oliver was sitting in his room, contemplating his problems over a bottle of claret, when he heard the sound of heavy footsteps in the hallway beyond.

'Mr Brandon?' the innkeeper called through the door.

Oliver didn't bother to get up. 'What is it?'

'Pardon me, sir, but there's a young lady downstairs asking to have a word with you.'

Oliver frowned. A young lady? At this time of night? Obviously not the kind of young lady he was interested in seeing. 'Tell her I've already gone to bed,' he called back gruffly.

'She said to tell you she was from the school, sir.'

*The school?* Good heavens, had Gillian come to see him?

Oliver jumped to his feet and shrugged on his jacket. 'Innkeeper, have you a decent parlour downstairs?'

'Aye, sir.'

'Good. Put the young lady in it and tell her I shall be there directly.'

As Oliver prepared to go downstairs, he wondered why Gillian had come. Was it possible she wished to apologise for her conduct? She certainly hadn't seemed inclined to do so this afternoon. Of course, she'd had a few hours to think things over. Mayhaps she had seen the folly of her ways and was hoping to make amends.

To his astonishment, however, it wasn't his disobedient young ward who awaited him in the privacy of the parlour. Instead, as the young woman slipped back the hood of her cape, Oliver was treated to the sight of the woman who had caused him an endless number of sleepless nights and an even greater number of disturbing dreams. 'Miss de Coverdale!'

'Pray forgive my calling upon you at so late an hour, Mr Brandon, but it was imperative that I speak with you.'

'Have you no care for your reputation?'

'I have little enough reputation left to worry about,' Helen said. 'I felt that what I had to say was worth the risks in coming.'

It took a moment for Oliver to gather his wits about him. Damn it, why did the mere sight of her cause his insides to turn to liquid? 'I thought Gillian had come to pay a call,' he said huskily. 'Had I known it was you, I would not have agreed to a meeting.'

Helen flushed at the harshness of the rebuke. 'I know. That is why I did not give the innkeeper my name. But I had to come, sir. I had to talk to you about Gillian's future.'

Oliver's eyes darkened. 'It seems to me you should be more concerned with your own, Miss de Coverdale. I am sure Mrs Guarding informed you of my ultimatum.'

'She did, and I shall deal with that at the proper time. But how you deal with Gillian's future is far more important to me right now.' Helen took a hesitant step forward. 'Mr Brandon, is it your intention to take Gillian back to Hertfordshire and settle her in an arranged marriage?'

'I fail to see that what I do with my ward is any business of yours.'

'Oh, but it is, sir. Because I fear that what you are about to do is a terrible mistake. Gillian puts a greater value on love than she does on anything else. Indeed, she believes it to be the most important thing in the world.'

'Unfortunately, you and I have both seen what happens when Gillian puts that much stock in love,' Oliver drawled. 'And I think it should be obvious why I would not wish to see her make her own decision again.' He turned and walked towards the window. Why was this so damned difficult? Why couldn't he just be angry with her and stay that way? 'Why did you go against my wishes and allow her to see Wymington?' he asked softly. 'You knew better than anyone how I felt about the man.'

'Yes, but I had to see for myself what Mr Wymington was like.'

'Why would you think to question my own assessment of the man?'

'Because I could not be sure that your reasons for disliking him were sound.'

Oliver whirled to face her, and his expression was a study in anger. 'Do you think I am completely insensitive, Miss de Coverdale, or just supremely stupid?'

Helen flushed, but valiantly held her ground. 'I think that, as Gillian's stepbrother and guardian, you might have been jealous that she was giving her affections so completely to someone else. To listen to Gillian speak of him, Mr Wymington is a paragon amongst men.'

Oliver gave a short burst of frustrated laughter. 'I have had the acquaintance of many men, Miss de Coverdale, and I have yet to meet a paragon. However, I do not expect Gillian to have a great deal of sense when it comes to matters like this. She is young and foolish, and has been indulged far more than she ought. But I do expect those in my employ, and those in whom I put my trust to abide by my wishes. You have not. And however justifiable you feel your actions to be, it still does not change the fact that you deliberately disobeyed me.' He turned back towards the window, and his voice dropped away. 'I trusted you, Miss de Coverdale. I believed you to be a good influence on Gillian. I knew how much she respected you and as I came to know you better, I felt that same respect myself. Indeed, I agonised over the mistake I had made in believing you to be…something you were not,' he said quietly. 'And yet, what did I discover today but that you are not to be trusted at all.'

Helen blinked as a soft shimmer of tears appeared in her eyes. 'Mr Brandon, I know there is nothing I can say to excuse my own conduct, but I did not come here to plead my case. I came here to talk to you about Gillian's.' She took a tentative step closer. 'Is it your intention to find Gillian a husband without her knowledge or consent?'

Oliver was silent for a moment, his eyes fixed on the deserted street below. Did she truly care so little about her own predicament that she would not even seek his forgiveness? 'Yes, it is.' His voice was flat, his tone lacking in emotion. 'It is clear that Gillian wishes to be married, so the sooner I settle her in the wedded state, the better off we shall all be.'

'She will resent your intrusion into her life,' Helen said quietly. 'Gillian needs to be in love with the man she marries. She will suffocate in a relationship that exists in name only.'

'We have already agreed that people marry for reasons other than love, Miss de Coverdale,' Oliver replied in the same, bland tone. 'Gillian needs guidance in her life. She needs the firm hand of a husband to tell her what she can and cannot do. And since I cannot trust her to find the kind of man who will do that, I shall have to do it for her.'

His words fell into the heavy silence between them; a silence broken only by the faint sputtering of the candle on the table.

'Mr Brandon, you told Mrs Guarding that you...wanted my resignation. If I agreed to leave the school, would you consider allowing Gillian to stay?'

Oliver sighed, and then slowly turned to look at her. She was such a beautiful woman. In the dim light of the candle, her loveliness seemed to him almost ethereal. He gazed in silence at the gentle oval of her face and at the long, dark hair falling in glistening waves past her shoulders. His eyes lingered for a moment on the inviting curve of her mouth and upon the ripe fullness of her lips. And he knew that, had it been possible, he would have done anything he could to banish the expression of fear and uncertainty from her eyes.

But he could not. He could not back down from the stance he had taken. And in acknowledging that, he also acknowledged that, after tonight, he would never see Helen again.

'I do not see that leaving Gillian at Guarding's will serve any useful purpose.' Oliver's voice was firm, yet tinged with regret. 'Mr Wymington has been able to see her and to correspond with her easily enough during the past two months. What makes you think he would stop just because you were no longer there?'

It was, Helen supposed, a logical answer. Until Gillian made up her own mind not to see Mr

Wymington, there would be little anyone could do to stop her. Which meant, she realised sadly, that there was nothing more she could do here.

'Mr Brandon, I deeply regret the disappointment I have caused you. I care about Gillian, and would hate to see her throw herself away on a man like Wymington. But I fear that in my efforts to help, I have managed only to exacerbate the situation, and for that I am truly sorry. It was not my wish to make things more difficult for you than they already were.'

Oliver gazed across the room at her, and was seized by a sudden, inexplicable longing to take her in his arms and hold her close. He wished he could make the suffering he saw so plainly etched upon her face go away, for in truth, he knew how deeply she cared for his ward. He knew that what she had done, she had done with the girl's best interests at heart. But still something held him back. The knowledge that Helen had betrayed his trust by going against his wishes would not allow him to take that step forward. For while he could accept that her heart had been in the right place, he still could not bring himself to accept that she had deceived him.

'What do you intend to do now, Miss de Coverdale?' he asked.

Helen offered him a half-hearted smile. 'Mrs Guarding has told me that she will give me her decision in the morning. I shall make my own then. For now, I shall take up no more of your time.' She drew the hood up over her head and started for the door. 'Thank you for listening to me, Mr Brandon.'

'Shall I walk you back to the school?' Oliver asked, taking an unconscious step towards her.

Helen quickly shook her head, her eyes suspiciously bright. 'Thank you, but I know the way. Goodnight, Mr Brandon.'

As the door closed behind her, Oliver closed his eyes and drew an unsteady breath. 'Goodnight, my dear Helen,' he whispered into the silence. 'And…goodbye.'

Long before the sun rose to brighten the morning sky, Helen knew what she had to do. She had lain awake most of the night, restlessly tossing and turning as she reviewed in painful detail the events of the past week. And after considering all of the options, she settled on the only one that she felt suitable to resolving the situation.

She sat down at her desk and wrote out two letters. She did not stop to consider her own feelings as her pen flew across the paper. She knew in her heart that what she was doing was right, because this wasn't about her. It was about doing what she had to for the people she loved.

Her first letter was to Mrs Guarding. In it, she thanked the headmistress for being such a faithful ally, and expressed at length her gratitude for having had the opportunity to be a part of the Guarding Academy for Girls. She then went on to say that, given what was at stake, she felt it best that she resign her position and leave the school as quickly as possible. That way, Mr Brandon's demands would be met and hopefully, it would ensure that any plans for future retribution would be set aside. He might even be persuaded to reconsider his position and allow Gillian to remain at the school.

Helen's second letter was to Oliver, and it was considerably more difficult to write. Her feelings for him had only deepened in the past weeks, and she knew that she had fallen in love with him. It was foolish, yes, but she had long since given up believing that anything to do with love was logical. Unfortunately, she also recognised that the way she felt about him could have no bearing on what she had to say. Because this too, had to be done for the best of all concerned.

Helen sealed the two letters and then quickly took them down to the kitchen. She gave Oliver's letter to one of the young lads with instructions to deliver it to the Angel, and then slid the other one under Mrs Guarding's sitting-room door. Then, returning to her room, she began her preparations for the day to come.

She had learned to live without the love of a man once in her life. Surely she could learn to do it again.

Helen's letter was delivered to Oliver just as he was preparing to leave. He read it over slowly, a deep groove appearing in his forehead as he realised what she was saying.

Dear Mr Brandon

I am sure it will come as no surprise to you that I have tendered my resignation to Mrs Guarding. I should have accepted your instructions without question, and I regret that my desire to do good has caused so much heartache. I can, however, assure you that your suspicions with regards to Mr Wymington are correct.

The gentleman freely admitted to me that his interest in your ward was largely financial, and that he is convinced of his power over her; a power I believe he will not hesitate to use. In that, I can agree with your wish to remove Miss Gresham to Hertfordshire as soon as possible. But I would advise you to be cautious even there, for I am not convinced that he will so easily give up his pursuit.

I would ask only one thing of you, sir. That is, that you reconsider your decision to force Gillian into a marriage of convenience. I cannot stress how detrimental I feel this would be, both to her, and to your continuing relationship with her. Gillian believes that love is the most important thing in the world, and as a result, her view of marriage is somewhat idealistic. I would suggest that if she is to be married, let it be to someone of her own choosing. She is far more likely to forget Mr Wymington if the gentleman who takes his place is one for whom she can feel genuine affection, rather than someone for whom she feels nothing.

Again, please accept my heartfelt apologies for the problems I have caused.

Yours most sincerely,
Helen de Coverdale

Oliver sighed. So, she had resigned. Good. That was what he'd wanted, wasn't it? After all, if teachers and servants were allowed to take matters into their own hands, the result would be social anarchy. There had to be some control exercised over their conduct.

But if that was the case, why did he feel so damned wretched about the entire affair?

Oliver tossed the letter on to the bed and slowly walked around the room. What would Helen do now? Go back into service? He thought it likely. But this time, she would hardly do so with a letter of recommendation to ease her way. Mrs Guarding would not be able to provide her with one, given the circumstances under which she was leaving.

Which meant that Helen would have no choice but to seek a lesser position in a large house, perhaps as a lady's maid or a companion. He doubted she would wish to serve as a governess again. A woman so beautiful would never truly be safe in any man's house.

Oddly enough, Oliver didn't like to think of Helen in such a position. He could not bear the thought of her having to fight for her virtue against men like Lord Talbot, or even Sidney Wymington. Of course, why he'd give a damn about what other men did to her made absolutely no sense at all. She was nothing to him.

So why should the idea of another man making love to her make him want to run out and do everything he could to stop it from happening?

Reluctantly, Mrs Guarding accepted Helen's resignation.

'What will you do now, Helen?' she asked as she slowly folded up the letter.

Helen tried to put a brave face on the situation. 'I'm not sure. Perhaps I shall apply to a domestic agency for work. I thought perhaps a position as a companion might be suitable.'

'You would not consider going into service as a governess again?'

'Not as long as there is anything else I can do, no.'

Mrs Guarding nodded. 'I suppose I can understand your feeling that way, given everything that's happened. But I am so very sorry to lose you, Helen.'

Helen nodded tightly. 'I am very sorry to be going.'

'I will, of course, prepare a letter of recommendation for you. Hopefully it will make matters easier.'

Helen stared at the headmistress in astonishment. 'You would do that for me? But…I don't understand. You were not able to give Desirée such a letter.'

'No, because her situation was not the same as yours. In Desirée's case, there were witnesses to the incident with Lord Perry. Here, the evidence is strictly circumstantial, and you yourself were not involved in any act of impropriety. I fail to see why you should be penalised for trying to help Miss Gresham, simply because it was not in the accepted way.'

Helen gulped hard, hoping the older woman would not see how close to tears she really was. 'You are…too kind, Mrs Guarding. I had not expected such charity, given everything I have done.'

'It grieves me to see you leave under conditions like this,' the headmistress admitted, her own voice brusque. 'Nor am I entirely pleased with Mr Brandon's decision to take Gillian back to Hertfordshire, now that you have sacrificed your position here.'

Helen smiled faintly. 'Thank you, but my being here has nothing to do with his decision. He would have done that whether I stayed or not. No, it is his plan to settle Gillian in a marriage of convenience that causes me the greatest concern. Because I truly believe that, in the long run, *that* will be the straw that breaks the proverbial camel's back.'

# Chapter Twelve

*October, 1812*

In the drawing room at Shefferton Hall, Sophie regarded her brother with an expression of doubt and concern. 'Are you sure there is nothing else to be done, Oliver? It seems a rather drastic measure.'

'Drastic it may be but I fear it is our only choice.' Oliver stood with his back to her and stared through the window into the darkness. 'I want you to find Gillian a husband by Christmas.'

'That does not give us much time.'

'It need not take much time. You must know of an eligible gentleman who is looking for a wife.'

'Well, yes, but not necessarily one of whom Gillian will approve.'

'I do not intend to study Gillian's wishes in the matter.' Oliver's voice was terse. 'She cannot be trusted to use her head in choosing a husband, so we must use ours. And I will tolerate no interference from anyone in this.'

'If you are referring to Miss de Coverdale, I think

you are being unnecessarily harsh, Oliver,' Sophie observed. 'It seems to me the woman was only trying to help.'

Oliver's face stiffened. 'I do not wish to discuss Miss de Coverdale's participation in this, Sophie. I gave explicit instructions beforehand and I expected them to be obeyed.'

'Yes, but by not doing so, Miss de Coverdale has given you proof of Mr Wymington's deceitfulness. Proof you yourself said you were in need of.'

'Proof it may be, but it has done little to change Gillian's mind. She is still of the opinion that the man is a paragon.' Oliver all but spat the word. 'That is why I want her here at Shefferton, where I can keep my eye on her. At least until she is safely married.'

It was clear from the expression on Sophie's face that she was far from happy, but as though sensing it would be impossible to change her brother's mind, she merely lifted her shoulders in a graceful shrug. 'Very well, if this is what you wish, I will see what I can find out.' She stopped and thought for a moment. 'There is young Nigel Riddleston, I suppose.'

Oliver turned. 'The baronet's son?'

'Yes. He is a pleasant young man. Perhaps not as dashing as Mr Wymington, but he is certainly handsome enough. And if I do not miss my guess, he has been harbouring a tendre for Gillian ever since Lady Tingley's musicale last summer.'

Oliver slowly nodded his head. Yes, he knew the lad. He was a good-natured chap with a keen wit and a well-grounded sense of duty and obligation. And there was both money and property in the family. Yes, he might be just the man, Oliver thought with relief. Hopefully, in time, Gillian would come to love

him. For while Oliver was loathe to commit his stepsister to a loveless marriage, he was determined to
protect her from the Sidney Wymingtons of the
world.

'Thank you, Sophie. If you would be so good as to
meet with Mr Riddleston and see if there is any interest on his part, I shall begin to prepare Gillian.'

Sophie glanced towards him, and the concern was
evident in her eyes. 'She will not be happy about this,
Oliver. You do know that, don't you?'

Oliver sighed. 'I am well aware of the fact, my
dear. I also know that I do not have your complete
agreement to the plan. But I cannot help but feel that
the sooner Gillie is safely married to a man we can
trust and respect, the less likely we are to suffer consequences that will make more than just Gillian unhappy.'

Helen was clearing out the small cupboard in her
classroom when Gillian appeared in the doorway. She
was holding a letter in her hand, and her face was as
white as a ghost's.

'Miss de Coverdale, is this true? Is Oliver really
going to marry me off to a man I do not even know?'

Helen sighed as she slowly got to her feet. It was
the first time Gillian had spoken to her since the dis-
astrous events of that fateful Sunday. Obviously, her
concern over her guardian's plans was more than
enough to make her forget her anger.

'I fear that is his intent, Gillian. He was very upset
about what happened with Mr Wymington and he is
anxious to see you happily settled.'

'But how can you say that? He is not concerned

with my happiness at all!' she cried, waving the letter in the air. 'He simply wishes me off his hands.'

'I do not believe that for a minute. Neither would you if you had seen how unhappy he was the last time I spoke with him.'

Gillian collapsed into a chair, her face a picture of despondency. 'Oh, it is all going so horribly wrong. First Oliver tells me I am to go back to Hertfordshire, and now I learn that I am to be married by Christmas. On top of that, I have been suffering agonies of guilt over having accused you of trying to lure Mr Wymington away. What must you think of me!'

'Gillian, there is no need—'

'There is every need,' the girl cried. 'How could I have accused you, my dearest friend, of behaving in such a manner? You, who have done nothing but show me kindness ever since I arrived. I am ashamed of myself for even thinking such a thing.' Gillian got up and flung herself into Helen's arms. 'Can you ever forgive me, my dear Miss de Coverdale?'

Nearly overcome with relief, Helen gave a shaky laugh. 'Dear child, of course I can forgive you. It was a very emotional day for all of us, and I think we all over-reacted a little. But now we must think of your future and what you are going to do about it.'

'I don't want to go back to Hertfordshire, Miss de Coverdale. I don't want to be married to someone I have never met. I would far rather stay here with you.'

Deciding for the moment not to tell Gillian that she wasn't going to be staying herself, Helen merely smiled and brushed the hair back from Gillian's face. 'Well, I cannot say for certain, my dear, but perhaps

if you were to promise your guardian that you would
not see Mr Wymington again—'

'Not see him! But—'

'Gillian, listen to me, it is the *only* way your guardian will allow you to stay. Understand that now, or
know that you will have no choice but to return to
Hertfordshire with him and do as he asks.'

Helen held her breath as Gillian slowly turned
away. It was impossible to tell from the expression
on her face what she was thinking. 'I doubt I shall
ever find anyone as wonderful as Mr Wymington.'

'I know. But you will never know unless you try.
Perhaps you will find someone even better.'

Gillian smiled, but Helen could tell her heart wasn't
in it. She gave a half-hearted nod, and then turned
and walked out of the room.

The entire episode left Helen feeling distinctly out
of sorts. She could not bring herself to believe that
Gillian would do something reckless in the short period of time she had left, but something about the look
on the girl's face worried her excessively.

'Oh, Oliver, I do hope you're doing the right thing,'
Helen whispered into the silence. 'And I do hope you
get Gillian away from here before she has a chance
to do something we will all live to regret!'

Oliver decided not to make the Guarding Academy
his first stop upon his return to Northamptonshire.
Instead, he headed for Abbot Quincey and the cottage
reputed to belong to Mr Wymington's uncle. He assumed he would find Mr Wymington there. By all
accounts he had not returned to his rooms in
Hertfordshire, nor had he shown his face in London.

Which probably meant he was still in the area, waiting for an opportunity to see Gillian.

Well, he would find no success in that quarter, Oliver reflected grimly. Wymington would be told that if he didn't stay the hell away from her, he would be made to suffer the consequences. It was long past time someone put the man in his place. And if he refused, Oliver intended to demand satisfaction. After that, he planned to carry on to Guarding's and tell Mrs Guarding that he had rethought his decision with regard to Helen.

Oliver had wrestled long and hard with his conscience and in the end, had come to the conclusion that there was nothing to be gained by his forcing Helen to leave Mrs Guarding's employ. He hadn't changed his mind about removing Gillian from the school. And given that he and Sophie had already met with the younger Mr Riddleston and found him as delighted with the prospect of courting Gillian as they were of seeing it happen, there seemed to be no reason to exact further vengeance. It was enough that Gillian's life would be turned upside down, without doing the same to Helen's. She had already suffered enough. Oliver had no wish to be the cause of any further grief in her life.

Unfortunately, when Oliver arrived in Abbot Quincey and eventually located the cottage he was looking for, he was dismayed to find it securely locked, and seemingly in want of an owner.

'Are you looking for the old man who lived there, or the younger one?' a voice called to him from the street.

Oliver turned around and saw a middle-aged woman standing by the gate. She was plainly dressed and carried a baby on one ample hip. A little girl of about four clutched at the fabric of her skirt, while a blond-haired boy played in the dirt behind her.

'The younger one,' Oliver replied. 'I understood he was here visiting his uncle.'

'I don't know about that, sir,' the woman said. 'Gorse Cottage's been empty this six months or more. The old man died beginning of the year. Landlord found him when he came to collect the rent. Of course, nobody much bothered with him. They said he had relatives in London or somewheres about, but we never saw no visitors come.'

Oliver frowned. 'What about the young man who came here? When did you last see him?'

'Not for a week or so now, I shouldn't think. Hush Jane, I'll see to you shortly.' The woman sighed as she hiked the baby higher on her hip. 'Nice-looking young man, but definitely one for the ladies. I saw him come here with two of the girls from the village, and they all acting silly and giggling, as young girls will.'

Anger rose in Oliver's breast, but he struggled not to show it. 'I am grateful for your help, my good lady.' He walked back towards her and reaching into his pocket, pulled out a sovereign. 'Take this and buy something for you and your family.'

The woman looked at the gold coin in disbelief. 'A *sovereign*?' she whispered. 'You'd give so much to a stranger?'

Oliver smiled. 'What you just told me is worth that much.'

'Then I wish I could have told you more.' The woman winked at him as she tucked the coin in her pocket. 'I bid you thanks, sir, and a fine day to you.'

Oliver tipped his hat and watched her walk away. Then he turned to glance at the empty building behind him. So he had uncovered yet another of Wymington's lies. He wondered how many more there would be. For while it might well have been his uncle's cottage, it certainly wasn't to *visit* the old man that Wymington had come. Obviously he was using the cottage for his own purposes, not the least of which included a love nest—perhaps even one where he had hoped to lure Gillian.

A dangerous light glinted in Oliver's eyes. Yes, it was well he had set out on his course of action. Because he would find Sidney Wymington. And when he did, he would give him the thrashing he so richly deserved.

The only question was—where the hell was Wymington now?

*'Non credo di aver avuto il piacere,'* Helen said as she wrote the words on the chalkboard. 'Which means, I do not believe I have had the pleasure. Now, if you knew the person to whom you were being introduced, you would say—'

*'Credo che ci conosciamo,'* Oliver recited from the doorway.

As the girls began to giggle, Helen felt her cheeks grow warm. 'Mr Brandon!'

'Miss de Coverdale. Forgive my interrupting you in such a manner.'

Helen went to put the piece of chalk down—and promptly dropped it on the floor. 'That is quite all right.' She bent to pick it up, and stepped on the hem of her gown. 'We were just…finishing for the day.'

Blushing furiously, she smiled at her class. 'Thank you ladies. *A domani.*'

The girls offered a chorus of replies and then gathered up their books and filed out of the room. Oliver waited until the last of their footsteps had faded into silence before advancing further into the room. 'So, you have decided to leave Guarding's.'

Helen inclined her head. 'Mrs Guarding asked me to stay on until Christmas because we are still short-staffed. Otherwise I would already have gone.' She averted her gaze, wishing it wasn't so hard to see him like this. 'Have you come to…take Gillian home?'

'Yes. I would have been here earlier but I thought to pay a call on Mr Wymington. I went to the cottage where his uncle supposedly lived.'

Helen started. 'Supposedly?'

'A woman passing by told me that the man who owned the house died at least six months ago.'

'Six months!' Helen blanched. 'But…if that is the case, Mr Wymington must have intended—'

'Yes, I think we both know what Wymington intended,' Oliver interrupted darkly. 'He did have a key, so I can only assume it was his uncle's cottage, but he certainly did not come here to pay him any visits.'

'Mr Brandon, I hardly know what to say.'

'There's nothing to say, except to acknowledge that we were both correct in our assumptions about him. Which is why I think it best I take Gillian back to Hertfordshire as soon as possible. I cannot trust Wymington to keep his distance, and at the moment, I'm not sure I trust Gillian to keep hers either.' Oliver drew a deep breath. 'Nor am I convinced she would not agree to do something foolish if Wymington were to suggest it.'

Helen blanched. 'You think they might elope?'

'I cannot rule the possibility out. What I have learned of Wymington's character over the past few weeks has only served to deepen my dislike of him. He hasn't an honourable bone in his body, and for what it's worth, I am grateful to you for having confirmed my suspicions.'

'Is that why you came here now?' Helen asked.

'That, and to tell you that I intend to speak to Mrs Guarding about reinstating your position here.'

Helen gazed at him in confusion. *'What?'*

'There is no reason for you to leave the school, Miss de Coverdale,' Oliver said, his tone reflecting both warmth and concern for her. 'I was…angry when I spoke to Mrs Guarding. I was disappointed by what I perceived to be your betrayal. But I realise now that it wasn't a betrayal at all. You were simply doing what you thought best for Gillian. And in light of what you told me about your own past, how could I fault your motives? That is why I intend to speak to Mrs Guarding and assure her that I would be most pleased if you would return to your position here.' His mouth pulled into a thin-lipped smile. 'I only hope you will not think too badly of me for what has happened.'

'I could…never think badly of you, sir,' Helen said, painfully aware of the truth of the statement. 'I am just…surprised by the sudden turn of events. Are you going to see Gillian now?'

'I intend to speak to Mrs Guarding first. Then I shall see Gillian. Well, I suppose this really is goodbye, Miss de Coverdale.'

Not trusting her voice, Helen bent her head and curtseyed. There was so much she wanted to say to him, and yet not a word of it was appropriate. Likewise keeping his silence, Oliver merely bowed from the waist, and then turned and left the room.

After he had gone, Helen slowly sank down at her desk. She thought about everything he had told her, including the forgiveness he wished her to have, and then sadly closed her eyes. What was she to do? The man she loved was walking out of her life.

And there was absolutely nothing she could do to stop him.

As expected, Mrs Guarding was greatly relieved to hear that Oliver no longer wished to see Miss de Coverdale leave. His assurances that nothing would be served by her resignation were warmly received, as were his hopes that the slight breach of conduct could be discreetly overlooked. The headmistress did express her regrets that Gillian would be leaving them, but she did not try to change Oliver's mind. She merely thanked him for his leniency in allowing Helen to stay, and then sent one of the girls to fetch Gillian.

'She retired to her room with a megrim last night,' Mrs Guarding informed him. 'I understand she has stayed to her bed this morning with it as well.'

Oliver nodded his understanding. 'No doubt as a result of my coming to take her home.'

Unfortunately, it was with considerable surprise that they both learned a short while later that Gillian was, in fact, not in her room.

'Perhaps she was feeling better and decided to come downstairs, Mr Brandon,' the headmistress said.

'I believe she is scheduled for a class with Miss de Coverdale. I shall send a note and ask her to bring Gillian here.'

'That is quite all right,' Oliver said, already heading for the door. 'I shall go and fetch her myself.'

But Gillian was not in Helen's room, nor had Helen seen her that morning. And upon hearing as much, Oliver began to feel the first real stirrings of alarm.

'I think we should commence a search of the building,' he said, 'followed by a thorough check of the gardens and the—'

'Excuse me, Miss de Coverdale, Mr Brandon.'

Oliver broke off and turned to see Elizabeth Brookwell standing in the doorway. She was holding something in her hand and it was clear from the expression on her face that she was far from happy.

'What is it, Miss Brookwell?' Helen said quickly.

'I have a letter, Miss de Coverdale. For Mr Brandon.' The girl's voice was noticeably subdued. 'Gillian asked me to…give it to him when he arrived.'

'When did you last see Gillian?' Helen asked as Oliver went forward to take it.

'Very early this morning, Miss. She was dressed for going out, but when I asked her where she was going, she wouldn't tell me. She just gave me this letter and said I was to make sure Mr Brandon received it.' Elizabeth's bottom lip quivered. 'She said I wasn't to give it to him until this evening, but I thought it best not to wait that long.'

'Thank you, Miss Brookwell, you may go.'

As the girl silently departed, Oliver broke the seal and read the letter aloud.

Dear Oliver:

I am sorry to disappoint you, but I have left with Mr Wymington. I know you do not approve of him, but I love him, and I could not bear the thought of being forced into marriage with someone else—especially someone I do not even know. Please do not worry about me. Mr Wymington loves me and has promised to take good care of me. He assures me this is the only way we can be together. I shall write again once we are husband and wife.

'Love, Gillian,' Oliver finished on a whisper.

Helen felt as though the room was spinning all around her. 'Dear God, we must stop them!'

'We must indeed, but how much of a head start have they?'

Thankfully, a visit to the stables provided them with the answers they needed. One of the lads had chanced to see a closed carriage drawn by a single horse pull up to the back door of the school around five o'clock that morning, and minutes later, a young lady dressed in a travelling cloak and carrying a small case emerge from the school and climb up beside the gentleman.

It seemed that Mr Wymington had indeed, persuaded Gillian to elope with him.

Helen began to tremble. 'They will head for Scotland.'

Oliver nodded. 'Without question. Which is why I must set off immediately.' His expression was bleak. 'Wymington has only one horse, but the gig is light and they have the advantage of a considerable head start.'

'Poor foolish girl,' Helen whispered. 'She has no idea what she is doing.'

'Of course not. To her, it will all be some great adventure. I only hope to God I can catch them before it is too late.'

'Let me come with you, Mr Brandon,' Helen cried suddenly. 'I can't help but feel that I am partially to blame for what has happened.'

'This isn't your fault, Miss de Coverdale, but I would be grateful for your company. It is imperative that we find them!'

Helen did not voice her unspoken thoughts as she hurried towards his waiting carriage. They had to find the miscreant pair indeed. All they could do was hope that it wasn't already too late.

# Chapter Thirteen

Drawn by a pair of fleet-footed blacks, Oliver's carriage made excellent time along the dusty road. Assuming that Wymington would head for Gretna, they set out on an identical path and drew comfort from the fact that they could travel the road faster with two horses than Wymington could with one. But Wymington had the advantage of time, and in a race like this, every second counted!

Helen said very little on the frenzied drive north. She was too wrapped up in her own thoughts to offer aimless conversation. Oliver too was restrained, fixing his concentration on the team and on maintaining a steady pace.

'They cannot be so very far ahead of us,' he said, his eyes scanning the horizon. 'Thank God they set off this morning and not last night. Otherwise we would be too late to save her, even now.'

Helen knew all too well what Oliver was referring to. Had Gillian been forced to spend even one night at an inn with Mr Wymington, her reputation would have been irrevocably lost. The best they could have hoped for then was marriage.

They passed through a number of small villages as they headed for the border. Oliver stopped at one coaching inn to enquire about the passage of a gig carrying a young lady and a gentleman, and described them as best he could. Most fortuitously, he was given the very good news that yes, a young couple matching their description had stopped there a little while earlier, but that they had carried on after only a brief delay. And no, they had not gone in for a meal or anything else, as far as the man could remember. Oliver had nodded his satisfaction, and then urged the horses on.

Finally, a few hours later, Helen gasped as she spotted a small carriage drawn by a single horse away in the distance ahead of them. 'Look, Mr Brandon, there!'

'Yes, I see them.' Oliver flicked the whip over his horses' heads with renewed vigour. 'It would seem we are to be spared a considerable amount of grief. Tell me, Miss de Coverdale. Would you be able to drive this carriage if forced by circumstances to do so?'

Surprised, Helen glanced at him. 'Yes, I am sure I could.'

'Good. There was a decent-looking inn in the last village we passed. Perhaps you would take Gillian back there and wait for me while I deal with Mr Wymington.'

'Yes, of course.'

'Good. Now, I suggest you hold on. I am going to try to overtake them.'

It was a daring move. The road was considerably narrower here than it had been in other places, and Helen gasped as Oliver closed the distance and then urged his carriage alongside Mr Wymington's, causing them both to sway and bounce precariously. She forgot her nervousness, however, when she saw Gillian's white face staring back at her.

'Draw to a halt, sir!' Oliver shouted. 'You can go no farther!'

Wymington turned to glare at them, an ugly expression marring the handsome lines of his face. For a moment, Helen wondered if he would ignore Oliver's order and push on regardless. But he must have seen something in Oliver's face that convinced him of the futility of continued flight. Reluctantly, he drew the lathered bay to a halt.

Oliver sprang down and ignoring Wymington, went immediately to see to Gillian. 'Are you all right?' he asked as she shakily emerged from the carriage.

Gillian's eyes were the size of saucers. 'Of course, but…what are you doing here?'

'I have come to take you home. Surely you did not think I would allow this abomination to take place!'

'But I love him!' she cried desperately.

'I will hear no more of this, Gillian,' Oliver snapped. 'Go with Miss de Coverdale. She will see you safely back.'

'Why? What are you going to do?'

'I am going to have a word with Mr Wymington.'

Impulsively, Gillian reached for his arm. 'He did not force me to come, Oliver. Please, you must believe me. I am here of my own free will!'

'Yes, no doubt after he convinced you of how wonderful your life together would be.' Oliver glanced at Helen and she saw the anger shimmering in his eyes. 'Take her back to the inn and wait for me.'

Helen nodded, and moved towards Gillian. 'Come, my dear. We must leave here.'

'Oliver, please don't hurt him!' Gillian cried.

'Do as I say, Gillian!'

Sobbing, Gillian put her hand to her mouth. She ran back to Oliver's carriage and flung herself into the seat.

'Take me away from here,' she cried as Helen climbed up beside her.

Suppressing a sigh, Helen gathered up the reins and set the pair to a brisk trot. Gillian obviously had no desire to stay and listen to what Oliver had to say to her beloved Mr Wymington.

Gillian was very quiet on the ride back to the Rose and Crown, and wisely, Helen did not press her for conversation. A great deal had happened over the past twelve hours and she had no doubt that Gillian was trying to make sense of it all. Only a short time ago, she had been headed for Scotland with the man she planned to marry. Now, she was driving back to an inn with a former teacher at her side, after having left her dashing young man at the side of the road to face a very angry and displeased guardian. Indeed, there was much for her to think about.

Helen, however, was not sorry for the silence. It gave her ample opportunity to focus her attention on her driving. While she was relieved that the blacks had such responsive mouths, they were spirited creatures demanding of her full attention. She did not wish to put them at a hole and risk possible injury to the animals or to themselves.

Fortunately, it wasn't long before she got the feel of the reins back and was able to relax a little. But

she could not relax her mind, filled as it was with the
enormity of everything that had happened. What
would Oliver do now? What was he saying to poor
Mr Wymington? Helen knew she was probably foolish to feel any kind of pity for the man, but she would
not have wished to be in his place. Oliver's anger
would be frightful, and while she knew that duels
were seldom fought in England any more, this would
be a matter of honour. Helen was quite sure that,
given the type of man Oliver was, he would demand
justice.

At the Rose and Crown, Helen asked the landlord
for a room where they might rest awhile and then
ordered a light meal for Gillian. The poor child had
not eaten anything, given that Mr Wymington had
been anxious to reach his destination. Helen had no
stomach for food, and ordered nothing for herself.
Instead, she sat next to Gillian at the table and tried
to break through the girl's wall of silence.

'Did you really think about what you were doing?'
Helen asked gently. 'Your brother was nearly beside
himself with worry.'

Tears bubbled in Gillian's eyes. 'Sidney told me
he loved me. He said he…wanted to marry me.' She
looked up at Helen and her mouth began to quiver.
'He even showed me the ring he had bought.'

As Gillian began to weep in earnest, Helen pulled
her into her arms and held her close. Poor child. How
hard it must all seem to her. Indeed, Helen remembered all too well the pain and the grief she had suffered in the days following her separation from
Thomas. At times, she had wondered if she would
ever stop crying.

'I know this seems like the end of the world,

Gillie,' Helen whispered against her hair, 'but you must believe it is for the best. Mr Wymington was dashing and handsome, but he was not an honourable man. I know that is hard for you to accept, but I am telling you the truth, dearest. He would have taken advantage of you.'

'He t-told me you would t-try to turn me against him,' Gillian blubbered. 'He told me you would t-try to make me…think ill of him.'

'Yes, because Mr Wymington is a very smart man.' Helen brushed the blonde hair back from Gillian's forehead. 'Men like him always know what to say to impressionable young women. He knew how to make you believe everything he said.'

Gillian sniffed. 'I hate Oliver for doing this. I *hate* him!'

'Hush, child,' Helen crooned, rocking her close. 'You mustn't say things like that because I know you do not mean them. Oliver did what he did because he loves you. He was very worried about you.'

'But there was no need. We were going to be married.' Gillian's face crumpled into tears again. 'He bought me a ring…'

Helen knew there was nothing she could say to make the pain go away, so she just let the girl cry. Time would heal the raw edges, but for now, the wound was too fresh, the pain too deep. Gillian would suffer much before she came to terms with the reality of Mr Wymington's deceit, and for a while, it would be difficult for all of them. Helen only hoped Oliver would have the patience and the understanding to deal with it.

Oliver joined them at the inn a short while later. Helen met him at the door of the small, cosy parlour and knew without having to ask that it had been a difficult interview. His eyes were dark, his lips pressed together in a tight, angry line. But he said not a word about Mr Wymington, asking only after Gillian's welfare, and her own.

'I am fine, sir, and thankfully, Gillian is asleep,' Helen assured him as she closed the door. 'She had been crying ever since we arrived.'

'Thank you for bringing her back here, Miss de Coverdale, and for taking care of her.'

'There is no need to thank me, sir; I would have done it without your asking. But…where is…Mr Wymington?'

'On his way to London.' Oliver's face closed down. 'We shall not be hearing from him again.'

Helen's eyes opened wide. 'Did you threaten him?'

'Not in so many words. I gave him the choice of settling the matter with pistols at dawn, or by writing a letter of confession to Gillian in which he told her the truth of his intentions.' Oliver withdrew a letter from his pocket. 'Needless to say, he chose the latter. I assured him he had made the right decision, since at least this way he was able to escape with his life.'

Helen looked at the letter but did not ask to read it. 'What will he do now?'

'Take the money I gave him and use it to buy his commission.'

'You *gave* him money?'

'I wanted to make sure he had enough to go on his way. But I assured him that if he ever tried to contact Gillian again, I would kill him.'

Helen shuddered. She had no doubt Oliver meant it. There was something in his tone that convinced

her it was not an idle threat. Mr Wymington had made
the mistake of trifling with someone Oliver loved. If
he valued his life, he would not make that mistake
again.

Within the hour, they set off for Steep Abbot.
Gillian was very quiet getting into the carriage. Her
eyes were red-rimmed and swollen, and Helen knew
it was because Oliver had shown her the letter. The
poor child had clutched it almost pathetically to
her breast, the look of hurt and confusion on her
face heartbreaking to see. Clearly, the truth of
Wymington's defection had come as a crushing disappointment.

It was well after dark by the time they reached the
school. Helen took Gillian up to her room and spent
a few minutes with her there before returning downstairs. Then, together, she and Oliver went to see Mrs
Guarding.

Not surprisingly, the headmistress was in a rare
state of agitation.

'Helen, Mr Brandon, I am so relieved that you have
returned.' Mrs Guarding glanced from one to the
other with a look of deep apprehension. 'Is everything
all right?'

'Everything is fine,' Oliver assured her. 'Thankfully, we were able to intercept Gillian and Mr
Wymington in time to stop them from marrying. Or
from anything worse happening.'

The headmistress sagged noticeably against her
desk. 'Thank God for that. Where is Mr Wymington?'

'The gentleman will not be troubling us again,'
Oliver said quietly. 'He is even now on his way to
London to secure a new position with the militia.'

'And Gillian? How is the poor child?'

Oliver sighed. 'Disappointed. Broken-hearted. Mr Wymington wrote out a confession admitting to his true motives in courting her. Needless to say, when Gillian read it, she was devastated. She'd believed all along that we had conspired to make Wymington sound like a fraud. It shook her to learn that we had been telling her the truth.'

'Poor child.' Mrs Guarding's kindly face was filled with compassion. 'How terribly confused and be-trayed she must be feeling right now. It is never easy to recover from disappointments of the heart. But she is young and time will heal the wounds she has suf-fered today. Eventually, she will be as bright and happy as ever.'

'Yes, but I think it is still best I take her back to Hertfordshire with me,' Oliver said. 'I will feel better knowing that she is close during these next few weeks. I know she doesn't like me very much right now, but I want her to know that I care about her regardless.'

Mrs Guarding sighed. 'Yes, I think it is important that she does know that, Mr Brandon. Well, I shall make arrangements to have her cases brought down. When do you wish to leave?'

'I think the sooner the better. With luck she will sleep in the carriage.'

Helen listened to the conversation in silence. She refused to allow herself to dwell on what it meant, because she knew that if she did, she would be every bit as heart-broken as Gillian. Oliver was taking his ward back to Hertfordshire. Which meant that he would have no reason to return to Steep Abbot.

Ever.

*   *   *

The pattern of Helen's days soon fell back into their former routine. It was a rhythm that had been established long before Oliver Brandon had come into her life—and her heart. The girls had all been sorry to see Gillian go, of course, but Helen knew their grief would pass and that life would go on for all of them. Such was the way of the world. But it was hard to pretend that everything was all right in *her* world. Helen felt as though her heart had been torn asunder, and that her life had become a sad and empty vacuum; a vacuum where love should have existed.

Mrs Guarding continued to be supportive. She gave Helen extra time away from school, and surprisingly, Helen found herself eager to take advantage of it. She was finding it increasingly difficult to concentrate on her studies. She could not muster the same level of enthusiasm for her classes. Instead, she took to wandering through the woods near Steep Abbot, enjoying the freshness of the crisp autumn air and savouring the peace and quiet to be found in the shelter of the huge old trees. Somehow, she took comfort in the familiarity of nature.

On a beautiful clear day near the end of October, Helen wandered down to the pond where Desirée had first met her dashing Lord Buckworth. She had never ventured this far into the Steep Wood before, and for a moment, she just stood in silent admiration of the beauty all around her. No wonder Desirée had come here so often. There was a kind of serenity about the place. A feeling of peace. It was almost as though the problems of the outside world had no place within these leafy bowers.

She sat by the grassy edge of the river and threw

stones into the water, watching the ripples fan out in ever-increasing circles. As she did, Helen tried not to think about Oliver. She tried not to remember the sound of his voice, or the breathless way he'd made her feel every time he spoke to her. Because to remember those things only brought it all back.

Funny. He had never even spoken her name, and yet Helen knew how sweet it would sound upon his lips. She often whispered his own name aloud, lingering over it, wondering if he would smile at hearing her say it. He never would, of course, because there would never be anything between them to allow such familiarities. He would always be Mr Brandon to her, and she Miss de Coverdale to him. A wealthy gentleman, especially one with connections to the aristocracy, would never contemplate marriage to a lowly schoolmistress.

Helen sighed as she watched a single leaf drop from an overhead branch and land on the glassy surface of the water. Oh yes, he was well-connected. Gillian had told her as much during one of their last conversations. She had informed her that his aunt was Viscountess Endersley, an imperious lady who lived with her husband on a magnificent estate in Kent. Apparently, Lady Endersley travelled north at least six times a year to visit her family, and it was widely known that Oliver was her favourite. She had, over the last little while, presented several young women to him in the hopes he might find one amongst them who would be suitable to becoming his wife, and she had been *most* disappointed when he had declined them all.

Helen's lips curved in a wistful smile. She could only imagine what Lady Endersley would say if

Oliver were to express interest in a schoolmistress. She would never condone such a *mésalliance*. For Oliver to marry so far beneath him would be unthinkable.

Still, all of that meant nothing in the overall scheme of things, because Oliver had not *expressed* any interest in her. Oh, he had been charming in her company, and even flattering upon occasion. But there had been nothing in his conduct to convince her that he held her in any particular esteem. She had enjoyed the brief time they had spent together, but he had not misled her in any way, nor allowed her to believe there was anything between them. She was his ward's teacher. He was her pupil's guardian.

There was really nothing more to it than that.

It was the middle of November before Helen heard from Gillian again. The letter arrived innocently enough with the midday post, but as Helen read it over in the privacy of her room after classes that night, her eyes began to widen in a mixture of shock, fascination and bewilderment at the unexpected news.

My dear Miss de Coverdale

You will no doubt be surprised at receiving this, but I simply had to write and tell you. I am in love with a wonderful young man and engaged to be married! Yes, I know you will be shocked, but it has all happened so quickly I can scarce believe it myself. My betrothal celebration is to take place on the nineteenth, and I am writing to ask if you will attend. Oliver has already secured Mrs Guarding's approval for the visit, and if you are agreeable, he will send a carriage to bring you to Shefferton Hall on Wednesday next, where you are to remain with us until Saturday.

I do hope you will agree to make the journey. I have missed you terribly, and hope you are as eager to see me as I am to see you. I have so much to tell you! Oliver too, is anxious to renew his acquaintance.

Your dear friend
Gillian Gresham

Helen let the letter fall to her lap and then stared at the wall in disbelief. Gillian was *in love*? But how in the world had such a thing come to pass—and so quickly? The child had barely been back in Hertfordshire a month. How could she have met someone and fallen in love with him in such a short period of time? More importantly, was this the arranged marriage Oliver had spoken of?

Helen picked up the letter and read it over again:

…Oliver has already secured Mrs Guarding's approval for the visit, and if you are agreeable, he will send a carriage to bring you here to Shefferton Hall on Wednesday next, where you are to remain with us until Saturday.

Goodness, Oliver certainly wasn't leaving anything to chance, Helen reflected. He had gone to Mrs Guarding and gained her approval for the visit before Helen had even been made aware of it. He was even sending a carriage so that transportation might not be an issue. '…Oliver too, is anxious to renew his acquaintance.' Helen decided not to read too much into that. While she wished with all her heart that the sentiment might be a genuine one, she knew better than to allow herself the luxury of believing it. Gillian was the one who wished her to be present at the betrothal celebration, so it was only natural that it was she who would have persuaded Oliver to invite her. And relieved that Mr Wymington was no longer the object of her affection, Oliver had probably been willing to do anything to make Gillian happy, even to allow her dear Miss de Coverdale to be present at the celebration.

Still, it was flattering to know that Gillian cared enough to invite her *and* that Oliver had no serious objections to her being there. And surely if the Brandons saw nothing wrong with a schoolmistress mingling with polite society, neither should she.

# Chapter Fourteen

*November, 1812*

Shefferton Hall was a fine old house, built before the time of Elizabeth I and mellowed even further by the relentless passage of time. It slumbered against the natural beauty of gently sloping hills and wide-open meadows bordered by dense hedgerows and the occasional low stone wall. The gravelled drive was long and lined on either side with tall trees, the branches of which joined together to form a canopy of green overhead. It cut through a fine timber bush and then curved towards the Hall, finally allowing Helen her first glimpse of the majestic house, and causing her to catch her breath in wonder.

She had expected a lovely property. She had not expected anything like this.

A sudden movement drew Helen's attention towards the impressive front entrance. Gillian was standing on the top step, dancing up and down and waving her hands. Helen smiled and waved back, trying not to admit to the excitement she was already beginning to feel.

It was hard to believe that she was actually here in Hertfordshire. That she had been invited to stay at this magnificent home by the family of one of her former pupils. Harder still to believe that within moments she would be face to face with Oliver again. How would she feel upon seeing him? Helen wondered as the carriage finally drew to a halt and a liveried footman let down the stairs. What would she say to him, and how would he respond? More importantly, would she be able to keep the depth of her feelings from him for the several days she would be called upon to be in his company?

'Miss de Coverdale!' Gillian cried as she ran forward. 'How splendid to see you again! I am so very pleased you have come.'

'And I am very pleased to have been invited,' Helen said, returning the girl's affectionate embrace. 'But I must say the news came as something of a shock.'

'Yes, I knew it would.' Gillian laughed as though it were all a wonderful joke. 'Oliver said you would be astonished. But we can talk of that later. Right now you must come and meet Sophie.' Gillian linked her arm through Helen's and turned to lead the way back inside. 'I have told her all about you and she is most anxious to make your acquaintance.'

The trepidation Helen felt at the thought of meeting Gillian's stepsister vanished within moments of their being introduced. Mrs Sophie Llewellyn was every bit as delightful as Gillian had led her to believe. Striking in appearance, she was very tall and slender, and was possessed of the warmest, most gracious

smile Helen had ever seen. She immediately set about
to making her feel at ease, and as the conversation
flowed between them, Helen couldn't help but like
the elegant lady whose bright green eyes seemed to
contain a perpetual twinkle.

'I am so glad you agreed to come, Miss de
Coverdale,' Sophie said when they were all comfortably seated in the beautifully appointed drawing-
room. 'We have heard a great deal about you since
Gillian returned from Steep Abbot, and I must say, it
has all been of a most flattering nature.'

Helen felt the warmth rise to her cheeks, uncomfortable at being the centre of attention. 'I cannot
imagine what Miss Gresham could have said to elicit
such praise, Mrs Llewellyn, but I can assure you that
I enjoyed having her as one of my pupils. She is a
gifted watercolourist and did a credible job with her
Italian. I am very pleased at having been invited to
celebrate this wonderful occasion with her.'

'Good afternoon, Miss de Coverdale.'

The voice that fell so sweetly on her ears caused
Helen to jump and her heart to turn over in her breast.
*Oliver.* She turned slowly and saw him standing in
the doorway. His dark hair was windblown and his
cheeks were ruddy from the cold. He looked to have
just returned from a ride, and it seemed to Helen that
he was even more dashing than he had been upon the
occasion of their last meeting.

Surely it was not possible for a man to grow so
very much more handsome in the space of only a few
short weeks?

'You smile at my greeting,' Oliver observed as he
walked into the room. 'Was it something in my choice
of words?'

'Forgive me, Mr Brandon. My amusement had nothing to do with what you said or with anything about you,' Helen hastened to say. 'I was merely thinking about something Gillian said to me a few weeks back.' She cleared her throat and wished that her quickened pulse would settle so that the annoyingly breathless quality of her voice would also disappear. 'Thank you for all the trouble you have gone to on my behalf. Both in speaking to Mrs Guarding and to arranging transportation for bringing me here.'

Oliver tipped his head. 'Neither was in any way troublesome. Mrs Guarding informed me that you had forgone the pleasure of a trip to London to see your good friend married, so she was more than happy to allow you this little outing in its place. And while I admit that Gillian's betrothal ball will hardly replicate the pomp and ceremony of a full-blown society wedding, I daresay we shall acquit ourselves reasonably well.'

'Dearest Oliver, you are being far too modest,' Gillian piped up. 'Considering all the arrangements you and Sophie have made, I am quite sure my betrothal ball will be the most elegant to be seen in Hertfordshire this year, and that my wedding will be the equal of any to be held in London. You will come to my wedding, won't you, Miss de Coverdale?' Gillian said, turning impulsively towards Helen. 'I cannot imagine getting married without you being there. In fact, perhaps you would like to—'

'Before you start making too many plans for Miss de Coverdale,' Sophie interrupted, 'perhaps I should show her to her room. I am sure she would like to rest before dinner. Travelling is such a tiresome occupation, is it not, Miss de Coverdale?'

'It is indeed, Mrs Llewellyn,' Helen said, smiling her gratitude. 'Thank you.'

'Oh, very well,' Gillian grumbled, clearly put out at having her friend whisked away so quickly. 'But we shall continue this over dinner. And then you must tell me what is happening at Guarding's, and how many of the girls miss me and ask after me.'

'Impertinent minx,' Oliver drawled affectionately. 'I doubt any of them have spared you so much as a thought since you left.'

'Oliver!'

'Pay him no mind, Gillian,' Sophie said, rising. 'You know how he likes to tease you. I am quite sure *all* the young ladies at Guarding's are anxious to hear how you go on, and to know all about your upcoming nuptials.'

'They are indeed, Mrs Llewellyn. In fact,' Helen said, wishing to set Gillian's mind at rest, 'you will be pleased to learn that I have brought letters from several of the girls who are anxious for news of her.'

Gillian's face brightened. 'Really? They have truly taken the time to write?'

'They have. I shall bring the letters down to dinner. Unless you would consider the timing inappropriate?' Helen said, glancing uncertainly at her hostess.

'It will not be inappropriate, Miss de Coverdale. Most of our guests will be arriving tomorrow, so I thought it might be pleasant to have a quiet, informal dinner this evening. It will give us an opportunity to become better acquainted with you.'

Grateful that she would be spared the rigours of a formal dinner, Helen inclined her head. 'There is little enough to know, Mrs Llewellyn. My life has been very quiet compared to most.'

'Well, I am sure we shall find something to talk about.'

'And we seldom find ourselves at a loss for conversation with Gillian about,' Oliver added. 'Even if we cannot vouch for the significance of its content.'

'Oh, now that is not fair, Oliver!' Gillian cried. '*You* have told me that I am a skilled conversationalist and that I find far more interesting subjects to talk about than most of my friends!'

'Come, Miss de Coverdale,' Sophie whispered. 'I shall take you upstairs and see you settled.' She drew Helen to her feet as Oliver and Gillian continued their good-natured bickering. 'Once these two get started on a discussion, there is no telling when it will end!'

The room Helen had been given for the duration of her visit was as pretty as she could have wished. It was bright and spacious, with mullioned windows that gave view towards the south-west, and walls that were papered in a soft lemon-coloured silk. The bedspread and curtains were of a slightly deeper hue, while the tapestry seat-covers and bed pillows all contained traces of the same warm shade. 'Oh, how lovely!' Helen exclaimed upon entering.

'Yes, it is nice, isn't it.' Sophie agreed. 'It was originally Catherine's room. Gillian's mother,' she explained at seeing Helen's look of confusion. 'She moved in here after my father died. Catherine loved yellow. She said it reminded her of daffodils and sunshine, and that she liked to have it around her as much as possible. Which was not in the least surprising.' Sophie glanced around the room and her lips curved in a smile of affection. 'If there was ever a woman blessed with a sunny disposition, it was Catherine Gresham.'

Helen nodded as she moved towards the elegant, four-poster bed and gazed around the room. It *was* exceedingly bright and sunny, and it certainly did make one feel cheerful. Unfortunately, one of the maids had already unpacked what few belongings Helen had brought with her out upon the bed and the comparison between her drab, dark school gowns and the sumptuous colours everywhere else was striking in the extreme.

'Well, I shall leave you alone to rest, Miss de Coverdale,' Sophie said, seeming not to notice. 'If you are in need of assistance, you have only to ring the bell for Trudy. She is a most accommodating young woman and will make sure you have everything you need.'

'Thank you, Mrs Llewellyn. I am sure I shall be very comfortable.'

'Good.' Sophie smiled then, and hesitated. 'By the by, I fear you may not have had time to prepare a new gown for Gillian's betrothal party. Indeed, you were scarce given time to ready yourself, let alone to acquire new clothes. But you need not concern yourself about such matters.' She walked towards the large wardrobe in the corner of the room and opened the doors. 'Perhaps you will be able to find something in here to your liking.'

The doors swung open and Helen gasped at the startling array of clothes that suddenly came into view. There were silk and satin evening gowns, elegant walking gowns and stylish riding habits, along with a veritable abundance of bonnets, boots, gloves, and shawls. Everything the well-dressed lady could possibly need.

'Gracious! Who do all of these clothes belong to?'

'Most of them were Catherine's,' Sophie told her.
'She absolutely adored clothes. She would sit for
hours pouring over copies of *La Belle Assemblee* or
*Ackermann's*. And she was most particular when it
came to having new things. She would not wear anything that was not of the first stare.' Sophie drew out
a lovely gown in a warm shade of apricot silk and
held it up for Helen's inspection. 'As you can see,
the styling is somewhat out of date, but the fabric is
excellent and the beadwork quite lovely.' She cast
Helen a sideways glance. 'Are you at all skilled with
a needle, Miss de Coverdale?'

Helen nodded, already assessing the degree of difficulty involved in altering the lovely garment. 'Yes,
I am.'

'Good. Then I think this gown—or any of the others—could easily be made wearable. Catherine was
not unlike you in size.' She offered Helen an apologetic glance as she laid the gown on the bed. 'I would
offer to lend you one of my own, but I fear the work
entailed in altering it would be far more extensive
than what you will encounter here.'

Helen bit back a smile. While the length of Mrs
Llewellyn's gowns would not pose a problem, the
width across the bodice—or the lack thereof—certainly would.

'You are exceedingly kind, Mrs Llewellyn,' Helen
said quietly, 'and I am more grateful to you than I
can say. I am sure I shall be able to find something
in the wardrobe that I can alter in time for tomorrow
night's festivities.'

'And for dinner this evening, if you like.' Sophie
held up the apricot silk again. 'With your dark hair,
this shade becomes you very well, and I do not think

there would be more than an hour or two's work to make it suitable.'

Helen bit her lip, wanting to take advantage of the lady's generous offer, but not at all sure she should. 'Will Gillian not mind me wearing her mother's clothes?' she asked. 'She might feel that I have…intruded on Catherine's memory in some way.'

'Gillian will be *delighted* to see you wearing them,' Sophie assured her. 'She has often remarked to me that it is a pity someone cannot make use of them, being that they are so very lovely. And I am quite sure Oliver will be happy to see you so attired.'

Helen hastily turned away, not wishing the other woman to catch sight of her burning cheeks. 'There is no reason why he should be, Mrs Llewellyn. Mr Brandon has been polite to me on the few occasions we have been in each other's company, but there is nothing to our acquaintance beyond that.'

'Perhaps, but my brother has made mention of you several times, Miss de Coverdale, and it is not like Oliver to speak of ladies with whom he has had so brief an acquaintance.'

'Well, I am sure he has only done so because I grew close to Gillian during the time she was at Mrs Guarding's Academy,' Helen replied. Then, desperately needing to change the subject, she smiled and said, 'I hope you will forgive me for asking, but what is the name of the gentleman Gillian has become betrothed to?'

'Good Lord. You mean Gillian didn't tell you in her letter?'

'No. She only said it had all happened very quickly, and that she could hardly believe it herself.'

'Well, yes, I think it caught us all a little off guard,' Sophie admitted with a chuckle, 'though not unpleasantly so since Oliver did ask me to arrange it. The gentleman's name is Nigel Riddleston. He is the eldest son of Sir John and Lady Riddleston of Kestwick Park in Wiltshire. My husband, whom you will meet at dinner this evening, knows the family very well and it was actually he who arranged their first meeting in London last year. Unfortunately, there did not appear to be any interest on Gillian's part, and not long after that, she met Mr Wymington. Strangely enough, however, this last time Gillian saw Mr Riddleston, everything was quite different.' Sophie smiled as she turned and walked towards the bedroom door. 'I think it safe to say that for Gillian, it was definitely a case of love at second sight!'

Helen spent considerable time debating whether or not to wear the elegant silk gown to dinner that night. Despite Mrs Llewellyn's assurances that no one would mind, she couldn't help but feel that she was intruding somehow; that she had no right to take Catherine Gresham's clothes and alter them to suit herself. But then, after further consideration, Helen decided that she was probably just being foolish. She had no wish to embarrass Gillian in front of her family and friends, and that was precisely what she would do if she were to appear wearing one of her dreary school gowns. Surely it would not be so very wrong to make use of one or two of the gowns hanging in the wardrobe. Certainly Mrs Llewellyn did not seem to think so.

In the end, Helen was exceedingly glad she did decide to wear the apricot silk because the meal was

neither the casual affair it was supposed to be, nor
the intimate family gathering Mrs Llewellyn had
planned. The unexpected arrival of the Viscount and
Viscountess Endersley and their two sons—one newly
married, the other accompanied by his noticeably increasing wife—along with all of their attendant
maids, valets and assorted underlings shortly before
five o'clock threw the carefully laid plans asunder and
the entire household into disarray.

Fortunately, the ever-efficient Sophie soon had
matters under control. She saw to it that the new ar-
rivals were warmly greeted and settled in their rooms
and then informed the butler that he should prepare
the formal dining-room for the evening meal, rather
than the common parlour where they had planned to
eat. Lastly, she went to the kitchens herself to advise
Mrs White of the last-minute guests, and to personally
apologise for the extra work involved in their arrival.

Helen was both relieved and dismayed by the ad-
vent of Oliver's toplofty relations. Relieved because
it meant she would not be singled out for attention
over dinner, but dismayed because she knew it would
be inappropriate for her to attend. She might well be
an invited guest to Gillian's ball, but she doubted the
Viscount and his wife would appreciate sharing dinner conversation with a schoolmistress from Steep
Abbot. And with that in mind, she hastily sent a note
to Mrs Llewellyn advising her that she would not
come down for dinner, but that she would take a tray
in her room.

Unfortunately, not long after despatching Trudy
with the message, Helen was herself summoned to the
drawing-room. To her surprise, it was not Mrs
Llewellyn who awaited her there, but Oliver.

'Oh! Mr Brandon.'

He turned at the sound of her surprised exclamation and offered her a tentative smile. 'I take it you were not expecting to see me, Miss de Coverdale?'

'No indeed, sir, I was not.' Helen felt the warmth steel into her cheeks again. 'I asked Trudy to extend my regrets to Mrs Llewellyn.'

'Which she did. But since I happened to be with my sister at the time the message was delivered, I volunteered to speak to you myself, since we were both in agreement as to the response.'

Helen bit her lip. 'I was not expecting a response.'

'Not even to be told that we would both very much like you to join us for dinner this evening?'

The sentiment was a generous one, but it was not what Helen had been hoping to hear. 'I do not think it would be appropriate, Mr Brandon. You have guests to attend to now.'

His mouth lifted a fraction. 'Are you not a guest?'

'Well, yes, but these are family members who I am quite sure would not appreciate the presence of a schoolmistress at their table.'

Oliver lifted one dark eyebrow in surprise. 'Are you forgetting that this is *my* house, Miss de Coverdale? And that I am the one who decides who sits down to my table?'

'I have not forgotten at all. Nevertheless, I am inclined to believe that your aunt and uncle's position in society—'

'My uncle is a jovial fellow,' Oliver interrupted smoothly. 'He drinks, perhaps a touch more than he ought, but he is happy enough when in his cups. And I have never heard him speak a harsh word to anyone, no matter what their position in life.'

Helen moved slowly towards the fireplace. 'Your uncle sounds like a most amiable gentleman.'

'Amiable indeed. As are his two sons.' Oliver stopped to run his fingers over a fine porcelain vase. 'Mr Richard Endersley, the eldest, has been married for two years. His wife is the middle daughter of Sir Geoffrey Netherby, late of Portsmouth. It was considered a good match, and my aunt was pleased. Mr Peter Endersley, my aunt's younger son, is only recently married and is anticipating the birth of his first child in the spring. His wife is the youngest daughter of a clergyman.'

Helen blinked her surprise. 'A clergyman?'

'A clergyman. From the North Country.'

'Really.' Helen felt a smile tugging at the corners of her mouth. 'And was your aunt as pleased with her younger son's choice of a wife as she was with her eldest's?'

'Not at first, but she has come to love Sarah as dearly as though she were a duchess.' Oliver's smile flashed. 'So you see, Miss de Coverdale, there is no reason for *you* to feel that your presence at the table this evening would be in any way lacking simply because you are a schoolmistress. Was your own father not a barrister?'

'Well, yes, but—'

'Then we need say no more. Except that I will be sorely disappointed if I do not see your lovely face gracing my table this evening.'

The unexpected compliment brought Helen's arguments to a halt—and the blood rushing to her cheeks.

'Of course, I realise it may not only be the early arrival of my aunt and uncle which has caused you this concern,' Oliver continued, his voice dropping. 'It may be that you are only using it as an excuse to avoid someone else's company at dinner this evening.'

Helen inhaled sharply. Surely he did not think she was desirous of avoiding *his* company, simply because of what had happened with Gillian?

'I cannot think what you mean, sir. I would certainly have no reason for avoiding the company of…anyone else who might be at your table this evening.'

'I am relieved to hear it. Because I should not like to think I have offended you in any way.' Oliver took a step closer to her, and rested his fingers lightly upon her arm. 'That would disturb me even more than would your absence from my table this evening.'

His sudden proximity was alarming in the extreme and Helen prayed he would not be able to see how rapidly her heart was beating. 'You need have no cause for concern, sir, for you have not offended me in any way. Indeed, you have been…all that is gracious. Now if you will excuse me, I think I should be…returning to my room.'

'Then you will be joining me…us…for dinner this evening?'

Helen closed her eyes. When he asked her in such a manner, how could she deny him? 'Yes, of course,' she whispered. Then, because she could think of nothing else to say, she dipped her head and all but ran towards the door.

# Chapter Fifteen

Georgiana, Viscountess Endersley, was a large woman, impressive both in size and in physical appearance. She had the most incredible red hair Helen had ever seen, a complexion that appeared almost white in comparison, and pale green eyes that watched the movements of all around her with the unblinking stare of a hawk. Her gown of dark maroon satin had surely been created by one of London's foremost modistes, and she carried herself with the air of a woman who was used to being in control—of herself *and* of everyone else around her.

'So, Gillian, you are to be wed at last,' the grand lady commented when everyone was gathered in the drawing-room before dinner. 'I am very pleased to hear it. And to young Riddleston, no less. Excellent. You have done very well for yourself, my dear. Very well.'

'Thank you, Aunt Georgiana,' Gillian answered dutifully.

'How old are you now, child?'

'Seventeen, aunt.'

Lady Endersley nodded. 'A good age for a gel to

be married. I m'self was married at seventeen. Doesn't do for a young woman to remain single too long. Would you not agree, Mrs Llewellyn?'

Sophie, who was standing in the company of her husband, Rhys, nodded her agreement. 'I certainly have no argument with that, Aunt Georgiana.'

'There, you see, Gillian. Your stepsister is happily wed and I daresay you shall be as well. Nigel Riddleston is a fine young man. One day, he will inherit the family fortunes and estates, and you shall become mistress of Kestwick Park. So, when is the wedding to take place?'

'In a fortnight's time,' Gillian told her, 'after which we plan to travel north to Scotland for a few weeks, and then spend Christmas in Wiltshire. We should be in London by March.'

'Splendid. You must call upon me there and I shall take you around. You will no doubt wish to refurbish a house, and my ability to acquaint you with which merchants to visit and which to avoid will go a long way towards saving you considerable time and money.'

'Thank you, Aunt Georgiana.'

Satisfied, Lady Endersley turned her attention towards Helen, who was standing quietly at Gillian's side. 'I do not believe I have made the acquaintance of this person, Gillian?'

'No, aunt, you have not. Pray allow me to introduce my very good friend, Miss Helen de Coverdale. Miss de Coverdale, my aunt, Lady Endersley.'

Helen gracefully curtsied. 'Lady Endersley.'

'*Miss* de Coverdale?' the Viscountess repeated in surprise. 'You are not married? But...surely you are of an age to be.'

'Yes, my lady, I suppose I am.'

'But how singular.' Lady Endersley glanced at Oliver, who had recently come over to join them. 'What is wrong with young men today, Oliver, that they would leave a beautiful young woman like this to sit on the shelf?'

Oliver turned to Helen and gave her a smile that made her go weak at the knees. 'I cannot imagine, Aunt. Except to say that perhaps Miss de Coverdale is not inclined towards marriage.'

'Not inclined towards marriage! Nonsense, all young women are inclined towards marriage. You have a most unusual surname, Miss de Coverdale,' the Viscountess remarked. 'Does your family reside in Hertfordshire?'

'No, ma'am. My parents are both gone and I live in…a small village in Northamptonshire.'

'Really. And have you other family there?'

'No, I live alone. That is—' Helen went to explain when she saw the look of concern on Gillian's face and abruptly stopped. Why was the child frowning? Was she worried about what Lady Endersley might say when she learned the truth of what she was?

'Miss de Coverdale is an exceptional watercolour-ist, Aunt Georgiana,' Oliver said in a conversational tone. 'She is also fluent in Italian, and is presently engaged in the teaching of those subjects at a private girls' school in Northamptonshire.'

'A girls' school!'

'Yes. The establishment has an excellent reputation and is run by a woman who is herself an acknowl-edged historian, poet and novelist.'

'Good Lord.' Lady Endersley's eyes widened in

astonishment. 'This young woman is a schoolmistress?'

'Yes. She is also Gillian's friend,' Oliver said in a voice that dared anyone to offer a criticism. 'Sophie and I were both very pleased that she accepted our invitation to come.'

There was a long, heavy silence. Lady Endersley glanced at Sophie, then at Helen, and then finally at Oliver, who was still standing relaxed and at ease in front of her.

'Well, I suppose it is not for me to comment upon who you invite to your house, Oliver, but in my day, we did *not* invite caper merchants and tutors to join in our family celebrations.' Lady Endersley looked down her nose at Helen, and then turned to address her next remark to her nephew. 'By the by, I saw Lady Merriot and her daughter in town last week. Constance has become quite the elegant young lady. So poised and refined. And of course, she always was beautiful. In fact, I seem to remember you saying that she was the most beautiful young lady you had ever seen. Is that not correct?'

Oliver's mouth curved in a knowing smile. 'I likely said as much, yes.'

'I thought so. I told her I would pass along her greetings. I also told her you would likely call upon her when you were next in London.'

The last remark was accompanied by a look at Helen that no one—including Helen—could fail to understand. Clearly, Lady Endersley was informing everyone that while Oliver might think well enough of Helen to invite her to celebrate his ward's betrothal, she was *not* to be mistaken for a lady who might engage his affections in any other way.

And Helen knew there was nothing Oliver or anyone else could say that was going to change her mind
about that!

The rest of the evening did not improve. Though
the meal was excellent, the wines exceptional, and the
conversation filled with details about wedding break-
fasts and house plans, the atmosphere was still
strained. Mrs Llewellyn's seating arrangement thankfully put Helen at the opposite end of the table from
the Viscountess, but it did not lessen her discomfort
at being there. Because every time Helen looked up,
she saw people staring at her, their expressions rang-
ing from mildly pitying to outright condemning.

Was it any wonder she pleaded a headache and
retired as early as possible?

Gillian, of course, had valiantly tried to ease the
situation. She had caught up with Helen at the bottom
of the stairs and tried to assure her that she mustn't
pay any attention to Lady Endersley's remarks, reminding her—as Oliver had done—that one of the
Viscountess's own daughters-in-law was the offspring
of a lowly clergyman. But Helen had merely smiled
and assured Gillian that she was not offended by the
woman's remarks, and that she truly was suffering
from a headache. What would have been the point in
saying anything else?

Lady Endersley was Oliver's aunt; a member of the
aristocracy, and a woman of considerable influence
and power in society. How could Helen blame her for
harbouring cynical opinions about her, an impoverished schoolmistress? The Viscountess obviously
viewed her as an unmarried woman who was desirous
of bettering her circumstances in life, and who saw

in Oliver a way of making that happen. Perhaps she even believed that the only reason Helen was here was so that Oliver might be able to visit with her under the guise of her being a guest at Gillian's betrothal party. The fact that Oliver had intervened on her behalf would only have served to confirm the woman's suspicions. After all, why else would her beloved nephew—a man who could have had any lady he desired—defend the reputation of a penniless schoolmistress unless she already meant something to him?

No, it was better that she have as little to do with Lady Endersley as possible, Helen decided. She had no desire to be humiliated in front of Oliver or Mrs Llewellyn again, and if she kept to her room and did not venture downstairs, there would be no chance of that happening.

As to the ball tomorrow night, she would mingle as little as possible, make sure that she kept as far away from the Viscountess and her family as possible, and first thing Saturday morning, she would climb back into the carriage and head for home, where her associations with Oliver Brandon would become nothing more than a collection of bittersweet memories.

Helen found the gown she intended to wear to the betrothal party tucked away at the back of the wardrobe and wrapped in layers of tissue thin paper. Curiosity compelled her to draw it out, but from the moment she removed its wrappings and held it up to the light, Helen knew it was perfect.

The rich, ivory-coloured silk was exquisite, its fine overlay of silver net shimmering in the morning sun.

Hundreds of tiny beads had been sewn into the bodice and down the front in a narrow line, and though the styling of the gown was years out of date, its uncomplicated design made it relatively simple to alter. All that was required was some gathering of the fabric around the bust line, the application of some lace around the sleeves and neck, and the shortening of the hem to make it appear *au courant*.

Mrs Llewellyn, after deciding not to press Helen into coming downstairs, personally brought her something to eat, and after seeing what she was working on, kindly sent up a pair of long ivory gloves for Helen to wear. Gillian also appeared at her door late in the afternoon with the gift of a beautiful, hand-painted fan, something Helen knew would go perfectly with the gown and which Gillian assured her she was delighted to see her wearing.

'And I shall send Marie to assist you this evening,' the girl said as she flounced down upon the bed. 'I am positively dying to see what she will do with all that wonderful long hair of yours.'

Helen smiled, but the expression in her eyes was wistful. 'I haven't had anyone dress my hair in years. Since I was your age, in fact.'

'Really?' Gillian's eyes went wide. 'Then you haven't always been a teacher?'

Helen set the fan on the bedside table and shook her head. 'At one time, my life was not unlike yours. I went to parties and to musicales. I even sang and played the piano forte.'

'You never told me!'

'I had no reason to. My life is not what it once was.'

'But you were obviously comfortable with this sort

of thing once, so there is no reason for you to feel uncomfortable tonight. And I do so want you to have a good time, Miss de Coverdale, the presence of my aunt notwithstanding.'

'I shall have a wonderful time, whether your aunt is there or not,' Helen said as bravely as she could. 'Because more than anything, I am looking forward to seeing *you* dance with the young man whom Mrs Llewellyn tells me you are very happy to be marrying.'

Gillian sighed. 'Yes, I am really most fortunate. Mr Riddleston treats me ever so well, and he is very handsome. Did Sophie tell you we met in London last year?'

'Yes. She also told me you were not taken with the gentleman upon first acquaintance.'

Gillian tipped back her head and laughed. 'Yes, is that not a good joke? I cannot even recall what he was like the first time I met him. But strangely enough, when I saw him again last month, it was almost as though…I was seeing him for the first time. As though he was a different person altogether.'

Neglecting to point out that it was probably Gillian who was the different person, Helen said only, 'Do you love him?'

Gillian's smile slipped ever so slightly. 'Yes. Perhaps not in the way I loved Mr Wymington, but I would never tell Oliver that. He has been so good to me since we've been back, Miss de Coverdale. He's taken me out nearly every day, and he has spoiled me even more than he did before. In fact, I shall almost be sorry to leave Shefferton Hall,' she admitted with a laugh. 'As to Mr Wymington…well…I know that he was only interested in my fortune, and I know that should make it easier for me to get over him, but a person never *really* forgets their first love, do they?'

Unbidden, an image of Thomas's face flashed into Helen's mind, and for the first time in her life, she realised she couldn't see him any more. His features were beginning to blur, and the memory of his voice and of his physical appearance was becoming hazy in her mind. But she saw Oliver's face. She saw it as clearly as though he was standing right in front of her.

'We can if we allow ourselves to,' Helen said softly. 'In time, your memories of Mr Wymington will fade as new ones of your life with your husband and children move in to take their place. But no one can say how long that will take. Only you will know when it happens. But now, we must put the past aside and look to the future. I am here to celebrate your engagement to Mr Riddleston. And now before you dash away to get dressed and become the most popular young lady in the house tonight, I insist that you tell me everything you can about him!'

At twenty minutes to eight, Helen closed the door to her room and quietly tiptoed downstairs. She had no desire to be on the upper floors when the guests began to arrive. Better to be down here, tucked away in some quiet corner where no one would see her, and where she could lose herself in the crowds of people that would quickly gather.

Would she feel terribly ill at ease this evening, Helen wondered as she made her way into the deserted parlour? In truth, she failed to see how she could not. It had been years since she had moved in any kind of society, and though she had long ago learned the necessary social skills, she could only pray that she would remember how to use them.

Thank goodness she need have no concerns about her appearance. The gown had turned out even better than she'd hoped. The shimmering fabric now draped softly over the fullness of her breasts, fit snugly underneath and then fell in graceful folds to the floor. The elegant evening gloves Mrs Llewellyn had lent her for the occasion were perfect, and Gillian's beautiful hand-painted fan hung from a ribbon at her wrist.

True to her word, Gillian had also sent her maid to attend to Helen's hair, and the pretty French girl had worked wonders with it. She had exclaimed at length over its lush softness, and after studying it for a few moments, had decided to dress it in the antique Roman style, bringing the gleaming tresses together and confining them at the back of Helen's head. A single ribbon of ivory silk studded with pearl ornaments wound like a ribbon of starlight through the dark tresses.

Helen could scarce believe that she was the same woman who had left Steep Abbot only a day before. Certainly she did not look the same. In her beautiful gown and her upswept hairstyle, she looked as though she belonged in this magnificent house, with its beautiful, sophisticated people.

And just for tonight, Helen *wanted* to believe that she belonged. Because more than anything, she wanted Oliver to see her as something other than a schoolmistress wearing a plain old schoolmistress's gown. Just for tonight, she wanted him to see her as the privileged young lady she had once been.

'I vow the girls and the staff at Mrs Guarding's Academy would not recognise you, Miss de

Coverdale,' Oliver said softly from the door. 'I almost did not myself.'

The soft, caressing tone caused Helen to gasp as she spun around. She hadn't heard him come into the room, but now as she saw him standing opposite her, she could only thank the Fates for having given her this last opportunity to spend time with the man who had become so important in her life.

He had dressed formally for the occasion and Helen knew that he would be the most handsome man in the house. His double-breasted black cut-away coat, tailored, no doubt, by Weston or Meyer, fit his broad shoulders to perfection, while light kerseymere breeches and fine silk stockings outlined as fine a leg as Helen had ever seen. A snowy white cravat nestled against the lapels of his jacket, the arrangement of which she knew would have taken considerable time and skill, whilst nestled in the folds was an elegant sapphire pin.

Oliver's appearance was impeccable, and yet now, as in the past, there was nothing of the dandy about him. He appeared to her at this moment exactly as he always had; a simple man of taste and refinement. It was no wonder Lady Endersley held out such high hopes for him.

'You startled me, Mr Brandon,' Helen said, hating the breathlessness that had crept back into her voice.

Oliver bowed from the waist. 'Forgive me, Miss de Coverdale, it was not my intention to do so. I should have noticed that you were lost in your thoughts.' He smiled as he moved towards her. 'But I am surprised to find you hidden away in here. I thought to see you coming down the stairs. You would have created quite a stir looking as beautiful as you do now.'

Helen felt a blush heat her skin, and hastily opened her fan. 'I thought only to find an out-of-the-way place to hide. I am well aware my company is not so grand as many of the guests who will be here tonight.'

If possible, Oliver's smile grew gentler still. 'Ah, but your presence is more welcome than most, Miss de Coverdale, because *you* were invited out of affection. Would that I could say that about everyone who will be coming tonight.'

Helen's mouth curved in a grateful smile. 'Then I shall consider myself fortunate, sir, for I would far rather be thought of with affection than obligation.'

Oliver chuckled, and Helen was relieved to discover that she could still converse in the light, flirtatious manner expected of young men and women. The only problem was, she had no desire to flirt with Oliver. Her feelings went too deep for such trivial exchanges. As she moved around the room, she was extremely conscious of being alone with him. It seemed to her that his presence filled every inch of the room, and yet it was in no way suffocating or overwhelming.

But then, how could it be? He was the man she had fallen in love with. The man she would have chosen to spend the rest of her life with. As long as she could be in his company, there was no other place in the world she would rather be.

'You must be…very pleased that Gillian accepted Mr Riddleston's proposal so quickly,' Helen said, hoping to engage him in harmless conversation.

'Pleased *and* relieved,' Oliver admitted. 'I am delighted that Gillian is promised to a gentleman whom I can admire and who I know is marrying her for the right reasons. But at the same time, I am relieved that she genuinely cares for him and is happy to go through with the marriage for her own sake.'

'Go *through* with it?' Helen's expression reflected her surprise. 'You make it sound as though she was doing something she would rather not.'

Oliver sighed. 'Come, Miss de Coverdale, you and I know each other—and the situation—too well for that. Gillian is happy enough to be marrying young Riddleston, and I know she holds him in great affection, but I do not believe she feels for him the kind of breathless passion she felt for Sidney Wymington. Wymington was the kind of man whose appearance and manner would inspire such a response in the female breast. Even you cannot deny that he was a dashing fellow.'

'No, I cannot,' Helen admitted with a smile. 'But the flaws I discovered in his character soon blinded me to his good looks. My unfortunate conversation with him in Abbot Giles, and his attempts to discredit me in front of you and Miss Gresham, made me see him as a most unattractive man all around.'

'I would be lying if I said I was not glad to hear you say so,' Oliver said quietly. 'Fortunately, Nigel Riddleston has nothing of Wymington's ways about him, yet he is every bit as charming and a hundred times more sincere. In time he will inherit a grand estate and I know he has the intelligence and foresight to manage it well. He will not be one to fritter away his fortune on impulse and trifles.'

'And is he as…enamoured of Gillian as she is of him?' Helen asked, careful to use the same word he had.

'The poor lad is head over heels in love with her. Has been ever since the first time he saw her in

London.' Oliver's mouth curved in a smile. 'Yes, I am well pleased with the way events have turned out for Gillian, especially when I remember how perilously close we came to losing her. But what about you, Miss de Coverdale? Have matters turned out as well for you as you might have liked?'

Helen drew a long, deep breath. The question begged a cautious answer, for while she had no wish to lie to him outright, she could hardly admit the truth of her feelings.

'I am in the enviable position of having both a home and a job at the Guarding Academy,' she said slowly, 'and I am fortunate enough to have earned the respect and affection of a few good friends. What more could a woman in my position want?'

'The same things any woman might want,' Oliver replied. 'A home of your own. Children to care for. A husband to love—'

'Oliver, is that you I hear?' Mrs Llewellyn's voice called, seconds before she breezed into the room. 'The receiving line is forming and Gillian wishes you to take your place. You should—why, Miss de Coverdale, whatever are you doing here? And looking so very beautiful.' Sophie's eyes widened as she took in the magnificence of the skilfully altered gown. 'I vow, you have worked a minor miracle, my dear. Does she not look radiant, Oliver?'

'She does indeed.' Oliver's gaze fell softly on Helen's face. 'I told her as much only a moment ago.'

'But why are you not out in the ballroom where the gentlemen can see you?'

Helen felt the blush begin at her throat and spread upwards. 'I did not wish to appear too early amongst your guests, Mrs Llewellyn. Lady Endersley—'

'Oh, bother Lady Endersley,' Mrs Llewellyn interrupted. 'I intend to keep her fully occupied and well away from you this evening, my dear. But there will be many others anxious to make your acquaintance. And the sooner you take your place amongst them, the sooner you shall begin enjoying yourself. Now, Oliver, off you go. I shall attend to Miss de Coverdale.' Sophie marched forward and linked her arm through Helen's. 'It is past time we introduced this lovely young woman to society. And of course, to our delightful Mr Riddleston.'

# Chapter Sixteen

Nigel Riddleston was everything Helen hoped he would be. He was handsome, well-spoken, and so in love with Gillian that it nearly brought tears to Helen's eyes.

Oh yes, he would make her a wonderful husband. There was a quiet sincerity about him that was eminently appealing, and as the evening progressed, Helen was better able to understand why Oliver was so impressed with him. While Gillian tended to flit around the crowded room like a beautiful butterfly, Mr Riddleston took his time walking amongst the guests, stopping to speak to as many of them as he could and always with a kind word and a genuine smile. While Gillian was frequently sought out by other single gentlemen for dances, Mr Riddleston seemed perfectly content to watch from the side. But he always knew where she was. He was there, watchful, but never hovering, and Helen knew it was pride rather than possession that kept him glancing in her direction.

'Is he not a sweet man, Miss de Coverdale?' Gillian asked when the two of them at last had an opportunity to be alone. 'I admit, I did not expect to like him near so well as I do, but I find the more I come to know him, the more there is to admire about him.'

'He is a very likeable young man indeed,' Helen said, delighted at the note of happiness in Gillian's voice. 'I am more pleased for you than I can say. And you are to be married in a fortnight. How excited you must be.'

'Yes. I had originally thought the spring would be nice, but Nigel would like to be married by Christmas so that we can take up residence in London early in the new year. His mother and father keep a house in town and they have given it to us as a wedding present. Is that not exceedingly generous of them?'

'It is generous indeed.'

'And I expect *you* to come and visit us very often. You will come, won't you, Miss de Coverdale?' Gillian's eyes were softly beseeching. 'I should like that above all.'

'I shall do my very best,' Helen assured her. 'But you must remember that it is not always easy for a schoolmistress to leave her classes.'

'Then I must do everything I can to ensure that you do not remain a schoolmistress much longer! When you come to London, I shall introduce you to every handsome, eligible gentleman I know.'

Amused by the girl's emphatic if somewhat naïve declaration, Helen began to laugh. 'Oh, Gillian, that is a very kind sentiment, but I doubt any of the handsome, eligible gentlemen you are likely to know will have any interest in making the acquaintance of a one-and-thirty-year-old schoolmistress from Steep Abbot.'

Gillian looked appalled. 'But how can you say

that? Only look at the way the gentlemen are watching you tonight. Have you not noticed the way their eyes follow you around? Several perfectly amiable young men have asked me about you, and Sir Peter Rollings wishes to be introduced. He told me he thought you were quite the most beautiful woman he had ever seen.'

'What's this I hear, Gillie?' Oliver interrupted. 'Are you trying to lure Miss de Coverdale away? Mrs Guarding will not thank you for depriving her of yet another teacher.'

Gillian rolled her eyes. 'Really, Oliver. I would far rather see Miss de Coverdale married to a man who loves her than be locked away at some girls' school where she is forced to teach watercolours and Italian to a bunch of simpering young misses for the rest of her life. She is far too beautiful for that, don't you think?'

Helen blushed furiously. 'I am sure Mr Brandon has no opinion on the matter, Miss Gresham. But look there, I believe Mr Riddleston is attempting to secure your attention.'

Gillian turned and waved at the young man, who was indeed smiling and signalling in her direction. 'Yes, he wishes me to talk to his sister, the young lady standing there on his right. Amanda is a rather plain creature, but she has a sweet temper and I love her dearly. No doubt he will wish me to see to her Season once we are wed. But do not forget what I said, Miss de Coverdale.' Impulsively, Gillian reached up and kissed Helen on the cheek. 'I shall do everything I can to see that *you* are soon married as well. And thank you for being such a wonderful friend. I am so very glad you are here.' Then, in a rustle of silk skirts, she hurried away, leaving Helen, flushed and embarrassed, standing alone in the company of Oliver Brandon again.

'You must forgive Gillian for being a trifle outspoken,' Oliver said into the somewhat awkward silence. 'She tends to speak her mind about whatever happens to be on it at the time.'

'Yes. I suppose we must put it down to…the excitement of the evening,' Helen said, desperately trying to make light of the episode. 'She hardly knows what she is saying.'

'She is right about one thing, though. You are far too beautiful to remain a teacher for the rest of your life.'

Helen's pulse skittered as she opened her fan and plied it fervently to her cheeks. 'You are…too kind, sir.'

'I told you once before that kindness has very little to do with what I say to you, Miss de Coverdale.' Oliver clasped his hands behind his back in the gesture Helen had come to know so well. 'I am simply speaking the truth. You are a beautiful woman and there isn't a man in this room who doesn't know it.'

Helen swallowed hard. She knew she should offer some witty, sophisticated remark, but in the face of Oliver's compliment, she could think of nothing. What a pity. It seemed her newly reclaimed social skills had already deserted her.

'Gillian told me that…it was Mr Riddleston's wish that they marry before Christmas,' she said instead, saying the first thing that came to mind.

'Yes, he is anxious to get on with it. But then, as I told you, he has been in love with her for some time. Indeed, I think it was a case of love at first sight.'

Helen watched the young pair across the floor, and inadvertently, a soft sigh escaped her lips. 'I do hope it lasts, for both their sakes.'

'Oh, I think it will. It has happened in our family a number of times.'

'Yes, I remember you telling me that your sister and her husband fell in love that way.'

'Yes. As did I.'

A bolt of lightning striking the floor beside her could not have startled Helen more. The quietly offered words, spoken in a conversational tone of voice, caused her pulse to quicken and her breath to come in short gasps. 'I...beg your pardon?'

'You sound surprised, Miss de Coverdale. Did you not think I was the type who could fall in love at first sight?'

'I'm sure I have...no idea what type you are, Mr Brandon.' *Oliver was in love?* Oh, dear God, how could such a thing be true! Why hadn't Gillian told her? Surely the girl had known that her own stepbrother was harbouring a *tendre* for someone. Especially one that had been going on for some time. Why had she led her to believe there had been no one in his life?

'I must confess to being...surprised, Mr Brandon,' Helen stammered, fighting to keep her voice steady. 'Gillian did not...tell me you were involved with anyone.'

'She did not tell you because she did not know,' Oliver said with a smile. 'No one does. It happened a long time ago.'

'I see. And what of the...young lady?' she asked,

forcing herself to say the words. 'How does she feel about your keeping silent for such a long time?'

'I have no idea,' Oliver replied. 'Because the young lady doesn't know how I feel either.'

Helen could barely hear him over the strange buzzing in her head. 'But how can that be, sir? If you were…in love with her, she must have had *some* indication as to your feelings?'

'In truth, she had none. Because at the time, she didn't know me from Adam.'

The buzzing was replaced by a dull roar. 'Surely there was something in the way you spoke to her—'

'I said not a word to the lady,' Oliver admitted quietly. 'It would not have been…appropriate at the time. Nor was I given an opportunity to do so. But the memory of her face and the manner of our first meeting has stayed with me to this very day.'

Helen wished she could think of something to say, but her mind had gone totally blank. What was she supposed to say upon learning that the man she had fallen in love with was in love with someone else?

'I know it sounds strange, Miss de Coverdale, but you have to understand that my feelings were of the kind I thought best kept to myself,' Oliver continued as the silence between them lengthened. 'As I said, I was not even willing to acknowledge my own awareness of them at the time. And because so many years went by before I saw the lady again, I had no reason to believe they still existed. But then, under the most amazing of circumstances, I saw her again and I realised that, to my great astonishment, nothing had changed. I felt the same way about her as I had upon seeing her that very first time.' Oliver shook his head in wonderment. 'It was unsettling to say the least.'

Unsettling indeed, Helen echoed silently, aware that any pleasure she might have taken in the night was now completely gone. All she felt was sick at heart; numbed by the painful realisation that Oliver would never be anything to her but the most casual of acquaintances. Saddened, because she had foolishly allowed herself to believe since coming to Shefferton Hall that he held her in some esteem. Now, knowing that he did not, she wanted nothing more than to run away and hide before she made a complete fool of herself.

'Mr Brandon, would you please…excuse me? I find it very warm in the room all of a sudden.'

'Of course, Miss de Coverdale, but is everything all right? You seem a little distressed. Perhaps you would care to take a stroll on the terrace?'

'Yes. That would be…most welcome,' Helen said, grasping at anything that would serve as a means of escaping his company.

'Then allow me to escort you outside.'

She blanched. 'No! That is…thank you, sir, but the offer of an escort is not necessary. I can manage…quite well on my own.'

'I think not, dear lady,' Oliver said softly. 'Your face has suddenly turned the colour of your gown and I fear you are in danger of fainting away if you keep breathing like that. Come, allow me to escort you on to the terrace. A change of scenery and a breath of fresh air might be just the thing to revive you.'

Helen wanted to tell him it was going to take a great deal more than fresh air and scenery to revive her, but what would be the point? Nothing was going to change the fact that Oliver Brandon was in love with someone else.

Thankfully, the evening air did help restore her equilibrium, if not her spirits. Helen closed her eyes and drew a few deep breaths of the cool night air into her lungs and felt the light-headedness begin to ease. But it did nothing to lessen the feelings of despair within her heart. That only grew stronger every time she looked at Oliver's dear face and knew that he was lost to her.

She gripped the stone balustrade hard, desperately trying to hide the trembling in her hands, knowing that the sooner she could get away from him, the better.

'There, do you not feel a little better for having come outside?' Oliver asked, his voice low and filled with concern.

Helen dropped her head to hide the expression in her eyes, and wished she might be anywhere but here. She did not even have the strength to *look* at him. 'Thank you, Mr Brandon, you are very kind to be so attentive. And yes, I…believe I am feeling…a little better. Forgive me. I am not used to crowds and it has been…a very long time since I attended a function like this. I think the excitement of the evening quite overwhelmed me.'

'Of course. Your reaction was only to be expected. But are you warm enough? There is a chill in the air tonight.'

'Thank you, I am fine. But it would probably be best if you were to…return to your guests, Mr Brandon. People will be wondering where you are.'

'Let them wonder. It is Gillian's celebration, not mine,' he reminded her. 'And right now, I don't care about anyone else, Miss de Coverdale.' He put his hands on her shoulders and gently turned her to face him. 'I only care about you.'

Helen gasped, dismayed to feel tears trembling on her lashes. 'But you *don't* care. You are in love with…someone else. You just told me as much!'

His burning eyes held her still. 'Does that disturb you?'

'Yes. *No!* I mean…of course it doesn't disturb me.' She dashed her hand across her eyes, wiping the traitorous moisture away. 'Why should it?'

'Because my dear Miss de Coverdale, I am hoping that you are *not* as indifferent to me as you have been trying to make me believe.' His fingers tightened on her arms. 'Please tell me you aren't, *amore*.'

Stunned, Helen gazed up into his face. 'I *beg* your pardon?'

Slowly and seductively, Oliver's eyes slid over her face, lingering on her eyes before coming to rest briefly on her lips. 'Do you not know the word?'

'Of course I know the word. But…why would you call me your beloved when you have just finished telling me that you are…that you are…'

'In love with someone else? Why indeed? Unless it is because I thought it was time the young lady was made aware of it herself.'

Helen stared up at him, wondering if she had somehow fallen asleep and was dreaming all this. 'Mr Brandon, pray do not tease me. In my present state, I am ill-equipped to deal with the subtleties of your phrasing. Please, tell me what you mean—'

'I mean, sweet Helen, that *you* are the woman I'm in love with. The same woman I've been in love with for so many long, empty years. Do you find that so very hard to believe?'

At that moment, Helen was extremely grateful for the strength of his hands on her arms. Otherwise, she feared she might have sunk to the ground in a heap. Oliver Brandon was in *love* with her? With *her*?

'But…you thought I was…immoral,' she whispered as the tears began to roll down her cheeks. 'You accused me of having…a bad influence on Gillian.'

'Yes, because I had convinced myself you would. But in my heart, I knew differently.' He reached into his pocket and drew out his handkerchief. 'I never forgot the first time I saw you, Helen. That night, in the library, when you looked up and saw me, I knew then that something had happened to me. That the memory of your face would stay with me for the rest of my life. But I never put it down to my being in love with you.'

Helen sniffed. 'You didn't?'

'Of course not. I thought I had been bewitched by a pair of beautiful dark eyes.' He smiled as he gently wiped away the traces of her tears. 'I convinced myself you couldn't possibly be the kind of woman I wanted to marry because it seemed to me that we were different in so many ways. And yet, when I saw you again that morning at Mrs Guarding's Academy, I knew it to be a lie.'

'But when you spoke to me in the carriage,' Helen persisted, 'when you came to take me driving, you told me that I…that I—'

'I know what I said,' Oliver cut in. 'And I wish to God I could take back every single word I uttered. I never meant to hurt you, beloved. I think that in some way, I was still fighting what I was feeling for you. I couldn't deny that Fate had brought us back together again, but I was tempted to think of it as a cruel joke rather than the best thing that could have happened to me.' He reached for her hand and held it in his. 'Tell me I'm not harbouring foolish hopes, dearest. Tell me that you care for me, even if only a little. For even that will give me a reason to keep on trying to make you love me.'

'Oh, Oliver, you have no need of such foolish hopes,' Helen told him weakly. 'I love you more than you know. More than I can possibly tell you. But I never imagined you were in love with me. I never thought—'

It was as far as Helen got. Oliver silenced her words with a kiss of such soul-searing passion that it left her breathless and trembling with emotion. Everything and everyone else faded away as his lips closed over hers and his arms drew her close, bringing their bodies into intimate contact and arousing feelings and sensations that Helen had never experienced before. It was as though they were the only two people in the world. The only two people who mattered.

'I never want to hear that mentioned between us again,' Oliver said when at last he raised his head and gazed down into her eyes. 'I never want to hear you talk about Lord Talbot or your poor clergyman, or any other man who has ever spoken to you in a disrespectful way, lest I be tempted to seek out every one of them and challenge them all to a duel!'

'Dear me, challenge them *all*?' Helen's laughter escaped as a soft ripple of sound. 'If that is the case, I fear you will be too busy fighting to spend any time with me.'

'Ah, but if you will have me, dearest Helen, I intend to spend the rest of my life as close to you as I am now. And I guarantee, there will be times when you may wish me far away, so devoted will my attentions be.'

'Never! I could never wish you far away from me again. In fact, if I had only one wish, it would be that you would not be more than ten paces from my side. I love you, Oliver. A separation of even a short time would be cruel punishment indeed.'

'Then…will you marry me, Helen?' he whispered, as his fingers touched her face and moved tenderly along her cheek. 'Will you consent to be my wife?'

Helen closed her eyes and leaned into his caress. 'I would marry you in an instant, beloved, but…I must ask if you have given this question the consideration it deserves.'

'What is there to consider, other than how we feel about each other?'

Helen sighed. 'There is much to consider, given that our positions in life are so different. You must know there are others who will not be as well pleased with your decision as I.'

'Others?' His brow darkened. 'What others?'

'Lady Endersley for one.'

'Lady Endersley be damned!'

'No, you must not say that, Oliver,' Helen said, gently pressing her fingers to his lips. 'She is not wrong to care about you, nor is she wrong to wish to see you marry well. She is your aunt, and she loves you. But by marrying me, you may risk losing her affection, and I would hate to be the cause of such a rift between you.'

Oliver stared at her for a long time. So long, in fact, that Helen began to wonder if he was indeed reflecting upon the wisdom of his choice. But when he spoke again, she knew that nothing had changed.

'Dearest Helen. With everything you say, you only make me love you more. You are not wrong in wishing to make me look beyond my own feelings. And you are not wrong in saying that others may not be pleased with my decision. But it is *my* decision to make, and our happiness that is at stake. I've found the woman I want to marry. She teaches watercolours and Italian at a girls' school in Steep Abbot. And if my aunt or any other members of my family will not receive her, then they shall not be received by me.' Oliver drew her close and with infinite tenderness cupped her chin between his fingers and tipped it back. 'I love this lady so very much. And if she will agree to have me, I intend to spend the rest of my life showing her exactly how much I do love her, in every way I can. Do you think, under the circumstances, that will be convincing enough?'

Helen's eyes glowed with a deep and abiding sense of happiness. 'Oh yes, my darling Oliver. I think that, under any circumstances, that is probably all the convincing the lady is ever likely to need.'

# Lord Exmouth's Intentions

*by*

*Anne Ashley*

**Anne Ashley** was born and educated in Leicester. She lived for a time in Scotland, but now lives in the West Country with two cats, her two sons and a husband, who has a wonderful and very necessary sense of humour. When not pounding away at her keyboard, she likes to relax in her garden, which she has opened to the public on more than one occasion in aid of the village church funds.

# *Chapter One*

A distinct lack of enthusiasm induced Robina to allow the half-folded garment to slip through her fingers, and her attention to wander as she peered through the window to follow the progress along the street of a very smart racing curricle, pulled by two superbly matched greys.

Considering the Season had officially come to an end the week before, London remained surprisingly bustling with life, its many springtime visitors seemingly reluctant to return to their country homes, or to move on to those coastal towns which had become such fashionable summer retreats in recent years.

It just so happened that she would have been more than happy to return to her Northamptonshire home, to sample once again the sweetly fresh country air, and be reunited with her father and sisters once more. She was not so foolish as to suppose that it would not take a little time to adjust to the tranquillity of the vicarage in Abbot Quincey again, after spending more than three months here in the capital, thoroughly enjoying all the delights of a Season which, even though she said so herself, had been something of a success.

For a simple country parson's daughter, with no dowry to speak of, she had managed to attract the attention of two very worthy gentlemen, either of whom, she didn't doubt for a moment, would have made a very considerate husband. She had been encouraged by her mother to turn down both offers for her hand, which she had dutifully done without, she hoped, causing lasting hurt to either erstwhile suitor. And certainly none whatsoever to herself!

Neither Mr Chard nor the Honourable Simon Sutherland had succeeded in igniting that illusive flame which every romantically inclined young woman longs to experience. She had come through what was likely to be her one and only London Season a little more worldly-wise and certainly heart-whole. An involuntary sigh escaped her. Whether or not she would be able to say the same by the end of the summer was a different matter entirely.

Without the least warning she experienced it yet again: that sudden surge of blind panic. Why, oh why, hadn't she flatly refused when the suggestion had first been put to her? Why had she allowed herself to be persuaded into accompanying the Dowager to Brighton, when she had in her heart of hearts known from the very first that what Lady Exmouth truly wanted was not a young companion for herself, but a biddable little wife for her son?

Abandoning the packing entirely now, Robina

slumped down on the bed, not for the first time cursing herself for not being a little more assertive on occasions.

It wasn't that she had taken the Dowager's son in dislike. Nothing could have been further from the truth. Lord Exmouth was a very personable gentleman. If he was not quite the dashing, handsome hero of storybooks, he was certainly most attractive, blessed with a good physique and noble bearing. Just because he happened to be the wrong side of five-and-thirty was not such a drawback either, for older gentlemen, she had been reliably informed, tended to be rather more dependable.

That he rarely smiled, had more often than not a cynical glint in those very attractive dark brown eyes of his, and frequently relapsed into periods of brooding silence were traits, she didn't doubt, to which she would grow accustomed in time. What she knew she could never reconcile herself to, however, was always figuring as second best in the eyes of any man she agreed to marry. And that, she very much feared, would be precisely her fate if she was ever foolish enough to consent to a union with Lord Daniel Exmouth!

A sympathetic sigh escaped her this time as the many rumours concerning the very personable widower filtered through her mind. If half the stories circulating about him were true then the poor Baron was a mere shadow of his former self.

His heart, according to many, had died with his first wife in that tragic accident eighteen months ago.

Many believed that, because he had been tooling the carriage when it had overturned, killing both his wife and the nephew of a near neighbour, the combination of both grief and guilt had changed him from the most companionable of gentlemen into a die-hard sceptic who now attained scant pleasure from life. Yet, for all his brooding glances and frequent periods of self-enforced solitude, he could still on occasions be both affable and charming. Sadly, that didn't alter the fact that whoever agreed to become his second wife would always live in the shadow of the beautiful Clarissa, who, many believed, had taken her husband's loving heart with her to her grave.

Her mother's unexpected appearance in the bedchamber put an end to these melancholy reflections, and Robina automatically rose to her feet to continue her packing.

'Great heavens, child! Haven't you finished yet? What on earth have you been doing all this time? You know full well that Lady Exmouth's servants will be here at noon to collect your trunk.'

Robina cast a glance in her mother's direction, not for the first time wishing that she were more able to assess her moods. The tone she had used had been mildly scolding, but her expression betrayed no hint of annoyance.

Would now be an appropriate moment to admit that she, too, would much prefer to return to Northamptonshire at the end of the week? Could she possibly succeed in making her mother, who was not always the most approachable of people, understand her grave misgivings about spending the summer in Brighton? Or had she foolishly left it rather too late?

'Mama, I have been having second thoughts about accompanying Lady Exmouth,' she said in a rush, before she could change her mind. 'I should much prefer to return with you to Abbot Quincey at the end of the week.'

The seconds ticked slowly by while Robina scanned her mother's face in the hope of glimpsing some visual reaction to the belated confession, but as usual Lady Elizabeth's expression remained as inscrutable as ever.

'Why this sudden change of heart, child?' Once again there was just the faintest hint of impatience in the beautifully cultured voice. 'Not so very long ago you were overjoyed at the prospect of spending the summer weeks by the sea. No pressure was brought to bear when the suggestion was first put to you. It was entirely your own decision to accept Lady Exmouth's very kind invitation.'

Robina could not argue with this. She had never made any secret of the fact that she had liked Lady Exmouth from the first moment they met, and the prospect of extending the period of frivolous enjoyment by spending several weeks as the guest of that delightful and highly sociable lady had been just too much of a temptation for the country parson's daughter, who had discovered that she had rapidly acquired a taste for the finer things in life. It was only when she had paid that short visit to Hampshire to be amongst the select few who attended the small party

to celebrate the engagement of the Duke of
Sharnbrook to Lady Sophia Cleeve that grave doubts
had begun to assail her.

'In that case we shall not be seeing each other
again until the autumn,' her good friend Sophia had
remarked, after Robina had casually divulged her intention of spending the summer in Brighton as the
guest of the Dowager Lady Exmouth.

They had been standing outside the glorious ducal
mansion, bidding each other a final farewell, and
there had been an unmistakable teasing glint in
Sophia's eyes as she had added in an undertone, 'So,
do I congratulate you now, or wait until the an-
nouncement is officially made, you sly old thing?'

Even now Robina could recall quite clearly gaping
like a half-wit at her lifelong friend. 'I—I do not
perfectly understand what you mean, Sophia. You
are the one to be congratulated, not I.'

'At the moment, yes,' she had laughingly agreed,
'but it is quite obvious to anyone of the meanest
intelligence that it will not be too long before you
also are sporting a splendid betrothal ring on your
left hand.'

Robina clearly recalled also her friend's teasing
laughter before she had gone on to add rather taunt-
ingly, 'Why, you cannot possibly go about refusing
reasonable offers of marriage, while encouraging the
attentions of a certain party, and happily accepting
an invitation to spend the summer with that favoured
gentleman's mother, without causing a deal of speculation. Surely you don't suppose that people haven't

already put two and two together and realised that your affections are engaged! I have fallen desperately in love myself, and so am able to read the signs, my dear. But if you would prefer that I wait a little longer before offering my heartfelt congratulations, you only have to say so.'

Robina had been too stunned to say anything else at the time, and had been prey to the most guilt-ridden reflections and fearful conjecture ever since.

Had she in truth actively encouraged Lord Exmouth to suppose that a proposal of marriage from him would not be unwelcome? She had asked herself that selfsame question time and time again in recent days, and even now wasn't perfectly sure that she knew the answer.

She couldn't deny that, up until she and her mother had paid that short visit to Hampshire, she had not once refused to stand up with Lord Exmouth whenever they had happened to be attending the same party. Which, she now realised, had occurred far too frequently to have been mere coincidence. She could only marvel at how credulous she had been for supposing that pure chance had brought them together so often, and not, as she now strongly suspected, the designs of their respective mothers.

If her suspicions were correct then the Dowager believed that in the quiet and undemanding vicar's daughter she had found the ideal person to care for her two motherless granddaughters, and make the life of her heartbroken son more bearable, without de-manding too much of him in return. It was also fairly safe to assume that her own mother was of a similar mind, and that she had every expectation of her eldest daughter receiving a very advantageous offer of marriage in the not too distant future.

'May I ask you something, Mama?' She did not wait for a response. 'Are you hoping that Lord Exmouth will make me an offer before the summer is over?'

Lady Elizabeth's expression remained inscrutable, and yet Robina sensed that her mother had been momentarily taken aback by the directness of the question. In truth, she had rather surprised herself that she had summoned up enough courage to ask such a thing. She was wont to treat her mother with the utmost respect as a rule, and had never been encouraged to query any decision she had chosen to make.

Evidently Lady Elizabeth did not deem the question an impertinence, for she said after a moment's quiet deliberation, 'I certainly believe he is not indifferent to you, Robina. And I cannot deny that, should he decide to make you an offer of marriage, I would be delighted, yes. It would be a truly splendid match, far better than I could ever have hoped for you. Carriages, jewels, fine clothes would be yours for the asking. You would want for nothing, child.'

Nothing except love, Robina longed to retort, but remained silent as she watched her mother move in that graceful way of hers across to the window.

'You must appreciate of course that if you did

marry Exmouth, your sisters' chances of finding suitable husbands would be vastly improved. By reminding you of this, I hope you realise that I would
never expect you to forfeit your own happiness in
order that your sisters might attain theirs. Nothing
could be further from the truth! And if I thought that
your feelings were already engaged, I would not suggest for a moment that you further your acquaintance
with the widower... But your affections are not engaged, are they, Robina?'

'No, Mama, they are not,' she responded, scru-
pulously honest, but with a hint of wistfulness which
Lady Elizabeth's sharp ears had little difficulty in
detecting.

She turned away from the window to look directly
at her daughter once more. 'But you wish they were,
is that it? You wish that during your time here in
London you'd met just one young man who had succeeded in sending your heart pounding...? A knight
in shining armour who might have swept you off
your feet?' The sudden shout of laughter, though unexpected, lacked neither warmth nor sympathy. 'Ah,
child, I was your age once and know what foolish
fancies pass through a young girl's mind. Remember,
my dear, that very few members of our class marry
for love. And perhaps that is no bad thing... Love,
after all, is a luxury few can afford.'

After a moment she moved slowly across to the
door. 'Your father and I would never dream of forcing you into a marriage with a man you could neither
like nor respect. I do not believe for a moment that

you are indifferent to Lord Exmouth, child. So I would ask you to think long and hard before you turn down what might well prove to be your one and only chance of making a truly splendid match.'

Robina, watching the door being closed quietly, realised that her mother had divulged far more about herself during the past few minutes than ever before.

She had long held the belief that her parents' union had been a love-match. Lady Elizabeth Finedon, proud and aristocratic, the daughter of a duke, no less, had chosen to marry the Reverend William Perceval, a younger son of an impoverished baronet. If love had not been the reason for the union then Robina was at a loss to understand what it might have been. Maybe, though, during the passage of time, there had been occasions when her mother had regretted allowing her heart to rule her head.

Her father, a worthy man of rigid principles, had made no secret of the fact that it had been his wife's substantial dowry which had enabled him and his family to live in relative comfort, if not precisely luxury. Even so, it had been only the practising of strict economies over the years that had enabled the Vicar of Abbot Quincey and his wife to fund a London Season for their eldest daughter.

Robina knew that her parents had every intention of offering her three younger sisters the same opportunity as she herself had received. The twins, Edwina and Frederica, would have their come-out next year, an even greater expense with two of them to launch. Little wonder, then, that her mother was wishful to

see her eldest daughter suitably established before
next spring.

Her conscience began to prick her as she gazed at
the half-filled trunk. Her parents had found it no easy
task to finance this enjoyable London Season. Her
mother especially had deprived herself of so much
over the years to ensure that each of her children
possessed at least a small dowry to offer a prospec-
tive husband. Was it not time for the eldest daughter
to show her appreciation by doing something in return?

She reached for the lovely gown which she had
allowed to slip through her fingers a short time before and, folding it with care, placed it neatly on top
of the other garments in the trunk.

Those perfectly matched greys which had momentarily captured Miss Robina Perceval's attention were
brought to a halt some twenty minutes later outside
a fashionable dwelling in Curzon Street. The middle-
aged groom, sitting beside his master on the seat,
willingly took charge of what he considered to be
one of the finest pair of horses he'd seen in many a
long year, and watched with a hint of pride as the
greys' highly discerning owner jumped nimbly to the
ground.

Although perhaps no longer in his first flush of
youth, his master was none the less in the same prime
physical condition as the animals he had purchased
that very morning. Tall, lean and well-muscled, Lord
Exmouth was still a fine figure of a man who, most
people considered, was at last beginning to show def-

inite signs of recovering from the tragic blow life had dealt him.

But there were those who knew better. There were those who knew the truth of it all and whose respect and devotion continued to hold them mute, Kendall mused, watching his master disappear inside the house.

Another prominent member of this touching band of loyal retainers was in the hall, ready to relieve his lordship of his hat and gloves. 'Her ladyship's compliments, my lord, and could you possibly spare her a few minutes of your time before incarcerating yourself away in your library.' The butler permitted himself a thin smile. 'Her ladyship's words, sir, not mine.'

'Where is the Dowager? Not still abed, I trust?'

'No, my lord. But still in her bedchamber, supervising the—er—packing of her trunks, I believe.'

White, even teeth flashed in a sportive smile. 'I didn't suppose for a moment, Stebbings, that she was undertaking the task herself,' his lordship responded and, swiftly mounting the stairs, did not notice the butler's slightly stooping shoulders shaking in appreciative laughter.

Her ladyship, now well into middle age, was not renowned for exerting herself unduly, not if she could possibly avoid it. So it came as no great surprise to her lean, athletic son to discover her prostrate on the *chaise longue*, one podgy, beringed hand poised over the open box of sweetmeats too conveniently positioned nearby.

She paused before reducing the box's contents further to turn her head to see who had entered her room. 'Daniel, darling!' She greeted him with every evidence of delight, proffering one soft pink cheek upon which he might place a chaste salute, and then waiting for him to oblige her. 'I was informed you went out bright and early this morning. I sincerely trust you didn't forgo breakfast.'

'No, ma'am. You will be pleased to learn my appetite remains hale and hearty.'

'Yes, you do take after your dear papa in that, as in so many other things. He was not one to pick at his food, and yet he never seemed to put on an ounce of superfluous fat.' Her sigh was distinctly mournful. 'And yet here am I, eat like a bird, and have a girth like a Shetland pony!'

'Mmm, I wonder why?' his lordship murmured, casting a brief glance at the half-empty box at her elbow, before lowering his tall, lean frame, the envy of many of his friends, and much admired by more than one discerning female, into the chair nearby.

'You wished to see me, Mama?' he reminded her.

'Did I?' She looked decidedly vague, but as her son knew very well the Dowager's appearance was deceptive. She might have grown quite indolent in recent years, rarely bestirring herself if she could possibly avoid it, but little escaped the notice of those dreamy brown eyes. 'Ah, yes! It was only to remind you that the trunks are being sent on ahead today. We don't wish to be burdened with piles and piles of luggage when we set forth on Friday.'

'I believe Penn has seen to everything in his usual efficient way.'

'What a treasure that valet of yours is, Daniel! Just like my own dear Pinner.' She turned to the birdlike female, busily occupied in folding clothes into a size-able trunk, and gave the faintest nod of dismissal.

'I trust you are looking forward to the forthcoming sojourn in Brighton, dear?' she continued the instant they were alone. 'And quite content to bear your fee-ble old mama company for several more weeks? I must confess I have thoroughly enjoyed our time to-gether here in London.'

His lordship's eyes, so very like his mother's in both colour and shape, held a distinctly sardonic gleam. 'You are neither feeble-minded nor old, my dear. And neither am I a moonling. So you can stop trying to hoodwink me, and voice the question which is quivering on the tip of that occasionally ungov-ernable tongue of yours! Which is, of course, am I looking forward to furthering my acquaintance with Miss Perceval. The answer to which is…yes.'

His mother's gurgle of appreciative laughter was infectious, and his lordship found it impossible not to smile. 'Possibly just as well that I am anticipating a pleasant time by the sea, since Montague Merrell, together with half my acquaintance, is firmly con-vinced that the Reverend's delightful daughter would make me an ideal wife.'

'And so she would!' her ladyship agreed, not re-luctant to add her voice to those which in recent weeks had urged the personable Baron to consider seriously taking the matrimonial plunge once again. 'She is without doubt the sweetest-natured gel you could ever wish to meet.'

'I wouldn't argue with that,' he agreed amicably.

'She is compliant and dutiful. She would never interfere with your pleasures, or cause you the least concern.'

'I should wish to know her a little better before voicing an opinion on certain aspects of her character.' He took a moment to study the nails on his left hand. 'I strongly suspect that Miss Robina Perceval possesses rather more spirit than most people realise.'

Her ladyship was inclined to take this as a criticism, but was not one hundred per cent sure that it was. Her son was one of those irritating people who always managed to conceal what they were thinking and feeling remarkably well. A disturbing possibility, and one which had never occurred to her before, did suddenly pass through her mind, however. 'I hope, my dear,' she said gently, 'that you were not hoping to find a second Clarissa. You never would, you know.'

His lordship regarded her in silence for a moment, his expression inscrutable, then he swiftly rose to his feet and went across to stand before the window, his body straight, but not noticeably tense.

'I realise that,' he said at length, his voice level and, like his expression, giving absolutely nothing away. 'Clarissa was undoubtedly a rare creature. I have yet to meet her equal in beauty… And I doubt I ever shall.'

Her ladyship, masterfully suppressing the threat of tears, looked across the room at him, at a loss to know quite how to respond. Not once since the tragedy occurred had he attempted to talk about the accident, at least not to her, and on the few occasions Clarissa's name had been mentioned she had watched him withdraw within himself, shrouding himself in his own private gloom.

'Do not look so stricken, my dear,' he advised gently, turning in time to catch that unmistakable expression, that look he had seen flit over scores of faces during these past months. 'I didn't come to London with the intention of searching for a mirror image of my dead wife. I came for the sole purpose of finding someone who would happily take care of my daughters, be kind to them and yes, I suppose, take the place of their dead mama.'

If this admission was supposed to relieve the Dowager's mind, it fell far short of the mark. 'I had hoped, Daniel, that you might have taken account of your own feelings in the matter, and not just your daughters' needs. Do you feel nothing for Miss Perceval at all?'

He was silent for so long that she thought he would refuse to satisfy her curiosity, but then he said, 'I think Robina Perceval is one of the most charming, good-natured and innately honest people I have ever met. I would feel a great deal easier in my mind, however, if I thought she really did wish to spend the summer with us in Brighton?'

'Daniel, whatever do you mean?'

She looked so utterly bewildered that it was as much as he could do not to laugh outright. 'Mama, I have always had the utmost respect for your acute understanding, but I must confess there have been occasions when you have allowed preconceived notions to cloud your judgement.'

'But—but...' The Dowager was momentarily lost for words. 'I'm sure you are wrong, Daniel. The dear child simply jumped at the opportunity to bear me company when I first asked her.'

'I do not doubt for a moment that she did, ma'am,' he concurred. 'It took me a short time only to discover that, although Miss Perceval possesses an innately charming reserve, she is by no means averse to socialising and has attained a great deal of pleasure during her time in London. Therefore it is quite natural that she would wish to continue the period of frivolous enjoyment if the opportunity arose. What appears to have escaped you completely, however, is the slight constraint in her which has been quite apparent to me since her return from Hampshire.'

The Dowager had not observed this. Which was extremely remiss of her, she decided, for she didn't doubt for a moment that her son, discerning demon that he was, had spoken no less than the truth. 'I wonder what could have occurred to make her have second thoughts about accompanying us?'

The look he cast her was more than faintly sardonic. 'Come, come, ma'am, isn't it obvious? Something or someone has made her realise what your real motive was for asking her in the first place.'

'How thoughtless some people are! And just when things were progressing so nicely too!' She looked as annoyed as it was possible for someone with her naturally amicable disposition to appear. 'Why must people interfere, Daniel?'

'Strangely enough, Mama, I have been asking my-self that selfsame question during these past weeks,' he murmured, casting her a smile which managed to convey both loving affection and exasperation in equal measures. 'The damage has been done, how-ever. She now knows what fate both you and her own mother have in store for her.'

'Daniel, that simply is not true!' She managed to hold his openly sardonic gaze for all of ten seconds before she made a great play of rearranging her shawl. 'I admit I may possibly have mentioned in passing that, now your official period of mourning had come to an end, you might be considering a sec-ond marriage.'

He raised his eyes heavenwards. 'You do surprise me!'

'And Lady Elizabeth may possibly have remarked on the fact that her eldest daughter, clearly betraying all the signs of truly motherly instincts, was unfail-ingly patient with her younger sisters,' she continued, just as though he had not spoken. 'But I assure you, Daniel, that I never suggested for a moment that I thought she would make an ideal wife for you. I would never dream of doing such a thing! You are far too much like your dear father. You are always willing to listen to someone else's viewpoint, but will make your own decision in the end.'

'I'm pleased you appreciate that at last, Mama, because it makes what I have to say to you now a great deal easier.' Although he was still faintly smil-ing, there was no mistaking the note of hard deter-mination edging his deep, attractive voice. 'I was quite willing for you to cajole me into accompanying you to Brighton, even though I knew from the first your real motive for doing so... No, kindly allow me to finish,' he continued, holding up a restraining hand when she was about to interrupt. 'I wish to further my acquaintance with Miss Perceval, as I've already mentioned. She intrigues me. I believe there is much more to that young lady than either you or I realise. One thing I'm firmly convinced of, however, is that she had no thought of becoming the future Lady Exmouth until some well-meaning individual pointed out to her that that might well be the fate which awaits her. She may yet come to welcome that eventuality with open arms, but I am resolved that it shall be her decision, and not yours or her mother's... Now, do I make myself clear, my dear?'

'Perfectly, Daniel. You wish me to sit back, and allow nature to take its course.'

'Precisely!'

The Dowager once again turned her attention to the tempting delicacies in the pretty box at her elbow. 'Very well, Daniel. You may woo Miss Robina Perceval in your own way, and without any interference from me.'

Narrow-eyed, Daniel watched a gooey confection disappear between smugly smiling pink lips. For some obscure reason he was not totally convinced that she would be able to keep that promise.

# Chapter Two

Leaning back against the comfort of the velvet squabs, Lady Exmouth stared through the carriage window at the passing countryside, recalling quite clearly a time in the not too distant past when the road to Brighton had been little more than an uncertain track, frequently impassable. All that had changed, of course, once the Regent had discovered that the air at the small, insignificant resort tended to benefit his health. Now Brighton was a centre of fashion, and could be reached by many different routes, one of which was considered by many to be the finest posting road in England.

Her ladyship had happily left all the travel arrangements, and choice of route, in the hands of her very capable son. Since the age of one-and-twenty, when he had come into the title, Daniel had displayed a natural aptitude for organisation, and a keen sense of responsibility far beyond his years. Little wonder, the Dowager reflected, that only a very small number of people had voiced certain doubts when, just two years after his father's demise, he had calmly announced his intention of marrying his childhood sweetheart.

What a beautiful creature dear Clarissa had been! her ladyship mused, her mind's eye having little difficulty in conjuring up a clear image of limpid blue eyes set to perfection in that lovely heart-shaped face, the whole framed in a riot of the prettiest guinea-gold curls.

The only child of an impoverished country squire, Clarissa would undoubtedly have become the toast of any Season had her father ever been in a position to finance such a venture. From the age of sixteen she had had most every eligible young bachelor in the county dangling after her at one time or another. Yet she had remained touchingly devoted to the only son of her nearest neighbours. They had seemed such an ideal couple, perfectly suited in every way. When little Hannah had been born, within a year of their marriage, their happiness had seemed complete.

It had been shortly after the birth of her first grand-child, the Dowager clearly recalled, that she had first broached the subject of her making her home in Bath. It was most touching, of course, that neither her son nor daughter-in-law would hear of such a thing, so she had remained at Courtney Place until after the birth of their second child three years later. Then no amount of entreaties had persuaded her to remain in the beautiful ancestral home, where in many ways she had continued to feel as though she was still its mistress.

She had never experienced any regrets in the choice she had made. Bath suited her very well. She had made many friends there, and was looking forward to the day when she could return to her comfortable house in Camden Place.

Much depended, of course, on how matters progressed during these next few weeks in Brighton, for she had no intention of allowing her son to return to the ancestral pile alone, once the summer was over, to continue brooding over the loss of his lovely Clarissa. If this meant that she must delay her return to the West Country to bear him company, then so be it! She could not help hoping, though, that matters would resolve themselves in a far more satisfactory manner, and that her son would soon be sharing his lovely home with quite a different lady.

Drawing her eyes away from the pleasing landscape, her ladyship darted a glance at the only other occupant of the well-sprung travelling carriage to discover her companion sitting quietly staring out of the other window, seemingly lost in a world of her own.

Daniel, the astute demon, had not been wrong when he had suggested that something had occurred to disturb the normally very calm waters of Miss Robina Perceval's mind. Something most definitely had! If, as Daniel himself suspected, the vicar's daughter was not at all sure that she wished to cement an alliance with the noble Courtney family, then it would, indeed, be most unfair to bring pressure to bear upon the dear girl during the forthcoming weeks to do just that.

It was so difficult to know how best to proceed in a situation such as this, her ladyship decided, absently running a finger back and forth across a faint crease in her skirts. She had no real desire to interfere in such a delicate and personal matter, while at the same time she had no intention of allowing her only child to dwindle into middle age a lonely and grieving man, when at hand was the very being who could bring great contentment back into his life, even if she failed to make him perfectly happy.

It wasn't as if she was foolish enough to suppose for a moment that Miss Robina Perceval could ever take the place of the beautiful Clarissa in Daniel's eyes. That would be hoping for far too much! There was no denying, though, that he had perceived something in the vicar's daughter that appealed to him, for she was the only female he had displayed the least interest in throughout his entire sojourn in the capital.

She cast a further glance across the carriage to the opposite corner. Only this time she discovered that she was being observed in turn by a pair of blue eyes which, although of a similar hue, betrayed a deal more intelligence than the late Baroness Exmouth's had ever done.

'I was beginning to think you'd fallen asleep,' her ladyship remarked for want of something better to say. 'So quiet had you become.'

'Oh, no, my lady. Merely lost in admiration for

this part of the country. I've never travelled this far
south before, so everything is new and interesting.'

Although the poor girl might be experiencing
grave doubts about this forthcoming sojourn in
Brighton, it was quite evident that she was not prepared to brood about it to the extent that she became
taciturn, the Dowager thought, mentally adding a further tick to that long column of Miss Robina
Perceval's excellent qualities.

'I can recall a time, my dear child, not so very
long ago, when many abandoned their attempts to
reach the small fishing village, which Brighton used
to be not so very long ago. Much is said these days
to the Regent's discredit, but if he had not purchased
his "little farmhouse" on the coast, I very much fear
that this and many other roads in this part of the
country would have remained those frequently impassable tracks, full of potholes and littered with
abandoned carriages.'

Evidently the vicar's eldest daughter was much
struck by this viewpoint, for her pretty face wore a
very thoughtful expression, as it so often did when
she was turning something over in her mind.

'Yes, one tends to forget that not so very long ago
travelling about the country was something of a dangerous undertaking, and that journeys that used to
take very many hours are now completed in a fraction of the time.'

'And in far greater comfort, too!' her ladyship assured her. 'Carriages are so well sprung nowadays,

and there are always plenty of hostelries *en route* where one can refresh oneself.'

As if on cue the carriage turned off the post road a moment later and came to a halt in the forecourt of a very superior posting-house. The door was thrown wide, the steps were let down, and his lordship stood, hand held out, ready and appearing very willing, to assist them to alight.

'Why is it, Mama,' he remarked, guiding them into the inn, 'that two ladies can travel the same distance, in the very same conveyance, and yet one can look none the worse for her ordeal whilst the other resembles nothing so much as a ruffled hen which has spent much of the day ineffectually flapping about a farmyard?'

'Odious boy! No need to enquire which of us in your opinion needs to set her appearance to rights, I suppose.' The Dowager tried to appear affronted but failed miserably. 'Where may this overheated hen refresh herself?'

His lordship beckoned to a serving-maid, and Robina, having somehow managed to keep her countenance, accompanied her ladyship into one of the upstairs chambers to effect the necessary repairs to her own appearance.

It was by no means the first time she had heard Daniel utter some provocative remark. Her ladyship never failed to take her son's teasing in good part, and Robina couldn't help but feel a little envious of the special bond which existed between mother and son. She would never have dreamt of saying such things to either of her parents, especially not to her mother, who, unlike the Dowager, did not possess much of a sense of humour.

That was perhaps why she liked her ladyship so much. Lady Exmouth was such an easy-going soul, fun-loving yet in no way light-minded, though she tried, Robina had frequently suspected, to give the impression that she was a trifle featherbrained.

They had got on famously from the first, and Robina did not doubt that she would have derived much pleasure from the Dowager's delightful company during the forthcoming weeks, had it not been for the fact that that dear lady would be bitterly disappointed if, by the end of their stay in Brighton, her son's engagement to the Vicar of Abbot Quincey's daughter had not been announced.

She ought to feel flattered, she supposed, that the Dowager's son had taken such an interest in her, and maybe she would have been if she thought for a moment that she had succeeded in capturing his heart. But she flatly refused to delude herself. There was little hope of her, or anyone else for that matter, ever taking the place of his late wife.

After removing her bonnet, she took a moment to study her reflection in the glass as she tidied an errant curl. She was well enough, she supposed. At least she had been assured that she was pretty enough to turn heads, but that did not make her a beauty. Yet, there had been beauties enough gracing the Season that year, she reminded herself, her friend Sophia Cleeve to name but one. So wasn't it rather odd that

Lord Exmouth had displayed precious little interest in any one of them if he was indeed the connoisseur of beauty he was reputed to be?

'Something appears to be troubling you, child?'

Jolted out of her puzzling reflections, Robina discovered that she was the focal point of a deceptively dreamy brown-eyed gaze. 'Er—no, not really, my lady. I was just thinking of certain persons I had seen during the recent Season in London, and was wondering how many would be following our example by removing to Brighton.'

Robina salved her conscience by telling herself that it was not a complete lie, and fortunately the Dowager seemed to accept the explanation readily enough.

'A great many, I shouldn't wonder. Certainly the Carlton House set, one of whom, as you probably know, is none other than my son's particular friend, Montague Merrell. We'll ask Daniel who is likely to be paying a visit to the town, should we? No doubt he'll enlighten us.'

This, however, he seemed unable, or disinclined, to do, when they joined him a few minutes later in a private parlour. He merely shrugged, saying, 'You know I'm not one of the Regent's cronies, Mama. And I cannot say that I'm in the least interested in who'll be trailing after him this summer.'

'For a young man who has been considered one of the *ton's* most fashionable members all his adult life, you display precious little interest in what goes on in polite society,' his mother remarked, casting an approving glance over the delicious fare awaiting her on the table.

Daniel was not slow to observe the rapacious gleam in those dark eyes, and obliged her by pulling out one of the chairs. As far as he could recall his mother had always been blessed with a healthy appetite. Which was no very bad thing, he didn't suppose, so long as one did not permit food to become a ruling passion.

He had not been slow to note, either, that Miss Perceval had not opened that immensely kissable mouth of hers since entering the room; had noticed too that she appeared increasingly ill-at-ease in his company these days. A decidedly sorry state of affairs which must be rectified without delay!

'Permit me to help you to a slice or two of chicken, Miss Perceval.' He did so without offering her the opportunity to refuse. 'You must be hungry after spending so many hours in a carriage. Travelling any great distance often makes one feel peckish.'

'It certainly has that effect on me,' the Dowager put in.

'That goes without saying, Mama.'

'Rude boy!' she admonished good-humouredly. 'Your dear papa did not beat you enough when you were a child.'

Daniel noticed that sweet, spontaneous smile, hurriedly suppressed, at the foolish banter, and was fairly sure that it would be no hard matter to restore the delectable Robina to her former composed state. Perhaps it might even be possible to achieve a closer bond between them before the day was out, he decided, swiftly setting himself a new goal.

'I dare say you are right, Mama. However, permit me to point out that there is a delicious game pie lurking by your right elbow which appears to have escaped your notice.'

'Thank you, my dear.' A flicker of a knowing smile hovered around her ladyship's mouth, clearly betraying to her son that she knew precisely what he was about. It appeared to be having the required effect too, for their guest began to help herself to the various tempting dishes on offer without the least prompting.

'I must say, my dear boy, you have surpassed yourself. This is a most marvellous repast you have ordered, catering for all tastes.'

'Nothing whatever to do with me,' he surprised them both by admitting. 'If you wish to express your appreciation, then thank Kendall. He was the one who bespoke this late luncheon to be served in a private parlour when he arranged for the stabling of my greys here two days ago.'

'Have we very much farther to travel, my lord?' Robina enquired, deciding that it was high time she added something to the conversation.

'There's about an hour's journey ahead of us, certainly no more. My latest acquisitions will accomplish it easily.'

'You are delighted with your greys, are you not, my son?'

'Exceedingly, ma'am!' he concurred, looking extremely pleased with himself. 'It was very gratifying to pip no less a personage than a duke to the post in purchasing them. I was reliably informed that Sharnbrook was more than a little interested,' he informed them in response to their enquiring glances, 'but he delayed too long. Possibly had more important things on his mind, like his engagement to Miss Perceval's friend, for instance.'

'Now that rather insignificant affair surprised me,' her ladyship remarked. 'I do not understand at all why they held such a small party at Sharnbrook to celebrate the event. After all, the Duke is reputed to be one of the richest men in England. It's not as if he couldn't afford a large affair. Your friend's papa too, Robina, is held to be very plump in the pocket, so I fail to understand why the engagement wasn't celebrated more lavishly.'

'It was what Sophia and Benedict both wanted,' Robina divulged. 'I know it was only a small party, but it was a most enjoyable occasion none the less.'

'I'm all in favour of keeping these highly personal celebrations as small and informal as possible,' his lordship announced, surprising his mother somewhat. 'I could almost feel guilty now at depriving Sharnbrook of those superb greys. I should imagine we have much in common. Just because one happens to be comfortably circumstanced does not mean that one needs to make a vulgar display of the fact.'

'You do surprise me, my son. You insisted that half the county be invited to the party celebrating your engagement to Clarissa.'

The Dowager had spoken without thinking, and cursed herself silently for every kind of a fool. She had rarely mentioned her late daughter-in-law's name when in public, and never in front of the young woman who now sat silently at the table and who appeared totally absorbed in devouring the food on her plate.

'Very true, Mama,' his lordship responded, swiftly breaking the ensuing silence, and betraying no visible signs of distress at touching on such a poignant subject. 'But a person's taste can change over the years. 'I would at one time never have considered driving myself above a few miles in an open carriage, but have very much enjoyed the experiences of this day.'

His dark eyes flickered momentarily in Robina's direction. 'Perhaps I can persuade you, Miss Perceval, to bear me company for what remains of the journey. You might find travelling in the fresh air a more pleasurable way of completing the journey. Added to which, it will permit her ladyship to close her eyes, as is her custom in the afternoons, without appearing rude.'

Robina hesitated, but only for a moment. There was no earthly way that she was going to be able to avoid his lordship's company for any appreciable lengths of time during the forthcoming weeks, so she might as well be sensible and accustom herself to his presence at the outset.

'Yes, my lord, I think a spell in the fresh air would be most welcome.' She cast him a smile which somehow managed to display both a hint of shyness and a touch of roguery. 'I might end looking slightly windswept, but at least I hope I shall avoid resembling some demented hen.'

His deep rumble of appreciative laughter succeeded in putting her at her ease to such an extent that when, a short while later, she was seated beside him in the curricle, she was more than content to be in his company, and not in the least nervous over placing her well-being in the hands of a man who had, reputedly through the dangerous tooling of a carriage, succeeded in killing his beloved wife.

It was only, after happily following the comfortable vehicle containing his mother for a mile or so, when his lordship unexpectedly turned off the main post road and on to a much narrower lane, bringing the spirited greys to a halt beneath the shade of some roadside trees, that she began to experience those stabs of blind panic which had plagued her from time to time during recent days.

'Miss Perceval, I had a particular reason for wishing you to bear me company for the remainder of the journey,' he announced, staring straight ahead down the deserted road, while with little effort, it seemed, masterfully controlling his spirited horses. 'If my mother performs her duties as your chaperon conscientiously, there ought not to be too many occasions when we find ourselves quite alone together, and there is something I particularly wished to say to you before we embark on what I hope will be a most enjoyable stay for us both in Brighton.'

If Robina had not felt as if she were being slowly

throttled she would quite happily have betrayed her feelings by giving vent to a loud and protracted groan. She had forced herself to come to terms with the fact that sooner or later the subject of a marriage between them would be raised, but she had hoped that the occasion would arise later rather than sooner, thereby permitting her to enjoy a brief period in Brighton without encumbrance. His lordship began speaking again, and she forced herself to listen.

'We both know why our respective mothers wished us to spend the summer together. They are both hoping that I shall—to resort to the modern-day vulgar parlance—come up to scratch. Well, let me assure you, Miss Perceval, that at this present moment in time I have not the slightest intention of making you an offer of marriage.'

Turning his head, Daniel discovered a look of such utter bewilderment on her sweet face that he was forced to exert every ounce of control he possessed not to take her into his arms and totally confound her by kissing her breathless.

'You look slightly stunned, Miss Perceval.' An understatement if ever there was one. The poor girl looked as if she were about to swoon! 'I'm sorry if my plain speaking has offended you.'

'Er—no, not at all, sir,' she responded so softly that he had a little difficulty in catching the words.

'But I think we would rub along much more comfortably if we cleared up one or two matters at the outset.' Again he was forced to exert the utmost control, only this time to stop himself from laughing.

She was regarding him much as defenceless rabbit might a snake which was about to strike for a second time. 'I think you must realise, Miss Perceval, that I have grown quite partial to your company during our time in London. I should like to think that we have become…friends.'

'Er—yes,' she responded guardedly.

'And as such, I think we can be honest with each other without causing offence.'

'It—er—would be nice to think we could, certainly,' she agreed, in a voice that was growing progressively stronger, though remaining slightly wary at the same time.

'As you may have gathered by now, my darling mother, together with most of my friends, has decided that it is high time I consider a second marriage.'

No response was forthcoming this time, so he continued undeterred. 'It seems that most are in agreement that you would make me the ideal wife.'

Again there was no response.

'They may possibly be correct, but I reserve the right to decide for myself. Just as I believe that you deserve the chance to make up your mind about me, without the least pressure being brought to bear upon you. That could be difficult in the present circumstances, with a certain person watching our every move, waiting with bated breath for us to announce our betrothal, unless we both work together to turn the situation in which we now find ourselves to our mutual advantage.'

She appeared merely bewildered now as she said, 'And how do you propose that we do that, my lord?'

'Simply by just being ourselves, and doing precisely what we wish to do. It would be foolish to attempt to avoid one another, as we'll be residing in the same house, don't you agree?'

'Most assuredly.'

'So what I suggest is that we keep the world guessing by being seen in each other's company quite frequently, while at the same time not denying ourselves the pleasure of other people's.' He continued to hold her full attention. 'Then, if by the end of the summer, when we have come to know each other a good deal better, we both decide that we should suit, all well and good, and if not...'

He reached for one of her hands and felt those slender, tapering fingers momentarily tremble in his clasp. 'Either way, child, I want the decision to be ours, yours and mine. Not your mother's, or mine, or anyone else's, understand?'

It took a monumental effort, but Robina forced herself to meet his concerned and kindly gaze, and made a rather startling discovery. His eyes were not just a deep, warm brown but were flecked rather attractively with gold.

'Yes, my lord, I do understand... And—and thank you,' she said softly, blissfully ignorant of the fact that it had cost him dearly to suggest what he had, that the last thing in the world he had wanted was to release her from any obligations she might feel to marry him.

'For what, silly child?' His expressive brows rose. 'For suggesting something that will benefit us both? Well, if you wish to show your appreciation, you can kindly stop calling me my lord. My name is Daniel.'

'Oh, I couldn't possibly address you like that, sir!' She was genuinely shocked. 'Mama would never approve.'

'I'm not particularly interested whether she would or not,' he returned bluntly. 'You'll be residing under my roof for the next few weeks, my girl, so you'll do what I tell you, especially if you know what's good for you.'

She gave an uncertain laugh. By repute he was a kind-hearted, considerate man, and yet some inner feminine wisdom warned her that there might be a less agreeable side to him if he was ever crossed. She had already discovered that he was not afraid to speak his mind, and couldn't help wondering what other interesting facets to his character would emerge before this day was out.

'Very well, little bird, we'll compromise. When in private I insist you call me Daniel, and when in public you may call me what ever you like...' white teeth flashed in a playful smile '...providing it is polite, of course.'

Giving the little hand a last reassuring squeeze, Daniel turned his attention back to the greys. 'We had better catch up with my darling mama, otherwise she might imagine we've eloped.'

'Oh, how excessively romantic!' Robina exclaimed without thinking, and then turned a glowing crimson when she discovered herself on the receiving end of a startled glance.

'Excessively uncomfortable, I would have thought,' he contradicted, slowing his team down as they approached a busy little village, 'especially if undertaken in an equipage such as this one, and it should come on to rain.'

'People in love would not consider such a mundane thing as the weather, if they were considering running away together,' she pointed out, rather enjoying his teasing banter, and liking too the way his eyes were brightened by that wickedly provocative glint.

'I should,' he argued, 'but then I'm a practical sort of person, not given to mad starts. Besides which, having attained the great age of almost six-and-thirty, I enjoy my creature comforts and am far too old to go careering about the country. So I can tell you now, I shall never consider eloping with you.'

'In that case, I think you were very wise to have second thoughts about making me an offer,' she informed him quite deliberately, knowing that even half an hour ago she would never have considered saying such a thing to him. Now, however, she felt as if a very close friendship was on the verge of springing up between them. 'It is quite evident to me at least that we would not have suited. I should very much like a gentleman to go careering about the country with me.'

'I never said that I had had second thoughts about

making you an offer, my girl,' he corrected. 'I merely said— What the devil!'

For a moment Robina was startled, then she saw it too—a great brute of a man beating a donkey with a stout stick, and very much appearing as if he was enjoying the exercise, while a woman, with two children frantically clutching at the folds of her skirts, was alternately shouting and pleading with him to stop.

Without a second thought Robina accepted the reins Daniel tossed into her hands, and then watched him stalk across the road. Easily capturing the stick, he proceeded to lay it about the bully's shoulders before calmly knocking him to the ground with one superbly aimed blow to the jaw.

She was a little too far away to hear clearly what was being said, but a great deal of gesticulating, and swearing, she suspected, especially on the part of the felled bully, followed as Daniel calmly took something from inside his right boot. A moment later the pile of pots and pans which had been tied to the donkey's back fell to the ground with a clatter, and a further heated altercation between the man and the woman ensued, before Daniel stepped into the breach once again.

Robina was only vaguely aware of what followed, for her attention was taken up with calming the greys, which had taken exception to the noise of the pots and pans clattering on the road. By the time she had them well under control again, the unkempt rogue was trudging off up the village street, carrying his wares on his own back, the two children, no longer sobbing, were leading the donkey into a paddock, and Daniel was accompanying the woman into a charming thatched cottage.

He reappeared a few minutes later, the woman at his heels this time, desperately striving to keep up with his long-striding gait, while attempting to offer her grateful thanks.

'Not at all, my good woman. Only too pleased to be of assistance,' Robina heard him say, before he doffed his hat, and came hurriedly across the road towards her.

'My dear girl, I cannot apologise enough!' There was an unmistakable flicker of concern in his eyes as he clambered up on the seat and relieved her of the reins. 'What on earth must you think of me, deserting you in such a fashion! I sincerely trust you weren't too nervous at being left in charge of the greys?'

'Not at all,' she assured him. 'I frequently tool Papa's one-horse gig when at home.' She caught the slight twitch at the corner of his mouth, but didn't attempt to enquire precisely what he had found so amusing, and merely asked for an account of what had taken place.

'You saw what happened, I am ashamed to say, but there was little I could do to avoid your witnessing that unfortunate encounter.' He gave the greys the office to start, once again handling the spirited pair with effortless ease. 'I am not accounted a violent man, and yet I would be the first to admit that I

have an almost pathological hatred for persons who
inflict needless cruelty. It wasn't sufficient for that
oaf to pass by the gate of the donkey's former, caring
owners each day, he must needs stop to torment those
children further by abusing a creature that they both love,
and had looked upon as a pet.'

'How dreadful! I'm very glad we happened along.
And now the donkey, I assume, has been restored to
its former owners.'

'Not quite.' His smile was decidedly rueful. 'He
now belongs to me. I decided, all things considered,
that it would be for the best.'

Robina managed to keep her countenance, but it
was an effort. It was quite evident that he wasn't
precisely enthusiastic over this latest acquisition, and
she could not resist the temptation to tease him a
little.

'I have observed during my weeks in London that
it is not unusual for a gentleman of—how shall I
phrase it?—an eccentric nature to indulge in rather
queer starts from time to time. I suppose you suddenly discovered that you had need of a beast of
burden?'

'I am beginning to discover that there is a strong
teasing element in your nature, my girl!' The swift,
narrow-eyed glance he cast her managed to betray
both amusement and faint exasperation. 'No, you
provoking little baggage! I did not suddenly take it
into my head that I wished to own such a creature.
And if you dare to tell another living soul, you'll

regret it! I would become a laughing-stock, and the talk of the clubs for weeks!'

She did not suppose for a moment that he would care a jot what the world at large said or thought about him, but she gave her solemn promise none the less, before demanding to know why he had taken it upon himself to make such an odd purchase.

'Because I discovered that it was in fact that poor woman's idle husband who sold the beast, before calmly going off and leaving her and their children to fend for themselves. She hasn't seen him since and doesn't expect to. There is, however, always the chance that he'll turn up again, like the proverbial bad penny, and repeat the procedure, leaving her without the means to transport her goods to market, and depriving the children of their pet. So to overcome this possibility, I have given her a letter which states that, on condition she takes good care of the animal, she has my full permission, as its owner, to use the donkey to transport her goods to the local market, but on no account must my property be sold without my written consent.'

How exceedingly kind and considerate he was! Robina decided, as they rejoined the post road and she caught sight of her ladyship's carriage in the distance. He had been generous to three perfect strangers and no less generous towards her.

By demanding only friendship, he had now made it possible for her to enjoy the weeks ahead without fear that at the end of her stay she would be asked for recompense.

So why then, she wondered, a frown of puzzlement creasing her brow, wasn't she feeling deliriously happy at this precise moment? Furthermore, why had she suddenly developed this peculiar hollow feeling deep inside?

# Chapter Three

Robina, still very much enjoying the novel experience of having her hair expertly dressed each day by Lady Exmouth's skilful abigail, sat quietly before the dressing-table mirror, contemplating yet again how much her life had changed since she had left rural Northamptonshire behind her on that cold day in early March.

For a simple country girl, accustomed to comfort rather than luxury, and to lengthy periods of solitude, given to quiet reflection, or the pursuit of some useful occupation whereby she might be of some benefit to her fellow man, it was quite surprising the ease with which she had conformed to a hectic and purely social life, where the pursuit of personal pleasure was the only thing that need concern her to any degree. Her mother's presence, understandably, had been a steadying influence during those heady weeks in London. Since her arrival in Brighton no restrictions had been placed upon her whatsoever. In fact, not to put too fine a point on it, she was being thoroughly

spoilt by the darling Dowager and her no less considerate son. And she was shamefully loving every
moment of it!

'It's simply no good at all. It must stop!' she announced, with as much determination as she could
muster, and without really realising that she had spoken her guilty thoughts aloud until she happened to
glance up and noticed the middle-aged abigail's
slightly puzzled expression in the dressing-table mirror.

'What's the matter, miss? Don't you care for this
style any longer? We can always try something different if you'd prefer.'

'I have no fault to find with the way you dress my
hair, Pinner,' Robina hurriedly assured her.

'Well, that's a blessing, miss!' One could almost
sense that the highly skilled and conscientious servant was suppressing a sigh of relief. 'For one dreadful moment there I thought you were going to ask
me to cut it. And that I would never willingly do,'
she announced, easing the brush almost reverently
through the long shiny dark strands. 'Beautiful, it is,
and a sheer delight to dress, miss, just like the rest
of you. There aren't too many blessed with such a
perfect figure as yours. You're an abigail's dream,
Miss Robina, so you are! You'd look wonderfully
turned out in a scullery-maid's apron!'

'You're the one who deserves the credit, not I,'
Robina countered, desperately striving not to allow
this fulsome praise go to her head.

As her father, the Reverend William Perceval, had

always considered vanity amongst the very worst of
sins, compliments were rarely uttered back at the
vicarage in Abbot Quincey, and yet Robina, who had
been taught to consider inner beauty far more meaningful than any shallow outward trappings, could not
help but feel gratified by the compliment.

'It is no good, Pinner,' she announced, rising to
her feet when the last curls had been carefully pinned
into place. 'I must face the fact that, unless I begin
to exert a deal of self-control, I stand in the gravest
danger of becoming thoroughly corrupted whilst I
continue to reside under this roof. Why, I shall be of
no earthly use to man or beast when the time comes
for me to return to Abbot Quincey! I never used to
think twice about mending a tear in a gown, or dress-
ing my own hair. Now I wouldn't even contemplate
doing such a thing, and am more than content to sit
back and allow others to do everything for me.
Thoroughly indulged, I am, and loving it! What
would dear Papa say?'

It was all very well to make light of it, Robina
decided, as the bedchamber resounded with Pinner's
highly amused chuckles, but really it was no laughing matter. She had adapted to this life of ease, this
life of pure self-indulgence, as though she had been
born to it, which of course was far from the truth.
Although life at the vicarage could never have been
described as one of drudgery, she had been expected
to undertake a variety of light duties, which had included a certain amount of time given to the entertainment of her three younger sisters, ensuring that

they didn't get into mischief by setting a good example herself.

And a fine example she would set for them now!
she mused, unable to suppress a rueful half-smile.
There was no denying that the highly complaisant
and faintly indolent Dowager was an appalling influence. To be fair, though, she ought to accept the
lion's share of the blame herself for not displaying
more strength of character and halting her meteoric
descent into that wicked pit of dissipation. On the
other hand, it had to be said in her own defence that
she had been battling against tremendous odds during
these past days. Why, even his lordship had actively
encouraged her to do precisely as she wished!

Although Daniel had made his feelings on the matter perfectly clear at the outset by announcing that
friendship was all he demanded from her at this present moment in time, since their arrival in Brighton
he had been unfailingly thoughtful, touchingly attentive to her every possible need.

She paused as she reached the bottom of the stairs,
and stared thoughtfully in the direction of the breakfast-parlour door, unaware that her expression had
been softened by a quite spontaneous, tender little
smile.

She found it hard to believe now, but it was true
none the less that, although she had readily agreed
to the suggestion when it had first been made, she
had, surprisingly, not found it easy to look upon
Daniel merely as a friend. Which was all the more
curious because she had never found it in the least

daunting to converse with him, not even when they had first met in London.

Her father's particular calling had ensured that throughout her life she had, on a fairly regular basis, come into contact with people who had suffered recent bereavement. Consequently she had known precisely what to say to Daniel from the first, and had never experienced the least awkwardness in his presence. A slightly closer relationship had initially, she was forced to own, proved a different matter entirely, however.

Not having been blessed with any brothers had, she supposed, substantially limited her experience of the opposite sex, and although her Perceval cousins, Hugo and Lowell, had been frequent visitors to the vicarage, she had acquired precious little knowledge of the workings of the male mind from either of them. During childhood she had been inclined to look upon Hugo, some ten years her senior, as a most superior being, sophisticated, charming, and slightly unapproachable; Lowell, being some six years his brother's junior, had always seemed to her, and still did for that matter, little more than an endearing scamp, always ripe for any lark. Consequently, living under the same roof as Lord Exmouth had turned out to be something of a revelation.

Daniel, she had swiftly discovered, possessed the most wonderful sense of humour. He certainly appeared to enjoy indulging in bouts of light-hearted banter, and the frequent exchange of the swift repartee, but there was nothing of the mischievous schoolboy in his nature. Far from it, in fact! He was every inch the fashionable gentleman, accomplished and refined, and yet not remotely high in the instep. This was perhaps why she had managed eventually to dispense with those last barriers of reserve, and had come to feel so completely relaxed in his company, more so, surprisingly, than in her own father's.

No one would have supposed for a moment that Robina held her new-found friend in such high esteem when she entered the breakfast-parlour a moment later to discover him, as expected, already seated at the table; least of all Daniel himself, who was not slow to perceive the slightly troubled look in her strikingly pretty, clear blue eyes.

'What's the matter, my little bird?' Ever the polite gentleman, he rose to his feet and waited until she had slipped into the chair beside his own before resuming his repast. 'Did you have trouble sleeping last night?'

'How could I possibly have trouble sleeping, Daniel, when I have been given, I do not doubt, the most comfortable bed in the house?' Without the least show of reticence, Robina began to help herself to coffee and a delicious hot buttered roll. 'And that is precisely what concerns me. If I'm not very careful, I'm likely to be ruined by both you and your mother.'

'Now there's a tempting thought!' he muttered before he could stop himself, but fortunately she appeared not to have heard. 'How precisely have Mama and I fallen from grace?'

'You both spoil me shamefully. Yes, you do,' she reiterated when he looked about to refute this. 'You have been so kind, giving up so much of your time in order to keep me entertained. And as for your mother... Oh, Daniel! She came to my bedchamber after we had retired last night, bringing the box containing that lovely garnet necklace of hers and matching earrings.' There was no mistaking the agitation in her voice. 'She insisted on making me a present of them, and I found myself in the position whereby to have refused would have made me appear so very ungrateful. And that I assure you I am not! But she really ought not to give me such things.'

'I couldn't agree more!' he announced, surprising her somewhat, for he sounded genuinely annoyed.

'Then—then, you'll have a word with her on—on my behalf?' she ventured, fervently hoping that she would not be causing trouble between mother and son. 'Suggesting kindly, I hope, that she ought not to—to give me such things?'

'Most assuredly I shall, child. You may rely upon it,' he responded, frowning dourly as the door opened. 'And there's no time like the present,' he added as the object of his evident displeasure, joining them early for once, entered the breakfast-parlour.

'What's this I've been hearing, Mama!' he demanded the instant she had seated herself in the chair opposite. 'What do you mean by presenting Robin with that set of garnets, may I ask?'

'Why shouldn't I, dear?' the Dowager replied, betraying no obvious signs of resentment at the faintly dictatorial tone. 'They were mine to dispose of as I saw fit, and they will look much prettier displayed against young skin.' Glancing across the table, she was not slow to notice the twinkling mischief in his dark eyes. 'What is the matter, my son? Do you disapprove of my giving Robina such a gift?'

'Most assuredly! Why didn't you present her with the rubies?' Daniel almost burst out laughing as Robina's knife fell from her fingers to land on her plate with a clatter. 'I've always considered garnets trumpery gauds, as well you know.'

'Well, dear, I couldn't give her the ruby set, now could I?' the Dowager pointed out in her defence. 'They are amongst the family jewels, and are kept safely locked away at Courtney Place. Besides which, they are not mine to give.'

Ignoring the flashing look of reproach from a certain highly disgruntled quarter, Daniel leaned back in his chair, looking for all the world as if he were giving the matter due consideration. 'I do not think I would give Robin the ruby set in any case, not unless she had her heart set on them, that is. No, I would be more inclined, with her delicate colouring, to deck her out in sapphires. What do you think, Mama?'

'Oh, for heaven's sake!' Robina buried her face in her hands, not knowing whether to laugh or cry. 'I give up!'

'Yes, you may have a point there, dear,' her ladyship agreed, sublimely ignoring the muttered interruption. 'Sapphires certainly emphasise blue eyes and a fair complexion, but don't discount the rubies, my son. With that beautiful dark hair, she could carry that particular stone very well, too.'

Wickedly enjoying himself at his darling guest's expense, his lordship finished off the last mouthful on his plate before reaching for the journal conveniently placed nearby. 'By the by, Mama. Darling Robina, here, feels that we are spoiling her, and being far, far too kind. So I have decided to remedy this misconduct on our part by taking her out in the curricle this morning.'

A brief glance in Robina's direction was sufficient to inform the Dowager that the girl was as much puzzled by this pronouncement as she was herself. 'I'm evidently being foolishly obtuse, but I do not immediately perceive how jaunting about the town in an open carriage is likely to remedy the situation, my son.'

'Because yesterday, when Robin and I were strolling about the town, our attention was momentarily captured by the sight of that outrageous Lady Claudia Melrose making an exhibition of herself again by tooling a high-perched phaeton down the middle of the street. And young madam here, far from scandalised by such behaviour, was not slow to express her admiration of the dashing lady's skill, nor her wish that she too could tool a racing vehicle with such flair. So, after due consideration, I've decided to offer the benefit of my no little experience and instruct her.'

Robina, swiftly forgetting her grievances, gave

vent to a tiny squeal of delight. 'Truly, sir…? You'll teach me?'

'Yes, child, but only because it will offer me the golden opportunity of scolding you unmercifully, you understand? And woe betide you if you dare to damage my greys' delicate—'

He broke off, staring fixedly for a few moments at the article in the newspaper which had unexpectedly captured his attention, before handing the journal over to Robina, indicating the section he wished her to read by prodding the precise spot in the column with one well-manicured finger. 'Am I right in thinking that the Marquis of Sywell heralded from your neck of the woods, child?'

Her expression changing to one of incredulity, Robina swiftly apprised herself of the item of news, and then automatically turned to Daniel for corroboration. 'Heavens above! Do you suppose it can possibly be true?'

'I am on occasions very sceptical about what I read in the newspapers, most especially about what appears in the gossip columns. But I doubt very much that such a detailed account as that one would have appeared in print if it were not true.'

'What on earth has happened?' the Dowager enquired, gaining her son's attention.

'The Marquis of Sywell is dead. He was discovered by his manservant lying flat on his back on the bedchamber floor, with a razor—er—stuck in his chest. It may have been an accident of course. Sywell was, after all, a notorious drunkard who could well have tripped and fallen on the implement. The authorities, however, cannot rule out foul play.'

'No, indeed,' Robina agreed, focusing her attention on an imaginary spot on the wall opposite, wondering why she felt not the smallest degree of remorse.

Undeniably, the Marquis had been a cruel, thoroughly selfish man who had gone through life taking what he wanted, when he wanted, with no consideration whatsoever for the feelings of others. The name Sywell had become a byword for debauchery among the inhabitants of the four Abbey villages. He had been despised by many; liked by none. He had not, however, inflicted any harm on her personally, nor on any member of her immediate family, as far as she was aware. So surely she ought to feel at least a twinge of remorse, if not for his death, then at least for the manner of his passing? The truth of the matter was, though, she felt absolutely nothing at all, and was not quite comfortable with herself for this sad absence of feeling. Had her weeks in London so changed her that she now cared not a whit whether or not a fellow human being had met his end in so violent a manner?

Daniel, watching her closely, was not slow to note the slightly perturbed expression. 'Were you well acquainted with him, child?'

'No, not at all.' She shook her head in wonder. 'It is a shameful thing to admit to,' she announced, not thinking twice about sharing her thoughts with him, 'but I think the world will be a better place without the Marquis. If my sympathies rest with anyone, then it is with the possible perpetrator of the deed. What he must have suffered at Sywell's hands to induce him to seek revenge and commit such an act one can only wonder at.'

'Very true,' the Dowager agreed, much struck by this. 'And if he was indeed murdered, I doubt there will be any lack of suspects.'

'I didn't realise you were so well acquainted with him, Mama?'

'We were slightly acquainted, Daniel,' she corrected him. 'We met on one or two occasions many years ago. Your maternal grandfather was not in favour of a closer association. Even in those days Sywell had a somewhat unsavoury reputation. He was undeniably a most disagreeable man, who went through life making enemies—far more, I dare say, than there will be mourners at his funeral to lament his passing.'

'You may possibly be right,' Daniel agreed, rising to his feet. 'But I for one have no intention of fruitlessly trying to speculate on which of his numerous enemies might have been the perpetrator of the crime—if indeed a crime was committed, for that in itself has yet to be proved. I have a far more important matter taxing my poor brain at this present moment in time—namely, how to pacify Kendall for the ordeal ahead of him.

'You may or may not be aware of it, ma'am,' he continued, in response to the faintly bewildered glance his mother cast up at him as he passed her chair, 'but my most loyal retainer, being a confirmed bachelor, retains one or two preconceived notions where the fair sex is concerned. He is not a total misogynist, for he has on the odd occasion been overheard to utter mild praise when observing some female equestrian displaying a modicum of skill. He is, however, old-fashioned enough to deplore the present vogue for ladies tooling their own carriages.'

'Why not simply leave him here when you take Robina out?' her ladyship enquired, at a loss to understand why her son was making such an issue of an easily resolved problem.

His expression was faintly mocking. 'Because unlike you, Mama, who have proved to be possibly the most negligent chaperon on the face of the planet since we took up residence here in Brighton, I'm endeavouring to ensure that Robina's hitherto spotless reputation does not become slightly tarnished in the eyes of this censorious world of ours by being observed leaving the town's limits solely in my company.'

Although the explanation appeared to satisfy the Dowager, Robina was not quite so certain that she fully understood the reason behind his lordship's resolve to observe the proprieties wherever possible. Whose reputation was he striving to protect—hers or his own? she couldn't help asking herself. Was he doing everything within his power to ensure that she was not forced into a union with him? Or was he determined that he would not be obliged to offer her the protection of his name because of any gossip

which might arise from their being observed together? And why was it, she wondered, had the latter
possibility brought a return of that very uncomfortable hollow feeling deep inside?

By the time she had taken her place beside his
lordship in the curricle later that morning, Robina
had come very close to convincing herself that
Daniel's determination to have a third person present
as much as possible whenever in her company was
prompted by entirely unselfish motives. Yes, she had
almost convinced herself, but not quite. She refused,
however, to permit the remaining lingering little
doubt to mar the pleasurable excitement she was experiencing at the prospect of being taught to handle
such a fine pair of horses.

Having been expected to perform many tasks over
the years under her mother's watchful eye had certainly stood her in good stead for just such an occasion as this, Robina reflected, happily taking
charge of the equipage as they reached the outskirts
of the town and the open countryside lay before them
beckoning invitingly. At some point in her young life
she had acquired a dogged determination not to allow
fear of failure or an expert's critical opinion to prevent her from attempting something new. Consequently, she was able to concentrate fully on the task
in hand, even though she had been forewarned that
the small, stocky individual perched on the seat behind her was undoubtedly watching her every move,
just waiting for the opportunity to give his opinion

of 'uppity' females who thought themselves capable of handling the ribbons by giving vent to a loud snort at any foolish mistake she might make.

Thankfully no such derisive sound reached her ears. More satisfying still was the fact that only once, before she was requested to draw to a halt at a convenient spot in the lane where there was room enough for two carriages to pass quite comfortably, did her tutor feel the need to correct a slight error by placing his hand over hers, though why the fleeting and unexpected contact should have resulted in her heart momentarily beating a little faster she was at a complete loss to understand.

'That performance was extremely creditable for a person who has only before ever handled a one-horse gig,' Daniel announced, sounding genuinely impressed. 'What say you, Kendall?'

An ominous silence, then, 'Miss Perceval, m'lord, 'as a pair o' good light 'ands, I'll give 'er that.'

'Praise, indeed!' murmured Daniel for his pupil's ears only. Then louder, 'Do you wish to continue, or would you like me to take over now?'

Although highly delighted with her progress thus far, and with the praise she had received, even the groom's mild offering, Robina knew her limitations. Her arms felt a little tired, and her head was beginning to throb with the sheer effort of concentrating so hard, so she decided she'd had enough for one day and willingly handed back the reins.

'Do you wish to return to the house, or would you,

perhaps, enjoy a further exploration of the country-side?'

She certainly would have enjoyed that, but felt she ought not to impose on his lordship's good nature further by taking up any more of his time, and echoed her thoughts aloud.

'You are not imposing, I assure you,' he countered. 'If I hadn't wished to drive you about, child, believe me, I would never have offered.'

There was an undoubted glint in his eyes which in a child might have been taken for devilment. 'You appear to have gleaned, undoubtedly from my endearing mama, a very false impression of my character, my little bird. It is worth remembering that doting parents frequently refuse to see faults in their offspring.'

'Is that so, my lord?' Robina parried, a rare dry note creeping into her voice. 'In that case, all I can say is that you have been blessed, for my mama, loving and caring though she has unfailingly been throughout my life, has never been slow to point out my many failings.'

Having found himself in the punctilious Lady Elizabeth Perceval's company on numerous occasions during those weeks spent in London, and having become in recent years something of an astute judge of character, Daniel was not surprised by this innocent disclosure, but chose not to comment, and merely said,

'Besides which, I have a very good reason for pandering to your every whim. I am hoping that you will grant me a favour in return.'

He watched the questioning lift of delicate brows. 'You see, I've written to Miss Halliwell, my daughters' governess,' he explained, 'expressing my wish that she breaks the journey to Lyme Regis by spending a few days here in Brighton with us. My daughters, Hannah and Lizzie, spend a month each summer visiting their great-aunt Agatha in Dorset. She was my father's youngest sister and simply dotes on the girls.'

That lovely and totally spontaneous smile, which never failed to reach her eyes, and which was the very first thing he had ever noticed about Miss Robina Perceval, curled up the corners of that perfectly shaped mouth of hers.

'How delightful! I had secretly hoped that I might be given the opportunity of making your daughters' acquaintance. Lady Exmouth has told me so much about them that I feel I know them already.'

Daniel smiled to himself as he recalled that the second thing that had occurred to him about Robina in those first meetings in London was that she always managed to say precisely the right thing. She really was a darling!

'Well, I'm relieved to hear you say that, because I hoped you would assist me by keeping them amused whilst they're here. Lizzie, I'm afraid, is easily bored. It may well yet prove to be a grave error of judgement on my part, but I've tended to be rather indulgent since their mother's demise, and Lizzie,

I'm afraid, can be something of a handful on occasions.'

It wasn't the admission itself which momentarily deprived her of speech, for she had learned from the Dowager that her son was both a loving and lenient father. It wasn't the fact that this was the first time, as far as she could recall, that he had ever mentioned his wife, either. What had come as a complete surprise was the fact that there had not been, as far as she could detect, so much as a hint of sadness in his deep, mellow voice.

She cast a fleeting sideways glance up at the strong contours of his wholly masculine profile to discover that, although he wasn't precisely smiling, there was nothing in his expression to suggest that mentioning his wife had caused him the least distress.

'Having three younger sisters myself, I can appreciate the mischief young girls can get into from time to time. I shall be only too happy to offer any assistance I can, my lord,' she assured him, and was surprised for the second time within the space of a few short minutes to discover that her willing offer of help did not appear to please him very much. In fact, if anything, he looked faintly annoyed.

The reason behind the unexpected frown was soon made clear. 'I thought we had agreed that we would dispense with formality when in private, Robina.'

'We did,' she agreed, unable to forbear a smile, or to resist the temptation to tease him a little. 'But might I remind you, sir, that we are not alone. Kendall is with us.'

Only for a moment did Daniel take his eyes off the road ahead to cast her a narrow-eyed, deeply assessing stare. 'I am beginning to realise that when my daughters arrive I shall have not just one unruly little baggage residing under my roof. Thank heavens my Hannah is always well behaved!'

Robina frankly laughed. She had been called many things in her young life, most notably a sweet, biddable girl, which in recent years she had found increasingly irksome. It always made her feel as if she were a complaisant half-wit, some mindless creature without a will of its own. So it was little wonder that his lordship's observation had come as something of a refreshing change, more like a compliment than any slur on her character, though she doubted very much that he had intended it as such.

Feeling marvellously content, a state which she had been experiencing very frequently of late, she leaned back in the comfortable seat and gazed about with interest at the unfamiliar landscape, something which she had not dared to do whilst tooling the curricle herself, lest she lose her concentration and make some foolish mistakes. His lordship, on the other hand, seemed quite capable of doing both. He really was most accomplished at handling the ribbons, controlling the spirited greys with effortless ease.

On the few occasions she had been privileged to sit beside him in the curricle, she had not once witnessed him give way to temptation with displays of dashing flair. He had never, for instance, attempted to feather-edge a corner or manoeuvre the curricle between two vehicles with only an inch to spare. She didn't doubt for a moment that he could easily accomplish such feats, but she could never imagine him putting either his horses or any passenger he might have taken up beside him at risk by making the attempt, unless the manoeuvres were totally unavoidable. Which made her ponder yet again on what must have occurred eighteen or so months ago that had resulted in the tragic accident which had killed his wife.

She was not so foolish as to suppose for a moment that only careless exhibitionists met with accidents. Where horses were concerned anything might happen at any time. Why, one only had to consider the many occasions her good friend Lady Sophia Cleeve, a fine horsewoman by any standard, had taken a tumble from her mount, or the occasional mishap her cousin Hugo, a most notable whip, had experienced over the years, to appreciate that the most skilful handlers of horseflesh could, and often did, come to grief from time to time. None the less she found it difficult to believe that a momentary lack of concentration or gross negligence on Daniel's part had resulted in the death of his much beloved wife.

It was all rather pointless trying to speculate on what might have occurred, she reminded herself. She had never been given any details about the accident whatsoever. Which, now she came to consider the matter, was most strange. The Dowager simply adored her son and never required much encouragement to begin talking about him. From things she had let fall from time to time, her ladyship had been touchingly fond of her late daughter-in-law too. Whether the truth of the matter was simply that the Dowager wasn't in possession of all the facts herself, or that she found the subject of the beautiful Clarissa's demise too painful a topic to discuss, was anyone's guess. It was strange, all the same, that Lady Exmouth had never once attempted to touch on the subject.

Robina came out of her reverie to discover that they had, at some point, turned off the narrow twisting lane, and were now bowling along a much wider road and at a much brisker pace. From the position of the sun, she judged that Daniel had decided to head back to Brighton to enjoy the light luncheon which no doubt awaited their return. She was just beginning to feel that she could do justice to whatever the excellent cook had prepared for them, when she caught sight of a great deal of activity in a field just up ahead.

'Oh, what is taking place over there, do you suppose?'

'It'll be one of the horse fairs held in these parts every summer. The main one takes place in August.' He couldn't mistake the faint look of interest in her blue eyes. 'Would you care to stop and take a look? There are bound to be some side-shows.'

Robina very much looked forward to the annual summer fête held in the grounds at Perceval Hall, her uncle's estate in Northamptonshire. She would miss it this year, as it always took place in July, so she would not have minded in the least making up for the loss of that particular yearly treat by enjoying this unexpected event now. Nevertheless, always considerate to the feelings of others, she expressed her wish not to upset Cook by being late for one of her delicious luncheons.

'There's no need to concern yourself on that score,' Daniel assured her, after expertly turning the curricle into the field and quickly finding a sheltered spot beneath some trees. 'I made it clear before I left the house that I was unsure of precisely when we would return.'

'But what about Kendall?' Robina said, willingly accepting his lordship's helping hand to alight. She turned towards the groom, who now stood at the horses' heads. 'Do you not care to browse too?'

'No, thank you—er—Miss Robina. I'm more than 'appy to bide a while 'ere in the shade, and enjoy me pipe.'

Daniel cast a brief glance at his trusted henchman, before easily capturing Robina's hand, placing it in the crook of his arm, and leading her towards the first of the side-shows. She was perhaps sublimely unaware of it herself, but Kendall's familiarity had not been a token of disrespect, far from it. Robina had undoubtedly found favour in the loyal retainer's eyes.

'I rather fancy that Kendall was more impressed with your display this morning than he would have you believe, my little bird.' That and your undoubted consideration for the feelings of others, he added silently.

'I must confess I was rather pleased with my performance myself,' she admitted, smiling faintly as the thought occurred to her that, had her dear father been present to hear that particular disclosure, he would probably have approved of her honesty, but the self-gratification might well have earned her a frown of disapproval.

Evidently her present companion did not appear to think that she was being in any way conceited, for he smiled down at her like some indulgent uncle. He had a delightful smile; she had thought so from the first. It emphasised that rather attractive cleft in his firm chin, and crinkled the corners of those warm brown eyes.

'Yes, well,' she said faintly, amazed at her wayward thoughts, and fervently hoped that the sudden heat she could feel in her cheeks might be attributed to the warmth of the day. 'I do realise, of course, that I've still a great deal to learn. Tooling Papa's one-horse gig, with dear old Bessie between the traces is one thing; trying to control a pair of spirited horses is quite another.'

While she had been speaking, she had been taking a keen interest in the various attractions and the wide variety of wares for sale on the stalls, but now her sweet countenance unexpectedly betrayed a hint of distaste. Daniel followed the direction of her disapproving gaze to see a brightly coloured sign inviting people to step behind the screen to inspect the wondrous sight of a calf with two heads, a goose with three legs and various other oddities.

'Evidently you disapprove of such spectacles, child.'

'I find them distasteful in the extreme, not to mention needlessly cruel. Not many of those poor creatures are destined to live for very long. It would be much kinder to put them out of their misery at birth. On the other hand, though,' she sighed, 'who am I to criticise or condemn? I have never known hunger. I cannot truly blame any poor wretch for ensuring that his children have food in their bellies, no matter how distasteful the means by which he achieves this might be.'

Her smile swiftly returned as they reached the next attraction, a rough wooden structure housing, if the sign outside were to be believed, the world's fattest lady. Two yokels suddenly emerged from behind the screen, both, it appeared, decidedly unimpressed after witnessing the spectacle.

'She weren't as fat as the one they 'ad 'ere last year,' the taller remarked in a carrying voice, after fortifying himself from the jug he carried.

'No, she weren't,' his companion readily agreed. 'She weren't nearly so fat as your wife, come to that.'

'No, she weren't. I were thinking the selfsame— 'Ere, what do you mean?' the first demanded, evidently realising at last what his friend had just said. 'I'll 'ave you know my Betsy ain't fat, just got plenty o' meat on the bone, that's all.' He fastened one grimy hand on his friend's shirt, spilling some of the contents of the jug in the process. 'You takes that back!'

Swiftly drawing his highly amused companion away before the ex-friends came to blows, which looked imminent, Daniel gazed down at her smiling face, thinking what a wicked sense of humour she possessed, something which he had suspected from the first.

He was convinced, too, that Lady Elizabeth Perceval had instilled strict codes of conduct in her eldest daughter, and this he considered highly commendable. He knew from experience that children needed to be kept under control and taught how to behave, as long as one remembered not to take discipline to extremes, and thereby run the risk of crushing a child's natural vivacity. He would not go so far as to say that this is what had happened in Robina's case, but he had felt increasingly, as he suspected his far from obtuse mother had too, that Robina had been reared to maintain a strict control over emotions and inclinations. She would no doubt always continue to do so to a certain degree, but since their arrival in Brighton there had already been a very noticeable change in her. She seemed far more relaxed and outgoing, and he couldn't help wondering how many more interesting facets of her character would emerge during the forthcoming weeks.

They continued their inspection of the stalls and side-shows, but none of the attractions, or the variety of gaudy fairings for sale, tempted Robina to untie the string of her reticule and part with the small quantity of money that Daniel did not doubt she carried with her. Only when they approached a brightly coloured caravan, with a sign on its door bidding one and all to enter and have their fortunes told by the all-seeing Madame Carlotta, did Robina hover for an instant, a wistful expression fluttering over her features before she made to move on.

'Go on,' he prompted. 'Why not indulge yourself?'

'Oh, no. I couldn't possibly do that. Papa would never approve. He considers all fortune-tellers charlatans.'

'Undoubtedly some of them are,' Daniel agreed, still gently preventing her from moving on. 'But any father who takes the trouble to teach his eldest daughter both Latin and Greek,' he continued, making use of a surprising fact he had discovered himself since their sojourn in Brighton, 'must surely consider her intelligent enough to form her own opinion, and would not, I feel certain, deny her the opportunity to do precisely that.'

Seemingly much struck by this viewpoint, she appeared to debate within herself. 'What harm can it do? Go along, child,' he urged again, and she finally gave way to temptation, quickly moving away before he had the opportunity to delve into his pocket for his purse and pay for the harmless experience.

Evidently the gypsy was a true professional, conveying her predictions with lightning speed, for in no time at all, it seemed, Robina was descending the caravan's steps, a look of wry amusement on her face.

'Let that be a lesson to me to attend my father in the future,' she announced, as she reached Daniel's side and, without the least prompting, slipped her arm through his. 'Papa was absolutely right, as he so often is—a fool and his money are soon parted!'

'You must allow me to pay. It was my suggestion, after all.'

'Certainly not!' she countered, retaining a firm hold on his arm, thereby preventing him from reaching for his purse without an undignified struggle. 'It will serve as a salutary lesson not to be so gullible in the future.'

'From that I infer you are not altogether pleased with what yours holds in store.'

'On the contrary, if what I have just been told is to be believed, it seems I am destined to enjoy a truly blessed existence. Madame Carlotta told me precisely what any girl would wish to hear.'

'Which is?' he prompted, unable to prevent a twitching smile at the wry cynicism.

'Oh, the usual highly improbable things—my path will very soon be crossed by a tall, handsome stranger. Both adventure and danger lie ahead. Whatever that is supposed to mean! Madame Carlotta didn't choose to divulge any details for some reason. Now, what else did she tell me?' Her finely arched brows drew together for a moment. 'Ha, yes! Not too many weeks will pass before I will find myself married to the man of my dreams. Furthermore, I am to give birth within a year to the first of the three sons my husband and I are destined to have during our long and excessively happy life together.'

Daniel turned his head away, thereby concealing his expression of utter delight. Three sons, by gad! he mused. And here I would happily have settled for just one.

The future was beginning to look very rosy indeed!

# Chapter Four

Although she most certainly did consider that she had been more than a little foolish to waste so much as a single penny of her small allowance on having her fortune told, Robina was destined to experience a change of heart before her second week in Brighton had drawn to a close, and was even to begin to wonder whether Madame Carlotta truly did possess the rare gift of second sight.

The week turned out to be a very hectic one, with many more people arriving in the town and many more visitors calling at the house. Invitations were received in increasing numbers, and in the middle of the week Lady Exmouth arranged the first of several small and informal parties she planned to hold that summer.

Well into middle age she might have been, but the Dowager proved that she was certainly not behind the times by ensuring that the trio of musicians hired for the evening played a selection of waltzes.

Although the dance had nowhere near achieved

universal acceptance, it was being performed increasingly at private functions. Nevertheless, woe betide any young woman embarking on her London début caught swirling about a room on a gentleman's arm. She might well be considered fast, thereby risking social ruin.

This, however, Robina considered, hardly applied in her case any longer. She had behaved with the utmost propriety throughout her Season in London, and as it was highly unlikely that she would ever be privileged to enjoy another, unless she married well, her reputation was hardly likely to suffer to any significant degree as a consequence of performing the *risqué* dance at a private function.

None the less, she was very well aware that her mama, not so complaisant, nor anywhere near as forward-looking, as the irrepressible Lady Exmouth, would have staunchly disapproved of her taking part. Surprisingly enough she didn't allow this fact to deter her. After a brief battle with her conscience, she agreed to partner Daniel, a gentleman who, she was swiftly beginning to realise, possessed the innate ability of persuading her to do precisely what she knew she really ought not to do.

The instant he placed one shapely hand lightly on her waist and captured her fingers gently in the other, Robina was reminded vividly of that morning when she had paid a visit to her very good friend Lady Sophia Cleeve at Berkeley Square, and had witnessed the dance performed for the very first time. It had been Sophia's intention to ask her brother to help demonstrate the steps. Unfortunately Lord Angmering had unexpectedly left town, and Sophia, never easily thwarted, had swiftly secured the services of her personal groom.

Robina had suspected at the time that her good friend had not been as indifferent to the handsome man swirling her about the elegant drawing-room in Berkeley Square as she had tried to appear, and that Sophia had been in a fair way to losing her heart. That the groom had turned out to be none other than the Duke of Sharnbrook was a fact known by very few; and although the fashionable world at large had been surprised by the speed of their engagement, no one who had attended the small, very select party, held at the Duke's ancestral home, had doubted for a moment that the newly betrothed couple were genuinely in love.

All this, of course, Robina was forced silently to concede, had little to do with the strange reaction she now found herself experiencing as Daniel expertly swirled her about the salon. It wasn't as if there had never been any physical contact between them either, she reminded herself. His lordship had never failed to offer a helping hand to get in and out of a carriage. Somehow, though, this experience felt completely different.

By the time Friday evening had arrived, and she found herself once again comfortably established in his lordship's well-sprung carriage, Robina had managed to convince herself that the peculiar fluttering in her breast and the increased pulse rate had been the result of nothing more disturbing than a natural nervousness at performing the waltz in public for the very first time, and had nothing whatsoever to do with her partner's prolonged and wholly masculine touch.

The explanation was reasonable enough as far as it went, but it could hardly account for the fact that, when her hand had been claimed a little later for a second waltz by a very charming male guest, she had experienced no reaction at all. She had decided, however, not to dwell on this very curious detail, and had succeeded up to a point in thrusting it from her mind.

She was very much looking forward to the evening ahead. It promised to be most enjoyable, not only because it would grant her the opportunity of furthering her acquaintance with several people she had met in London, but also because it meant that Lady Exmouth would be reunited with the hostess, a friend of many years standing, and one whom the Dowager had not seen for more than two decades.

'Am I correct in thinking that Lady Phelps, like yourself, has just one son?' Robina enquired when there was a lull in the conversation.

'Yes, that's right, dear. Just one of the many things we were destined to have in common throughout our lives.' Leaning back against the squabs, her ladyship quickly relapsed into a reminiscent mood. 'We took the matrimonial plunge within a month of each other, both marrying men much older than ourselves, and both sadly losing our husbands within weeks of each other. We were destined to have just the one child too, although Augusta had to wait many more years before her marriage was finally blessed. I have never met her son Simon, but am reliably informed that she simply dotes on the boy.'

'Lucky Simon,' his lordship remarked sardonically. 'I was little more than a poor, neglected waif, quite unloved.'

'Yes, and it shows, I'm afraid,' Robina responded, somehow managing to keep her countenance, unlike the Dowager, who offered her opinion of her son's grossly inaccurate remark by giving vent to a very unladylike snort.

'You were thoroughly spoilt. Your dear papa was nowhere near strict enough with you. Prematurely grey I went because of you, my boy! You were forever into mischief,' his own very loving mother declared. 'Still, I would far rather have had you that way than like poor Augusta's son. I gather he was something of a weak, sickly child, forever suffering from some ailment or other. That, I suppose, is one of the reasons why Augusta and I saw nothing of each other after Simon was born. That, and the fact that she married an Irish peer, and visits to England were, understandably, few and far between.'

'That and lack of funds, you mean,' his lordship corrected, revealing not for the first time in Robina's presence his streak of ruthless honesty. 'It is common knowledge that the late Lord Phelps was a dissolute rake and inveterate gambler. It was only his marriage to your friend Augusta Davenport that saved him from ruin.'

'True, I suppose,' her ladyship was forced to concede. 'From what I have gleaned from the letters Augusta and I have exchanged over the years, her son fortunately does not appear to have inherited his father's weaknesses. He spends most of his time painting and writing poetry, I believe.'

Daniel was decidedly unimpressed, as his expression clearly showed. 'Byron has a deal to answer for. Since the publication of Childe Harold every Tom, Dick and Harry fancies himself a dashed poet! Look at the rubbish we were forced to endure at Lady Tufnell's soirée in London. Never heard such a load of twaddle mouthed in one evening in my life!'

'Oh, it was not as bad as that, Daniel,' her ladyship countered. 'The trouble with you is that you completely lack a romantic soul. One or two of the offerings were most moving, don't you agree, Robina?'

'Unfortunately, ma'am, I find myself quite unable to offer an opinion.' There was just a suspicion of a twitch at the corner of her mouth. 'If my memory serves me correctly, on that particular occasion I was seated beside your son, and found my attention all too frequently straying in my attempts to prevent him from dropping off to sleep.'

The only response to this gentle teasing was a deep rumble of masculine laughter, a sound heard far more frequently of late, and one which was music to the Dowager's ears.

How glad she was now that she had used every ounce of self-control she possessed, going against her natural inclinations, and had not interfered in the developing relationship between her son and Robina, she reflected, turning her head to gaze sightlessly through the carriage window.

Anyone observing them together might be forgiven for supposing that a wonderful bond of friendship had developed between them. Which of course was precisely what had occurred. There was undeniably a genuine fondness on both sides, which was plain for anyone to see, but certainly no hint of any lover-like affection between them. Daniel treated Robina as he might have done some favoured younger sister, and Lady Exmouth very much suspected that Robina, in her turn, was beginning to look upon Daniel as the brother she had never been blessed to have.

She smiled to herself. Her son, with the patience and understanding that was so much a part of his nature, was being immensely cautious by slowly, very slowly, winning the regard of the woman he had chosen to marry. There wasn't the smallest doubt left now in Lady Exmouth's mind that her son truly did wish to marry the parson's daughter, though precisely why he was determined to do so was not quite so clear.

Unlike his first wife Robina was a very restful young woman, who always appeared sublimely content sitting with Daniel in companionable silence in the library or the parlour, reading her book. She was intelligent too, and was not afraid to venture an opinion on a great many important topics. On several occasions during the past two weeks the Dowager had come upon them when they had been debating some controversial issue, something which her ladyship could never recall Daniel ever doing with his first wife.

Yes, she mused, there wasn't the slightest doubt that they were admirably well suited. There wasn't the least doubt in her mind, either, that Daniel was managing to conceal the depth of his feelings, though whether he had, against all the odds, fallen in love for the second time in his life was a question which she was quite unable to answer.

The carriage drawing to a halt brought an end to the Dowager's pleasurable deliberations. She did not delay in alighting and leading the way into the house her childhood friend had taken for the duration of her stay in Brighton. She was very much looking forward to the reunion and, quite naturally, was prepared to find her friend vastly altered.

It just so happened, however, that it was not the first glimpse of Lady Phelps, now pale and gaunt, and looking every one of her five-and-fifty years, which almost brought Lady Exmouth to an abrupt halt in the doorway leading to the elegant drawing-room, but the sight of the blond-haired Adonis standing sentinel-like beside her.

Lady Exmouth was not so advanced in years that she could no longer appreciate a fine specimen of manhood. She had known numerous truly handsome gentlemen in her lifetime, and yet she could not bring one to mind to equal the young man standing before her now, bowing over her hand with seeming effortless grace. With his perfectly proportioned physique and a face whose features resembled those on some classic Greek statue, he might almost, she decided, be described as beautiful.

She tried to assess her protégée's reaction to such a rare specimen, but apart from a slight widening of those clear blue eyes, Robina betrayed no visible sign that the outstanding young man was having the least effect on her young heart.

The arrival of more guests ensured that exchanges of pleasantries were kept to a minimum, and Daniel, smiling a trifle wryly, shepherded the ladies further into the room. 'I am well aware that appearances quite frequently are deceptive, but I wouldn't have supposed for a moment that our young host suffers unduly from ill health.'

'No, indeed,' his mother agreed. 'Quite the contrary, I would have thought, unlike his poor mama. The years have been less than kind to dear Augusta. How thin and jaded she has become!' She turned to Robina. 'What did you think, my dear? Did you not find Lord Phelps excessively handsome?'

'Yes, very. And singularly lacking in conceit too, I noticed, which I rather admired.'

The Dowager nodded in agreement, secretly pleased by this response. She ought to have known that a sensible girl like Robina would not permit herself to be beguiled by a handsome face. 'And what is your opinion of the young man, Daniel?'

'I'm afraid, ma'am, I am a poor judge of masculine charms. Or lack of 'em, as the case may be,' he returned, taking a glance about him. 'Ha! I see your faithful admirer is amongst the guests. If you'll excuse me…'

Was that a hint of impatience she had detected in his pleasantly mellow voice? Robina wondered, following his progress across the room. She didn't doubt for a moment that he, like anyone else, experienced it from time to time, and anger too, she supposed, though she had noticed precious little evidence of either during the time she had been privileged to know him.

She transferred her attention momentarily to the portly Baronet whose companionship Daniel had sought. A close friend of the Regent's and a long standing member of the so-called Carlton House set, Sir Percy Lovell had by all accounts been a serious contender for the Dowager's hand many years ago, and had remained a lifelong friend.

Robina had met him on several occasions during her Season in London, and again here when he had been amongst the guests at the Dowager's dinner party on Wednesday evening. She rather liked him herself, and wasn't in the least unhappy to find herself a short time later seated beside him at the highly polished table which had been prepared for the dozen or so privileged guests who had been invited to dine before the party officially got under way.

'I must say,' he remarked, helping himself to generous portions from several of the tasty dishes on offer, 'Augusta has arranged a decent spread here. Or her excellent cook was determined to display her skill.' His eyes momentarily strayed in their hostess's direction. 'By the looks of old Gussie she don't concern herself overmuch about food any more. Never was more shocked in my life than when I clapped eyes on her earlier! To look at her now you'd never believe she was a plump little pullet in her younger days. Still, the years bring some changes to all of us, I suppose.'

Robina could not forbear a smile at this. The years had certainly wrought changes in Sir Percy, if what she had been told was true. He had been, by all accounts, a fine figure of a man in his youth. Sadly this was no longer the case. A carefree bachelor existence and an undoubted weakness for the finer things in life had taken their toll on his physical appearance. His girth, according to the Dowager, had more than doubled in size during middle age, and his permanently high colour was testament to his love of fine old port and brandy.

'I think Lady Exmouth was slightly shocked by the changes she perceived in Lady Phelps too,' she divulged. 'But, as you remarked yourself, people are bound to change in two decades.'

'Lavinia hasn't to that extent. Put on a bit of weight in recent years, though, I suppose.' He glanced briefly at his own opulent midriff. 'Still, who hasn't?' He transferred his merry, round eyes, which, Robina was becoming increasingly aware, very little escaped, to the much slimmer form sitting at the head of the table. 'I must say young Phelps came as something of a surprise, also. Never would have supposed that Augusta, never much to look at even in her youth, and the late Lord Phelps could have produced such a handsome fellow.'

Unlike most of the other young ladies present, Robina had refrained from glancing too often at the head of the table, but did so now. 'He is without doubt the most handsome man I have ever met in my life,' she responded, betraying what she had thought when first setting eyes on the young lord. 'The mere sight of him is enough to send any young maiden's heart a-fluttering. He is still young, of course. Just four-and-twenty, I believe the Dowager said. I think when the time comes for him to marry, there will be no shortage of young ladies wishing to become his wife.'

'Mmm,' was the only response forthcoming before Sir Percy refreshed himself from the glass at his elbow.

'You do not agree, sir?'

'I wonder whether the next Lady Phelps will be entirely of his own choosing, m'dear.'

Robina was not slow to follow the Baronet's train of thought. Although Lady Phelps had greeted her warmly enough on her arrival, Robina had managed to detect a certain calculating look in the lacklustre eyes, and had wondered whether Lady Phelps's rather lethargic demeanour, like Sir Percy's frequently vague, childlike gaze, might well prove to be quite misleading.

'Would you be suggesting by any chance that he

might be obliged to seek his mama's consent before
he places a betrothal ring on any lady's finger?'

Sir Percy beamed approvingly. 'I suspected you
were a clever little puss the very first time I met you,'
he disclosed. 'Yes, m'dear, you have the right of it.
That is precisely what I do think. I also think that
she'll not be in too much of a hurry to give her consent, either.'

Robina was not granted the opportunity to comment further, even had she wished to do so, for the
personable young gentleman seated on her left, a certain Mr Frederick Ainsley, whom she had met for the
very first time that evening, claimed her attention.

It transpired that Mr Ainsley was actively seeking
a career in the church. Consequently they had little
difficulty in maintaining a conversation, and some
little time had elapsed before Robina once again
turned to the amiable Baronet to discover him working his way through a large portion of fresh straw-
berry meringue, liberally covered with large dollops
of thick cream.

'Exmouth appears faintly subdued this evening,'
he remarked, surprising her somewhat, and she quite
naturally transferred her gaze momentarily to the
place at the table where Daniel was seated, only to
discover him looking directly back at her. She
smiled, and for the first time ever won no answering
smile, before he transferred his attention back to the
lively damsel on his left.

'He was fine earlier. Quite jovial, in fact,' she divulged, clearly recalling the cheerful conversation

during the short carriage journey. 'I suppose, though, past tragic events are bound to intrude into his thoughts, especially on an occasion such as this, when his wife would undoubtedly have accompanied him. I cannot imagine that one ever fully recovers from such a devastating blow, no matter how hard one might strive to do so.'

'Perhaps not,' Sir Percy conceded, after finishing the last morsel of delicious meringue on his plate, and with praiseworthy control not replacing it with a further helping. 'Clarissa was certainly a very sociable creature, much more so than Exmouth ever was. She loved to attend balls and parties, whereas Daniel is happiest when at home, looking after his estate.'

Sir Percy took a moment to fortify himself from his glass before continuing his interesting disclosures. 'Increasingly, as I recall, Clarissa would pay visits to London, staying with friends, or come here to Brighton, leaving Daniel back at Courtney Place to join her later. The marriage on the surface, though, appeared a happy one.'

Was that an element of doubt she had detected in his voice? Surely not! 'You knew the late Baroness very well, I presume.'

'Been a friend of the Exmouth family for years, m'dear. Yes, I knew her very well. She was exquisite. A diamond of the first water!' He stared down into the remaining contents of his glass, a slight frown puckering his wispy grey brows. 'Can't help thinking myself, though, that Exmouth married far too young. He'd only just attained the age of three-

and-twenty, after all, and although he was always a very level-headed young man, mature beyond his years, there's no trying to get away from the fact that the passage of time brings changes to us all, and not just physically.

'Clarissa, though, was outstandingly beautiful. No one could disagree with that. Would have succeeded in capturing any young man's heart. But there ain't much else you can do with a beautiful work of art except look and admire it, if you follow my drift. I don't mean to imply that she was a simpleton,' he added hurriedly, 'far from it, in fact, but her interests were a trifle limited, as you might say. Still,' he shrugged, 'as I've already mentioned, she seemed to suit young Exmouth well enough.

'Then came the accident,' he continued, while Robina was still digesting what he had already disclosed. 'All very tragic, as you've remarked yourself, m'dear. But something has always troubled me about it all… Something just never seemed quite right to me.'

Robina's interest was well and truly captured. 'Do you mean you were there at the time and witnessed the tragedy?'

'Oh, no, no! I was staying close by at the time, though, with a neighbour of Exmouth's. When news reached us, we jumped into the carriage and travelled over to Courtney Place. We learned then that Clarissa had died, and young John Travers, who had been paying a short visit to a maiden aunt residing nearby, had also been very badly injured in the accident. He never regained consciousness, poor fellow… Died the following day.'

Robina took a sip from her own glass, glancing across at Daniel as she did so. He was thankfully smiling now, that wonderful easy smile which he had so frequently bestowed upon her, while he happily conversed with the lively Lady Smethurst.

When she had first met him all those weeks ago in London, she had naturally felt saddened to learn about his bereavement, as much as one could experience sadness on hearing about the tragic loss suffered by a virtual stranger. Now, however, he was no longer a stranger, but her dear and wonderful companion whose friendship she had swiftly come to value far more than any other. Now the mere thought that he might be suffering hurt her unbearably too. It was almost a tangible thing, like a knife being thrust deep inside and cruelly twisted.

'When we arrived at Courtney Place, Daniel himself was not there,' Sir Percy went on to divulge, seemingly locked in the past. 'We were told he could be found at the scene of the accident, so we went along to see if there was anything we could do.' He shook his head sadly. 'Dreadful, it was. Clarissa's own carriage, the one Daniel had bought her the year before for her own private use, twisted and broken, lying at the bottom of the ravine, with the horses, both of which Daniel himself had shot to put an end to their suffering, lying alongside it.'

'What was it precisely about the accident which

puzzled you, Sir Percy?' Robina prompted when he
fell silent again.

'The location, m'dear,' he didn't hesitate to enlighten her. 'It happened on a stretch of road known
locally as Snake Pass, for obvious reasons. It's a picturesque little run, but seldom used nowadays, not
since the new road was constructed, except by farm-
ers and sightseers, and then only during the summer
months. It's virtually impassable during winter, and
dangerous too. It follows the line of the hillside, and
weaves in and out, hence its name.'

'Well?' she prompted again, determined to discover precisely what troubled him about the incident.

'Well, m'dear...I can't help asking myself what
an intelligent man like Daniel was doing tooling his
wife's carriage along a road he knew to be highly
dangerous. Furthermore, I discovered that he had returned from London a matter of only an hour or two
before the accident occurred. It just isn't the act of a
sensible man to go gadding about, tooling a carriage,
when one must surely be quite weary already after
travelling from London.

'And sightseeing...?' he continued, deliberately
keeping his voice low so that the conversation could
not be overheard. 'Who in his right mind goes gadding about sightseeing on a filthy day in late
October? Answer me that if you can! I clearly remember that it had been raining all that morning, and
although the afternoon was dry, it was dull, damp
and thoroughly dismal. Daniel informed me that it
had been young Travers's idea. He had been keen to

see something of the county before he returned to his home in Derbyshire. Well, I suppose that's feasible enough,' he conceded. 'But what I cannot swallow is that Daniel accepted the wager in the first place.'

'Wager?' Robina echoed, not clearly understanding what Sir Percy had meant.

'Seemingly, m'dear, young Travers suggested that any man who considers himself a capital whip ought to be able to tool a carriage competently in any weather, in any conditions and with reasonable speed. Exmouth certainly doesn't lack skill when it comes to tooling a carriage. You know that from experience yourself.' He shrugged his plump shoulders again. 'I'm not suggesting that he would never accept a wager—gentlemen do from time to time. But he would never have put his horses at risk, let alone his wife, by tooling a vehicle along that particular stretch of road. That to me totally lacks the ring of truth!'

Indeed it does, Robina silently agreed. Daniel would never do such a foolhardy thing, least of all for a wager. Sir Percy was right—it just didn't ring true somehow.

Later that night, as she climbed into bed, Robina was to recall again the conversation she had had with Sir Percy over dinner. It had proved most enlightening and had provided much food for serious thought.

That conversation was by no means the only interesting aspect of what had turned out to be a most enjoyable evening, she reflected, snuggling between the clean sheets. She had very much enjoyed the company of Mr Frederick Ainsley and had danced with him twice during the evening. The only slight disappointment was that Daniel hadn't once offered to lead her out on to the floor. The devastatingly handsome Lord Phelps most certainly had, though, making her feel the envy of every other young female in the room, and the cynosure of all eyes.

She frowned suddenly, as a thought suddenly occurred to her. The gypsy woman at the fair had predicted that a handsome young man would cross her path in the near future. And one most definitely had! The odd thing was, though, the experience of dancing with Lord Phelps had had little effect upon her, unlike two nights before, when Daniel had expertly guided her about the floor.

How very odd that was!

# *Chapter Five*

The following morning it seemed to Robina that the door-knocker was never still. The first caller to the house was Mr Frederick Ainsley, who came for the sole purpose of inviting her to take a walk with him in the park. Ordinarily she would have been delighted to comply, but as she had already arranged with Daniel to go out with him in the curricle later that morning, a treat she would never willingly forgo unless wholly unavoidable, she politely declined, although she was more than happy to agree to the suggestion that they enjoy a promenade together the following afternoon.

No sooner had the very amiable Mr Ainsley taken his leave than their hostess of the previous evening, accompanied by her son, arrived at the house. The cruel light of day did little to improve Lady Phelps's world-weary appearance, unlike her sole offspring's. Seating himself beside Robina on the sofa, he resembled some golden Apollo with the sun's rays streaming through the parlour window, enhancing the bright guinea-yellow of his curls.

Daniel, who had retired to his library directly after breakfast in order to write a long letter in response to the one he had received that morning from his steward, must have detected the sound of the door-knocker this time, for he joined them a few moments later. The conversation quickly turned to the present vogue in paintings, and other works of art, a subject on which, Robina had discovered the night before, the young Lord Phelps proved most knowledgeable. Daniel promptly enquired whether his young visitor would care to accompany him into the library to inspect the fine landscape hanging above the hearth. The invitation was speedily accepted, though whether it was a desire to view the painting which prompted the eager acceptance or Daniel's suggestion that they might partake of something rather stronger than the tea which the butler was at that moment carrying into the room, Robina was not perfectly sure.

Lady Exmouth was not slow to note the secretive little smile hovering about the sweet mouth of the young woman whom she very soon hoped to call daughter, and couldn't help wondering precisely what was passing through that quick little mind. Her ladyship was nothing if not a realist, and was very well aware that the unexpected arrival of such a handsome young man on the scene might well give rise to some unforeseen problems, so it was with some satisfaction that she noted that her young protégée did not appear in the least downcast at having the young Adonis removed from her sphere.

Unlike Robina, Lady Phelps watched the gentlemen leave the room and waited for the door to be firmly closed behind them, before turning to her friend and offering her condolences on the death of Daniel's wife. 'Simply a dreadful tragedy. Clarissa was such a beautiful girl! So full of life, as I remember.'

'Indeed she was,' Lady Exmouth agreed, handing her visitor a filled china cup. 'Daniel, thankfully, is recovering well. His weeks in London did him a great deal of good.'

Lady Phelps's dull grey eyes flickered momentarily in Robina's direction. 'I'm pleased to hear it. He is still a relatively young man, not yet six-and-thirty, if my memory serves me correctly. He must not be allowed to mourn forever.'

She turned her eyes once again in Robina's direction, only this time her gaze was considerably more direct. 'And you, my dear, are you enjoying your stay in Brighton?'

'Very much so, ma'am. Both Lady Exmouth and her son have been so very kind.'

'Nonsense, child! It's a joy having you with us. Male company is all very well for a time, but one still needs the companionship of one's own sex. Robina is the eldest daughter of Lady Elizabeth Finedon, that was, and William Perceval, Augusta,' Lady Exmouth explained, after she had finished dispensing the tea.

'Ha, yes! Yes, of course. Your papa is a clergy-man, is that not so, my dear?'

'Yes, ma'am. He is the Vicar of Abbot Quincey.'

'A worthy gentleman, I'm sure. I remember your mama very well. You have younger brothers and sisters, I presume.'

'Three sisters.'

'How very lucky your parents are! I was only blessed with the one child.' She turned to her friend. 'But we have been most fortunate in our children, Lavinia, have we not?'

'Very. And Simon is such a very handsome young man, Augusta!'

Lady Phelps permitted herself a thin smile. 'But, alas, never strong.'

This brought a faint flicker to one corner of the Dowager's mouth, Robina noticed. No doubt her ladyship thought, as she did herself, that Lord Phelps looked the very picture of health, with his fresh complexion, clear, sparkling eyes and shining crop of guinea-gold curls.

Although the Dowager had certainly not admitted to it in so many words, Robina had gained the distinct impression that the reunion had not turned out to be quite the joyful occasion for which Lady Exmouth had hoped. From odd little snippets she had let fall during the carriage ride home the previous evening, it was quite evident that she considered that her old friend had changed out of all recognition in many ways, and not for the better. Robina remembered too the look she had glimpsed on the

Dowager's face when her ladyship and Lady Phelps had been seated together on the sofa, enjoying a dish of tea after the delicious dinner served the previous evening. Robina had thought she had detected a hint of impatience in the Dowager's eyes, and a touch of boredom too.

There was no hint of boredom now, merely suppressed amusement, as she said, 'All children become ill from time to time. It's unavoidable, Augusta. I'm sure Simon cannot cause you concern, now, however. He looks the very picture of health.'

'Ah, but looks can be deceptive, my dear. He is nowhere near as robust as he might appear. And he carries a great deal of responsibility on those young shoulders of his. It is no secret that the estate came to him in a sorry state. Thankfully Simon has not inherited his father's weaknesses, and things are much improved.' The woebegone expression was noticeably more marked. 'It is still necessary, however, for Simon to marry well.'

'In that case, Augusta,' her ladyship returned bluntly, 'I cannot imagine what on earth prompted you to come here to Brighton. The real prizes are to be captured during the London Season.'

Lady Phelps's trill of laughter sounded more than a little forced. 'Oh, no, my dear! We did not come here with the intention of finding Simon a suitable wife. He is still very young, and has no intention of taking the matrimonial plunge quite yet. Of course, if he did happen to meet the right sort of girl, and fall in love, all well and good, but we really came to

enjoy a change of scenery and take advantage of the
healthy sea air.'

This in all probability was quite true, for the
widow, at least, looked as though she could do with
recouping her strength. The lady might not be in
prime physical condition, but Robina didn't suppose
for a moment that she lacked ambition, or cunning,
come to that, and couldn't help wondering whether
Lady Phelps would willingly allow a golden opportunity to ensnare a rich prize for her son to slip
through her bony, mercenary fingers, if a suitable
heiress did happen to arrive on the scene during their
stay in Brighton.

Whether or not Lord Phelps himself wholeheartedly approved of these plans for his future, Robina
had no way of knowing. As the days passed, and she
found herself in his company quite frequently, unavoidable in a town such as Brighton, where the
same people were continually invited to the same
social events, she swiftly came to the conclusion that
he was a remarkably complacent young man, with
few ambitions, and few interests outside those of
poetry and art.

He certainly never appeared particularly interested
in pursuing any masculine outdoor activities, and
seemed quite content to accompany his mother wherever she wished to go: social events in the evenings;
about the town during the day to visit her friends.
Not surprisingly they were regular visitors to Lord
Exmouth's home, and it didn't take Robina very long

to notice that their arrival at the house usually sig-
nalled Daniel's immediate departure from it.

Consequently she began to see far less of him.
Lady Phelps's frequent calls were by no means solely
responsible for this. July's arrival had brought a further influx of visitors to the town, which included
good friends of Robina's from Northamptonshire,
Olivia Roade Burton and her recently married sister
Beatrice and her new husband, the very charming
Lord Ravensden. Her visits to the Ravensden household, and her growing friendship with Frederick
Ainsley who, unlike Lord Phelps, was fond of fresh
air and regular exercise, ensured that Robina was frequently away from the house too.

Daniel's very good friend Montague Merrell also
arrived in town, and quite naturally Daniel was keen
to spend time with him, pursuing wholly masculine
interests. Understandably enough, he did not always
make himself available to squire Robina and his
mother out in the evenings. This in itself caused no
particular problems, except that Robina did miss him,
a circumstance that she was not prepared to admit to
until she was forced to do precisely that, when
Daniel, one morning over breakfast, unexpectedly
announced his intention of moving in temporarily
with his friend Mr Merrell.

'For heavens' sake why, Daniel?' the Dowager responded, voicing Robina's particular thoughts very
succinctly.

'It may have slipped your memory, Mama, but
your grandchildren are due to arrive today.'

'Well? What of it? We've room enough to house them very comfortably. There's absolutely no need for you to move out.'

'Perhaps not,' he conceded, glancing at Robina, who was staring fixedly at the letter she had been reading, and had placed neatly beside her plate, 'but it would make things a deal more comfortable for you all if I do. Added to which, I flatly refuse to house Miss Halliwell in one of the attic rooms. She has been a constant comfort and support to the girls since their mother's death, and I will not have her treated like a servant. Hannah and Lizzie can share my room, and Miss Halliwell can occupy the one next door.'

Evidently the Dowager fully appreciated the kind consideration he was displaying towards his daughters' governess, and after a moment's deliberation she nodded in agreement.

'Good. That's settled then,' he responded, considering the matter now closed, and turned to Robina, who remained thoughtfully staring down at the letter by her plate. 'You're very quiet this morning, child. I trust your mother's missive brought no bad news?'

'W-what…? Oh, no. Not at all. Just a little local gossip. My family are eagerly awaiting the arrival of my cousin. She may already have arrived by now, of course.'

Robina forced herself to look at him, hoping the acute disappointment she was experiencing at his imminent removal from the house did not show in her face. 'You may remember I told you that Mama offered Cousin Deborah a home after her mama, my aunt Frances, passed away last year. I dare swear the vicarage will never be quite the same again once she takes up residence there. Darling Deborah has an unfortunate tendency to be—how shall I put it?—slightly accident-prone on occasions.' She glanced briefly at the letter once again. 'But apart from that, Mama only writes briefly that no one has been charged with Sywell's murder as yet.'

'It may well turn out to be one of those cases that never does get solved,' Daniel suggested, after a moment's thought. 'Although, from what Merrell was telling me t'other day, Prinny seems keen to have the thing cleared up.'

Lady Exmouth frowned at this. 'Why is that, do you suppose? Sywell was never a close friend of the Regent's, surely?'

'From what I can glean, the Marquis wasn't anybody's friend,' Daniel returned, his dry sense of humour coming to the fore. 'No, that isn't it. It's simply that Prinny ain't too happy when he discovers that a member of the peerage has been—er—bumped off. There's been enough of that going on in recent years across the Channel. Our future king don't want anything of that sort starting here, and I can't say I blame him. Can't have gangs of revolutionaries going about bumping off our aristos, now can we? It might be my turn next!'

'I am the only person likely to murder you, my boy, for deserting me in this fashion!' his mother retorted. 'Thank goodness I still have dear Robina to bear me company. I'm seriously considering persuading her to return with me to Bath, after the summer, to be my constant companion. She, I am persuaded, would never desert me!'

'If you are not very careful, Mama,' Daniel warned, his smile slowly fading, and his gaze unusually intense, 'you might succeed in persuading her to do just that.'

As Daniel's time was taken up with organising the removal of some of his more personal belongings to take with him to his temporary lodgings, Robina had of necessity to forgo her lesson in the curricle that morning. She remained in the house with the Dowager, receiving the steady stream of morning callers, a regular feature of the past few days, but after luncheon was determined to go out for a breath of fresh air, and was delighted when Mr Frederick Ainsley arrived on the doorstep just as she was about to set forth, and offered to accompany her.

Only just of average height and, with the possible exception of a pair of clear, intelligent grey eyes, having no looks worthy of note, Mr Ainsley might not have been to every female's taste. Unlike Lord Simon Phelps, who gained attention wherever he went, Mr Ainsley could attend a party of an evening and most other guests present might never recall his being there, and yet Robina much preferred his company to the handsome young Earl's.

His many wonderful qualities, Robina considered, more than compensated for any lack of striking physical attributes. He was very much the gentleman, both courteous and attentive. He was intelligent too, and a most interesting conversationalist, unlike Lord Phelps who seemed to drift off at a moment's notice into a world of his own, leaving Robina with the distinct impression that he had not heard a single word that she had said.

Robina found that time always passed remarkably quickly whenever she was with Mr Ainsley. This occasion proved no exception, and she arrived back at the house rather later than she had intended to discover the butler in the process of organising the swift removal of the variety of baggage which littered the hall. Therefore she wasted no time in going up to her room to remove her bonnet, and tidy her hair, and then went straight down to the front parlour to discover, as expected, Daniel's daughters sitting with their grandmother on the sofa, and a female in a plain grey gown seated nearby in one of the comfortable chairs.

Daniel himself was also present. He rose to his feet the instant she entered the room, and greeted her with, 'Ha! So the wanderer returns at last,' which might well have been meant as criticism. If it was he tempered it with a welcoming smile, and a raised hand beckoning her forward.

'Miss Perceval, permit me to present my daughters, Hannah and Elizabeth.'

Although she and her three sisters might differ slightly in looks, there could be no mistaking their close relationship. The same could not be said for the two girls who now stood before her, executing curt-seys with differing skills. Hannah, with her dark hair and soft brown eyes, certainly favoured her father in looks; whereas Lizzie, Robina suspected, was bidding fair to becoming the image of her lovely mother, having a pair of limpid blue eyes and a riot of bright guinea-gold curls.

She swiftly discovered that they were vastly different in temperament too. Hannah, seeming older than her twelve years, was quiet and refined; whereas Lizzie, it quickly became apparent, possessed all the boundless energy of a nine-year-old child, wanting always to be on the move. Her father, however, managed to persuade her with very little difficulty to sit quietly beside her grandmother once again, while he introduced Miss Halliwell.

Robina's experience of governesses was limited. Private tutors were luxuries her parents could ill afford, and she and her sisters had received their education at the vicarage from their parents, both of whom were highly intelligent and well read. There had been one or two governesses residing in the locale over the years, and of course her good friend Lady Sophia Cleeve had received private tuition from several different females during her formative years, all of whom, as far as Robina could remember, had been cast in a similar mould: gaunt, bespectacled and middle-aged. Miss Halliwell certainly did not conform to this stereotype, for she was, Robina judged, only in her mid to late twenties, and was very attractive, with a slim, shapely figure.

'Before you joined us,' Daniel said, once again seating himself after Robina had done so, 'we were discussing what we could do tomorrow to entertain the girls. Have you any ideas?'

'Well, if the weather remains fine,' she responded, after giving the matter a moment's thought, 'and it shows every possible sign of doing so, we might go into the country somewhere and have a picnic.'

The suggestion gained immediate approval from both girls, and Hannah in particular, who was keen to take her sketching pad to record the local scenery.

'That's settled then,' her father said indulgently. 'All that remains is for us to decide precisely where we are to enjoy this alfresco luncheon. Any thoughts on that score, Miss Perceval?'

Robina felt certain that her cheeks were growing quite pink with the warmth of the smile he cast her, and she could only hope that the added bloom might be deemed to be the quite natural outcome of her recent walk in the fresh air.

'There is that very pretty wooded area we passed when you took me into the country for my very first lesson in the curricle. It is situated very near where they hold the horse fairs,' she explained when he frowned in puzzlement. 'I seem to remember you said there was a ruined priory somewhere nearby, which I should imagine would make an ideal subject for sketching.'

'Ha, yes! I know where you mean. There were always several pairs of swans on the river there, as I recall.' She received a further warm smile of approval. 'Clever girl that you are, Miss Perceval, you have come up with the ideal spot—sufficient shade for Mama if it becomes too warm, and a wood for the more energetic amongst us to explore.'

'Have you been teaching Miss Perceval to tool your curricle, Papa?' Hannah enquired, resembling her father more closely still when she frowned. 'I cannot recall your ever teaching Mama.'

'Your mama never betrayed the least interest to learn, unlike Miss Perceval who continually astounds me by betraying a surprising interest in a wide range of things.'

'Will you teach me, Papa?' Lizzie asked, wide-eyed and eager.

'Perhaps. When you're a little older. And providing you can learn to sit still for more than two minutes at a time,' he teased gently, rising to his feet as the tea-tray arrived in the room. 'In the meantime, we shall leave your grandmama to enjoy her refreshments in peace, while we go out and enjoy ices and lemonade.'

'Am I right in supposing that you herald from this part of the country, Miss Halliwell?' the Dowager remarked, after her son and granddaughters had left the room.

'Yes, that is correct, my lady,' she responded in a well-spoken voice.

'I seem to recall, too, your mentioning that you still have relatives residing hereabouts.'

'Yes, my lady. My brother and his family. My

brother teaches in a school situated about five miles from Brighton.'

'In that case, my dear, why not take the opportunity whilst you're here of paying them a visit. In fact, why not spend the entire day with them tomorrow?' she suggested. 'My son would not object, I'm sure, to your making use of the chaise. We can easily manage with the travelling carriage. And I shall not be at all surprised if Exmouth decides to drive himself in the curricle.'

It was quite obvious by the sudden expression of delight that Miss Halliwell wished to accept the kind offer, and equally obvious that she was not one to neglect her duties when she said, 'But surely you will wish me to accompany you tomorrow in order to take care of the girls?'

'I'm certain that we can manage quite well. Miss Perceval has three younger sisters, and is quite accustomed to keeping young ladies entertained. So, we'll take it as settled.'

The Dowager smiled at Robina, as she requested her to pour out the tea, and then turned back to the governess. 'By the by, my dear, you and Miss Perceval have more in common than your ability to keep a watchful eye on young girls. Like yourself, Miss Perceval is the daughter of a clergyman.'

The conversation quite understandably turned to the busy and pleasant life to be had in a country vicarage. It transpired that Miss Halliwell had lost her mother some years before, and had been expected at a young age to take upon herself the duties of managing the household. When her elder brother had left the family home in order to pursue his chosen career as a teacher, she had remained with her father, until his demise four years ago, when the living had quickly been offered to another and she had found herself without a roof over her head. She had chosen to enter the same profession as her brother, and had been fortunate enough to find employment within a very short space of time in the Exmouth household.

After listening to this brief history of Miss Halliwell's life, Robina began to realise fully, for perhaps the first time, just how much she had taken for granted over the years, and how privileged her own life had been compared to that of the vast majority of clergymen's offspring. Unlike the late Mr Halliwell, her own father had been able to afford the luxury of employing servants to attend to the heavier household chores. She had not been asked to clean and cook, or lay fires. Nor had she been expected to grow an ample supply of vegetables in order to save a little money, as Miss Halliwell had been forced to do.

Furthermore, how many clergymen's daughters could boast to having enjoyed a Season in London? How many had found themselves sitting in a titled gentleman's parlour, dispensing cups of tea, as though they were mistress of the house and had every right to do so, just as she was doing now?

She had adapted so easily to this privileged way of life that she might have been born to it, which of course she had not. For the past few months, she told herself, she had been enjoying a fairytale existence, and it was high time she ceased her foolish dreaming and faced reality. If she returned to Abbot Quincey without receiving any further offers for her hand, she might well find herself having to seek some genteel employment in the not too distant future. After all, she could not expect her parents to support her indefinitely, and life as a governess might one day loom large on her own horizon. Miss Halliwell, it had to be said, seemed very contented with her lot. But how many governesses were lucky enough to find employment in the home of such a kind and considerate gentleman as Lord Exmouth? Precious few, Robina suspected.

## Chapter Six

It was a merry little group which gathered in the hall late the following morning. Miss Halliwell had departed an hour or so earlier, with Lord Exmouth's full approval, to spend the day with her brother and his family. Robina, who had already managed to win the new visitors' stamp of approval, most especially Lizzie's, who was beginning to think that in Miss Perceval she might have found something of a kindred spirit, was successfully keeping the girls in a high state of amusement by recounting yet another of her less than commendable childhood exploits, when the front door opened and Daniel entered the house. To the little gathering's surprise he was swiftly followed by the ample form of Sir Percy Lovell, wearing a wide-brimmed straw hat and sporting a garish yellow-and-green striped waistcoat, with a preposterously large nosegay tucked in his lapel.

'Great heavens!' her ladyship exclaimed, her gaze alternating between flowers and waistcoat. 'What in the world brings you here, Percy? Surely you're not to make up one of the party?'

'Most certainly am,' he assured her. 'When I ran across Exmouth last night, and he mentioned he was off on a jaunt into the country, I decided I wasn't prepared to miss out on the treat if I could help it, and so I invited myself.'

It was quite apparent that neither Hannah nor Lizzie, who joyfully greeted him, objected to his company. Sir Percy, beaming like some highly indulgent great-uncle, promptly presented Hannah with the nosegay, telling her that she was turning into a devilishly pretty gel, before informing Lizzie that she was a naughty little puss who ought to be kept on leading-strings, which only succeeded in making her chuckle and dance about him all the more.

'You are an appalling influence, Percy,' Lady Exmouth informed him, before casting a playfully accusing glance in quite another person's direction. 'But you are by no means the only one.'

Daniel, having instructed the footman to place a clean rug in his curricle, turned in time to overhear these latter remarks. 'Is that so!' he announced, slanting a look of mock severity directly upon the miscreant.

The only response forthcoming was a wickedly provocative blue-eyed glance which instantly produced a smile of such loving tenderness to transform his lordship's features that Sir Percy, blinking several times, stood transfixed.

The full import of what he was witnessing quickly

permeated his brain. He was very well aware of
course of precisely where his good friend the
Dowager considered her son's future lay or, to be
more precise, with whom. Nonetheless up until that
moment he had not fully appreciated just how successful she had been in her endeavours. He glanced
in her direction for confirmation, only to discover her
making a great play of searching through her reticule,
an unmistakable smile of satisfaction tugging at the
corners of her own mouth.

'By Jove! Yes—er—well. Shall we be on our
way?' he suggested, turning to lead the way outside.

Quite understandably both the girls had wished to
travel in the curricle with their father. He was in the
process of offering them a helping hand to scramble
up on to the seat, when a lone horseman, trotting
down the street in their direction, happened to catch
his attention.

There was no hint of tenderness in the glance he
directed at Robina this time. She looked as surprised
as everyone else by the rider's approach, and her
ladyship hurriedly stepped into the breach before her
son's evident annoyance prompted him to say something which he might later come to regret.

'Why, good morning, Lord Phelps,' she greeted
him, when at last he drew level with the small cav-
alcade. 'I sincerely trust you did not intend to pay us
a morning call, for as you can see we are just about
to depart for a jaunt in the country.'

'Yes, ma'am, I know. Hoped I might catch you
before you left. Discovered earlier from my mother

that you were organising a sketching party, and decided I'd come along. If you've no objection, that is?'

'Why, of course not,' she announced, with as much enthusiasm as she could muster, while hoping her slightly raised voice would conceal Sir Percy's string of muttered oaths. 'I'm certain Cook will have provided us with ample provisions.'

'What on earth possessed you to permit that fellow to tag along, Lavinia?' Sir Percy demanded, climbing into the coach after the ladies, and slamming the door firmly closed in case the new arrival should take it into his head to leave his mount and request a seat in the carriage. 'Damned impertinence turning up like that, and virtually inviting himself!'

'Well, that's rich coming from you!' she retorted. 'You did precisely the same thing yourself.'

'Ah, but that's different. I'm an old friend of the family. Knew you'd have no objection to me making up one of the party.'

'And what makes you suppose that I've the least objection to Lord Phelps doing precisely the same thing?'

'Should have thought that was obvious, m'dear,' he muttered, casting a meaningful glance at the sole occupant of the seat opposite, who had remained interestedly staring out of the window from the moment the carriage had moved off. 'Daniel wasn't best pleased. Any fool could see that.'

'Oh, I don't supposed he minded to any great extent,' she countered, not making the least attempt to lower her own voice. 'Why should he, for heaven sakes! Lord Phelps is quite harmless, you know.'

'Hopeless, maybe!' Then, again in an undertone, 'But devilish handsome.'

'Undeniably so.' The Dowager then decided to prove to her old friend that his obvious concerns were quite without foundation, and turned at once to Robina. 'Did you notice the look on Hannah's face, dear, when Lord Phelps came trotting down the street towards us?'

Robina could not forbear a smile. 'I did as it happens. I wish I had a shiny golden guinea for every occasion I'd glimpsed that particular expression since the young Earl arrived in Brighton. I'd be a very rich woman by now!'

'I cannot recall your gaping at him in just such a fashion when you were first introduced.'

Robina's eyes twinkled with amusement. 'That is because I had been forewarned, you see. A gypsy accurately predicted, as things have turned out, that a handsome man would cross my path.'

'Good heavens!' Lady Exmouth betrayed genuine surprise, and not just mild interest too. 'I did not realise you'd been to a fortune-teller, child. When did you go? Was it recently?'

'Yes, quite recently. When Lord Exmouth took me out for my very first lesson in the curricle, we came upon a horse fair and decided to take a look around. The fortune-teller was amongst the attractions.'

'How very exciting! What else did she tell you, my dear?'

Robina felt that she had been dwelling rather more than she should of late on what that gypsy woman had told her, secretly hoping, she supposed, that perhaps more than just one of the predictions might come true. It would be comforting to think that she was destined to enjoy a full and happy life, but she was desperately striving to be sensible about it all.

'Oh, not very much, ma'am.' She shrugged. 'One must not take these things too seriously.'

'She was certainly right about the handsome young man,' her ladyship pointed out, slightly disappointed by Robina's distinct lack of enthusiasm. 'Did she predict a marriage for you, by any chance?'

'Bah!' Sir Percy interjected rudely, thereby earning himself an impatient glance from his friend. 'Well, it's all stuff and nonsense, Lavinia, as you very well know. And if she did happen to predict a marriage for the gel, I hope to high heaven it wasn't to that buffoon riding alongside us.'

It was an effort but the Dowager did manage to suppress the chuckle rising in her throat. 'Now, that is unkind, Percy. I wouldn't suggest for a moment that Lord Phelps is a stimulating orator, but he certainly isn't a simpleton.'

'Seems one to me. Have you ever tried to hold a conversation with the halfwit? Why, he goes off into a world of his own at the drop of a hat. Still,' he shrugged, 'I suppose he has been forced to adopt such tactics in order to get away from that mother of his, if only to mentally distance himself,' he continued, striving to be fair. 'She never leaves the boy alone. Drags him about with her everywhere.'

'Yes, I had noticed that myself,' the Dowager was forced to concede.

'And I'll tell you another thing,' he went on, warming to the subject. 'Don't let those die-away airs of Augusta's fool you. She's as sharp as a razor, that one! And as mean as a moneylender to boot! I've had it on the best authority that the only reason she's in Brighton now is because she hasn't had to dip into her own purse to pay for the house she's staying in. It was her sister who hired it originally. Only when the sister became ill late in the spring, she offered it to Augusta. She snapped up the chance by all accounts. And hasn't paid her sister a penny piece, if I know anything!'

Lady Exmouth had not heard this particular tale, but wouldn't have been in the least surprised to discover it was true. 'I'm afraid Augusta has changed. She isn't the friend I remember.'

'Very true. So you be careful, m'dear,' Sir Percy warned. 'I've also heard a rumour that she intends to stay over in England until next year. The family no longer owns a property in this country, so I wouldn't put it past her to sponge off her friends. If you're not very careful, she'll be inviting herself to Bath in the autumn and inflicting her company on you.'

'She'll be out of luck if she tries,' her ladyship responded. 'My plans are still uncertain. I should like to return to Bath after the summer, but there is every chance that I shall be returning to Courtney Place with Daniel.'

Sir Percy did not attempt to hide his astonishment. 'Why on earth are you considering doing that? Daniel's fully recovered—happier than I've seen him look for years.'

'Do you really think so?' The Dowager was much struck by this. She valued Sir Percy's opinion more than he realised. 'Perhaps, then, there'll be no need for me to return to Kent.'

'No need whatsoever,' he assured her. 'I'll admit I thought he could do with your support after the accident happened. That's why I took it upon myself to travel to Bath to collect you.'

'And very grateful I was too,' she responded, casting him a fond smile.

'Well, it was little enough at the time.' He shook his head at the all too vivid memory. 'But as I've said, Exmouth's fully recovered now and more than capable of arranging his own future, Lavinia, old girl. So, if you take my advice, you'll allow him to do so. He'll not thank you for interfering,' he added, casting her a meaningful glance.

Robina, who had sat quietly digesting everything that had been said, was of a similar opinion. She wasn't so certain as Sir Percy appeared to be that Daniel had fully recovered from the tragedy of losing his lovely wife, but she was sure that he was more than capable of running his own affairs without his mother's help, kindly though her ladyship's intentions were always meant.

At least Daniel proved himself very capable of finding his way to the spot Robina had suggested for the picnic without any trouble at all, for within what seemed a very short space of time he was drawing his curricle off the road, coming to a halt beneath the shading branches of a large yew.

Whilst Robina and the Dowager consulted on the exact spot to hold the picnic, Daniel organised the removal of the food baskets and rugs from the coach. The delicious aroma of roast chicken wafted through the air as the baskets were carried across the grass, making Sir Percy feel decidedly peckish, and he wasn't slow to voice the opinion that the contents of the baskets should be sampled before the champagne had chance to grow warm.

As no one objected to this, the Dowager ordered the servants to serve the food and drink immediately. Everyone, with the exception of Lord Phelps who ate sparingly, eagerly sampled each of the tempting offerings Cook had taken the trouble to prepare. Consequently, no one felt particularly energetic afterwards, and the game of cricket which Daniel had proposed earlier to keep his younger daughter entertained was postponed until the food had been given time to settle.

Hannah decided to follow Lord Phelps's example and sketch for a while. It was decided that the best view of the ruined priory could be obtained from a position close to the large wood which covered a substantial part of the landscape. A river meandered its way across the countryside close to the wood's edge, and nestling between a clump of trees on the far bank was what remained of the priory.

After spreading a blanket on the lush grass several yards from where Lord Phelps had chosen to position himself, Robina settled herself between the two girls. Hannah, a keen sketcher, was very quickly absorbed in the subject across the river, unlike her sister who swiftly lost interest, but who was persuaded to continue with her effort until she saw her father approaching.

Daniel paused to stare over Lord Phelps's shoulder, and was sufficiently impressed by what he saw to nod his head several times in approval, before he turned and moved slowly towards the girls.

'Phelps undeniably has talent,' he remarked in an undertone as he reached them.

He was generous in his praise of his elder daughter's effort too. He even managed to say something complimentary about Lizzie's rather hurried, half-hearted attempt, before finally coming to stand behind Robina.

'Well, now, what can one say about this effort, I wonder?' he remarked, after peering long and hard over her shoulder.

Robina, managing to school her features, continued with her drawing, just as though he were not there. Sketching had always been a favourite hobby of hers, an enjoyable way of passing those miserable, wet days when she could not venture out of doors. She had been told by many people, including her mother who was a severe critic when it came to judging the so-called female accomplishments, that she had undoubted talent. She knew her limitations, but was also very well aware that the subjects of her drawings were always instantly recognisable, and so was prepared to take any teasing in good part.

'That—er—object in the centre is the priory, I presume… Yes,' he muttered, turning his head on one side. 'If you look at it from this angle it does resemble a building…vaguely.'

'Oh, Papa! That is most unfair of you to make fun,' Hannah reproved. 'I wish I could sketch half so well as Robina.'

His brows rose. 'Robina?'

'Yes, well—but Robina gave me permission to call her by her first name.'

'And me too, Papa,' Lizzie informed him, abandoning her drawing completely now and scrambling to her feet. 'Did you know she has three sisters, and her papa gave them all boys' names, because he really wanted them to be boys?'

'No, he didn't, silly,' her elder sister corrected. 'He chose names for boys, and then changed them slightly when they all turned out to be girls.'

'He still wanted a boy. Robina said so,' Lizzie argued, before casting an enquiring glance up at her father. 'Did you want us to be boys, Papa?'

'No, sweetheart. I was more than happy with you and Hannah.'

This perfect response won him a bright smile from his younger offspring, as she caught hold of his hand. 'Come along, Papa. Let's go and explore the wood.'

'Very well, Lizzie, I'll come with you presently,' he responded, disengaging her hold. 'But first I must go and see if either your grandmama or Sir Percy wishes to accompany us. Don't you go off without me,' he warned, before striding back across the grass.

Lizzie, evidently not content to sit and await her father's return, decided to make use of a conveniently fallen tree to practise her balancing skills by walking back and forth along the length of the trunk, leaving Hannah and Robina in peace to continue with their sketching.

'I think that was very rude of Papa to say those unkind things about your picture,' Hannah remarked, once she knew her father was safely out of earshot. 'I never ever heard him criticise any of Mama's drawings. And yours is much better than any of hers that I ever saw.' She frowned suddenly. 'Mama didn't like it when people said unkind things about her pictures.'

Robina had gained the distinct impression already from odd remarks the girls had made that both of them remembered their lovely mother with deep affection, most especially Hannah who, being the elder by some three years, recalled things about their mother rather better than Lizzie did. Both had coped remarkably well with their sad loss, and both were touchingly close to their father.

Robina didn't suppose for a moment that Hannah's last remark had been intended as a slur on her mother's character. Evidently, though, the late Lady Exmouth either did not appreciate criticism, or objected most strongly to being teased. Robina had grown accustomed to both throughout her life, and so had not taken his lordship's less than flattering remarks to heart.

'Your papa, I've discovered, is a great tease. He certainly enjoys tormenting me from time to time.'

'He certainly teases Lizzie and me.' Hannah's frown returned. 'I cannot recall his ever teasing Mama, though.'

She looked across at Lord Phelps, who had remained quietly absorbed in what he was doing since he had selected his spot on the grass. 'He's very handsome, isn't he?'

'Very,' Robina agreed, thinking that girls grew up rather quickly these days. She could not recall ever noticing whether a gentleman was handsome or not when she had been Hannah's age. She could, however, remember wandering off by herself, when she had been specifically requested not to do so, just as Lizzie, the little monkey, appeared to have done.

'Your sister hasn't bothered to await your father's return, I see,' she said, placing her sketch pad carefully to one side, before rising to her feet in one graceful movement. 'I had better go and check she isn't getting into mischief.'

'She's always doing that,' Hannah grumbled. 'I had better come with you. One of these days she's going to get herself lost. Then she'll be sorry!'

As they entered the wood, they could see no sign of the girl. Experienced in the ways of her sister, Hannah voiced her suspicion that Lizzie had possibly gone down to the river. 'She would do that, as Papa particularly requested her not to do so.'

Robina could not forbear a smile. She could fully appreciate the girl's chagrin. Having three younger sisters, she knew well enough how annoying they could be on occasions, but she had never been tempted to play the talebearer, and she doubted that Hannah would ever consider doing so either.

'In that case we'd better search there first,' Robina suggested, leading the way through the undergrowth.

The long grass and bracken brushed against her skirts, but there was little she could do to protect them from the inevitable staining. Besides which, she was more concerned about Lizzie than her own appearance.

They arrived at the riverbank without catching a glimpse of the truant, but thankfully after a few moments Robina detected a gleeful chuckle in response to Hannah's calling. 'She's further along the bank,' she said, swiftly locating the direction of the faint noise.

Keeping a safe distance from the edge of the slippery, sloping bank, they continued to forge a path through the thick undergrowth, and eventually spotted the girl, clinging monkey-fashion to the overhanging branch of a tree which leaned some way out across the river.

'Come back at once, Lizzie!' Hannah ordered, a clear note of alarm in her voice, which Robina could quite understand. The branch was swaying precariously under Lizzie's weight. 'Come back at once, do you hear, or I'll go and fetch Papa!'

'Oh, very well,' Lizzie responded, evidently having taken her sister's threat seriously, and was just beginning to edge her way slowly back when there was the unmistakable sound of splintering wood. Hannah let out a scream as Lizzie, immediately losing her grasp, dropped into the water, quickly disappearing into the murky depths.

Refusing to panic, Robina quickly dispatched Hannah to collect her father. Lizzie had landed in the water several yards from the bank, too far out to reach with a substantial stick, so Robina did not waste precious time in trying to make the attempt and swiftly removed both bonnet and shoes.

Only that morning she had been entertaining Exmouth's daughters with amusing tales of her own childhood exploits, some of which she was forced to admit she was now less than proud. However, one secret pastime in which she had never regretted indulging was learning to swim.

Her good friend Lady Sophia Cleeve had been taught to do so by her elder brother Lord Angmering, and had been eager to share this rare female accomplishment with her good friend the vicar's daughter. The lake on the vast Cleeve estate had been an ideal place to learn, and Robina, after a tentative beginning, had soon lost her fear of the water and had surprisingly excelled at this outdoor pursuit. Never had she been more grateful for this natural ability than now, for the instant she dived into the water her worst fears were confirmed.

The river looked peaceful, gently flowing, but beneath the surface were hidden currents and, worse still, beds of tangled reeds, just waiting to entwine themselves round an ankle or leg and slowly draw some poor unsuspecting soul slowly downwards to his death. Robina could feel those perilous green tendrils flicking against her skirts as she began to tread water, frantically searching for a sign of the little girl who moments before had been gasping and spluttering above the water line, but who now was nowhere to be seen. Then, blessedly, she noticed a stream of bubbles rising just a few yards away, and detected a flash of blue just beneath the surface.

She reached the exact spot in seconds. The water was murky, heavily silted, and visibility was poor, but thankfully after one swift plunge beneath the surface she made contact with the girl and, holding fast to the sleeve of the bright blue dress, she brought Lizzie to the surface.

Coughing, spluttering and understandably terrified, Lizzie entwined her little arms vicelike about Robina's neck, almost sending them both plunging into the murky depths once more. Somehow Robina managed to disengage those frantically clutching arms and manoeuvre the petrified girl into a position whereby she could manage to get them both safely back to the bank.

Fighting the current, and Lizzie's continuing frantic struggles, Robina was almost spent by the time she reached her goal. Even at the river's edge the water was too deep for her to stand, and the bank too steep for her to climb, even if she had possessed sufficient strength to make the attempt. The only thing she could do was hold fast with her free hand to one of the gnarled tree roots protruding from the earth, and pray that help was not slow in coming.

Thankfully her prayers were answered. Just when she thought she could hold neither Lizzie nor her lifeline a moment longer, a deeply reassuring voice sounded from just above and a strong masculine hand reached down to relieve her of the heavy burden she had successfully saved from a watery grave.

The next moment her own wrists were encircled by long, masculine fingers and she was blessedly raised from the water herself, and held fast to a stone hard chest. She clung to her rescuer, entwining her arms about the strong column of his neck in much the same way as Lizzie had done to her only minutes before. Her deliverer did not appear to object in the least, for he made not the least attempt to remove them as he murmured words of comfort, none of which she could clearly hear above the pounding in her temples and her valiant efforts to regain her breath.

Only when her breathing became more regular, and she felt she could stand without assistance, did she disengage herself from the gentle hold in time to witness the Dowager arrive on the scene, carrying a blanket, and Sir Percy, breathing harder than she was now doing herself, bringing up the rear.

The Dowager, wasting not a moment in wrapping the frightened and sobbing Lizzie in the woollen rug, glanced across in Robina's direction and let out an exclamation of dismay.

'By Jove!' Sir Percy muttered, following the direction of her gaze, and promptly felt for his quizzing-glass.

'Daniel, your coat…quickly,' her ladyship ordered in rapidly fading accents. 'The poor child must be freezing.'

After one brief glance in Robina's direction, Daniel could appreciate fully his mother's concern, and quite understand too why Sir Percy's gaze betrayed an earthy masculine appreciation. Robina's wet gown clung to her like a second skin, leaving absolutely nothing to the imagination.

Quickly suppressing his own strong desire to look his fill, and sublimely ignoring Robina's half-hearted attempt not to accept the garment, he slipped the jacket about her shoulders, and then wasted no further time in getting the perpetrator of what might well have turned out to be a tragic incident back to the coach.

Scooping Lizzie up in his arms, he led the way out of the wood, leaving Robina to the tender care of his mother. By the time they had arrived at the edge of the wood, Robina had managed to assure the Dowager that, apart from a slightly bruised and grazed right hand, and the fact that she was now feeling a little chilled, she was none the worse for her ordeal.

'Well, at least we can do something about making you a little warmer,' Sir Percy announced, and went striding across the grass towards Lord Phelps.

'Miss Perceval has a greater need of this than you, sir!' he snapped, a distinct note of impatience in his voice, and did no more than literally tug the rug from beneath the startled young Earl, almost sending him toppling over on to the grass.

'Good heavens!' he remarked, turning startled eyes towards Robina.

For someone who appeared to be living in another world most of the time, his gaze on occasions could be most disconcerting, and remarkably acute, noting the smallest detail. 'Has there been an accident?' he asked, thereby betraying the fact that he hadn't taken the faintest interest in anything going on about him since the moment he had positioned himself on the grass. 'Did you fall into the river, Miss Perceval?'

Sir Percy clapped a hand over his eyes. 'Heaven spare us!' he muttered and, without attempting a further explanation, escorted the highly amused ladies back to the coach.

Later, after being stripped of her sodden, mud-stained garments, Robina eased her aching limbs in a bath of warm scented water. Pinner, who had always betrayed a great fondness for her, fussed about like a mother hen, nothing being too much trouble. Robina accepted this exaggerated cosseting with a good grace, but when Pinner, having helped the her-oine of the day to restore her normally faultless appearance, announced that the doctor had been asked to call and would undoubtedly be paying a visit to the room very shortly, Robina decided that she had received more than enough attention for one day.

'I have no wish to see any doctor, Pinner. Besides, except for a sore hand, there's nothing whatsoever the matter with me, and I've absolutely no intention of wasting the doctor's valuable time over such a trivial matter.'

'The master insisted, miss.'

For the first time ever Pinner saw the light of battle flash in a pair of blue eyes, but whatever the normally even-tempered vicar's daughter might have been about to retort was held in check, for the door opened and a round little man, carrying a leather bag, entered the room.

Smiling like some indulgent uncle, the doctor listened patiently to all Robina's assurances that she was perfectly well, and then promptly set about his work, declaring when he had finished the brief examination that she was in excellent health, and that he would send his man round with a jar of salve for the injured hand.

'Have you had chance to examine Miss Courtney, Doctor?'

'Yes, ma'am. She's none the worse for her ordeal.' He tutted. 'Always been an excitable child, of course. Just like her dear mama—highly strung. I've left something to help her sleep tonight, and I shall call again in the morning, but I do not envisage any complications arising from the day's unfortunate escapade.'

'His lordship was very cross with her,' Pinner divulged when the doctor had left the room. 'Administered a proper scold, so I've been told. Said she had to stay in bed for the rest of the day, and if she dared to defy him, he'd pack her straight back to Courtney Place.'

'Oh dear,' Robina muttered, feeling a little sorry for the girl, but Pinner was of a different mind.

'If you ask me, she's been allowed to get away with things for far too long, miss. I'm not saying that one oughtn't to have made allowances after her mother died, but Miss Lizzie's always had a tendency to be naughty. I think the master now realises he must start to take a firmer hand with her before she becomes thoroughly spoilt. Why, I overheard his lordship telling the mistress that if you hadn't been there to save Miss Lizzie, it would have been too late by the time he'd reached the river.' There was a suspicion of tears in the maid's eyes. 'A real heroine you be, miss.'

Feeling acutely embarrassed by this unmerited praise, Robina did her best to try to assure the maid that she wasn't in the least brave, and that she had done no more than most other people would have done in similar circumstances, but Pinner would accept none of it. As far as she was concerned the vicar's daughter was one of those rare beings touched by God: someone special, someone to be revered, and nothing Robina could say would detract her from this belief.

So, deciding the best course was to allow the passage of time to restore the maid's sound common sense, Robina took herself off to the girls' room to check on Lizzie's progress for herself. She was not unduly worried about the child. The girl, quite naturally, had been very frightened by the ordeal, and her subdued state throughout the entire carriage journey back to the house had been understandable in the circumstances. Robina didn't suppose for a moment that Lizzie was in the least danger of succumbing to this unusual lethargy for any great length of time, and was not in the least surprised to discover her sitting up in bed, quite happily listening to her elder sister reading a story.

Her arrival certainly gave rise to mixed reactions: Hannah, rising from the chair placed by the bed, and smiling brightly, was obviously delighted to see her; Lizzie, after one very guilty glance across the room, lowered her eyes, suddenly finding the bedcovers of immense interest.

Being vastly experienced in the ways of young girls, Robina understood the reason behind this distinct lack of enthusiasm on the part of the younger sister. 'I haven't come here with the intention of scolding.'

The assurance won an instant response: a decidedly mischievous smile, swiftly followed by a wicked chuckle. 'Wasn't it exciting, Robina! A real adventure we've had today!'

'Exciting…?' Hannah glanced at her sister in dismay. 'You might have died, you silly little idiot! You know what Papa said—if Robina hadn't been there to save you, you wouldn't be here now.'

'Well, yes…I know that,' Lizzie reluctantly conceded. 'But she was there, so it was all right, wasn't it?'

Hannah, much to Robina's intense amusement, raised her hands ceilingwards in a despairing gesture. 'I give up! You're hopeless…completely hopeless. You know what Papa told you would happen if you ever disobeyed him again,' she reminded her. 'And he means it. He was very cross.'

'I know,' Lizzie mumbled, absently plucking at the bed covers. 'And I've promised him I won't. I shan't go near a river again until he's taught us how to swim.' She raised excited eyes to Robina, as her rescuer came forward to stand by the bed. 'Papa has said that he's going to teach both Hannah and me how to swim when he returns home in the autumn. Was it your papa who taught you how to swim?'

'Er—not exactly, no,' she admitted, wondering how her father would react if he was ever to discover his eldest daughter's unusual accomplishment. She doubted very much that he would display quite the enthusiasm which Lord Exmouth was betraying for his own daughters to learn how to swim. 'No, it was a friend of mine who taught me.'

'Papa says that girls ought to learn as well as boys, and he cannot think why he never thought of teaching us before,' Hannah divulged, appearing less enthusiastic than her younger sister at the prospect of taking to the water. 'I shouldn't mind learning if...well, if you were to teach me, Robina,' she admitted at last, colouring slightly. 'After all, it isn't very seemly, is it?'

'Don't be silly!' Lizzie scoffed, when Robina, quite understanding the older girl's modesty, was about to suggest that, if she could swim, perhaps Miss Halliwell might be persuaded to offer instruction. 'After all, Papa didn't take any notice at all of Robina when he pulled her from the river,' Lizzie continued, blithely ignoring her sister's swift warning glance. 'And she looked as if she wasn't wearing any clothes at all.'

'Lizzie, how could you!' Hannah reproved, but the damage was already done. Poor Robina's face had turned a bright red, for she knew the girl had spoken no less than the truth.

She had noticed herself the look of blatant admiration on Sir Percy's face, but at the time had thought that perhaps he had been much impressed by her act of bravery in rescuing Daniel's daughter from the murky depths of the river. How foolish she had been! She ought to have realised that her thin muslin gown, though modestly styled and perfectly respectable for a young lady to wear, would become virtually transparent when wet.

She remembered something else too: the way Daniel had clasped her to him; the way she had clung to him in return, experiencing in those few moments a wonderful feeling of being protected, cherished.

Had he merely held her that way in order to conceal her less than modest state? The thought that this might indeed have been the case was, strangely, considerably more daunting than discovering that she had quite innocently been displaying her charms to appreciative masculine eyes.

Suddenly aware that two pairs of young eyes were regarding her now, she tried to make light of the matter, and then quickly changed the subject by suggesting things they could do together whilst the girls remained in Brighton. She might well have succeeded in thrusting the memory of that embarrassing incident from her mind completely had she not a few minutes later, when she had left the room, come face to face with Daniel mounting the stairs.

There was absolutely no way of avoiding the encounter. To have turned and run back up the staircase to the sanctuary of her own room would, she didn't doubt for a moment, have given rise to the most appalling conjecture on Daniel's part. Much better to face him now, she decided, and try to make light of the day's escapade.

'I have just popped in to see how that little mermaid of yours goes on. I do not think she is any the worse for her ordeal.'

'And you?' he asked gently, coming to a halt two steps below, and staring up at a sweet face that betrayed becoming rosy tints of embarrassment.

'Oh, I'm fine. We Northamptonshire girls come from good earthy stock, you know,' she said airily. 'We're remarkably robust.'

'Remarkably brave too,' he responded softly. He reached for her right hand, noticing it trembling slightly in his light grasp, as he studied the broken nails and the several grazes across the palm. He did not doubt for a moment that such a modest girl as Robina would rather forget the experiences of this day. She was undoubtedly embarrassed about something, for she seemed quite reluctant to meet his gaze, so he decided not to prolong the encounter, and merely said, 'I could never possibly hope to express my gratitude, so I shan't attempt to try. Suffice it to say, I salute your courage, my little bird.'

And raising her hand, he brushed his lips lightly across her fingers before continuing on his way up the stairs and leaving Robina, for the second time that day, breathless and in the grip of some powerful force which had her instinctively grasping the banister rail for support.

# Chapter Seven

Robina would never have supposed for a moment that any action of hers would result in such recognition. The servants, she quickly discovered, simply couldn't do enough for her, treating her with a kind of reverence whenever she emerged from the bedchamber. She noticed that more of her favourite dishes appeared on the menu, and was repeatedly informed by both Stebbings and Pinner that Cook was more than willing to prepare any other little delicacies that Miss Perceval might be wishful to sample.

Unfortunately this unexpected attention was not limited to members of the household. An account of the incident by the river, possibly divulged initially by Sir Percy Lovell, quickly spread throughout Brighton society, and not a day went by without the house being invaded by a stream of inquisitive visitors, determined to discover for themselves if there was any truth in the story circulating about Miss Robina Perceval's courageous act.

Vases of beautiful flowers began to appear in

every room in the house, including a huge arrangement of highly scented white lilies, sent by Lord Phelps and his mother. Daniel's brow was seen to darken considerably each time he passed by them in the hall, though whether it was the powerful scent of which he disapproved, or from whence they came, no one was very sure.

Robina comforted herself in the knowledge that shallow society would find a new source of interest given time, and that she would not forever remain an object of attention wherever she went. Thankfully, there had been a noticeable reduction of interest displayed when the day arrived for Hannah and Lizzie to leave Brighton and continue their journey to Dorset.

Robina was sorry to see them go, for she had become genuinely attached to the sisters, but she was happy to think that their departure would herald their father's return to the house. No matter how enjoyable she had found the girls' company, she couldn't deny that she had missed very much those times she and Daniel had spent together, happily reading in companionable silence, or playing cards.

Sadly he betrayed no signs of desiring an immediate return to the house, and appeared more than content to remain for the time being at least with his good friend Montague Merrell. Strangely enough the Dowager did not appear particularly concerned over her son's seeming reluctance to take up residence with them again. In fact, she appeared too excited by their invitation to dine at the Pavilion to concern herself with much else.

The Regent's arrival in Brighton brought a further influx of visitors to the town, and a noticeable increase in social events. Not an evening passed without Robina spending an hour or so in her bedchamber, preparing to attend some party or other, and on the day they were due to dine at the Pavilion, Pinner took longer than ever to dress Robina's hair and to fasten her into the lovely kingfisher-blue silk gown which she had donned only once before, when she had worn it on the occasion of her good friend Lady Sophia Cleeve's engagement party.

Daniel had kindly consented to escort them, and kept Robina in a high state of amusement throughout the short carriage journey by passing rather disparaging remarks concerning the Regent's garish taste in décor, and the deplorable alterations His Royal Highness continued to make to his 'little retreat' by the sea.

Robina, although excited at the prospect of dining at the Pavilion, could not but agree with Daniel's opinions. Each room she passed through in the famous building was richly decorated and sumptuously furnished, no expense having been spared. The choice of décor, however, certainly wouldn't have been to everyone's taste, and most certainly wasn't to her own. Simplicity and sobriety were not words in the Regent's vocabulary it seemed. There was evidence of his extravagance everywhere, most especially in the dining-room, where an amazing number of richly dressed dishes were placed on the table.

As the evening wore on, and many, many more guests began to arrive, the atmosphere in the Saloon, where dancing was being held, became increasingly oppressive. Robina managed to locate a slightly cooler spot in one corner, and attempted to conceal herself behind the gracefully spreading foliage of a conveniently positioned potted palm, while she studied the dancers, all dressed in their finest, their clothes and bodies glimmering with precious jewels.

Unfortunately, as had happened more frequently of late, her mind began to dwell on what the future might hold in store for her once she had left all the delights of Brighton behind her, and she quite failed to notice a certain tall, athletic figure quietly approaching.

'And what's all this?' The familiar, attractive voice made her start. 'It isn't like you, my little bird, to skulk away in a corner.'

'I was not skulking, as you call it,' she responded, wondering if he had been watching her for some little time, 'merely trying to make myself as inconspicuous as possible. It's so very warm in here, Daniel. I wouldn't dare risk a further period on the dance-floor, and was doing my level best to avoid being asked.'

He appeared to accept this explanation readily enough. 'Yes, it's certainly oppressive. Would you care for a stroll in the conservatory? You might find it a little less uncomfortable out there.'

She didn't need to think twice about it, and linked her arm through his, willingly accepting his escort into the huge glass construction which was noticeably cooler and far less congested, though there were more than one or two couples lurking amidst the greenery.

'What were you thinking about, Robin?' he asked, after they had strolled to the end and seated themselves in two of the wicker chairs. 'You appeared to be in a world of your own. Aren't you enjoying these opulent royal surroundings?'

'Very much, though I do find them a little overwhelming.'

The answer came swiftly enough, but to one who had made an intense study of her moods, Daniel found the reply just a little too mechanical, as though part of her mind remained elsewhere. 'Is something troubling you, Robin?' he asked gently, but she made no attempt to respond this time. 'Come, child, we are friends, are we not? True friends should never be afraid to confide in each other.'

Friends…? Once she had found it such a comfort to think of him in that light, but now… 'I was thinking of how very much I've enjoyed my time here in Brighton. Surprisingly enough, much more so than I did my weeks in the capital.'

He appeared decidedly sceptical. 'You'll forgive me for saying so, Robin, but you looked anything but contented a few minutes ago.'

She couldn't help but smile at the swiftness and honesty of his response. 'If that is so then it was the

thought of having to leave all this behind when I
return to Abbot Quincey.' She discovered she was
equally powerless to prevent a sigh escaping. 'I'm
becoming far too contented with this kind of life,
Daniel. It is quite worrying.'

He regarded her in silence, his expression quite
unreadable now. 'What convinces you that you must
abandon this kind of life? If you do not relish the
prospect of returning to Northamptonshire, there
must surely be other options open to you.'

'Such as what?'

'Marriage.' There was more than just a hint of
cynicism in the smile he cast her. 'After all, it was
with the intention of finding yourself a husband that
you left Abbot Quincey in the first place.'

She wasn't in the least offended by this. Daniel
would never be deliberately hurtful, but at the same
time he was never afraid to speak his mind, and she
had grown quite accustomed to the occasional blunt
remark.

'You make it sound so very mercenary,' she responded, not attempting to deny it. 'Which, of
course, it is. Most young women who embark on a
London Season do so with that very goal in mind.
And I was, I suppose, luckier than most,' she continued, after a moment's reflection. 'I did at least receive two proposals of marriage, neither of which I
regretted refusing.'

She decided not to add that this was done with her
mother's full approval, and in the hope that a third
and far more advantageous offer might be forthcom-

ing from Daniel himself. 'Both gentlemen were very respectable, but my feelings were not engaged.'

Once again she found herself on the receiving end of one of those penetrating brown-eyed stares. 'And has no suitable gentleman succeeded in capturing your interest since your arrival in Brighton? Mr Frederick Ainsley, for instance? He has been increasingly attentive in recent weeks, and you do not appear averse to his company.'

She certainly wasn't averse to the gentlemanly Mr Ainsley's company. She liked him very well, had done so from their very first meeting. Whether she would be content to spend the rest of her life with him was quite another matter entirely.

Strangely enough, Robina had never once seriously considered the possibility of a union with Frederick Ainsley. She didn't doubt for a moment that he would make both a considerate and loving husband. In many ways he reminded her of her own father. Both were intelligent and both were sincerely dedicated to their chosen profession. Therein, she supposed, lay the reason why she had no intention of allowing her relationship with Mr Ainsley to deepen.

She had never made any secret of the fact that she had enjoyed a very happy childhood in Abbot Quincey. None the less, she experienced no desire whatsoever to exchange life in one vicarage for life in another.

She had now grown accustomed to a completely different lifestyle. And she loved it! It wasn't that she wished for a future that was just one long round of socialising and parties. Oh, no, that would not appeal to her in the least! She wanted marriage and children. But most important of all she wished to marry a man whom she could love and respect. Her perfect mate was out there somewhere, she felt certain of it, and yet his image continued to elude her, remaining just a blur in her mind's eye.

'Yes, I should like to marry, Daniel. But, if and when I do, it will be to a man I love,' she admitted at last, thereby betraying her inmost thoughts. 'I would never marry just for security, or just to have a home of my own.'

There was a discernible note of self-consciousness in her little trill of laughter. 'Oh, I don't know, Daniel. Perhaps I expect too much from life. I've been luckier than most, I know. It's just that… How can I explain it?…I suppose it's just that nothing very exciting has ever happened to me. Every girl dreams of meeting her knight in shining armour, a brave Sir Galahad who will rescue her from danger, and then fall hopelessly in love with her.

'Yes, well, may you laugh,' she went on when a rich masculine rumble greeted this confession. 'You're a man. No doubt you've enjoyed a deal of excitement in your life; whereas mine, up until a few weeks ago, has been singularly uneventful.'

Daniel's smile remained, but there was no mistaking the sincerity in his voice as he said, 'Yes, I rather fancy I do understand, my little bird. A little excitement from time to time does no one any harm. So, you're hoping to meet your Sir Lancelot.'

'Galahad,' she corrected, feeling extremely foolish now at having confessed to a rather childish fancy. 'But as that is unlikely ever to happen, I'm desperately striving to resign myself to life as a governess.'

'Dear me,' he murmured. 'That's a comedown from a life with a brave knight.'

'True,' she agreed, 'but possibly more realistic.'

Easily removing the fan from her clasp, Daniel opened it to its fullest extent to study the decoration of delicately painted flowers. 'Have you forgotten Mama's suggestion that you might like to consider becoming her permanent companion?'

Robina clearly recalled the subject being raised, but hadn't taken her ladyship's remarks seriously. 'She was jesting, surely?'

'No, I do not believe so, child. She's extremely fond of you.'

He looked as if he was about to say something further, but then evidently thought better of it, and promptly handed back her fan before rising to his feet. 'There will be time enough for you to consider my mother's proposal. The Brighton Season is far from over, so let us return to the Saloon now and continue to enjoy it.'

They were halfway down the huge glass construction when they noticed a number of persons beginning to gather near the door. The little group suddenly parted, and into the conservatory strolled

Daniel's very good friend Montague Merrell, accompanied by none other than the Regent himself.

Robina knew, of course, that Mr Merrell was a close friend of the future king. She had seen Mr Merrell, together with several others, enter the room with the Regent shortly before it was time to go in to dinner. There had been no opportunity of being introduced to the Regent then; there was no chance of avoiding it now. His Royal Highness took one glance down the conservatory and his plump features creased in a smile of instant recognition.

'Exmouth, old fellow!' He came forward, moving with surprising grace for a gentleman of his ample proportions. 'Monty here informed me that you were amongst the guests tonight. How good it is to see you in society once more!'

'Thank you, sir.' Daniel noticed the future monarch's eyes stray in Robina's direction, and hurriedly presented her before the totally wrong conclusion could be drawn.

Robina, executing a graceful curtsey, discovered her hand captured in warm, podgy fingers. 'Delightful! Delightful!' beamed the Regent, eyeing her approvingly, and making her feel like a particularly tasty morsel presented to him on a plate.

'Miss Perceval is at present residing with us in Brighton, sir... And is here under my mother's protection,' Daniel added, just in case the Regent should still be harbouring any doubts as to Robina's respectability.

'Excellent!' The future king, after one last squeeze

of the slender fingers, released his hold on Robina's hand. 'And how is your dear mother, Exmouth? In good health, I trust?'

'In fine fettle, sir, as always.'

'Excellent, excellent!' he said again, before turning to Merrell. 'Well, Monty, let us leave Exmouth to escort this delightful young lady to the safety of his mother's side, and go and find Wilmington. You said he was also here tonight, I seem to remember.'

'Indeed he is,' Mr Merrell responded and, after casting a sly wink in Daniel's direction, accompanied the Regent back to the Saloon.

Daniel and Robina followed at a discreet distance, and eventually found the Dowager amidst a small group at the far end of the room.

'I have been ordered by no less a personage that the Regent himself to restore Robina to your protection,' Daniel divulged, after extricating his mother from the small group. 'And as I wouldn't dare to disobey a royal command, here she is.'

'Where on earth have you been, child? The last time I saw you, you were dancing with Lord Farley.'

'Oh, she has gone up in the world since then, Mama,' Daniel put in before Robina could even attempt to offer an explanation for her long absence. 'She has been hobnobbing with royalty.'

'Truly?' The Dowager's excited glance darted between the two. 'You've met the Regent, child? Did you introduce her, Daniel? I was hoping to present you. What did you think of our future king?'

'Rather overwhelming, ma'am.'

'Rather overweight, you mean,' the Dowager corrected.

'Careful, Mama,' her son warned. 'There are those who have been banished for saying less.'

Lady Exmouth was about to say that she had spoken no less than the truth, when an undignified squeal reached her ears, and she turned to discover a vivacious damsel, dressed in an amber-coloured gown, bearing down upon them.

'Heavens above!' she exclaimed, wrapping her arms about the perpetrator of the unladylike squeal. 'What on earth are you doing here, child?'

'The same as you, I should imagine, Aunt Lavinia.'

Disengaging herself from the loving embrace, the new arrival turned to Daniel and unashamedly placed a smacking kiss on his cheek. 'Never expected to bump in to you here, my dear cousin,' she admitted, staring up at him with more than just a hint of devilment in her dark eyes. 'Always thought you had more taste. My, my, how you have changed!'

'Which you patently have not, you outrageous baggage!' he retorted, smiling down into twinkling brown eyes. 'Now, behave yourself for a moment, and allow me to present Miss Robina Perceval to you…Robin,' he added turning to her, 'this is my cousin, Lady Arabella Tolliver, the scourge of my life.'

'Horrid creature!' Laughing, Lady Tolliver reached for Robina's hand, and held it fast in both her own. 'How very pleased I am to make your ac-

quaintance, Miss Perceval. I had heard rumours that
dear Aunt Lavinia had taken a pretty girl under her
protective wing.'

'And before you are tempted into further indiscretion,' her ladyship put in hurriedly, 'I think we had
better find ourselves some quiet corner, preferably
somewhere where we are able to sit down.'

She turned to her son in time to catch the amused
glint in his eyes, and hurriedly asked if he would be
kind enough to fetch them refreshments. Then without further ado, she ushered the young ladies to the
farthest corner of the room, where she was lucky
enough to find three vacant chairs.

'Now, Arabella,' she began, when they had all
seated themselves. 'What brings you to Brighton?
You never mentioned you were planning a visit in
your last letter.'

'Good gracious, Aunt Lavinia! You ought to know
me better than that by now. I never make plans. I do
everything on the spur of the moment. Besides, why
shouldn't I be here? My period of mourning was over
weeks ago.' She cast a rather wistful glance down at
the skirts of her fetching amber-coloured gown. 'Pity
really…I looked quite becoming in widow's weeds.'

'Arabella, really!' her aunt reproved, striving not
to laugh. 'What are people to think when you talk
that way!'

She then turned to Robina, who was also doing
her level best not to laugh at the lively Lady
Tolliver's remarks. 'If you have not already guessed,
my dear, this outrageous young woman is my niece,

the only daughter of my dear departed sister Emily. Sadly my sister died giving birth to a stillborn child, and my niece spent long periods during her childhood with us at Courtney Place. I believe she looked upon the house as her second home, and Daniel as her brother.'

'I certainly looked upon the Place as home, Aunt, but whether I ever thought of Daniel as my brother is quite another matter.'

Robina certainly detected the wry edge in Lady Tolliver's voice. Whether the Dowager did or not was difficult to judge, for her attention was diverted in the next moment by her son's approach, bringing with him a footman, bearing four glasses of champagne on a silver tray. Once they had all sampled their refreshments, Daniel turned to his cousin, asking where she was staying.

'Dear Roderick rented a house for the duration of the summer. The poor dear would not hear of leaving me behind when I contracted a troublesome cold, which I simply could not shake off. We planned to arrive in the middle of June, but only succeeded in leaving Devonshire a few days ago.'

'And you are fully restored to health now, I trust?'

'Yes, Cousin, and eager to make up for all the time we've lost.' Her rather wide mouth curled into a sudden smile. 'Oh, there's dear Roddy now,' she announced, glancing in the direction of the main door. 'Do go over and rescue him from Lord Crawford, Daniel. I do not wish for him to be persuaded into indulging in a game of chance with that inveterate gambler. Roddy's no card player, and I should hate to discover in the morning that he's lost the entire family fortune.'

She laughed as her cousin moved away to do her bidding. 'It is so amusing having a stepson virtually the same age as oneself. Most people seeing us together automatically assume that we're husband and wife.'

Robina, having followed his progress across the room, saw Daniel shake the hand of a sandy-haired gentleman of medium height, and thought it highly likely that most people who were not acquainted with them would possibly think that Lady Tolliver and Sir Roderick were married. She was intrigued to learn more about Daniel's spirited cousin, but was destined to discover nothing further that evening, for they were joined by several of the Dowager's particular friends, and Lady Tolliver soon afterwards drifted away to mix with the other guests.

Robina caught sight of her again on only three occasions throughout the remainder of the evening. Each time she was clinging possessively to Daniel's arm. He appeared not in the least displeased at being monopolised by her. In fact, he looked far happier than Robina had ever seen him look before. It ought, she knew, to have given her a great deal of pleasure to think that Daniel was blissfully contented in his cousin's company, but it did not. Perversely it had the opposite effect, and she left the Pavilion later that night feeling decidedly dispirited.

# Chapter Eight

The following morning Robina received a letter from her family, confirming the surprising notice she had read in the newspaper two weeks before, announcing her cousin Hester's betrothal to Lord Dungarran.

She shook her head, still finding it difficult to believe. 'Well, apparently it is true,' she declared to Lady Exmouth, who sat opposite her at the breakfast table, happily nibbling her way through a second delicious buttered roll. 'Yet I'm still finding it hard to believe. Hester never displayed the least interest in finding herself a husband. Her first Season was a complete disaster. It put her off the idea of matrimony altogether.'

'No, not entirely, my dear,' Lady Exmouth corrected. 'Evidently Lord Dungarran persuaded her to change her mind, though I must say I cannot recall your cousin betraying much interest in any gentleman on the occasions I saw her in London. But, then, some young ladies are more adept at concealing their feelings than others, are they not?'

After debating for a moment, she weakened and reached for a third buttered roll. 'Does your mother reveal any other details in her letter?'

Robina scanned the single sheet written in her mother's beautifully flowing hand. 'Only that the engagement was announced on the day of the fête. What a pity I wasn't there to celebrate with the family! Uncle James and Aunt Eleanor must be absolutely delighted.'

She shook her head, smiling to herself as a thought suddenly occurred to her. 'Do you know, ma'am, before we, Lady Sophia Cleeve, Hester and myself, that is, left Northamptonshire all those weeks ago, I never imagined that I would be the only one amongst us who would return home not betrothed. In fact, if I'm honest, I would be forced to admit that I considered it more than likely that I would be the only one to find herself engaged at the end of the Season.'

The hand raising the Dowager's coffee-cup to her lips checked for a moment. 'There's still plenty of time for you to become so, my dear. After all, you are not scheduled to return home until the autumn.'

'That is precisely what Daniel himself said,' Robina responded before she quite realised what she was disclosing, and noticed the sudden alert expression flicker over her interested companion's features.

That relaxed and easy-going manner of the Dowager's was extremely deceptive. It might lead one to suppose that she happily existed in a world of her own for the most part, content to let the more mundane day to day events pass her by; whereas, in fact, very little escaped her notice.

'Yes—er—well, as I mentioned to him last night,' she hurriedly continued, 'I would never marry simply for security and to acquire a home of my own.'

'Did you really say that to my son?' Lady Exmouth appeared genuinely impressed. 'Good for you, child!'

Robina stared across the breakfast table, puzzled by this surprising reaction to her disclosure. Surely, if Lady Exmouth continued to retain the hope of a marriage between her son and the Vicar of Abbot Quincey's daughter, she ought not to be happy to learn that the girl whom she considered highly suitable for a future daughter-in-law could not be persuaded to marry for either wealth or rank? Perhaps the Dowager had undergone a change of heart since her arrival in Brighton, and had come to the conclusion that her son and the vicar's daughter simply wouldn't suit, Robina mused, unexpectedly experiencing a feeling of bitter disappointment, and quickly changed the subject by enquiring if they could expect a visit from Lady Tolliver.

'Good gracious, child! I would never attempt to predict what that madcap niece of mine plans to do. She's a law unto herself!'

Disappointment was swiftly replaced by a strong feeling of resentment, as an image of Lady Tolliver, clinging like a limpet to Daniel's arm the previous evening, suddenly appeared before Robina's mind's eye.

'Daniel gave me the distinct impression that he is very fond of his cousin, ma'am,' she remarked in a casual tone, while desperately striving to control the wealth of strange sensations welling up inside. 'They are—er—more like brother and sister, didn't you say?'

'They always seemed so to me, and yet... Oh, I don't know, dear.' Her ladyship's lips curled into a reminiscent smile. 'I suppose at one time I imagined they might make a match of it. Arabella has no looks to speak of, but she has many other wonderful qualities to compensate for lack of beauty. She's intelligent and witty, and so full of life.' She shook her head, her smile quickly fading. 'I'm afraid, though, she could never compete with Clarissa, at least not in looks... Very few females ever could.'

Learning this ought to have improved Robina's state of mind; perversely, it did not. For some obscure reason she seemed incapable of controlling that unwholesome feeling of resentment. If anything it was increasing to encompass both Lady Tolliver and the late Lady Exmouth.

'Strangely enough Arabella was one of the very few people who thought Daniel was making a mistake in marrying Clarissa,' Lady Exmouth divulged, thereby instantly regaining Robina's full attention. 'And I do not believe her opinion was fuelled by jealousy. She genuinely seemed to feel that they would not suit. Of course there were others, like my good friend Sir Percy, who voiced their feelings of unease too, but their objections in the main stemmed from the fact that they considered Daniel too young for marriage.'

'What were your niece's objections, ma'am?' Robina prompted when the Dowager, with a faraway look in her eyes, fell silent once more. 'Did she ever offer an explanation for her disapproval?'

'No, I do not recall that she ever did, my dear. She and Clarissa played together a great deal when children, so Arabella knew her very well.' She shrugged. 'Perhaps my niece perceived something in Clarissa's nature that she didn't quite like. After all, no one is perfect. We all have our faults, little idiosyncrasies that others find irritating.'

This was certainly true. Robina had always been very close to her sisters, and loved them all dearly, but that didn't mean that she was blind to their faults, or did not find them quite annoying on occasions.

It would have been interesting to discover precisely what flaw Arabella had perceived in the late Lady Exmouth's nature, but as the Dowager evidently didn't know, there was little point in pursuing the subject, so Robina changed the conversation once again by remarking, 'From what Lady Tolliver was saying last night, I gained the distinct impression that her husband was a good deal older than herself.'

'Yes, dear, he was. It must be a trait with the females in my family to prefer older men. As I believe I've mentioned before, Daniel's dear papa was a good deal older than myself. Arabella's papa was much older than my sister, and Arabella herself married a gentleman old enough to be her own father.' Smiling, she shook her head. 'I must confess that I was surprised when my niece agreed to accept Sir Henry's proposal. She was always such a lively girl, never still for a moment, and I suppose I expected her to choose some dashing young blade. But no, she chose the quiet and dignified Sir Henry, whose only son was several months her senior.

'Surprisingly enough she adapted very quickly to married life, and settled down well in Devonshire. No matter what impression she may have given last night, she was touchingly devoted to Sir Henry, and utterly heartbroken when he died. She's still a relatively young woman, and I would like to think that she might one day marry again and have children, but I wouldn't be at all surprised if she did not.' She gave an unexpected gurgle of laughter. 'It isn't likely that too many gentlemen would be willing to put up with my niece's madcap ways.'

Perhaps not, Robina thought, trying to quell the sudden acrid taste rising in her throat by swallowing a mouthful of coffee, but one gentleman certainly gave the distinct impression last night that he might be willing to try.

In an attempt to rid herself of the totally unexpected melancholy state of mind which was increasingly plaguing her of late, Robina decided to pay a call on her friend Olivia. She would have much preferred to venture forth on her own, but as she knew that the Dowager, whose complacency did not stretch so far as to approve of young ladies wandering about the streets of towns and cities on their own, would deplore such behaviour, Robina asked Nancy, the young parlour-maid, to accompany her.

She arrived at the fashionable house Olivia's new brother-in-law had hired for the duration of their stay in Brighton to discover that her friend had had a similar idea, and had gone out for a walk. Olivia's sister Beatrice, however, was at home and, delighted by the unexpected visit, ordered refreshments to be brought to the front parlour at once.

For a while they discussed yet again the startling events which had taken place in recent weeks in Northamptonshire, before they went on to talk about more recent news—Hester Perceval's surprising betrothal, and the engagements of several other of their mutual acquaintances. Beatrice then went on to laughingly remark that she didn't suppose for a moment that it would be too long before her very welcome visitor found herself well and truly caught in parson's mousetrap, a suggestion which caused the most uncomfortable ache in a certain region beneath Robina's ribcage.

She swiftly assured her charming hostess that she had formed no attachment, and that it was much more likely that Olivia would be the next one to find herself engaged, a suggestion which instantly brought a troubled look into the new Lady Ravensden's eyes.

Robina was well aware that Beatrice was no fool, and that she had probably been aware for as long as

Robina had herself that Olivia had been showing a
marked interest in a certain Captain Jack Denning.

Having by this time met the gentleman on several
occasions, Robina had decided that she rather liked
him. He was undoubtedly handsome, and every
young girl's idea of the dashing storybook hero, she
supposed, which made her momentarily ponder anew
on why she, unlike her friend Olivia, had never been
particularly attracted to him.

There was no denying that he had a darkly brooding air. He had earned himself the reputation of being
abrupt on occasion, and there had also been considerable gossip in certain quarters concerning a rift between himself and other members of his family
which, quite naturally, might cause Beatrice some
concern, if she supposed that her young sister's affections were genuinely engaged.

This, however, was none of her affair, even though
she did consider herself a friend of the family, and
she had no intention of prying or becoming involved
in matters which were really none of her concern. So
she tactfully turned the conversation to less personal
issues, and a short while later declared that it was
time she took her leave.

Although declining Beatrice's kind invitation to
await Olivia's return, Robina decided not to go directly back to Daniel's house, and took a detour
through the centre of the town, which certainly
pleased the young parlour-maid.

Nancy, it quickly became apparent, enjoyed nothing more than gazing through shop windows to stare

with wide, admiring eyes at the beautifully trimmed dresses and bonnets. Robina, on the other hand, could work up little enthusiasm, and was in the process of trying to persuade her dawdling companion to increase her pace, when she heard her name being called in a bright, cheerful voice. Surprised, she turned to discover a very smart open carriage drawing to a halt a matter of a few yards away.

'Good day to you, Miss Perceval,' the instantly recognisable sole occupant of the carriage greeted her, as Robina approached. 'Can I tempt you to accompany me about the town. I intended to call on Aunt Lavinia, so shall see you safely home afterwards.'

To have refused would have seemed churlish. Furthermore, Lady Tolliver seemed genuinely pleased to see her. Robina wished she could have said the same, for Daniel's cousin had given her no reason whatsoever to take her in dislike.

Her conscience began to prick her, for she was very well aware that the Vicar of Abbot Quincey would have been most disappointed in his eldest daughter if he ever thought for a moment that she was capable of feeling antipathy without a very good reason.

'I should be delighted to accept,' she responded, desperately striving to sound as though she truly meant it, and then turned to the young maid, who declared that she was more than happy to continue walking, providing Miss Perceval had no objection.

'Just like the maids back home,' Arabella declared, after ordering her coachman to move on. 'They all seem to derive a great deal of pleasure from gaping into shop windows. Quite understandable, I suppose! Most young women enjoy looking at frills and furbelows.' Her eyes narrowed as she suddenly subjected her companion to a penetrating stare. 'You, on other hand, did not appear to be enjoying yourself.'

Robina, returning that steady gaze, realised suddenly that Lady Tolliver and the Dowager had much more in common than a mere family resemblance. Both ladies, it seemed, were acutely observant.

Deciding it might be wise not to attempt to deny it, she said, 'I had my fill of gazing into shops during my stay in London.' She shrugged. 'It is very nice to be able to wear and own pretty things, but I'm afraid I'm one of those people who cannot work up much enthusiasm for possessions, Lady Tolliver.'

'A rare female, indeed,' Arabella murmured, before suggesting that formality cease between them. 'I hope you will call me Arabella, for I fully intend to address you by your given name. I do so hate unnecessary reserve, so we may as well start as we mean to go on, don't you think?'

Evidently taking the silence for agreement, Arabella looked about her with interest. 'Good heavens!' she exclaimed, suddenly, catching sight of a familiar figure in a passing carriage. 'Isn't that Lady Milverton? What a quiz of a hat!' Chuckling wickedly, she turned her attention back to Robina. 'So, how are you enjoying your stay in Brighton?'

'Very much. Both Daniel and his mother have been so very kind, giving up so much of their time to keep me entertained. Daniel has even taken the trouble to teach me how to handle the ribbons.'

Arabella appeared genuinely impressed. 'My, my, wonders will never cease! Daniel must indeed think highly of you, my dear, to permit you to handle his precious horses. He always flatly refused to allow me to take charge of the ribbons whenever we ventured out together in the past. And I'm positive he never allowed his wife to drive herself about. Not that Clarissa would ever have considered learning how to handle a spirited pair,' she went on to divulge. 'Her interests, I'm afraid, were very limited.'

There had been no hint of malice in Arabella's voice. She had sounded quite matter-of-fact when disclosing those latter details, and yet something told Robina that Lady Exmouth had possibly been right when she had suggested that Arabella had not held the late Lady Exmouth in the highest esteem. It was also quite possible that Arabella had, indeed, secretly hoped to marry Daniel, and had resented the woman who had thwarted her ambition.

'You knew Daniel's late wife quite well, I understand,' she ventured in an attempt to discover a little more.

'Ha! So dear Aunt Lavinia has been discussing me, has she,' Arabella responded, a little knowing smile tugging at her full lips. 'She would! Yes, I knew Clarissa very well. I frequently paid visits to her home whenever I stayed at Courtney Place. We rubbed along together extremely well considering we had little in common. I was very much the tomboy, and enjoyed nothing better than climbing trees, and getting into all sorts of mischief, whereas dear Clarissa was very much the demur, young lady, quite happy to pass all her spare time sewing or drawing, or sitting at the pianoforte.'

The full lips curled into yet another effortless smile. 'She was certainly far more proficient at the so-called female accomplishments than I ever was, or ever could be for that matter,' she freely admitted. 'But she displayed precious little enthusiasm for much else, except perhaps socialising. Clarissa enjoyed being the centre of attention. To give her her due she wasn't in the least vain, but, I suppose, being so strikingly lovely, she had grown accustomed over the years to being the object of almost every gentleman's attention.'

She sighed, and after a moment added, 'Perhaps it was for the best that she died when she did. Her looks would undoubtedly have faded in time, and she would, I very much fear, have turned into one of those devilishly dull faded beauties who spend all their time lying on a couch, imagining that they have every sort of illness, while enjoying the doting attention of some foolish female companion.'

She laughed suddenly, an infectious gurgle that surprisingly had Robina chuckling too. 'Dear me, how old cattish I sound! Anyone listening to me would imagine that I disliked Clarissa, whereas in fact I liked her very well. She was immensely sweet and kind, and of course very, very lovely. I was not in the least surprised when Daniel became infatuated. Most gentlemen who met her fell instantly under her spell. But I was very surprised when he decided to marry her…I wonder how long it took him before he realised his mistake?'

Robina gaped in astonishment. Fortunately Arabella's attention was once again claimed by an acquaintance waving to her from a passing carriage, and by the time she turned back, Robina had succeeded in schooling her features.

'I must say, it is good to see Daniel enjoying life again. I wasn't able to attend Clarissa's funeral,' Arabella disclosed, glancing briefly at the golden band on her left hand. 'Dear Henry was fading fast at the time. He never fully recovered from that final attack, and died just a few months after Clarissa. Daniel came to his funeral. I was deeply shocked at the change in him. Now he seems a completely different man, happier than I've seen him look in years, I'm pleased to say. Though why in heaven's name I should continue to concern myself about the wretched creature I'll never know!'

Dark eyes, twinkling with mischief, turned towards Robina again. 'He's dragging my dear Roderick off to watch some fearful bout of fisticuffs the day after tomorrow, and leaving me quite without a protector. But I flatly refuse to wait at home for their return, so I've decided to organise an alfresco breakfast at some picturesque spot. Do say you'll make up one of the party. I'm determined to get to know you a good deal better, and determined too, that we shall become firm friends.'

Robina was not so very certain that they would ever become that close, and was even less certain why she felt that it might be wise to remain a little aloof where Lady Tolliver was concerned, for she was undeniably a most likeable woman whose innate honesty Robina could not help but admire.

That evening, when she saw Arabella again at a party given by yet another of the Dowager's close acquaintances, Robina began to feel even less inclined to make a friend of the lively widow.

When Lady Exmouth had mentioned, just before setting out, that she had received a note from her son expressing his regret that he now found himself unable to act as their escort, Robina had thought it most strange, for she had long since considered Daniel a man of his word. When he had pledged to do a certain thing, he invariably did do it.

As she entered Lady Maitland's stylish drawing-room, however, she understood fully why he had decided to break his word. There he stood, looking remarkably relaxed and happy, amidst a small group surrounding his lively cousin. There was no sign of Arabella's stepson, Sir Roderick, amongst the guests, and so Robina naturally assumed that Arabella had called upon her cousin's services to escort her to the party and, seemingly, he had been only too willing to oblige.

Robina could feel that unholy resentment returning

again with a vengeance, and seemed powerless to check it. She knew she was reacting like some over-indulged child to feel so aggrieved. Daniel had every right to escort whomsoever he chose. She was painfully aware, too, that she was being thoroughly selfish in begrudging him time with his cousin, but for some obscure reason she couldn't help feeling as she did.

She tried her level best to appear pleased to see him when he did eventually notice their presence and came across the room to greet them, but it was an effort, and it showed. Daniel instantly detected the faint brittle note in her voice, and asked outright if she was feeling quite well.

'Yes, dear, you do look a little flushed,' the Dowager put in before Robina could assure him that she was perfectly all right. 'I sincerely trust you haven't taken Lady Phelps's chill. What an inconsiderate creature Augusta has become! Fancy paying morning calls when one's eyes and nose are streaming, and one is forever sneezing! I wouldn't be at all surprised if we are not both forced to take to our beds within the next few days.'

Aware that if she remained, she might foolishly betray the resentment she seemed powerless to control, Robina scanned the room, frantically searching for a means of escape, and thankfully discovered one. 'Oh, there's Olivia Roade Burton, with her sister. I paid a visit to them this morning, but unfortunately Olivia had gone out. Would you both excuse me whilst I go and have a word with my friend? I haven't seen her for days.'

'Are you certain she's all right, Mama?' Daniel enquired, the instant Robina had scurried away. 'She seems a little tense to me.'

'If that is so, then it is quite evident that where Miss Perceval is concerned you are a deal more observant than I am, my son,' she responded, beaming with satisfaction. 'She was fine earlier. As she mentioned, she went out for a walk this morning, and was brought safely home by dear Arabella. Nothing untoward has happened this day, I assure you.'

But Daniel was not at all convinced. He had made too close a study of her in recent weeks not to be certain that something had occurred to disturb the calm waters of her mind, something which, unless he much mistook the matter, she was determined to keep to herself.

Leaving his mother happily conversing with several acquaintances, he wandered into the room set out for cards, selecting a seat near the door from where he was able to view proceedings taking place back in the drawing-room.

Robina, being an extremely pretty girl, had never been short of invitations to step out on to the floor, and this evening proved no exception. Each time Daniel raised his eyes from the cards in his hand it was to discover her lightly moving about the room, executing the steps of the various dances with effortless grace. On the surface at least she appeared to be enjoying herself hugely, but he was not fooled.

Her smiles, he had noticed, lacked that certain spontaneous warmth, and there was just a hint of tension about the set of those lovely, gently sloping white shoulders.

Declining the invitation to play yet another hand, he eventually wandered back into the drawing-room in time to see her latest partner returning her to the protection of the Dowager's side. 'I hope you will do me the honour of saving me the supper dance?' he asked, coming upon her completely unobserved and making her start. 'And, of course, permit me to escort you in to supper afterwards.'

Robina made not the least attempt to conceal either her delight or surprise. Daniel, although an excellent dancer for a man of his size, and surprisingly light on his feet, took a turn on the floor only rarely, declaring that, having almost attained the ripe old age of six-and-thirty, he considered it far more dignified to watch the spectacle rather than take any part in it himself.

That he had chosen to escort her in to supper in preference to his cousin brought immense satisfaction, and she only hoped the invitation was not by way of recompense for failing to escort her to the party, but because he genuinely desired her company.

The smile she bestowed upon him while accepting the invitation came effortlessly to her lips, but it quite failed to persuade him to remain by her side, and he wandered away directly afterwards to join a group of friends congregating by the door.

On several occasions, as the evening progressed,

Robina just happened to catch him staring in her direction, but he made no attempt to approach her again. Nor did he appear at her side to claim her hand shortly before the supper dance was due to begin.

'Do you happen to know where Daniel is hiding himself, ma'am?' she asked the Dowager, after scanning the room in a vain attempt to catch a glimpse of his tall, athletic figure.

'No, dear. I'm afraid I don't, unless he's still outside with Arabella. I thought I noticed them wandering out to the terrace a little earlier.'

Robina hesitated, but only for a moment. After all, it could do no harm to go in search of him, she told herself, making her way across to the tall French windows, which their thoughtful hostess had ordered to be left wide open to allow much needed fresh air into the room.

She was surprised to discover the terrace quite deserted, and turned, about to go back inside and search elsewhere, when a trill of feminine laughter floated up from the garden on the sweetly perfumed night air.

Her soft slippers made not a sound as she walked across the terrace towards the four stone steps leading down to a sizeable lawn. The two figures, silhouetted in the moonlight and standing close together, a mere few yards away, certainly appeared to remain oblivious to her presence. Despite the semi-darkness she had little difficulty in identifying them both, even before that easily recognisable female voice, heartbreakingly clear and carrying, announced,

'Oh, Daniel! I cannot tell you how happy that makes me! To think after all these years you have at last come to your senses... You have made the right choice this time, I think.'

Robina felt suddenly icy-cold, numb. Had she misheard...? Could she possibly have misunderstood? Then, as she watched Arabella wrapping her arms about that tall, muscular frame, and saw Daniel's willing response to the loving embrace, she could delude herself no longer.

Never before had Robina experienced so much gratitude towards her mother for insisting on such high standards of behaviour in her offspring than she did in those moments when the numbness began to leave her and her whole body was suddenly racked by the most agonising pain. Those strict lessons, instilled in her from childhood, could not be easily forgotten, and thankfully gave her the strength to suppress the agonised cry which rose in her throat, and to walk silently back into the house, dry-eyed, head held high, her unusual pallor the only indication that all was not well with her.

Nevertheless the distinct lack of colour didn't escape Lady Exmouth's notice, when at last she returned to her side. 'My dear, are you sure you feel quite the thing? You look quite dreadfully pale.'

'No, I do not feel very well, ma'am,' Robina answered, wondering how she could possibly manage to sound so natural when her throat felt as though it were being slowly squeezed by merciless fingers of steel. 'I have developed the most atrocious headache, and think it would be best if I leave at once.'

Lady Exmouth required no further prompting. But as Robina took her seat beside her in the carriage a few minutes later, thankfully escaping without having to face Daniel again, she was brutally aware that she would never be able to escape from the depths of her own feelings.

# Chapter Nine

'Grateful though I've been for your generous hospitality, and unrivalled masculine company, I think the time has now come for me to return to my own abode,' Daniel suddenly announced to his friend, as they paused in their stroll about the town to study half a dozen or so small fishing boats heading out to sea.

The Honourable Mr Montague Merrell didn't attempt to dissuade him. 'I expected you to go several days ago. It's been quite apparent to me for some considerable time that you're head-over-heels in love with the chit. Miss Perceval's a dashed lovely girl. I really cannot understand why you've delayed this long.'

'You above anyone else should know why caution has become a byword with me, Monty. I've fallen in love before, remember?'

Easily detecting the slightly bitter note in the pleasantly mellow voice, Mr Merrell cast his companion a sympathetic look as they moved on to continue their exploratory stroll about the town. 'You were very young, Daniel,' he reminded him. 'I know at the time I numbered amongst the few who were against your marrying, but that was simply because I considered it would have been wise to wait a year or two. Looking back, I cannot recall a single gentleman of my acquaintance who wasn't instantly bewitched by Clarissa. And believe me I was no exception.'

'Maybe not… But at least you, my dear friend, had the sense to know the difference between infatuation and love, whereas I…'

Daniel didn't attempt to finish what he was saying. There was absolutely no need for him to do so, for his companion was the only person in whom Daniel had ever confided; the only one to have been furnished with all the unsavoury facts concerning the late Lady Exmouth's unexpected demise.

Automatically keeping pace with his friend, as they turned down one of Brighton's many side streets to explore a part of the town where he at least had never ventured before, Daniel cast his mind back to one particular evening, shortly after Clarissa's funeral, when he had sat in the library at Courtney Place and had felt the need to confide in his friend Montague. He had openly confessed for the first time ever that his marriage had not been an unrivalled success, before he had gone on to relate all the details of Clarissa's tragic death. Daniel clearly recalled that his friend had looked genuinely shocked. Montague might have experienced reservations about his friend's marrying in the first place, but he, like everyone else, had believed the Exmouths' union had been a happy and successful one.

He cast his pensive companion a fleeting glance as they turned into yet another unfamiliar side street. 'Come on, Monty. Why don't you say, "I told you so". It's what's been passing through your mind, after all.'

'It most certain has not!' Merrell assured him, before a rueful smile tugged at one corner of his full lips. 'In point of fact, I was just thinking how very adept you've become over the years at hiding your feelings. I doubt there are half a dozen people residing in Brighton at the moment who might suspect that your feelings towards Miss Robina Perceval go rather deeper than that of mere friendship.'

'Yes, I have been most successful in my endeavours,' Daniel agreed, experiencing no small degree of satisfaction.

Montague regarded him in silence for a moment, and then asked, 'But surely you do not still harbour any doubts? Miss Robina Perceval is a darling girl, utterly delightful! I told you long before we left the capital that I considered that she would make you the ideal mate.'

'And you certainly ensured that you were given ample opportunity to form that opinion, as I remember,' Daniel returned, clearly recalling those occasions during the Season in London when he had chanced upon his friend seated in some secluded corner, conversing quietly with Robina. 'I might easily have been roused to a fit of jealous rage if I hadn't been quite certain that a confirmed old bachelor like yourself posed no threat.'

'And neither, from what I have witnessed during recent weeks, does anybody else,' Montague assured him, slanting a mocking glance. 'So why have you deliberately refrained from making your intentions perfectly plain?'

'Because, my dear inquisitive friend, I considered the time was not right, and that it certainly could do no harm to delay a few more weeks. Not for my benefit,' he went on to disclose. 'I had made my mind up to marry Robin long before we left the capital.'

That slightly rueful smile tugged at his lips once again. 'When, towards the end of last year, I first began to consider the suggestion put forward by several members of my family and many of my friends, including your good self, that I should marry again, I was thinking only of my daughters, not of myself. I finally decided that if I could find a female of good birth and gentle manners who would make a kind stepmother, and who would run my home efficiently, I would then seriously contemplate a second marriage. Needless to say, love never entered into my thinking… Then I came to London and met the Vicar of Abbot Quincey's daughter.'

'And instantly everything changed,' Montague suggested, but Daniel, truthful to the last, shook his head.

'No, not immediately. Not for several weeks, as it

happens,' Daniel surprisingly confessed. 'Oh, I liked her very well from the start. She was precisely what I was looking for—pleasing on the eye, unspoiled and sweet-natured. Furthermore, she had three younger sisters, and so was quite accustomed to caring for young girls. I became determined to get to know her better, and in doing so discovered, much to my utter astonishment, that the unimaginable had happened and that I had grown inordinately fond...' Again the rueful smile flickered. 'No, let us be totally honest—I was astounded to discover that against all the odds I had fallen in love. And not just with a lovely face this time. None the less, I was very well aware that, although my mother was very much in favour of the match, and was doing everything within her power to promote it, as was Robina's own mama, Robina herself...'

'Oh, come man! The girl simply adores you,' Montague assured him in a voice that clearly revealed that he at least was in no doubt. 'That lovely young face of hers positively lights up whenever you're nearby.'

Daniel's expression softened, and a warm glow sprang into his dark eyes. 'Recently I have begun to think that perhaps she's starting to see me in something more than the light of just a friend.'

'I'm positive you're right. So what's holding you back, for heaven's sake?'

'Oh, I don't know.' Removing his beaver hat, Daniel ran impatient fingers through his hair, as he took stock of their surroundings for the first time.

'Where in the name of heaven are we?' His eyes came to rest on a tavern on the opposite side of the narrow street. 'Let's go in there. Dashed thirsty work all this aimlessly walking about!'

Montague, wrinkling his long nose in distaste, followed willy-nilly into the tavern. It wasn't quite up to the standard to which he had grown accustomed, but he found the home-brewed ale very palatable, and was content to remain for a short while in order to sample more.

After seating himself beside Daniel on one of the rough wooden settles, he wasn't slow to return to their former topic. 'So, how much longer do you intend to wait before popping the question?'

'Inquisitive devil!' Daniel admonished, but without rancour. How could one resent the curiosity of someone who had only one's best interests at heart, someone who had remained touchingly loyal and had been an unfailing support when one had needed it most?

'As a matter of fact I had made up my mind to propose last night.' His forehead suddenly creased with a slightly troubled frown. 'Unbeknown to me, my mother decided to leave the party early. I spent some time with my cousin Arabella in the garden, and when I returned to the house I was informed by our hostess that Miss Perceval had not been feeling too well and that my mother had taken her home. I called at the house this morning, but Robina was keeping to her room. My mother seems to think that she may have contracted a chill, but I'm not so sure.'

He shrugged. 'She certainly didn't seem quite herself last night, but I wouldn't have said she was ill.'

'Probably just one of those mild female complaints,' his friend suggested. 'She'll recover soon enough, I dare say.'

Daniel cast him a faintly mocking glance. 'And what would a confirmed old bachelor like yourself know about women's troubles, may I ask?'

'A great deal more than you may think, old fellow,' Montague responded, with a distinctly self-satisfied smirk. 'I may never have been tempted into parson's mousetrap, but I ain't lived the life of a monk. The single state suits me very well, whereas it doesn't suit you, my friend. So do something about it! It ain't like you to be so indecisive.'

'I do not doubt the depth of my own feelings, Monty,' Daniel assured him after a moment's intense thought, 'but I cannot help wondering whether I am quite the right sort of person to make my little bird happy. Good God, man!' he exclaimed in response to his friend's derisive snort. 'She's nearer to my daughter Hannah's age than mine…Lizzie's, come to that!'

'Well, and what of it?' Montague responded, not considering the difference in ages in any way significant. 'You're in the prime of life—healthy, strong, a fine figure of a man.' He gazed down a little despondently at his own slightly thickening girth. 'I'm forced to admit that you're in far better shape than I am.'

'Maybe so, but that doesn't alter the fact that I'm

fast approaching middle age. I enjoy a quiet life, and maybe am a little too staid and set in my ways for Robina's taste.'

His features adopted a certain wistful expression as he stared down into the contents of his tankard. 'In many ways we are very alike, very compatible, both seeming to enjoy the same sorts of things. But that doesn't alter the fact that she is still a deal younger than I am, with a young heart that craves a little excitement from time to time.

'Believe me, it is so,' he reiterated when his friend looked faintly sceptical. 'To all outward appearances she seems very demure, every inch the well brought up young lady, but hidden beneath the surface lurk quite amazing qualities. She's an intrepid little thing, which she proved when she saved my daughter from drowning, for which I shall be eternally in her debt. She's always keen to attempt new things, too, which sets her quite apart from most other young females of her class who are quite content to remain indoors, plying their needles.'

He paused for a moment, recalling clearly a certain conversation he had had with Robina on the night they had dined at the Pavilion. 'Although her upbringing was on the whole a happy one, her life at the vicarage lacked adventure, and there is a certain part of her that yearns to meet the kind of man who could rectify this deficiency in her life before she settles down to a quiet married life.'

'Well, why don't you then?' Monty suggested.

'And how the deuce do you propose I do that?'

Daniel returned, a hint of exasperation creeping into his voice, making it carry further than he realised. 'I am not quite the swashbuckling type. Nor a knight in shining armour to ride *ventre a terre* to a damsel's rescue, even if the situation arose, which is highly improbable.'

'I'm not suggesting you wait for an opportunity to display your manly prowess, I'm suggesting you create one.'

'It is my considered opinion,' Daniel responded, casting his friend a faintly impatient glance, 'that that home-brewed ale has gone to your head.'

'Not a bit of it!' Montague assured him, laughing. 'Nothing could be easier. Simply arrange for dear little Robina to be abducted and then go gallantly dashing to her rescue. Tomorrow will do perfectly,' he went on, warming to the subject. 'She's to be amongst the guests invited to your cousin's alfresco breakfast out at Priory Wood, if my memory serves me correctly. The perfect opportunity for you to carry out the feat of daring.'

Daniel raised his eyes ceilingwards. 'A more addle-brained suggestion I have yet to hear!' he muttered. 'Even if I thought you were serious, which I know you're not, you don't suppose for a moment I'd lend myself to such a start.'

'Faint-hearted fellow!'

'Furthermore,' Daniel continued, ignoring the criticism, 'there is every likelihood that Robina will excuse herself from the outing. And even if she does decide to attend, there's not the remotest possibility that I could arrange her abduction in so short a time, even if I were foolish enough to contemplate doing such a senseless thing.'

He rose to his feet. 'Come, let us be gone from here, and trust that the fresh air will not be long in restoring your wits.'

Daniel turned, about to lead the way out of the inn, when he promptly collided with a small stocky individual who had been supping his ale at the very next table, and found himself on the receiving end of a rather direct, penetrating stare.

'Begging your pardon, guv'nor,' the stranger muttered, hurriedly stepping to one side. 'Didn't notice you standing there. No offence intended.'

'And none taken. It was as much my fault as yours,' Daniel responded, ever the polite gentleman.

It was only later, after he had arrived back at his friend's lodgings, that Daniel noticed his fob-watch was missing.

Trying not to dwell on the loss of a possession which he valued highly, simply because it was the last present his rapidly ailing father had bestowed upon him, Daniel accompanied his friend to a certain establishment where gambling for high stakes was the norm.

Mr Merrell, unlike Daniel himself, was a compulsive gambler, and was never happier than when seated at a table, glass of fine old brandy at his elbow, cards in his hand, pitting his skill against other gamesters. Considering he always played for high stakes, it was perhaps fortunate that Lady Luck had seen fit to favour him thus far. He certainly lost large sums on occasions, but never appeared unduly worried, for he felt certain that that beloved, fickle 'lady' would smile favourably upon him again before too long.

Daniel, standing behind his friend's chair, watched the play for a time, and then drifted away to enjoy a hand or two of piquet with an acquaintance. He distinctly lacked the faith in Lady Luck which his friend Montague possessed, and decided after half an hour to leave and seek out his mother who had planned to attend a large party being held at a house nearby.

The hostess, a friend of the family's for many years, was delighted by his unexpected appearance. After a brief exchange of pleasantries, Daniel did not delay very long in searching out his mother, and discovered to his intense disappointment that she had come to the party alone.

'Although Robina insisted that there was absolutely no need to summon the doctor, she didn't feel equal to accompanying me this evening,' her ladyship disclosed. 'I believe she has every intention of joining us on the picnic tomorrow, however.'

'If she feels well enough, then of course she may, but if not, do not hesitate to summon the doctor.'

The Dowager recognised that decisive note in her son's voice. Like his father before him, Daniel was a most charming, level-headed man, but could be quite determined and authoritative when the need arose. She smiled up at him. 'And have you definitely decided to return to us tomorrow, my dear?'

'Yes. I've given orders for my belongings to be taken back to the house during my absence. As you know, I've arranged to spend the day with Roderick. I expect to return to Brighton early in the evening, and will come directly to the house.'

Leaving his mother to return to her friends, he wandered about the room, stopping from time to time to converse with several acquaintances, but Robina's absence meant there was little inducement for him to remain, and he soon took himself off, deciding to have an early night as he had an early start in the morning.

Declining the footman's offer to find him a hired carriage, Daniel walked the relatively short distance back to his friend's lodgings, arriving just as a church clock somewhere in the distance chimed the hour. As he waited for his friend's very efficient manservant to admit him to the house, he thought he detected someone lurking in the shadows on the opposite side of the street. He paid little attention, however, and went straight into the house as soon as the door had been opened, taking himself into the library for a nightcap before finally retiring to his room.

No sooner had he poured himself a brandy than the sound of the door-knocker echoed in the small hall. To him it seemed a very odd time for someone to decide to pay a call, and therefore made no attempt to hide his surprise when the servant entered a minute or so later to inform him that there was a person at the door wishing to see him.

'What sort of person?'

Mr Merrell's very correct manservant sniffed loudly. 'A very common sort, my lord. He came to the house earlier whilst you were out. I would not have hesitated to send him about his business had it not been for the fact that he informed me that he had in his possession some property belonging to you.'

'Has he, indeed?' Daniel murmured, his thoughts automatically turning to the missing watch.

'So I am led to believe, sir. When I suggested that he might safely hand whatever it was over to me, he stubbornly refused to do so, declaring that he would place it in your hands personally, or not at all.'

'In that case, you'd better show the fellow in,' Daniel suggested, and a few moments later a small, stocky individual wearing a serviceable frieze coat, and twisting a somewhat battered and misshapen hat round and round in his hands, entered the room.

Daniel had a remarkable memory for faces, and instantly recognised the individual with whom he had momentarily collided in the inn that afternoon. 'So, we meet again, Mr—er…?'

'Higgins, sir. Honest Hector Higgins, at your service.'

'It is to be hoped, Mr Higgins, that you live up to your name,' Daniel remarked in a distinctly sardonic tone, as he gazed at the work-roughened fingers, which looked hard and clumsy, but which might well be nimble enough to remove an article from someone's pocket without the owner being any the wiser. 'You are in possession of an item belonging to me, I understand.'

'That I am, sir.' Delving into his pocket, Higgins drew out the treasured possession and promptly placed it into Daniel's outstretched hand.

He examined it briefly, noting with some relief that it was completely undamaged. 'It would seem, Master Higgins, that I am in your debt. Or at least I would be if I were not fairly certain that you quite expertly purloined this from my waistcoat pocket during our brief—er—contact in that inn.'

A decidedly wary expression flickered momentarily over the weather-beaten features. 'Now, guv'nor, I puts it to you…if I'd filched the watch, I wouldn't be giving it back, now would I?'

'You might if you thought you would attain more by way of reward than you would by trying to dispose of it by other means, especially as my name is clearly engraved in the back.'

'Pshaw! It'd be no bother to scratch that away, and no one none the wiser,' Higgins responded, determined, it seemed, to brazen it out. 'And I didn't bring it back 'ere, personal like, for no reward neither. I'm an 'onest cove. Weren't always, I'm ashamed to say, but I is now, and 'ave been since I met my Dora.'

Daniel couldn't help smiling at this artless disclosure, and was inclined to be generous and give the fellow the benefit of the doubt. 'That being the case, Master Higgins, and as you seem disinclined to accept a reward, the least I can offer you is a drink for your trouble.' He turned to the decanters. 'Will brandy serve?'

'Mighty hospitable of you, guv'nor. Yes, that'll do very nicely.'

Smiling in spite of the fact that he still strongly suspected that some recompense would be demanded for the safe return of the watch, Daniel obligingly poured a large measure of brandy and handed it to his visitor.

'Sit yourself down, Higgins, and tell me about yourself. What do you do for a living?'

'I'm a jarvey, sir. Been driving me own carriage these past ten year or more.' He sniffed, wiping his snub nose on the back of his hand. ''Course, the carriage is getting a bit worn and battered now, and the poor old 'orse ain't what she was.' He shook his head sadly. 'No, won't be long before she pays a visit to the knacker's yard.'

'How very unfortunate!' his lordship said faintly, wondering what in the world had possessed him to invite the visitor to remain.

'Aye, sir. It ain't easy being an 'onest cove. Gentry folk don't like to be seen driving about in a broken-down old carriage like mine, and when you don't pick up many passengers in a day, you can't afford repairs.'

'I sympathise with your plight, Higgins,' Daniel responded, wondering when the despondent jarvey would disclose his real motive for this visit. He did not have long to wait.

'Knew you would, sir.' His eyes never wavering

from Daniel's face, he consumed the contents of his glass in one go. 'Just like a soft-hearted cove like myself can sympathise with yours.'

Daniel took a sip from his own glass. 'I'm sorry, Higgins. I do not perfectly understand you.'

'Unrequired love, sir, can do terrible things to a man.'

'I'm sure you're right,' his lordship responded, while manfully suppressing a chuckle. 'But I believe you mean unrequited love.'

'Aye, that's it, guv'nor! But don't you be a'fretting no longer, 'cause Hector Higgins be the man to 'elp you there.'

Daniel blinked several times, wondering if he could possibly have misheard. 'I'm sorry, Higgins, I do not perfectly understand you. I am not in need of help.'

'Now, now, guv'nor, there's no need for you to be ashamed of yer feelings. Comes to us all in time. It 'appened to me, and now it's 'appened to you. Not that I likes to interfere, you understand, but I couldn't 'elp overhearing that little talk you had with your friend in the Crown, and knew I was the very man you was looking for.'

Daniel was becoming faintly bored, and it clearly showed as he said, 'And what service, pray, do you suppose you can render me?'

'Why, abducting the wench o' course! I knows the area round Priory Wood like the back of me 'and. Nowt could be simpler! All I needs to do is lurk in the woods tomorrow, awaiting the opportunity, like, nab the wench, and bung 'er in me carriage. Then you comes riding along, brandishing yer pistol. Mind, I wouldn't advise you discharge the firearm, m'lord,' he went on in all seriousness. 'Might frighten the old 'orse, and she ain't as young as she was. Might be too much for 'er.' He paused to cast a hopeful glance down at his empty glass. 'Now, what's do you think to that, m'lord?'

Daniel regarded him in silence for a moment, much as he might have done some half-witted child. 'I think, Master Higgins, that you have taken leave of your senses. Even if this plan of yours was not ludicrous in the extreme, I would still never countenance such a dishonourable act as abducting a young female and frightening her half out of her wits. Furthermore, what you overheard earlier today was my friend allowing the sportive element in his nature to get the upper hand, which he is sometimes inclined to do, but believe me his idiotic suggestion was never meant to be taken seriously. Unlike the one I am about to make, which is that we both seek our beds.'

In one graceful movement, Daniel rose from his chair, and relieved his highly disappointed visitor of the empty glass. 'Now, Master Higgins, I shall bid you goodnight... And consider yourself lucky that I'm not taking the little matter of the deliberate purloining of my watch any further.'

As the Dowager Lady Exmouth knew very well, there was an element of hard determination in her son's character which surfaced from time to time. It was clearly discernible now. Higgins opened his mouth to speak, thought better of it, and went disconsolately across to the door. 'No offence intended, m'lord,' he muttered over his shoulder and then, manfully resisting the temptation to place a well-aimed punch on the disdainful manservant's long nose, did not delay in leaving the house.

Life could be so unfair, he decided, as he trudged his weary way homewards. Here was he, an honest cove, doing honest work week in week out; year in year out. And for what? Hardly earning enough to keep body and soul together, he reflected, his spirits plummeting to an all-time low. He would be better off by far if he returned to his former profession... But no, he'd promised his Dora that his thieving days were over. He'd left that life behind him when he had moved away from London, and he had no real desire to return to a life of crime.

Not that he couldn't if he'd a mind to be so foolish, he reminded himself. His fingers were still as nimble as ever they were. He'd managed to take that gent's watch without his knowing much about it, he mused, with a certain grim satisfaction. Not that he had ever intended to keep it, though. That had never crossed his mind for a moment. He shook his head sadly, swiftly deciding that, as things had turned out, he might have been wiser to have done so. After all, what had all his good intentions brought him...? Absolutely nothing!

'Ahh well,' he muttered, crossing the street and entering the tavern. At least he had a few coins left in his pocket, enough to buy a tankard of ale to drown his sorrows.

The Crown was unusually quiet that evening, which suited his present unsociable mood very well, and Higgins had little difficulty in finding himself a secluded table in a corner, where he could continue to brood over life's iniquities without interruption.

Fate, it seemed, had other ideas, and was not even gracious enough to grant him the brief period of solitude for which he craved, for no sooner had he made himself comfortable on the settle than a sharp-featured man, sporting a bright red neckerchief clumsily knotted about his throat, and a blowsy female, whose low-cut gown left little to the imagination, plumped themselves, uninvited, on the settle opposite.

''Ere, what's all this, Hector, me old friend? Ain't like you to skulk away in a corner. Had a bad day, 'ave we?' The man's thin lips curled unpleasantly to reveal a set of rapidly decaying teeth. 'Now me, I've 'ad a good day. Told you afore old friend that you want to join forces wi' me.'

'And I've told you before, Jack Sharpe, that I gave up that kind o' life long since.'

'Aye, and where's it got yer, eh?' The decaying teeth showed again. 'Working all the hours God sends, and for what? I bet you ain't enough in your pocket for another tankard of ale.'

This was true enough, but Higgins had no intention of admitting to it, especially not to an unscrupulous little sneak-thief like Jack Sharpe who didn't

care how he got his grubby fingers on money. He
was not above sending his woman friend out on the
streets, and living off her immoral earnings when he
was without the price of a drink.

'Still,' Jack shrugged, 'I don't know why I'm
bothering wi' you. You wouldn't be much 'elp to me
n' more. You're not up to it no longer—too old and
too slow.'

'Oh, no I ain't!' the older man countered, the
goading just too much for him this time. 'I'll 'ave
you know I filched a fine pocket-watch this very day.
Had it off the waistcoat and into me own pocket in
a trice, and the gent none the wiser.'

'Oh, yeah!' Jack's tone was decidedly sceptical.
'Where is it, then? Show it to me!'

'I ain't got it no longer,' Higgins mumbled, going
slightly red in the face. 'I gave it back.'

'You did what!' Sharpe and his companion roared
with laughter, making Higgins feel more uncomfortable than ever.

He took an uneasy glance about him. 'Keep your
voice down, can't yer!' he snapped. 'Do you think I
want everyone to hear?'

'Frightened your little wife wouldn't like it if she
knew you'd been up to your old tricks again, is that
it, eh?' the woman goaded, and Higgins cast her a
look of distaste.

'Shut yer mouth, Molly!' Jack ordered, his gaze
suddenly intense. 'I reckon old Hector 'ere ain't spinning no yarn. I reckon he did filch the timepiece.

Though why in Hades 'e decides to give it back, I can't imagine.'

Half wishing now that he hadn't done so, and being made to feel incredibly stupid into the bargain, Higgins explained the reason behind his actions, relating the conversation which he had overheard earlier in the day and disclosing what had subsequently occurred.

Jack listened intently, absorbing every last detail. 'So, you actually went to this Lord Exmouth's house, hoping he'd agree to your plan, and he threw you out on your ear, did 'e?'

'No, not then,' Higgins countered. 'I told you, I went round to his 'ouse, round to the rear entrance, and discovered from the scatty kitchen wench that 'e weren't staying there. Only 'is mother and this wench he's got his heart set on is living in the 'ouse. He's staying with a friend. So I calls there, and the second time I goes, I sees 'im.'

'Pity he weren't interested,' Jack remarked, much to his female companion's intense amusement.

'Can't say I'm surprised!' she scoffed. 'If the gent's half as fond of this wench as you reckon 'e is, Hector, he wouldn't be so mean as to want 'er abducted in a broken-down old carriage like yourn. Why, I've travelled in the dratted thing m'self once, and I should know. Black and blue I was after I got back from me sister-in-law's funeral.'

'Shut yer gab, woman!' Jack growled. ''Ere, go and get us all another drink.' He tossed her a coin and waited for her to move away, before turning once again to Higgins.

'And you reckon this wench Lord Exmouth's a fancy for will be out at Priory Wood tomorrow?'

'I've already said so, haven't I?' He cast a suspicious glance across the table. 'Why are you so interested, anyhow?'

'No reason, I suppose.' There was a faint rasping sound as Jack rubbed his bony fingers back and forth across his chin. 'All the same, it's a damned shame the cove didn't take to the idea. Might 'ave been able to 'elp you out, there.'

Having had more than enough for one day, and more than enough of the present company, Higgins hurriedly tossed the contents of his tankard down his throat and rose to his feet. 'Thanks all the same, but I can do without your sort of 'elp, Jack Sharpe.'

'Oh! Hector gone, as 'e?' Molly remarked, as she returned, glasses in hand. 'Never mind, I'll soon drink 'is gin. The ungrateful dog!'

'Oh, no, you won't!' Jack whisked the glass from her fingers. 'You needs to be up bright and early in the morning. I've got a job for you.'

'Oh, yes?' She cast him a wary look. 'What kind of job?'

'I wants you to go to this Exmouth's house and keep watch. If this wench goes to Priory Wood, I wants to know about it.'

'But I don't even know what she looks like,' Molly pointed out, not relishing the prospect of rising early. 'Besides not knowing where she lives.'

'You'll find out easy enough.' He was thoughtful for a moment. 'You 'eard what Higgins said. Apart from the servants, only Exmouth's old mother and the girl are staying at the 'ouse. You wait outside and keep watch.'

'Then what?'

'Your brother's place is close to Priory Wood, ain't it?'

'Wel…? And what of it?'

Jack leaned back against the settle. 'I'll tell you in the morning, when I've had chance to think about it some more.'

## Chapter Ten

Lady Exmouth beamed with pleasure as she watched Robina, looking particularly enchanting in a powder-blue walking dress and matching pelisse, descending the stairs. She wished Daniel could have been there to witness the utterly charming spectacle. That lovely face, framed in a fetching bonnet, with its powder-blue ribbons tied in a coquettish bow beneath the delightfully pointed little chin, was a sight to take the most hardened gentleman's breath away.

Not that she thought for a moment that Daniel himself was in any need of further persuasion to convince him that Robina would make him the ideal wife. Unless she very much mistook the matter the wretched boy had made up his mind weeks before, no matter how hard he had tried to conceal the fact. And if any further proof of the exact state of his mind had been required, he had certainly betrayed himself the previous night, her ladyship decided, experiencing an immense feeling of satisfaction. Why, not even Arabella's presence could induce him to remain

at the party. If Robina herself had been present, of
course, it would have been a different matter entirely!

'Now, my dear, are you quite certain that you feel
up to this outing today?' the Dowager enquired as
Robina reached her side. The girl certainly appeared
perfectly restored, if a little paler than the Dowager
would have liked. 'It isn't too late to change your
mind,' she assured her. 'Arabella will quite understand.'

'I'm fine, really,' Robina answered, making a great
play of straightening a crease in one of her gloves.
'I cannot imagine what came over me. I'm not usually prone to those trifling megrims.'

'Well, we must just be thankful that it was nothing
more serious than an annoying headache which refused to go away. Had you contracted Lady Phelps's
chill you might have been laid up for days. I understand that Augusta, poor dear, is still keeping to her
bed. Which means, of course, that we shall be denied
her company, and that of her son's at the alfresco
breakfast.'

Robina clearly detected the faint hint of relief in
the Dowager's tone, but chose not to remark upon it,
and merely enquired who else would be travelling
out to Priory Wood that morning.

'I'm not perfectly certain, my dear. Several people
we are both acquainted with, I'm sure. I do know
Arabella invited Sir Percy Lovell, but he was otherwise engaged. And I do believe she asked that nice
young man of whom you're so fond, Mr Frederick
Ainsley, but he too was forced to decline. I under-

stand he has left town for a few days in order to visit a sick relative.' She shook her head. 'It is so difficult to arrange these things at a moment's notice, but I'm certain Arabella will have succeeded in persuading several people to come.'

The Dowager raised one hand, encased in a lilac-coloured glove. 'Ah! That sounds suspiciously like her now.'

Lady Exmouth's hearing was not defective. The footman opened the door in time to see the Tollivers' elegant open carriage drawing to a halt outside, and Arabella herself on the point of alighting.

'There's no need for you to trouble yourself,' the Dowager called, hurrying down the steps to greet her. 'We're ready and waiting, so we can leave at once, if you're agreeable?'

'Splendid! I do so admire punctuality!' Arabella announced, seating herself once again. 'And Robina too! Glad to see you felt able to accompany us. You and I, I'm afraid, are the youngest members of the party, so must keep each other company,' she went on, when Robina, at a far more decorous pace, arrived at the carriage. 'I'm rather surprised that not too many young people chose to accept my invitation. It would seem, though, that outdoor entertainment appeals more to the older generation.'

'I thought you might not find it so very easy to arrange your little picnic at such short notice, my dear,' Lady Exmouth remarked, making herself comfortable in the seat beside her niece. 'I find people these days tend to plan their schedules well in advance. Evening events are particularly difficult to arrange at short notice. One discovers that even one's friends refuse on the grounds of having prior engagements.'

'And that is precisely why I didn't attempt to organise a dinner-party,' Arabella responded vaguely, her attention suddenly drawn to a solitary figure on the opposite side of the street.

'What an exceedingly rude female!' she announced. 'That young woman has been pointedly staring in this direction from the moment I arrived.' She laughed suddenly, her sense of humour coming to the fore. 'I sincerely trust she's not hoping to see Daniel. She'll have a very long wait if she is.'

The Dowager, after one glance across the street, sniffed loudly. 'My son, I'll have you know, does not associate with persons of that—er—ilk.'

'Don't be so naïve, Aunt!' That mischievous sparkle of old was back in Arabella's eyes. 'Clarissa has been dead for almost two years… Though perhaps you're right,' she went on, after considering the matter further for a moment. 'Daniel has more taste than to associate with such a lowly sort. Or, perhaps, more respect for his health.'

Reaching forward she gave her coachman the office to start by tapping him lightly on the shoulder with her parasol, and the coach moved off, leaving the inquisitive female, Robina noticed, watching their progress along the street.

Robina, at least, had not been so naïve as not to know precisely to what Lady Tolliver had been alluding. She had swiftly discovered during her stay in the capital that it was certainly not unusual for a gentleman, widowed or otherwise, to keep a mistress. Whether Daniel himself did so, she wasn't so certain; wasn't sure either why it should matter to her one way or the other. After all, she told herself, it was no concern of hers. It would have been very much her concern if she had been in Arabella's position, and yet Daniel's future wife did not appear in the least troubled. How very unnatural that seemed!

'You're very quiet.'

The unexpected remark startled Robina out of her reverie, and she raised her eyes to discover Lady Tolliver's brown orbs firmly fixed in her direction.

'I do trust Aunty did not bully you into accompanying us today?'

'No such thing!' Robina assured her, managing a semblance of a smile. 'I was merely wool-gathering.'

Unable to hold that faintly unnerving dark-eyed scrutiny, all too reminiscent of Daniel's on occasions, she glanced skywards to discover not one single cloud lurking anywhere. 'I think you are going to be lucky with the weather. It looks set to be yet another fine day.'

'It certainly does,' she agreed. 'I just hope it doesn't become too warm. Still,' she shrugged, 'there ought to be plenty of shade out at Priory Wood.'

'I could have wished you had chosen a different spot for your outing,' Lady Exmouth put in. 'My memories of that particular idyllic place are not altogether pleasant.'

Arabella frankly laughed. 'Yes, Daniel told me all about it. What a little monkey Lizzie is! Not in the least like her mother. She must take after our side of the family.'

Tutting, the Dowager favoured her sportive niece with a reproving glance, and Arabella tried to look suitably chastened. 'Yes, you're quite right, Aunt. It is exceedingly naughty of me to make light of the matter. Daniel, I know, was most disturbed by the whole incident.' She looked directly across at Robina once again. 'And eternally grateful to you, my dear. He quite openly admits that he shall be forever in your debt.'

Perhaps Arabella did not notice the touch of sadness which just for one unguarded moment clouded those strikingly pretty blue eyes, but the Dowager most certainly did, and couldn't help wondering if her charming protégée was quite as restored to health as she would have people believe. Arabella was the dearest creature imaginable, but she could be a little tactless on occasions, and faintly overpowering, most especially to those who were not feeling quite equal to coping with her exuberance.

So she deliberately set herself the task of holding her niece in conversation by enquiring precisely who might be expected to join them at the alfresco breakfast that morning. Robina certainly did her best to contribute from time to time to the ensuing discussion, but Lady Exmouth sensed that it was an effort, and she became increasingly convinced that Robina would have much preferred to remain at home.

If the Dowager had suspected for a moment just how much of a trial Robina was finding the outing, she would have been appalled. The considerable strain of trying to behave normally lessened, of course, when they eventually reached the popular beauty spot, and the other guests began to arrive. Then Robina was able, without she hoped making it too obvious, to disengage herself from Arabella's side. She even managed to force several of the delicious delicacies the Tollivers' excellent cook had taken the trouble to prepare down her throat. As soon as she was able to do so, however, she drifted away from the few members of the party who had not succumbed to the heat of the day and the effects of several glasses of cool champagne by taking a nap, and sought the solace for which she craved.

The instant she felt certain that no one had decided to follow her example by going for a stroll, Robina ventured further into the wood. The river, she knew, was some distance away to her left, but she had no intention of venturing anywhere near it. The memories of that day, of far happier times, were all too firmly embedded in her mind.

But that was all she would be left with soon, a cruelly taunting voice in her head reminded her: bittersweet memories and the painful knowledge that events might have turned out so vastly different if she hadn't remained for so many weeks so insensitive to the desires of her own heart.

Tugging at the bow beneath her chin, she removed her bonnet and, holding it by its ribbons, absently

began to swing it to and fro as she ventured further
beneath the dense canopy of trees, not quite ready
yet to abandon this much needed period of solitude.

She had realised, of course, when she had agreed
to accompany the Dowager today that she would not
find Arabella's company easy to bear. She hadn't
realised quite how painful an ordeal it would turn out
to be. A sigh escaped her. But what choice had she?
She could hardly remain skulking in her bedchamber
indefinitely, giving way to bouts of weeping when
she felt certain she wouldn't be disturbed. Daniel
himself would be returning to the house that evening,
and although it might be distressingly hard, sooner
or later she would have to face him too.

No, she thought sadly, there would be no easy way
out for her. The next few days, or until she could
find some reasonable excuse to leave Brighton and
return to Northamptonshire would be agonisingly tor-
tuous. Today had been traumatic enough. Trying to
be at least civil to someone whom one resented bitterly had been no easy task, and yet she could not
find it within herself to hate Arabella, nor even remotely dislike her. How could she blame Arabella
for feeling a deal of affection for Daniel? Any
woman would wish to marry such a fine man.

That no mention had been made of the forthcoming marriage was rather odd, though, she decided,
frowning slightly as this puzzling thought occurred
to her. They might, of course, have reasons for wishing their betrothal not to become common knowledge. It was quite possible that Daniel wished to in-

form his daughters that he intended to remarry and was awaiting their return from Dorset before informing the world at large. It was still rather odd, though, that they had decided to keep their intentions a secret from the Dowager, for Robina felt certain that Lady Exmouth was completely ignorant of the fact that her son intended to wed again. Furthermore, Arabella had betrayed no obvious signs that a joyous event would very soon be taking place in her life. How very odd it all was!

The sound of hurrying footsteps nearby broke into her perplexing reflections. So, someone had chosen to follow her example, after all, she thought, swinging round to discover precisely which member of the party had seen fit to come in hot pursuit.

Setting his book to one side, Daniel consulted his pocket-watch, which informed him that it wanted only a few minutes to seven. His mother and Robina were rather late in returning from their alfresco breakfast. What an utterly ridiculous description to give a meal eaten early in the afternoon! he mused, returning the watch to his pocket and reaching for his book again.

The door opened, and the butler entered the library to set a decanter and a glass by his lordship's elbow. 'Shall you be requiring anything further, sir?'

'No, I don't think so, thank you, Stebbings... Yes, wait a moment,' he added, arresting the servant's progress across to the door. 'What time did her ladyship leave this morning?'

'Shortly before noon, sir.'

'Did she happen to mention that there was a possibility that she might be returning late?'

'No, my lord, she did not. Shall I delay dinner?'

'Yes, perhaps that might be wise. Inform Cook that we'll now eat at nine.'

Frowning slightly, Daniel reached for the burgundy at his elbow and poured himself a glass. It was most unlike his mother not to inform the servants if she thought there was a possibility that she might be late. What on earth could be keeping her? he wondered. Even if she had lost track of the time, there had been others present to remind her, most especially Robina who, unlike most females of his acquaintance, was an excellent little timekeeper.

Smiling to himself he leaned back in his chair, and sipped his wine while absently contemplating the shine on his Hessian boots. It was good to be back in his own home again. He had enjoyed his friend Monty's company very much, but he had missed not having his little bird around, missed her far more than he cared to admit.

What an unusual female his little Robin was! Never would he have believed it possible that in a simple country parson's daughter, whose upbringing had been, by her own admission, faintly constricted, and wholly conventional, he would have found a female so much after his own heart.

It had come as something of a revelation to discover just how much they did have in common. He could not prevent a further wry smile tugging at the corners of his mouth. To think that when he had first seriously begun to consider the idea of marrying again, his only objective had been to find a suitable mother for his daughters, and in doing so he had found the perfect life's companion, a female whom he was very sure he could no longer live without.

A sudden commotion in the hall disturbed these pleasurable musings, and he turned his head in time to see his mother burst into the room, with less than her usual grace, swiftly followed by his cousin who was looking unusually pale, and whose eyes distinctly lacked that teasing sparkle.

'Oh, Daniel, thank heavens you're here!' The Dowager almost fell upon his chest as he rose from the chair. 'It is all my fault. I blame myself entirely. I should never have taken her. I knew as soon as we set out that the poor child was not equal to the outing.'

'Now, Aunt Lavinia, you must not distress yourself so.' Placing her arm about the Dowager's shoulders, Arabella drew her across to the sofa. 'I'm certain there's some perfectly reasonable explanation for all this,' she said in a voice which, to Daniel's ears, sadly lacked any real conviction.

'Where is Robina?' he asked with deceptive mildness.

'That is just it, Daniel. We don't know,' Arabella answered, striving to remain calm. 'She has disappeared.'

His expression giving no hint of the anxiety rapidly rising within him, he transferred his gaze from his silently sobbing mother to his cousin. 'I think you had better explain precisely what has occurred.'

'What Aunt Lavinia said is perfectly true,' she began. 'Robina did seem unusually subdued today.' She shrugged. 'I thought, perhaps, it might be simply that there was no one of her own age at the picnic, and she was faintly bored. Which would have been in no way amazing. I was beginning to regret organising the wretched outing myself when most of my guests decided to take a nap after the meal. So when I noticed Robina wandering off into the wood, I was very tempted to join her.' She glanced down at the slightly misshapen, blue-trimmed bonnet she held in her right hand. 'Now, of course, I wish I had done just that.'

'So, when she failed to return, you quite naturally searched for her.'

Arabella watched him calmly reach for his wine, looking for all the world as though he hadn't a care. She, however, knew him rather too well to be fooled by this seeming display of unconcern, and couldn't help but admire the iron self-control he never failed to exert over himself in times of crisis.

'I thought at first that she had merely lost track of the time. I recall when I was younger I loved to wander through the wood at Courtney Place, and was frequently late in returning for meals. It was only when my guests began to depart that I really became concerned. Several of them offered to remain and join the search, but I assured them that there was no need.' She regarded him in silence for a moment. 'I didn't suppose that you'd want the whole of Brighton knowing that Robina had disappeared.'

A faint look of admiration sprang into his eyes. 'You acted very sensibly, Bella. Indeed I would not like the tattle-mongers to get wind of this.'

'No, I thought not. So, after everyone had gone, I ordered my servants to search the wood thoroughly, and my footman found this.'

She held out the bonnet for his inspection. One of the ribbons had clearly been torn off, and there was what appeared to be part of a large footprint on the brim.

'I thought she might possibly have met with an accident—fallen and twisted her ankle, perhaps. I dispatched one of my servants to the village nearby to enquire whether a young woman had gone there seeking assistance, but…'

She raised deeply troubled eyes to his. 'Oh, Daniel, I do not believe I'm a fanciful woman, but it almost seems to me as though she has been abducted.'

The Dowager, who had managed to regain control over herself at last, looked up at this. 'But that's nonsense, Arabella! Who on earth would want to abduct the dear, sweet child? Besides, who could possibly have known, apart from the guests, that we intended to go to Priory Wood today?'

'Who indeed?' Daniel murmured, eyes narrowing to slits.

Then, turning abruptly, he went striding across to the door. 'Stebbings!' he called. 'I want my curricle brought round from the stables at once!'

## Chapter Eleven

Robina turned her head in the direction of the small and decidedly grubby window to see the light was fading fast. How long had she lain here like this, trussed up like a chicken? And why had she been captured and imprisoned in this disgustingly filthy attic room in the first place?

It had all happened so quickly, too. One moment she had been ambling through that wood, minding her own business; and the next she had been accosted by two complete strangers. Before she had had time even to scream one of the men had grasped her arms and had tied them behind her back, while the other had wrapped a disgusting gag over her mouth. Then, after an evil-smelling sack had been flung over her head, she had been forced to suffer the indignity of being carried some distance across a brawny shoulder before being bundled none too gently into a cart.

By the jolting she had been forced to endure, they had obviously travelled along very uneven tracks. The journey had seemed to take forever, but she suspected she had travelled no more than three miles, if that. Then she had been carried in the same undignified manner up two flights of stairs and had been left here tied to this bed. Frowning, she looked about her. But where was here? Where on earth was she? More importantly, why was she here?

The sound of footsteps and voices interrupted these disturbing reflections. A moment later there was the noise of bolts being drawn back, the door swung open, and the two men who had abducted her came into the room, followed by a blowsy female whom Robina was convinced she had seen somewhere before.

'God's teeth, Jack!' the woman exclaimed, casting the captive a look of sympathy. 'Why did you leave her tied up like this?' Depositing the tray she carried down on a wooden box beside the bed, she began to undo the rope securing the slender ankles. 'How the devil do you suppose she can escape from up here?'

'It weren't me,' the smaller man answered testily. 'I left the tying up to yer brother.'

The woman cast the other man, who was leaning against the wall, and looking over at the bed with a decidedly lascivious gleam in his dark eyes, an impatient glance. 'She ain't no bird, Ben. She can't fly out of the window.'

'I weren't going to risk a pretty little morsel like that slipping through me fingers.' The leer became more pronounced. 'Don't gets the chance to 'andle such quality goods so often.'

'You can just keep your grubby 'ands to yerself,

Ben,' the woman snapped, knowing precisely in which direction her brother's thoughts were turning. 'She ain't to be harmed. We all agreed on that.'

'Aye, and so we did,' Jack concurred, moving forward to help untie the rope binding their captive's slim wrists. 'It's the money we're after, nothing else.'

Robina, having listened to this little discussion with interest, was able to sit up at last, and wasted no time in pulling the filthy rag from round her mouth. At least she now knew why she had been abducted. She was being held for ransom. But why had they chosen her? Was it simply a case of being in the wrong place at the wrong time, and just happening to cross their paths? Or had she been their intended victim all along?

She looked at each of her captors in turn. The men she felt certain she had never seen before they had snatched her from the wood, but the woman she most definitely had. She studied her intently. Like Daniel, she had a remarkable memory for faces, and it didn't take many moments before she suddenly realised precisely where she had seen her.

'You were in the street this morning, watching the house.'

The woman didn't attempt to deny it. 'Well, I 'ad to make sure we nabbed the right one, now didn't I, dearie? Lord Exmouth will pay right 'andsomely for your safe return, I'm thinking.'

'And why should you suppose that he would be willing to do that?' Robina asked cautiously. Surely if their objective was to attain a sizeable ransom they would have been wiser to have tried to abduct the Dowager.

'Don't try those little tricks on us,' the man called Jack scoffed. 'We 'appens to know that the rich lord plans to marry you.'

So that was it! If her own position had not been so precarious, she might well have found the whole situation highly diverting. The fools had abducted the wrong female! Arabella was the one they ought to have taken, but even so, she didn't doubt for a moment that Daniel would meet these scoundrels' demands in order to attain her safe release.

Perversely, this annoyed her more than anything else. Why should he be made to part with what may well turn out to be a considerable sum of money because of her bird-witted actions? If she had not foolishly gone wandering off by herself, she wouldn't have found herself in this predicament now. Yes, she had got herself into this situation, so it was up to her to get herself out of it, she decided. But how?

She took a moment to glance at each of her captors in turn once again, her gaze lingering a fraction longer on the man with the lascivious glint in his deep set eyes.

'Well, I suspect you're right,' she conceded at last, successfully controlling her rising ire. 'Providing, of course, that I come to no harm…of any description.'

The woman at least was not slow to follow her meaning, and her full lips curled into an unpleasant smirk. 'Don't you be a'worrying none about me

brother, dearie. He'll behave himself…so long as
you do the same. So eat up yer food like a good girl,
and we'll all leave you alone until morning.'

Robina took one glance at the unappetising broth
with its film of grease floating on the top, and decided to sample just the bread, which was at least
freshly baked, if slightly heavy.

'And what do you intend to do with me tomorrow,
if it isn't asking too much?'

'Inquisitive little thing, ain't she?' Jack remarked
to no one in particular. 'You're going to write a letter
to your lord, pretty lady. And if all goes well, you'll
be out of 'ere, and back in your own nice bed by
tomorrow night.'

'Or in 'is lordship's,' the other man sniggered, before turning to his sister. 'I don't see why we
couldn't 'ave got the thing done tonight. I told you
afore, Moll, I don't like the idea of keeping 'er 'ere.'

'I don't see why,' Molly scoffed. 'No one ever
comes 'ere n' more. And I can't say I blames 'em
neither. You've let this place fall into rack and ruin,
our Ben, since Betsy died.' Although not renowned
for cleanliness herself, even Molly was appalled by
the filthy state of the house. 'And as I've already told
you, I ain't walking all that way back to town tonight. Tomorrow will do fine. Besides, his lordship
might be more willing to part with 'is money, if he's
been left to fret for a while.'

Appearing quite smugly satisfied, she turned to
Robina. 'Had your fill then, dearie? That's good.
We'll just let Jack 'ere bind yer hands again. No need

to tie yer feet, though. I don't think you'll try to escape through the window. It's a mighty long way down.'

Robina's mind began to work rapidly as she obliged her captors by placing her hands behind her back. If she was going to effect an escape, she must make the attempt before morning. 'If—if I'm to remain incarcerated in here all night, might I not at least have a candle? It will be dark soon, and I could have sworn I saw something poke its head out of that hole in the corner earlier.'

'Ha!' Jack barked, securing the slender wrists with a merciless disregard for any pain he might be inflicting. 'Wouldn't be at all surprised if you did! The place is overrun wi' rats.' He seemed to debate within himself for a few moments. 'Don't see why she can't 'ave a candle, though. What say you, Molly?'

She merely shrugged before picking up the tray and carrying it from the room. Her brother, after one last ogling look in the direction of Robina's trim, shapely figure, followed, and then Jack went out, but came back a moment or two later with a lighted candle which he placed on the crate beside the small box bed. Without saying anything further, he went out again, the door closed, and Robina heard the bolts being securely slid into position.

Well, at least she had until morning to attempt an escape, she reminded herself, determined to think positively and not become too disheartened by her present predicament. She might be wise to wait an hour or so, or until such time as she could be sure that those three scoundrels below were asleep, which would not be too long if the odour of gin which had pervaded the room when they had entered was anything to go by. In the meantime it was only boredom with which she was forced to contend, and the pain in her wrists, where the cord rubbed against the soft flesh.

She couldn't prevent a protracted sigh escaping, as she turned to stare at the small window once more. It had grown considerably darker since the last time she had looked across at that grime-streaked single pane of glass. What time would it be now? Nine, perhaps nearer ten, she decided, and could not help wondering what had taken place with certain other persons during her long hours of incarceration.

The Dowager, poor darling, would be frantic with worry. They would have given up any search by now, of course; had possibly done so hours ago. It was possible that her ladyship had seen fit to inform the authorities, but it was much more likely that she would have returned to Brighton to apprise Daniel.

He would then have taken charge of the situation in that calm and sensible way of his. No doubt he would have informed the authorities, if his mother had not, and would have arranged for a further search to take place in the wood and surrounding area at first light. In the meantime, however...

Her eyes growing misty with tears she refused to shed, she turned her head to stare sightlessly across the dusty attic room, her mind's eye conjuring up a

clear image of the library back at the house in
Brighton, and of Daniel, concerned over her safety,
but outwardly appearing calm and collected as always, sitting there in his favourite chair.

It would have come as something of a surprise to
Robina had she known that at that precise moment,
far from comfortably ensconced in his book-lined
room, Daniel, his face set rigid with barely suppressed anger, was tooling his curricle at a neck-to-
nothing fashion through the streets of the town in an
attempt to find a certain jarvey.

Kendall, sitting on the seat beside him, cast his
master a concerned glance. Never had he seen his
lordship in such a rare taking—no, not even on that
dreadful day, almost two years ago, when the master
had ridden at the same neck-to-nothing pace along
the hillside track not far from Courtney Place. Not
that too many people had ever discovered that very
important fact, though, Kendall reminded himself.
Stebbings, he himself, and maybe one or two others
knew the truth of what had happened that day when
the late Lady Exmouth had died, but not one, as far
as Kendall was aware, had ever betrayed the master's
trust by disclosing what they had known.

'My lord,' he said in some urgency, as Daniel
overtook a lumbering coach with only an inch to
spare, 'are you sure you don't want me to take a turn
at tooling the curricle?'

This suggestion brought a glimmer of amusement
back into Daniel's eyes. 'Feeling somewhat nervous,

Kendall? I thought you had more faith in my abilities. I haven't even come close to scraping the paint work, I'll have you know.'

'It isn't that,' his trusty henchman hurriedly assured him, 'as I expect you well know, sir. It's just that I ain't being of much use to you at the moment.'

Kendall was well aware of precisely why they were scouring the streets of Brighton at this time of night, and was as concerned as everyone else over Miss Perceval's surprising disappearance.

'I don't know what this jarvey looks like, sir, nor what sort of carriage he drives, neither. If I were to take over the reins for a spell, it'd leave you free to look about for the cove.'

'Thank you for the offer, Kendall, but I've already come to the conclusion that I'm on a fool's errand. It would have been wiser for me to have remained at the Crown in the hope that he might put in an appearance, or I should at least have waited for the landlord's return.' And so saying, he turned the next corner and headed back towards the tavern he had visited earlier.

'What business do you suppose can that rascally landlord be engaged in that he must leave the running of his tavern in the 'ands of his brother?'

Daniel slanted the head groom a mocking glance. 'What business do you suppose, man? He's undoubtedly acquiring fresh supplies of rum and brandy from a reliable source, if I know anything.'

'Smuggled goods, you mean, sir?'

'I wouldn't be at all surprised. There's a deal of

free trading taking place all along this coast. The Preventive Officers are fighting a losing battle, and I suspect will continue to do so unless the laws are changed.'

They had by this time arrived back at the Crown. Daniel, willingly handing over the reins to Kendall now, wasted no time in alighting and re-entering the tavern, only to discover that the landlord had not yet returned. He realised at once that little would be gained in attempting to question the brother further. The man had freely admitted earlier that he helped out at the inn only rarely, and although he did know several of the locals by sight, he didn't know their names, and so couldn't say for certain whether Master Higgins had been in the inn already that evening or not.

Swiftly deciding that he had little option but to await the landlord's return in the hope that mine host was well acquainted with the jarvey, Daniel ordered himself a tankard of home-brewed ale, and had just carried it across to a corner table when the door opened and the very man he was intent on finding that night walked calmly into the inn.

His first impulse was to rush across and accost the jarvey, but he checked it. Higgins just didn't have the look about him of a man who was expecting to acquire a substantial amount of money in the very near future. In fact, he looked very sombre, thoroughly dissatisfied with life. Daniel was further confounded when Higgins, waiting for his ale to be poured, looked about him, his expression registering surprise, rather than fear or uncertainty, as he glanced in Daniel's direction.

Was it possible that he had totally misjudged Master Higgins, and that the man knew nothing of Robina's disappearance? Daniel wondered. Yes, there was just that possibility, he supposed. None the less, it seemed rather too much of a coincidence that on the very next day after Higgins had foolishly proposed abducting her, she should have disappeared, he finally decided, as he watched the jarvey come smilingly across to the table.

'Why, my lord! I didn't expect to be seeing you here again. Got a taste for our local landlord's home-brewed, have you? Well, can't say as I can blame you. He serves a good drop of ale.'

'He does indeed. Why don't you join me, Master Higgins?'

The jarvey did not hesitate, which only added to the rapidly growing conviction in Daniel's mind that the man was innocent of any wrongdoing this day. But he had to be sure.

'So, what does bring you back to our neck of the woods again, my lord?' Higgins enquired, looking and sounding remarkably composed. 'Ain't the usual haunt for gentlemen of your class. Not that you can't come and go as you please o' course. And it's always nice to see a friendly face round these parts.'

Leaning back in his chair, Daniel took a moment to sample the contents of his tankard before he said, 'As a matter of fact, I came here specifically to see you, Master Higgins.'

The jarvey's surprise was too spontaneous not to be perfectly genuine. 'Me...? But why should you want to see me, m'lord?' he asked before a sudden and decidedly hopeful expression flickered over his weather-beaten features. 'You ain't been giving a bit more thought to the little suggestion I put to you t'other evening, by any chance?'

Unlike his companion's, Daniel's smile was not pleasant. 'Believe me, Master Higgins, I have thought of nought else for the past few hours.' He leaned forward, his gaze intense. 'You see, Master Higgins, Miss Perceval has indeed been abducted, or at least her mysterious disappearance bears the distinct hallmark of abduction.'

Daniel watched the stubble-covered jaw drop perceptively, as the jarvey, all astonished incredulity, gaped across the table. Either he was the most gifted actor who ever drew breath, or he was genuinely astounded. He just had to be sure which it was.

'Now, Master Higgins,' he went on, his gaze never waving for a moment. 'Very few people knew for certain that Miss Perceval would be amongst the little party spending this afternoon out at Priory Wood. The lady who organised the outing knew, as did my mother and myself... And, of course, you knew, Mr Higgins.'

The jarvey did not pretend to misunderstand. 'But—but you don't suppose I had anything to do with the girl's disappearance, do 'ee?'

'Now that is precisely what I am endeavouring to discover,' Daniel responded smoothly.

'But I swear to you on my dear Dora's life, m'lord, I've never clapped eyes on the wench—I mean, the young lady—in my life. Furthermore, I ain't left the town all day. And there's plenty who'll vouch for that an all, iffen you don't believe me.'

'I'm not suggesting that you were actively involved in Miss Perceval's disappearance, Higgins,' Daniel assured him, no longer harbouring the slightest doubt as to the man's innocence. 'What I'm trying to discover is whether you mentioned to a third party that there was to be a picnic held at Priory Wood today at which Miss Perceval was to be present?'

'Now why the devil should I go and—' The jarvey's suddenly thoughtful expression was answer enough.

'So, you did mention the fact to someone,' Daniel prompted, when his companion remained silent, staring fixedly down into the contents of his tankard.

'Well, yes. Sort of, I did, I suppose,' he admitted at length. 'And Molly Turpin's brother lives out by Priory Wood, as I remember. Took her out there some months back in me carriage when her sister-in-law passed on. Right upset she was when she discovered she hadn't been left so much as the pearl brooch she had always admired. Wouldn't surprise me none if Molly's brother hadn't sold the brooch long since and spent the money on gin,' he continued after a moment's deliberation. 'A reet bad 'un is Ben Turpin. He'd do almost anything for his gin money.'

'Even going so far as to abduct a young woman

and hold her for ransom?' Daniel suggested, and Higgins looked gravely back across the table at him.

'Ain't saying he would, and I ain't saying he wouldn't. But it seems fishy to me m'lord that after I tells Molly and that ne'er-do-well man friend of hers in this very tavern all about my visit to you, the very next day that poor lass goes missing.' He looked decidedly shamefaced. 'I wouldn't like to think that any 'arm had come to the poor girl on account of me opening me big mouth.'

Daniel refused to dwell on this very real possibility. 'Do you happen to know where I can find these people, Molly and that male friend of hers? Do they live locally?'

'Close to me own place, sir.' Suddenly galvanised, Higgins tossed the last of his ale down his throat and was on his feet in an instant. 'If you don't object, I'd like to come wi' 'ee. I know these people. I'd get more out of 'em than you could ever 'ope to, sir.'

Daniel didn't need to think twice about accepting this offer of help. Quickly returning to the curricle, he very soon found himself amidst a mishmash of tightly packed dwellings, and began to appreciate why the man now sitting beside him on the seat would wish to grasp almost any opportunity to make some money and try to better himself. The area in which the jarvey resided was little better than a slum.

After requesting Daniel to draw up outside a dwelling that looked shabbier than most, Higgins jumped down from the curricle and disappeared up a narrow alley, only to return a matter of minutes later looking graver than ever.

'Jack and Molly ain't there. What's more, there ain't been a sign of 'em since morning. Which ain't usual, sir. Jack Sharpe tends to do—er—most of 'is business at night, as yer might say, and spends most days 'anging round the 'ouse or in the taverns.'

'I see,' Daniel responded, having a fairly shrewd idea of precisely which profession Jack Sharpe was engaged in, and now fearing the worst. That Robina might have fallen into the hands of an unprincipled sneak-thief and his doxy filled him with dread, but, as ever, he revealed little of this inner turmoil as he added, 'I think it behoves me to pay a visit to—er—Turpin's place of residence. Do you happen to know precisely where it is located, Higgins?'

'I've been out that way only once, sir, as I mentioned earlier. But I'm certain I could find it again, even in the dark. If you like, I'll willingly come with 'ee, and show 'ee the way. Just gives me a minute to pop in 'ome and see my Dora to tell 'er I'll be working late, otherwise she'll only fret.'

After watching the jarvey slip inside a dwelling which, from the outside, appeared in a better state than most, Daniel turned to his groom, seated on the back. 'I want you to return to the house. Inform her ladyship that I've gone out of town, and that I wish her to take no further action until I return. Which might possibly not be until morning.'

Although Kendall clambered down at once, his expression clearly betrayed unease. 'Are you sure you don't want me to come with you, sir? It sounds to me as if you might well find yourself having to deal with a right bunch of wrong uns.' He glanced briefly over his shoulder. 'And are you certain you can trust that jarvey, my lord?'

This evident concern for his safety succeeded in bringing a flicker of a smile to Daniel's lips. 'I would be the first to admit, Kendall, that where my fellow man is concerned my judgement has not always been faultless, but it has improved immeasurably in recent years. Yes, I am certain I shall not discover my trust in Master Higgins misplaced.'

By the light of the rapidly guttering candle, Robina examined the burns on her wrists. The discomfort she was being forced to endure now seemed rather a high price to pay for the removal of her bonds and the successful opening of the window. Had she been able to effect her escape by climbing down the ivy…well, that would have been a different matter entirely, but she steadfastly refused to give up hope quite yet.

In an hour or so, or when there was sufficient light to see clearly, she would consider again attempting to escape by way of the window. The ivy clinging to the house wall looked sturdy enough to support her weight, but she would be foolish not to be sure. The last thing she wished to incur now was further injury. She wouldn't get very far on a broken ankle.

Her only other option, of course, was an escape by way of the door. She glanced down at the stout piece of wood which she had managed to find under the bed, and which she had placed within easy reach upon the wooden crate. Any form of physical violence was abhorrent to her. None the less, it would not do to be faint-hearted in her present situation, she reminded herself. If the opportunity arose, she must be prepared to use that weapon, but, here again, she must wait until someone withdrew the bolts from the other side of the door. In the meantime she had at least one task to keep her occupied.

Sitting herself on the edge of the decidedly lumpy mattress once more, she tore two thin strips off her underskirt, and was in the process of binding up her left wrist when she distinctly heard a rustling noise and what sounded suspiciously like a grunt from just below the window. Then, to her horror, two large and shapely hands suddenly grasped the sill.

Stifling a scream, she darted forward. 'Who's there!' she demanded, half-fearing that it might well be the lecherous owner of the property come to pay a visit without his companions' knowledge. Reaching forward, she was seriously toying with the idea of bringing the small sash-window down hard on those two shapely, long-fingered hands when a distinctly amused and beloved voice drawled, 'Who the deuce do you suppose it is, my darling…? It is your Sir Galahad come to the rescue… Moreover, a Sir Galahad who is getting decidedly too long in the tooth for these sorts of starts.'

With a strange little sound, somewhere between a sob and a cry of pure joy, Robina almost flung herself into Daniel's arms the instant he had climbed into the room. He held her close, murmuring words of comfort, his recent exertions not wholly responsible for his rapidly increased pulse rate and erratic breathing.

'Here, let me look at you.' Reluctantly holding her a little away from him, he ran his fingers down her arms to capture her hands, and saw the slight wince. 'What's wrong? Are you hurt?'

'It's only my wrists. I was in the process of binding them up when you arrived.' Robina could not help but smile at his muttered oath, only half suppressed, as he examined her hurts. 'I did it myself,' she assured him softly, 'when I used the candle to burn through the cord that bound my wrists.'

'So the blackguards tied you up, did they?' He certainly did not appear best pleased to learn this, but made no further comment as he reached for the second strip of material, his fingers surprisingly gentle as he began to wrap it round the injured flesh.

'How many of the rogues are we dealing with, do you know?'

'Three… Well, I've only seen three,' she amended. 'A woman and two men.'

Somewhat bemused, Robina watched him secure the bandage deftly, still not quite able to believe that he was with her. 'Daniel, how on earth did you manage to find me?'

'Now that, my little love,' he responded, smiling as he released her wrist, 'is rather a long and involved story.'

'And you'd rather not tell me now. Yes, I quite understand.'

Moving over to the window, Robina poked her head out. From what she could see, it seemed a very long way down to the ground. But this was no time to be faint-hearted, she reminded herself once again. Besides, if Daniel could manage the climb up, surely she could manage to climb down?

'Should I go first, or you?' she asked, pulling her head back to find him surprisingly shaking his head.

'Neither of us, my dear.' Daniel moved over to the door to test its strength with his shoulder. 'I'm afraid I managed to dislodge a large portion of the ivy on my upward climb. It's a miracle I made it in one piece,' he admitted with brutal frankness. 'I wouldn't care to risk a descent.'

Disappointed, but not entirely downcast, Robina looked across at the door. 'Then it would appear we'll need to resort to my second plan.'

Daniel could not help smiling at this matter-of-fact attitude. What an amazing young woman she was! Most females would have succumbed to a fit of the vapours if they had experienced half of what his darling girl had been put through this day. Abducted, tied up, and locked in a filthy attic room for hours, she appeared, apart from her dishevelled appearance and injuries to her wrists, none the worse for her ordeal.

'Evidently you have already considered an alternative means of escape.'

'Well, yes,' she admitted guardedly, 'although I

haven't given much thought to how I'd actually achieve it.' She glanced down at the crate. 'But at least I managed to find myself a sort of weapon.'

'And would you honestly have been prepared to use it?' he asked, his dark brows rising sharply as he followed the direction of her gaze.

'I might have been forced to do so... Still might, if it comes to that. But at least I have until morning to think it over.'

There was no response, and Robina raised her eyes to discover him looking rather thoughtfully back across the room at her. He appeared suddenly very troubled. 'What's wrong, Daniel?'

'Nothing... Nothing at all,' he replied, but not very convincingly, before moving across to the window and surprising her further by taking a handkerchief from his pocket and waving it several times.

'Who are you signalling to?' Hope stirred. 'Is Kendall with you?'

'No, my dear. I have left my curricle and pair in the very capable hands of one Hector Higgins, about whom I shall tell you more presently. In the meantime, I would like to know whether or not you think all three of the rogues who abducted you are still in the house?'

'I believe so, but obviously I cannot be sure. I haven't heard any sounds from below for some considerable time, so I would imagine they must all be asleep...or drunk.'

'Maybe so. But I do not think we will alert them to my presence until morning.'

He evidently had his reasons, although Robina failed to see what they could possibly be. 'But what about your friend Mr Higgins? Could he not possibly alert the authorities, and tell them we're here?'

'He could, of course, but I would much prefer that he remain with the horses and await further instructions, as I've already advised him to do by my signal.' He noticed the puzzled expression. 'I am endeavouring to protect your fair name, my dear. The fewer people who know about this little escapade, the better.'

She smiled across at him, but he could easily detect the lingering puzzlement in her eyes. 'Trust me, my little bird. I have only your best interests at heart, believe me.'

Realising she was being very selfish to expect an immediate escape, Robina decided not to press him further. He had come in search of her, putting himself at risk, and was endangering himself still further by not enlisting outside aid in order to effect her escape, simply in an attempt to protect her good name. What more could she possibly ask of him?

Suddenly finding herself unable to hold that concerned, brown-eyed gaze, she turned away, once again finding herself having to fight the threat of tears. Why, oh why had she not recognised his true worth from the first? Why had it taken her so long to appreciate that in this kindly, level-headed gentleman she had found the very man for her? Yes, she had been given her chance, and had thrown it away… And now it was all wretchedly too late!

'Well, I suppose we may as well try to make ourselves as comfortable as possible until morning.'

This very practical suggestion forced Robina to abandon her heart-rending reflections, at least for the present, and she turned to discover him testing the thin mattress, and grimacing at its lumpiness.

'Come… Come and sit beside me, and I shall tell you all about my new friend, Honest Hector Higgins.' Daniel held out his hand, noting the slight hesitation before she obeyed.

After deliberately taking his time over the telling of the story, Daniel had the satisfaction of seeing that Robina was quite unable to keep her eyes open as she remarked in a distinctly sleepy voice, 'But what I don't quite understand is why Mr Merrell should have proposed that you abduct me in the first place.'

Smiling to himself, Daniel raised his arm and placed it about her slender shoulders so that she nestled comfortably against him. 'I think it might be wise to leave that particular explanation until morning, my love.'

# Chapter Twelve

Daniel glanced across at the window. It was morning, and still he wasn't sure whether he had done the right thing by choosing to spend the night here. But it was rather too late to do anything about it now, he reminded himself, transferring his gaze to the being who had caused him hours of soul-searching.

Still lying in the crook of his arm, Robina had slept soundly throughout the night; whereas he, plagued by a guilty conscience, had hardly slept at all.

It would have been a simple matter to attempt an escape at any time throughout the night. By using another of those prearranged signals, he could have instructed Higgins to leave the horses. Using those skills acquired in his misspent youth, the jarvey could easily have broken into the house. Higgins could then have located this room, unbolted the door, and with luck they might all have walked out without any one of those villains being any the wiser. But no, Daniel reflected, he had given way to temptation and chosen not to do so.

The instant Robina, in all innocence, had mentioned she was resigned to remaining incarcerated in this room until morning, the idea that she might be persuaded to marry him if they spent the whole night together had sprung into his mind. Well, perhaps he had not behaved like a gentleman, he was forced to concede, but at least he had not sunk so low as to make a marriage between them totally unavoidable by seducing her, although that too had certainly crossed him mind. And more than just once during the past few hours, he was ashamed to say!

He could only marvel at his powers of restraint. Holding that lovely, slender body pressed against him, feeling those firm, young breasts through the thin material of his shirt had been a sweet torment, and his subsequent frustrations little more than he deserved. A judgement on him, he supposed. If it had not been for the fact that he was certain in his own mind that they would make a blissfully contented couple once they were married, he might have been able to resist this golden opportunity of at least trying to persuade her to marry him.

As though sensing his thoughts, and wishing to torment him further for the subterfuge, Robina moved her hand in a feather-light touch across his chest and down to his stomach, igniting yet again that fire in his loins.

'Steady, boy, steady,' Daniel muttered to himself,

as he placed his hand over hers, instantly stilling those innocently tantalising fingers.

The brief contact of his restraining hand disturbed her. He could detect the slight movement of her eyes beneath those lids, with their ridiculously long, curling lashes which had caused such havoc with his senses when they had brushed against his chin during the night.

'It is perfectly all right, Daniel. I assure you I have them well under control,' she astounded him by unexpectedly murmuring.

'I beg you pardon, my darling?'

The delicate lids fluttered open, and she gazed smilingly up at him. 'The greys, Daniel, I...' She blinked several times as though trying to bring his features into focus, and then sat bolt upright, staring about in some confusion.

'I was dreaming we were out in the curricle.' She glanced about her again, the confused look slowly disappearing as she looked across at the window. 'Good heavens, it's morning!'

'You have been sleeping soundly in my arms all night,' some imp of mischief prompted him to tell her when she edged a little away from him.

'Good heavens!' she muttered again, looking so deliciously pink and flustered that Daniel was once again forced to exert that iron self-control and not pull her straight back into his arms. 'The last thing I remember was listening to some story about...about your acquaintance Mr Higgins.' The frown returned. 'Which, I seem to remember, didn't make very much sense, though I expect that was because I was tired and not attending properly.'

'I dare say.' Easing his aching back away from the wall, he got to his feet. 'Unfortunately I haven't the time to explain things more fully to you now, not if I stand the remotest chance of getting you safely back to the house before the whole of Brighton society starts parading the streets.'

'What time do you suppose it is now?' she asked, seeing his grimace as he flexed his arms. Little wonder he felt stiff. He must have spent the most uncomfortable night, with his back pressed against the wall, and her lying against him.

'As I left my pocket-watch, again, in Higgins's safe keeping, I can only guess, but I would imagine it must be around six.'

'In that case it is highly unlikely that our friends below have risen yet,' Robina pointed out. 'At least,' she amended, after listening intently for a moment, 'I cannot detect any sound of movement.'

'Well, they very soon will be awake.' There was a definite look of determination about him now, as he grasped the stout stick and began to pound it against the door. 'Come on, my dear, yell out. I don't wish them to be aware of my presence quite yet.'

Robina automatically did as she was bid. Taking the stick from him, she continued to hammer it against the door, shouting as loud as she could as she did so, until she detected the sound of heavy footsteps growing steadily louder.

'Now, what's all this, then? What's all this

racket?' a gruff and faintly annoyed voice demanded to know from the other side of the door, and Robina was fairly certain that it was none other than Molly's obnoxious brother who had come to investigate.

She glanced briefly at Daniel, who had positioned himself in readiness against the wall so that when the door was eventually opened, he would not be seen by their visitor. She guessed what she must do next.

'Let me out of here at once, do you hear me, or I'll scream the place down!' She must have sounded as though she had meant it too, for the bolts were immediately drawn back, the door swung open, and the obnoxious owner of the neglected farmhouse stomped into the room, but not before Robina had taken the precaution of backing away a few paces, her sturdy weapon held securely in her hand.

'Who untied you!' he growled, taking a threatening step forward, and reaching out a grubby hand to grasp the stick. 'Ere, let me have that!'

'I'm afraid we are unable to oblige you. But you can certainly have this,' Daniel said suavely, thereby making his presence known, and before Ben could do much else other than swing round, startled, Daniel placed a well-aimed blow on the flabby jaw, the force of which sent Ben sprawling to the floor.

'Come, my darling, no time to waste!' Grasping a bemused Robina by the hand, Daniel whisked her from the room, sliding the bolts across the door before she realised quite what was happening. 'I'm sorry you were forced to witness that, my dear, but I'm afraid there was no other way.'

'Oh, please don't apologise, Daniel. Besides, I've witnessed you perform the feat before,' she reminded him, sudden excitement adding an extra brilliance to her eyes.

'What a redoubtable young woman you are, Robin! A veritable breath of fresh air. Which is something I hope we'll both enjoy again, once we're away from this unwholesome place.'

Feeling inordinately pleased by the surprising compliments, Robina followed him along the musty-smelling passageway to the head of a steep and narrow flight of stairs. Hampered by petticoats, she wasn't able to descend as quickly as Daniel who, having reached a second narrow passageway, began to move cautiously forward. He was halfway along its length when a door behind him opened a fraction. Before Robina could gather her wits together to scream out a warning, Molly had darted out and had jumped on his back, clawing and hissing like a cat.

It had crossed her mind to wonder whether she would have the courage to use her weapon. Now that the moment had arrived, Robina didn't need to think twice about it. Unconcerned for her own safety, she darted down the last few stairs and, raising her arm, brought the wooden stick down hard across the cling-ing woman's shoulders. A loud scream of pain echoed along the passageway as Molly released her grasp and dropped to the ground to land in a huddle by the wall.

There was little pity in Daniel's eyes as he glanced briefly at the hysterically sobbing female whose features were contorted in pain as she clasped her shoulder. Nor did he betray even a moment's alarm as he turned to find his way barred by the third member of the villainous gang, brandishing an evil-looking knife.

'So, you thought to free the wench, did 'ee,' Jack sneered. He didn't seem particularly interested to discover precisely who Daniel was. Evidently his only concern was that a stranger was depriving him of some easy money.

He raised the hand holding the knife. 'Well, let's see how you'd like some of this.'

'No, I don't think so,' Daniel replied, his voice silky-smooth and as soft as velvet. 'Let us see, instead, how you'd like some of this.'

Calmly delving into his jacket pocket, he did no more than draw out a pistol and discharge it before the other man had taken more than a pace or two towards him. Robina, watching the knife fall from suddenly limp fingers, couldn't decide which of Daniel's startling feats had amazed her more—his ability to floor a powerfully built man easily with a single blow, or his unerring accuracy with a pistol. She didn't suppose for a moment that he had intended to mortally wound the man called Jack, who went stumbling back along the passageway to disappear from view, merely render him incapable of foiling their escape, which he had done with precious little effort, it seemed.

'Come, my darling.' Daniel recaptured a bemused Robina's hand, as she continued to gaze up at him in dawning wonder. 'I think it's time we left this den of thieves.'

'But—but, surely we aren't just going to leave them like this,' Robina protested, as Daniel hauled her willy-nilly along the remainder of the passage-way, down a second flight of stairs, and then out into blessed fresh morning air.

'I have no intention of sparing any one of them another thought,' he assured her, sounding sublimely unconcerned, as he continued to lead the way along a weed-covered path and into a narrow lane. 'None of them will suffer any lasting harm, I'm sure. They can think themselves very lucky that I'm not consid-ering bringing charges against them.'

Robina looked up at him, uncertain whether he was being quite sensible to leave matters as they stood. She didn't consider herself a vindictive person by any means, and would be quite happy to forget the whole unfortunate experience, but she couldn't help wondering whether, having been thwarted in their attempt to make some easy money, those three incompetent abductors just might try to wreak their revenge some time in the future, and echoed her fears aloud.

'They might, of course, but I very much doubt that they will. They're not hardened criminals, merely petty thieves and, by the looks of them, not very successful ones. Besides,' he shrugged, 'I am endea-vouring to ensure that your ordeal does not become widely known. Also, there is the welfare of someone else to be considered. I do not believe that I shall be troubled by those three again, but my friend Mr Higgins might not be so lucky if his part in this unfortunate business ever became common knowledge.'

Daniel continued to lead the way through a clump of trees and bushes, and eventually into a clearing beyond. 'And here he is, dutifully guarding my horses, just as he promised he would during my absence.'

Robina was delighted to make the acquaintance of the man who had made it possible for Daniel to accomplish his rescue in such fine romantic style, even if she still failed to understand why the good Mr Higgins should ever have imagined that Daniel should have wished to abduct her in the first place.

Little time was wasted in clambering into the curricle and heading back to Brighton. Thankfully at this early hour there were very few other travellers using the roads, and Robina was able to make a few necessary repairs to her appearance whilst she listened to Daniel recounting the events of the morning to his friend Mr Higgins, who had happily relinquished his seat to Robina and had climbed up on the back.

They bowled along at a sprightly pace until Daniel, quite without warning, drew the curricle to a halt. 'This is where we must part company,' he announced, turning to Higgins, who appeared as surprised as Robina by the unexpected stop as he obediently clambered down on to the road.

'In the field yonder, unless I much mistake the matter, are the first traders arriving for the horse fair. In an hour or two the place will be crowded. Take advantage of your early arrival by thoroughly examining the animals on offer before finally making your choice.'

Daniel paused to toss a bulging purse down to the jarvey. 'You'll find more than enough in there to purchase a fine animal, and to make all the necessary repairs to your carriage, if you don't choose to look round for a newer one. But before you go,' Daniel added, smiling at Higgins's expression of awe-struck wonder, 'I'll thank you for the return of my pocket-watch.'

This reminder appeared to restore the jarvey's faculties. Laughingly handing up the timepiece, he offered his grateful thanks, and then set off at a brisk pace in the direction of the fair-field.

'And now that we are alone,' Daniel remarked, after giving his greys the office to start, 'there are a few little matters which we must sort out before we arrive home.'

Robina instinctively put a hand up to her hair, which she had tied back with a ribbon torn from her gown. 'I realise I must look a fright, but there's not very much else I can do.'

'Your appearance does not concern me in the least,' Daniel assured her. 'Your reputation, however, most certainly does. You have spent the whole night alone in my company. Therefore I am in honour bound to offer the protection of my name.'

A long silence, then, 'No!'

Daniel had not expected his proposal to be accepted with a great deal of gratitude or enthusiasm, and he was forced to concede that he had not expressed himself as well as he might have done, but even he was shocked by the vehemence of the refusal.

Drawing his greys to a halt once again, he turned to discover her staring straight ahead, the lines of her sweet face held rigid, as though striving to maintain her composure.

'Come, my dear. We get along together so very well.' He reached for her hand, easily retaining it in his own when she struggled to free her fingers. 'I do not perfectly understand why you are so set against marrying me,' he continued, desperately striving not to betray the deep hurt he was experiencing at this surprising show of opposition. He simply couldn't…wouldn't believe that she was so indifferent to him!

'Come, surely you can stomach me as a husband?'

'Even if I could, you don't imagine for a moment that I'd be so cruel as to steal you away from Arabella.'

Her voice had been little more than a choked whisper, and Daniel wasn't perfectly certain that he'd heard correctly. 'Arabella, did you say…? What in the world has she to do with anything?'

Robina did turn to look at him then, her expression betraying both shock and bewilderment. 'Why, everything I should imagine! She's the one you truly wish to marry.'

'Marry Arabella…?' It was Daniel's turn to look

confused now. 'What in the world makes you suppose that I have any desire to marry my cousin?'

'Because I overheard you in the garden on the evening of the Maitlands' party.'

It was out before she realised what she was saying, but it was too late to do anything about it now. Daniel had digested her every word, and was now looking rather thoughtful, staring directly at her, and yet seeming to see something else.

'I don't know what you imagined you overheard, my little love,' he said at length, 'but unless I much mistake the matter that was the night I confided in Arabella, informing her that I had every intention of marrying again. Furthermore, that I had every intention of proposing that very night to the lady who had succeeded in winning my heart. She was delighted and wholeheartedly approved my choice. Unfortunately, my plans were thwarted by my future bride herself.' His tone had changed suddenly to one of gentle, teasing censure. 'Unbeknown to me, she had decided for reasons best known to herself—though I'm certain she will favour me with an explanation at some future time—to leave the party early, and has been hiding herself away and depriving me of the pleasure of seeing very much of her…up until last night, that is.'

Robina could only stare back at him in wonder. That tender look which she had so often seen in his eyes whenever he looked at her was unmistakably there again, confirming his every word. Unbelievably, he was every bit as much in love with her as she was with him, and all she could think of to say at such a moment of blissful enlightenment was simply, 'Oh.'

Daniel, however, seemed to find this precisely the right thing to say, and with great presence of mind decided to quash any lingering doubts which she might still be harbouring as to the true state of his feelings by taking her into his arms and ruthlessly kissing her.

Emerging from her first ever experience of masculine passion a little breathless, but very willing to sample a great deal more, Robina rested her head against his shoulder. 'Oh, Daniel, I've been such a fool,' she admitted, quite unable to stop those silent tears of happiness from escaping and rolling down her cheeks. 'It wasn't until I thought you wanted to marry Arabella that I realised how very much I loved you. But I never imagined for a moment that you were in love with me.' She felt that strong arm tighten about her as she inadvertently brushed his cheek with her long lashes as she peered fleetingly up at him. 'You managed to conceal your feelings very well.'

'And with good reason,' he responded, reluctantly holding her a little away so that he could look down into her face. 'Although I had decided, after our weeks in London, that you would make the perfect wife, I felt that you were being unfairly pushed into accepting an offer of marriage that you were not altogether sure you really wanted. I felt you needed more time to get to know me a little better.'

This had certainly been true, and yet now, after the heartfelt misery she had experienced during these past few days, Robina found it difficult to believe that there ever had been a time when she had experienced any reluctance in accepting an offer of marriage from him.

'I always liked you, Daniel, right from the first, and quickly grew to prefer your company to that of any other man. It was just...' She paused for a moment, unsure whether to confess her early doubts or not, and then decided that, if he was to understand her initial reluctance, only complete honesty would serve. 'It was just that I thought you could never possibly love me...any other woman, for that matter...not after...'

'Not after I had lost Clarissa,' he finished for her when her courage failed.

He glanced briefly at the slender fingers resting lightly on his sleeve, and took them gently into his own, while silently cursing himself for every kind of a fool. They were very alike in so many ways that he had instinctively known on numerous occasions precisely what she was thinking and feeling, and yet, idiot that he was, it had never once occurred to him to suppose that having to live in Clarissa's shadow was what his dear Robin had feared she must suffer if she married him.

'I should have told you the truth weeks ago, but I suppose,' he shrugged, 'the right moment just never seemed to arise. And the truth of the matter is, my darling, Clarissa hasn't entered my thoughts very often of late.'

He smiled at the frank puzzlement which sprang into blue eyes. 'Surprised…? Yes, of course you are. Because, like everyone else, you supposed I was desperately in love with my wife and utterly devastated when she died. And that is precisely what I allowed people to believe, my darling. But nothing could have been further from the truth.'

Retaining his hold on her hand, he began to rub his thumb absently back and forth across the soft white skin, as he turned his head to stare at the empty road ahead, gathering his thoughts.

'When I married Clarissa I was very young, and a trifle headstrong…arrogant, perhaps. I had been running the estate very successfully since my father's death, and felt that I was more than capable of making my own decisions, without outside interference. In many respects, I suppose, I seemed to many far older than my years—responsible, dependable. But emotionally I was not so mature. I have long since realised that I mistook infatuation for love.'

These revelations were so startling that Robina hardly knew what to say when he fell silent, as though expecting some response. 'But surely your marriage wasn't an unhappy one, Daniel?' she managed to ask, after a moment's intense thought.

'No, I wouldn't go as far as to suggest that,' he hurriedly assured her. 'It was simply that, after Lizzie was born, I was forced to face the fact that I had changed, matured, if you like, whereas my wife remained the child I had married. We simply had nothing in common. And as the years passed the differences between us became more marked, and we simply drifted further and further apart. Not to the extent that we went our separate ways, but we certainly spent less and less time together.

'I didn't object in the least when Clarissa wished to visit London, or our house here in Brighton,' he went on to disclose. 'In fact, I actively encouraged her to do so, little realising that maybe one day she just might succumb to flattery and attention which she no longer received from me. The gentleman who had captured her interest was a certain Mr John Travers who had a maiden aunt living within easy travelling distance of Courtney place, which of course proved mightily convenient for them both.

'You appear shocked,' he remarked, turning his head suddenly and noting the astonishment which she found impossible to conceal. 'Yes, my wife had a lover. And the truth of the matter is, my darling, I suspected as much, but chose to do absolutely nothing about it. Which is testament enough, I think, to the state of our union.

'I didn't realise to what extent my wife's feelings were engaged until I returned from London one day to find the house virtually deserted. The daughter of one of my estate worker's was being married that day, and my wife had given permission for the servants to attend the celebration. Only the butler remained in the house, and he informed me on my arrival that my wife had left the house in the company of Mr Travers an hour or so earlier to visit Mr Travers's aunt.' There was a distinctly cynical twist to his smile. 'My wife had taken to paying regular visits to the elderly lady, so I thought little of it until I learned from Kendall, who had accompanied me on my travels, that the stable-lad who normally tooled my wife's carriage was also at the wedding celebration, and Mr Travers's horse had been left in the stable. Now, that did strike me as being odd! What could be so urgent that Travers should feel the need to tool my wife's carriage himself, and not await the return of my stable-lad?'

'So you were not responsible for your wife's death at all,' Robina murmured, hardly aware that she had spoken her thoughts aloud, until he said,

'I was not tooling the carriage, no. Travers was in charge of that, and the young fool had chosen to take the hillside track, in an attempt to avoid meeting me on the road from London, I can only suppose. But I still hold myself, in part, responsible for Clarissa's death.'

'But why, Daniel?' Robina was at a loss to understand him. 'You were not even there at the time.'

There was a hint of sadness now about the smile he cast her. 'But had I been there, my darling, Clarissa would have been alive today. Had I given her more of my time, had I not been so wrapped up in my own interests, she would never have sought the attentions of John Travers.

'When Kendall and I rode out, and examined the wreckage, I realised at once that Clarissa had decided to leave me. I ordered Kendall to return to the house with my wife's baggage, so that people would merely believe that she had planned to visit Travers's aunt, although I never supposed for a moment that that had been her intention. I also instructed Kendall to say that I had arrived home before my wife had left the house and that I had been in charge of the carriage.'

'Because you didn't want the world at large to learn the truth?' Robina suggested, when he fell silent once more. 'Yes, I believe I can understand that, Daniel.'

'It wasn't so much for my sake, my darling. Although, if I'm honest, I would have to admit that my pride received a severe dent when I realised that Clarissa had grown to prefer Travers to me. But the decisions I made that day were for my daughters' benefit, rather than my own. I didn't want Clarissa's name dragged through the mud, or my children ever to discover that their mother was willing to abandon them. Everyone, including my own mother, had supposed our marriage to have been a very happy one for the most part, and I was more than willing to allow the world to continue to believe that. Only Kendall, my butler and my friend Merrell, who had travelled down from London with me that day, ever knew the truth… And now, so do you.'

'And no one will ever learn it from me,' she assured him gently, happy to think that he trusted her enough to confide in her.

'You think I didn't realise that?' The tenderness was back in his eyes as he held her close and kissed her again. 'To think that eventually I took the advice of all my friends and decided to marry again for my children's sake. I went to London to find myself a sweet, biddable girl, and found the Vicar of Abbot Quincey's daughter. Perhaps not quite such a biddable girl, as she decided that her choice of husband would be hers and not her mother's,' he said, gently teasing, 'but exactly the right girl for me.'

'I'm so very pleased that my future husband is prepared to accept me with all my faults,' she responded in an attempt to maintain this lighter mood.

'Then you'll marry me, and soon?'

'As soon as you please, my darling!' She laughed lovingly up at him. 'You see how biddable I can be when I choose.'

'Then let us hope it lasts until after the wedding.' He was suddenly serious again. 'Clarissa and I had a large wedding in London. I do not want the same for us. I should like just close family and friends to be present, and the wedding to take place in the chapel at Courtney Place, with your father conducting the ceremony, if he is agreeable.'

She approved wholeheartedly. 'That sounds simply perfect to me.'

'And soon...? You'll marry me soon?'

'As soon as ever you like,' she assured him once again.

'Then we had best not delay in making the arrangement. You may have forgotten what that gypsy woman foretold a few weeks ago, but I most certainly have not,' he announced, very reluctantly releasing his hold and turning his attention to his horses once more. 'Our first child is to be born within a twelve-month. And the way I'm feeling at the moment the prediction will very likely come true, so I think I had better return you without further delay to the protection of my mother's side.'

Robina edged herself a respectable distance away. 'Your not so biddable future bride is on this occasion in complete agreement with you, my darling.'

\*   \*   \*   \*   \*

# THE STEEPWOOD

# *Scandals*

*Regency drama, intrigue, mischief...
and marriage*

### VOLUME SEVEN

*Mr Rushford's Honour* by Meg Alexander

Gina, Lady Whitelaw left Steepwood as plain Gina
Westcott. Now, years later, she's returned home
– and has to face the man who stole her heart...

⚜

*An Unlikely Suitor* by Nicola Cornick

At three-and-twenty and a bluestocking to boot,
Miss Lavender Brabant feels her chance of marriage
has passed. But now she's met Barnabas Hammond,
a shopkeeper's son!

## On sale 4th May 2007

www.millsandboon.co.uk

*A young woman disappears.*
*A husband is suspected of murder.*
*Stirring times for all the neighbourhood in*

# THE STEEPWOOD

# *Scandals*

### Volume 1 – November 2006
*Lord Ravensden's Marriage* by Anne Herries
*An Innocent Miss* by Elizabeth Bailey

### Volume 2 – December 2006
*The Reluctant Bride* by Meg Alexander
*A Companion of Quality* by Nicola Cornick

### Volume 3 – January 2007
*A Most Improper Proposal* by Gail Whitiker
*A Noble Man* by Anne Ashley

### Volume 4 – February 2007
*An Unreasonable Match* by Sylvia Andrew
*An Unconventional Duenna* by Paula Marshall

*A young woman disappears.*
*A husband is suspected of murder.*
*Stirring times for all the neighbourhood in*

# THE STEEPWOOD

# *Scandals*

### Volume 5 – March 2007
*Counterfeit Earl* by Anne Herries
*The Captain's Return* by Elizabeth Bailey

### Volume 6 – April 2007
*The Guardian's Dilemma* by Gail Whitiker
*Lord Exmouth's Intentions* by Anne Ashley

### Volume 7 – May 2007
*Mr Rushford's Honour* by Meg Alexander
*An Unlikely Suitor* by Nicola Cornick

### Volume 8 – June 2007
*An Inescapable Match* by Sylvia Andrew
*The Missing Marchioness* by Paula Marshall

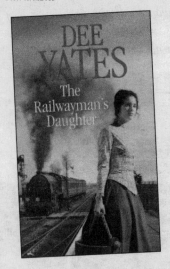

**In 1875, a row of tiny cottages stands by the tracks of the newly built York – Doncaster railway…**

Railwayman Tom Swales, with his wife and five daughters, takes the end cottage. But with no room to spare in the loving Swales household, eldest daughter Mary accepts a position as housemaid to the nearby stationmaster. There she battles the daily grime from the passing trains – and the stationmaster's brutal, lustful nature. In the end, it's a fight she cannot win.

In shame and despair, Mary flees to York. But the pious couple who take her in know nothing of true Christian charity. They work Mary like a slave – despite her heavy pregnancy. Can she find the strength to return home to her family? Will they accept her? And what of her first love, farmer's son Nathaniel? Mary hopes with all her heart that he will still be waiting…

**Available 16th March 2007**

www.millsandboon.co.uk

M&B

# *The* *Regency*

## LORDS & LADIES
### COLLECTION

*Two glittering Regency
love affairs in every book*

MILLS & BOON®

# The Regency

## LORDS & LADIES
### COLLECTION

*Two glittering Regency
love affairs in every book*

MILLS & BOON®

www.millsandboon.co.uk

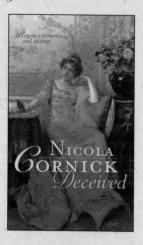

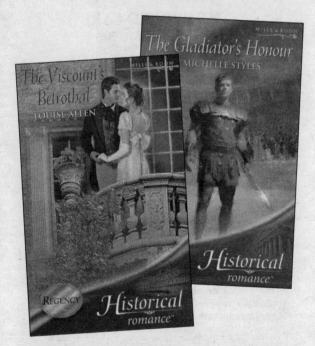

# MILLS & BOON

# *Romance*

### THE SHERIFF'S PREGNANT WIFE *by Patricia Thayer*

Surprise is an understatement for Sheriff Reed Larkin when he finds out his childhood sweetheart has returned home. After all these years Paige Keenan's smile can still make his heart ache. But what's the secret he can see in her whisky-coloured eyes…?

### THE PRINCE'S OUTBACK BRIDE *by Marion Lennox*

Prince Max de Gautier travels to the Australian Outback in search of the heir to the throne. But Max finds a feisty woman who is fiercely protective of her adopted children. Although Pippa is wary of this dashing prince, she agrees to spend one month in his royal kingdom…

### THE SECRET LIFE OF LADY GABRIELLA
*by Liz Fielding*

Lady Gabriella March is the perfect domestic goddess – but in truth she's simply Ellie March, who uses the beautiful mansion she is house-sitting to inspire her writing. The owner returns and Ellie discovers that Dr Benedict Faulkner is the opposite of the ageing academic she'd imagined…

### BACK TO MR & MRS *by Shirley Jump*

Cade and Melanie were the High School Prom King and Queen… Twenty years on Cade has realised that he let work take over and has lost the one person who lit up his world. Now he is determined to show Melanie he can be the husband she needs…and win back her heart.

## On sale 4th May 2007

*Available at WHSmith, Tesco, ASDA, and all good bookshops*
*www.millsandboon.co.uk*